The Year My Sister Got Lucky

By Aimee Friedman

Sea Change
The Year My Sister Got Lucky
South Beach
French Kiss
Hollywood Hills
Breaking Up: A Fashion High Graphic Novel
A Novel Idea

Short Stories in
Mistletoe: Four Holiday Stories
21 Proms

The Year My Sister Got Lucky

Aimee Friedman

For Natalie Joy,
who is a good dancer,
but an even better sister.

Library of Congress Cataloging-in-Publication Data

Friedman, Aimee.
The year my sister got lucky / Aimee Friedman.
p. cm.
Summary: When fourteen-year-old Katie and her older sister, Michaela, move from New York City to upstate New York, Katie is horrified by the country lifestyle but is even more shocked when her sister adapts effortlessly, enjoying their new life, unlike Katie.
ISBN-13: 978-0-439-92227-2 (HC) (alk. paper)
ISBN-10: 0-439-92227-5 (HC) (alk. paper)
[1. Sisters — Fiction. 2. Moving, Household — Fiction. 3. City and town life — New York (State) — New York — Fiction. 4. Country life — New York (State) — Fiction. 5. New York (State) — Fiction. 6. Friendships — Fiction.] I. Title.

PZ7.F89642Ye 2008   2007016416
[Fic] — dc22

ISBN-13: 978-0-439-92229-6
ISBN-10: 0-439-92229-1

12 11 10 9 8 7 6 5 4 3 2 1   9 10 11 12 13 14/0

Printed in the U.S.A.
First paperback edition, June 2009

Book design by Steve Scott

Of two sisters one is always the watcher, one the dancer. — Louise Glück, "Tango"

1

I'm an insomniac. Any sweet, deep slumbers I've had over the course of my fourteen years could probably be counted on one hand. Still, I manage okay during the day — school, dance class, dinner, homework. Most people wouldn't guess my little secret.

My sister, Michaela, is the only one who really knows.

"Michaela?" I whisper from my bed. My covers are kicked down around my ankles, my curls are piled up on top of my head, and I'm fanning myself with one hand to cool off.

Michaela lets out a long, weary sigh. Her big-sister sigh. It's the sound she makes when I try to talk to her at night, when I can't find the keys to let us into our building, or when I'm spacing out on the street and my foot misses the curb. Michaela never trips on the sidewalk. She's three years older than I am, and sometimes that gap feels as vast as the green swath of Central Park. Other times, it's as small as the space between our beds.

"Are you awake?" I persist, propping myself up on one elbow. I know the answer. For the past hour, I've been listening to her flip from side to side. This behavior, coming from Michaela, is completely weird. My sister is my exact opposite: a champion sleeper. She can crash as soon as her head touches a soft surface — or, sometimes, not even. Once, after a late dance class, I watched her doze off while we were riding home on the subway, standing squished between hordes of strangers. Her talent is awe-inspiring.

"Katie, come on." Michaela's voice — soft and light, even when she's annoyed — is muffled by the pillow over her head. "It's after midnight."

It's also thick, soupy August, and the apartment's air-conditioning broke today, so we've got the windows pushed open as high as they can go. Sirens and taxi horns and some hoarse girl yelling at her friend to meet her on the corner of East 5TH Street and 2ND float inside, but it isn't the noise that's keeping me up. I'm as used to the babble outside as I am to the stripes of light that passing cars paint on my ceiling. I remember when I was little, sitting in my parents' bedroom and watching my dad write, with his Frank Sinatra CD blasting in the background, and hearing the line about New York being "a city that doesn't sleep." I'd hugged my knees to my chest and felt a sudden, tugging connection to my hometown. That feeling's stayed with me ever since.

"You must be hot," I tell Michaela, and sit up entirely. Drops of sweat slip down my neck and beneath my white ribbed tank, the one I only wear at home because I worry it makes my boobs look too big. "Unbearably hot," I add. "Like, dying."

I'm not planning to leave my sister alone just yet. Having her awake is a rare, delicious treat; lying restless in the dark every night can start to get old after a while. Especially since Michaela is a sound sleeper who breathes in and out steadily and only occasionally murmurs nonsense. Sometimes I listen closely and hope that she'll spill something scandalous and awful in her sleep. No such luck so far.

"Mind over matter," Michaela mutters, all stoiclike. But then she flings the pillow off her face, which signals to me that she might be surrendering. Her straight, walnut-brown hair billows out behind her, and her hazel eyes flutter open. I can see them, bright and glistening, as they dart back and forth, quick as thoughts.

"What?" I ask, leaning forward to get a better look at her.

I see Michaela's brow furrow, ever so slightly. "What what?"

I roll my eyes. "You."

Michaela pauses, just long enough for curiosity to

stir in the pit of my stomach. "Nothing," she finally replies. Her left foot is dangling over the edge of the bed, and I watch as she points and flexes her toes, out of habit. Even in the shadowy half light, her arch is ridiculously beautiful.

"It's *so* not nothing," I retort, and swing my legs off the bed. For some reason, my heart is beating a little faster than it was a second before. "You've been acting different all night."

Because now I'm remembering Michaela's strange silence over dinner, the way she dragged her fork around and around her bowl of pasta without looking up at me. Our parents were arguing about rent checks or something equally dull, and I kept trying to catch my sister's eye. Normally, during meals, Michaela and I will ramble on and on about finding the right long-sleeved Danskin leotard, or creating the perfect iTunes mix, or did you see those dark indigo jeans in the window of Bloomingdale's? Not this time. And after dinner, she flounced off to our room to call our friend Sofia Pappas (who, okay, was technically Michaela's friend first, but we all hang out together in dance school), leaving me to wash the dishes.

"Katie, you're being overdramatic." Michaela closes her eyes and her long lashes rest against her cheeks. I want to ask her what's wrong with being overdramatic, but it's clear she's trying to distract me, and I can't allow that to happen. Silently, I get to my feet and begin to cross our tiny room, sidestepping Michaela's boxy pink toe shoes, which lie in a tangle on the carpet. I duck to avoid the low shelf that holds our hand-painted Russian nesting dolls, and then plunk down onto Michaela's bed. Her sheets feel crisp and neat, unlike mine.

"Katie!" Michaela bolts upright. "Get off!" She nudges me — hard — with her foot. It's a foot made strong from years of ballet training, so I know better than to mess with it. "What are you doing?"

I shrug, but scoot back. We sit on opposite ends of the bed, facing each other. "This way, you can't ignore me," I explain.

Michaela groans. "We have to get up early for dance tomorrow and —"

"I'm not going to fall asleep anyway so —"

"— Svetlana has been *on* me about nailing my pirouettes and —"

"— you'd better tell me whatever it is that's bugging you because —"

"— if I'm zonked in the morning it will be all your fault —"

"— since when do we keep things from each other?"

It's that last question that quiets Michaela. She holds my gaze, and I think we are both holding our breaths. Sometimes when I'm staring right at Michaela, I get the creeped-out sensation that I'm looking at *myself*. We don't have the same eyes, but I guess it's the expression in them that's the same: a look that our mom calls "penetrating." I'm not sure what that means exactly, but right now, I do feel as if Michaela is boring into me with her gaze, trying to read me, or maybe to read herself. Outside, a garbage truck is huffing and puffing, and I can hear our dad's rumbly snores from the next room.

"Okay," Michaela says, and her voice is less than a whisper, a feather of a whisper. I can smell her breath — minty and toothpaste-y — and see the faint shimmer of sweat on her upper lip. "Promise you won't tell Mom and Dad?"

I knew it!

"I promise, I promise. Can I guess?" Michaela half smiles, half shrugs, so I pounce. "It's about dance, isn't it?" Leave it to Michaela to have nightmares about pirouettes.

Michaela slowly shakes her head from side to side. "Not really. Sort of. No."

I lean back on my hands, wracking my brain. School is a distant memory in August, and we're not close enough to September for Michaela's coming senior year to be an issue.

And then a wild thought occurs to me.

My pulse flutters at the base of my throat. No. Impossible. But it *could* be. What else would keep my levelheaded sister up at night other than . . .

"A *boy*?" I whisper in shock. "You're thinking about a boy." I feel my stomach drop.

Boys. Such strange, alien creatures. Take the boys in my junior high, for example. They all chew with their mouths open, get into scuffling fights in gym class, and look at the floor whenever girls speak to them. Horrible. Sofia Pappas, who is sixteen, swears up and down that boys get cuter once they hit high school — *and* that kissing them feels nice — but I'm doubtful. After all, Michaela, who is seventeen and knows better, has never promised anything of the sort.

True, Michaela has only kissed one boy: Jason Rosenthal, the only boy in her dance class last year. Jason had wavy dark hair and a goofy smile, and was good at the big jumps. One afternoon, when I was home sick with a cold, Jason walked Michaela to the subway and kissed her just as the train was roaring in. The next day, he dropped out of dance school after some guys in his neighborhood found his tights in his bookbag and gave him a purple-black eye. Michaela never heard from Jason again, but she didn't seem to mind much. She's not the type to get all mopey and obsessive over boys — unless you count Ethan Stiefel, the so-gorgeous-it-hurts principal dancer of the American Ballet Theater. Michaela has a poster of him, leaping through the air, over her bed. Sometimes the two of us will lie back on Michaela's pillows and stare up at Ethan, wondering why we don't know any guys as perfect as him.

"Is Jason Rosenthal back?" I ask, studying Michaela's surprised face.

When she doesn't respond right away, dread seeps through me. So *that* explains why my sister's been avoiding me in favor of Sofia. Last year, whenever Michaela tried to talk to me about Jason, I'd swat the subject away like it was a mosquito.

"You can tell me, Michaela," I press on, trying to be brave. "It's okay — I promise I won't get weird or —"

"It's not about Jason," Michaela says flatly. "Or any boy."

Oh.

Before I can feel the full force of my relief, Michaela speaks again.

"We're moving," she says.

I look down at the bed on which we're sitting, as if I'm expecting it to up and glide away — a magic carpet. "No, we're not," I blurt, but my tongue feels stupid in my mouth.

Michaela is nothing if not patient. She reaches out and touches her warm hand to my hot arm. "Like, *moving*-moving," she murmurs. "Out of the apartment. Out of the city."

This idea is so insane that I start giggling, only the giggles come out more like nervous hiccups. Michaela watches me, concerned. "Um, when?" I snort, and my arm sort of flops as I gesture around our dark room. "Shouldn't we be packing? Or calling movers? Time's a-ticking!"

"At the end of the month," Michaela replies without a hint of wanting to laugh. I notice that she's twisting her thin blanket between her hands. It's this small detail that sends a cold knife through my belly. Maybe she's not joking. Or lying. Come to think of it, Michaela's never done much of either.

"Where?" I ask, and my voice is quieter now.

Michaela flicks on her bedside lamp, and I blink as she slides out of her bed and pads, catlike, over to her desk. Everything about Michaela is catlike, from her sloping eyes and her long, slender neck to her careful, graceful way of walking.

I think I'm more the hamster variety.

Michaela returns, holding her humming laptop, and sits down beside me. A Google map stares at us from the screen. The jumble of yellow and gold lines makes no sense to me. Give me a subway map, like the one that hangs on my wall, and I'll be able to figure out every orange squiggle and confusing transfer. Now, foreign names like KEENE and CROWN POINT pop out at me.

"Here." Michaela presses her finger to a small spot on the map. The screen dents when she touches it. "We're moving here."

Okay. This is feeling suspiciously less and less like a joke.

The map, I see, is titled ESSEX COUNTY, NEW YORK. Which, I'm guessing, is somewhere upstate. I've only been upstate once, to see a ballet performance in the cute town of Saratoga Springs. But the spot Michaela is pointing to isn't called Saratoga Springs.

"Fir Lake," I read aloud, my lips thick and slow. "What's a fir?"

"A kind of tree," Michaela replies instantly, ever the straight-A student. "It's like a pine tree. Green and bristly. Christmas. You know."

My mind sputters. My sister and I are sitting here, talking about trees, with a map of what may as well be the moon in our laps. How did this happen?

"Why?" I ask, my throat tight all of a sudden. I feel jumpy and wired, as if someone has plugged me into an outlet.

"There's a college right outside the town," Michaela says. "Fenimore Cooper College. And they needed a new professor to head up their Russian Lit department."

"Mom," I mumble, understanding.

"Mom," Michaela agrees. There's nothing more to say.

I think of our mother, who is no doubt awake next door, rubbing lemon-scented lotion into her hands, with some mammoth book on Tolstoy open in her lap while our father sleeps beside her. Anger flares up in me. My parents are so peaceful, so calm, keeping this huge, this momentous . . . *thing* from me. When were they going to let me know? When was anyone? Were they planning to leave me behind?

"How long have you known?" I whisper, snapping my head toward Michaela.

Her cheeks are as pink as the stripes on her night-gown. "Mom and Dad only told me last week. They said they wanted to wait to tell you until they cleared things up with the lawyers, about the house or whatever. They said there was no point in getting you upset until . . ."

"A baby." I am barely able to talk through my clenched teeth.

"What?" Michaela asks, and leans into me, as if she wants to give me a hug. I brush her off me, and stand, glaring down at her.

"A baby," I repeat, putting my hands on my hips. "That's all I am to you guys. It's disgusting."

"Katie." Michaela's voice takes on a worried, step-away-from-the-mental-patient quality.

I hold my hands up for added effect, and make my voice go high-pitched. "Oh, don't say anything to the *baby*! God forbid the *baby* gets upset! Maybe we'll have to change her diaper!" I'm not exactly sure who I'm imitating, but it doesn't matter.

"Speak louder, why don't you?" Michaela whispers, reaching up to tug on my arm. "I can't hear you over the *crazy*."

"I'm sick of it," I spit out, ignoring her. "Sick of

being the last one to find out stuff. Nobody ever tells me *anything*."

I'm not exaggerating. In fact, I'm remembering all the times this happened before — when our pet gerbil kicked the bucket; when my dance teacher decided I wasn't quite ready for toe shoes; when our dad couldn't sell his last manuscript and kept going into the bathroom to cry. My parents always act as if I'm too fragile, too head-in-the-clouds "sensitive" to bear any of this knowledge. But of course I'm not. I rely on Michaela — my spy, my confidante — to fill me in on the truth. This move, though, is bigger than any pet's passing. This is my *life*.

"I'm telling you now, aren't I?" Michaela is still attempting to whisper. Her face is growing more flushed by the second. "And by the way? You *are* getting upset. Don't you see?"

"Of course I'm upset," I bark, not caring who we wake up. I almost want our mom to come knock on our door, so I can grill her, too. "You waited a *whole week* with, oh, only the biggest news of our lives?" I know I am being overdramatic, but with good reason. Fragments from earlier in the summer are adding up, fitting together in my head. My parents, whispering in the kitchen. Their mysterious trips upstate to "visit antique shops," which they'd never done before. I clench my hands into fists. I'm such an idiot.

I gaze around the bedroom, which is bright and

lit up now: Nothing is hidden anymore. I try to comprehend that, in a few weeks, everything — our books, spilling off the shelves over my bed; the clothes jammed into our messy closet; the china dancer figurines on my desk — will be packed up and sealed off and shipped away. It's not to be believed. I'm still half waiting for Michaela to crack up and tell me that it's all a prank, revenge for my not letting her go to sleep.

Instead, Michaela looks tearful, which scares me. Michaela hardly ever cries. "Don't you think it's been driving me nuts?" she asks quietly, her voice cracking. She lowers her head, her hair curtaining her face. "Come on, Katie. You know I can't stand keeping secrets from you."

My heart squeezes. Suddenly, I feel so thankful toward Michaela that it overwhelms me. She *did* tell me. That's what counts. Instantly, I regret my hysterics. I'm an awful sister. Michaela and I are silent for a second as I stand, breathing shallowly, and she remains on the bed. Someone honks a horn and swears on the street outside.

"Why aren't *you* freaking out?" I ask when I'm feeling a thimbleful more normal.

"I'm not sure," Michaela admits, her tone thoughtful. She drums her fingers on the edge of her bed. I'm relieved to see her eyes look less teary.

"Did you lose it when they told you?" I entertain a brief, invented vision of Michaela throwing furniture.

"Of course not." Michaela gives me a small smile. "I'm not you."

"I resent that," I say. But I sit down beside her once more.

"Maybe I'm still in shock," she offers with a shrug.

"Very possible," I say, and we both laugh a little. Then I reach over and retrieve the laptop from Michaela's lap. Together, we stare and stare at the tiny spot marked FIR LAKE until I can feel my eyes smarting.

"Fir Lake," I say for the second time that night, and shake my head in disbelief. I imagine glassy water and rocky mountains; old, spooky houses decorated with cobwebs; giant, horned insects. All I know of nature is contained in the neat spaces of city parks, with their paved roads and ornate benches. My favorite book growing up was *Eloise*, because I, too, was a "city child." I still am, and so is Michaela. How am I — how are *we* — going to exist in a place called Fir Lake, when we've lived all our lives in apartment 4G, on 5TH Street, here in the East Village?

"It's not hicks-in-the-sticks middle of nowhere," Michaela says, clearly reading my mind. "It's a small town. They have their own high school right in the village, and Mom enrolled us there for the beginning of this year —"

"No," I tell her. I can't hear anymore. We're already enrolled in a new school? I've been on pins and needles to start at LaGuardia High School for the Performing Arts — Michaela's school — in September. Yes, it's true: I was dorkily excited about high school. Now, I'm filled with the deepest dread. Then I think of dance school, and all the friends and teachers I'll need to say good-bye to, and suddenly I'm too exhausted to think anymore. I close my eyes.

Wordlessly, Michaela shuts off her lamp, and the room is comfortingly dark once again. Going back to my own bed seems like too much of an effort, and Michaela seems to understand, because she clears a space for me beside her. We flop down onto our backs, staring up at the Ethan Stiefel poster. This time, when Michaela sighs, it's not her big-sister sigh. It's just a sigh.

"Hey, Mickey? I'm sorry," I say. Mickey is the name I gave my sister when I was four and she was seven, and I couldn't pronounce "Mick-ah-ella." My sister always called me by my real name — Katya — until I started school and my teachers (God bless them) transformed me into normal, American "Katie." I'm still Katya to my mother, no matter how much I beg her to make the switch. "Sorry I yelled at you," I add.

Michaela takes my hand and gives it a squeeze. "I'm sorry I didn't tell you sooner."

I nod against the cool pillow, feeling safe beside my sister. Even the heat seems less brutal here, and Michaela smells soft and familiar, like the powder she puts on after she showers.

"This isn't the end of the world, right?" I say, trying to convince myself. "Us, moving?"

"No," Michaela replies after a minute. "It could be the beginning."

And before I can ask her what she means by that, she's shut her eyes and fallen asleep.

2

Fir Lake is the first thing I think when I wake up the next morning. *Leotard* is the second, because one has just been thrown in my face.

"Get up!" Michaela calls, and I lift my head to see her standing in front of our mirror. She's dressed in her burgundy leotard with spaghetti straps (what the Advanced Girls wear), pale pink tights, and black leg warmers. Her bulging Capezio tote bag rests at her feet, stuffed with her toe shoes, lamb's wool, extra ribbons and elastic, and the filmy pink skirt she's going to tie around her waist once she gets to class. She is furiously twining her hair into a bun on top of her head. "If we're late, Svetlana is going to eat me for breakfast," she adds, sounding truly concerned that this might happen.

"You're too skinny — you wouldn't make a good meal," I mumble, pushing the leotard's shiny black material off my cheek. I'm hot and my mouth is cottony. I don't even know what time I drifted off last night, but my eyelids feel like paperweights. I am so not a morning person.

"Very funny." Michaela touches her tongue to her upper lip as she pushes a sharp-toothed pin through her bun, forcing it to stay in place. She's already wearing her Ballet Face — a serious, professional expression that makes her seem very different from the close, cuddly Michaela of last night.

Last night.

I roll out of Michaela's bed, suddenly eager to start the day. I can hear my parents in the kitchen, Dad fiddling with the espresso machine while Mom gripes about some spelling error in *The New York Times*. I know I promised Michaela I wouldn't give her away, but that doesn't mean I can't ask Mom and Dad a few leading questions. I yawn and loosen my hair from its band, letting my thick dark curls spring free. Getting them into a respectable bun every morning is a task worthy of Hercules.

Or worthy of Michaela, a can of hair spray, and several torture weapons disguised as pins.

This morning, though, I need to build in extra time for the parental chitchat. Quick as can be, I strip, grab my tights from off the floor, tug them on, and step into the black leotard Michaela helpfully threw at me. This is my gear, my uniform, and in some ways, it feels more comfortable than the boxers and tank

I wore to bed. I fling on what us dancers call "street clothes" — a denim pencil skirt, a thin yellow T-shirt with the words MUSEUM OF MODERN ART across the front, and my silver flats. Finally, I bind my hair up into a sloppy bun before heading for the door.

"Where are you going?" Michaela gasps. "I need to fix your hair! Claude will chop your head off if he sees you looking like that."

Michaela believes that all ballet instructors are capable of inhuman violence.

I pull my black tote off the hook on the door — I packed my ballet slippers and water bottle last night — and turn the knob. "I have business to take care of," I reply casually, then dash out of the room before she can stop me.

"Katie! You promised!"

Really, we know each other way too well.

My parents glance up, all innocence, when I skid into the kitchen. My mom is standing at the counter, pouring milk into her coffee, and Dad is carefully pulling his charred bagel out of the toaster. Our kitchen is so narrow that my parents' backs are pressed together, and if anyone tried to open the refrigerator door right now, there would be a terrible accident.

"Katya, what is the matter? Why haven't you girls left yet? You know how angry Svetlana gets when Michaela is tardy." My mother shakes her dark bangs out of her eyes, glances down at her wristwatch, and clucks her tongue to show me how disappointed she is.

"Morning, kiddo." My dad cheerfully drops a kiss on my forehead as he squeezes his way out of the kitchen with his bagel in hand; it's obvious his writing is going well today. But I grab his arm before he can escape.

"If something, um, really important was going to happen to our family, you and Mom would tell me, right?" I ask my father, widening my eyes at him meaningfully. I hear the *clink* of my mother's spoon as she stirs the milk into her coffee.

My dad blinks once, twice, then gives a hearty nod. "Of course I would, love," he says, his face breaking into a smile. "Now, if you'll excuse me, I have to get started on my third chapter while the opening line's still fresh in my head."

I frown. The annoying thing is, he *hasn't* blown me off: My dad is really just that spacey. As Dad ambles off, he nearly collides with Michaela, who is running full tilt toward the kitchen, dressed in her street clothes. He greets her, then heads into my parents' bedroom while Michaela joins me on the threshold, shooting me an am-I-going-to-have-to-kill-you? look.

"Michaela, why did you tell your sister about our move when I explicitly asked you not to?" our mother asks coolly, and both Michaela and I turn to face her, openmouthed. "Stop looking at me so surprised," Mom says to me with her crooked smile. "I understood very well what you were asking, Katya. I am not your father."

"Sorry, Mom," Michaela says softly, and bows her head. "But I realized that it wouldn't be fair —"

"Whoever said life was fair?" Mom asks, which is, hands down, her favorite expression. It's been drilled into my brain since childhood, right along with the fact that *Anna Karenina* is the best novel ever written and that American kids never learn proper geography. Normally, I don't notice my mom's accent, but I hear it when she speaks that phrase. It's the way she says *was*, as if it's spelled with a *v* instead of a *w*.

"I'm sorry," Michaela says again, her eyes downcast.

"I'm not," I mutter. "I have a right to know things. It's like I'm not a citizen in this house." I'm hoping Mom will warm up to the word *citizen*, since she only recently became one.

But Mom barely seems to hear me. She comes forward and puts her hands on Michaela's shoulders, looking my sister in the eye. "It's okay, sweetheart," she says, her voice smooth as milk now, when before it was as sharp as black coffee. "I spoke to the lawyer this morning, and it's all been finalized." She checks her watch once again. "But we'll talk about this later. Go on now, both of you." She squeezes Michaela's shoulder. "Show Svetlana how you've been practicing your pirouettes."

I wonder if, when my mother looks at my sister, she remembers herself as a teenager, all dressed up for *her* dance class. Back in Saint Petersburg, the snowy city where she grew up, my mom studied dance at a super-prestigious school that spit most of its students out into the Kirov Ballet. But one day my mom's teacher pulled her aside and told her that really, she didn't have a dancer's figure, and she should probably give up on the dream and just become a schoolteacher or something. I totally inherited my mom's body — not too tall, with breasts that sprung up overnight, and hips that wiggle even when I don't want them to. I have "curves," like my closest dance-school friend, Trini Cortez, says. In America, you can still have curves and become a real ballet dancer. At least, I hope so. Otherwise I'm out of luck.

Since Mom is Mom, she gritted her teeth and burned her toe shoes and studied until she became a professor of literature. Schoolteacher wouldn't have been good enough for her. Then she came all the way to America to teach at New York University, married a semi-famous American writer, and had two daughters, whom she enrolled in ballet lessons as soon as they could walk.

I use the story of my mom's life to explain to my friends at regular school why ballet is "such a big deal" to my family. I'm not sure that kids who have ordinary American mothers could ever understand. In Russia, ballet means so much — it's more than just tutus and little girls wanting to look pretty. It's considered the highest of high-art forms, and there, nobody would beat up a boy because he decided to wear tights. I've only been to Russia once, and I don't even speak the language, but sometimes I like to imagine myself there, wearing a fur hood, and running tragically across a stone bridge in toe shoes while a beautiful boy-dancer named Sasha chases after me. Maybe it will happen one day.

"So it's true, then," I say to my mom as she ushers me and Michaela to the door. Deep down, there was still a lingering piece of me that hoped Fir Lake was all a giant misunderstanding. Perhaps our parents had decided to purchase a vacation home there — not that we have the money for that sort of thing — and Michaela had interpreted it all wrong. But Michaela isn't like me; she doesn't invent stories.

"This is a dream opportunity," Mom tells me briskly. "You'll see how much happier we'll all be, once I have a higher salary, and we have more space, and —" she lowers her voice and glances over her shoulder — "it will be nice for your father to have a change of scene, to write his books in the fresh air."

"We're happy here," I protest, looking around our small, cluttered living room, with its modernist paintings on the wall, towering bookshelves, and view onto the bars and restaurants of 1st Avenue. Dad writes in the bedroom or in Starbucks, Michaela and I lounge in our room, Mom has her office at NYU. Who needs fresh air?

"There's even a dance school in town," Mom

adds, her eyes intent. "We made sure of that." She kisses Michaela on the cheek as my sister leaves the apartment, and she quickly kisses me, too, but the gesture feels meaningless and mindless — like an afterthought.

"Mom and Dad can't stand me," I announce once Michaela and I are walking toward the Astor Place subway station. Pounding the pavement all around us are young women in strappy heels, clutching sweating cups of iced coffee; guys in blue button-down shirts arguing into their cell phones; rope-thin models trotting along in chunky platforms; a grungy-looking man playing a harmonica while jingling a hat full of change.

Michaela rolls her eyes. "Please, Katie. You don't see it, but you're so their favorite."

"You are," I reply automatically. This is an old, old debate. And though I let Michaela win sometimes, I know I'm always right. Someone deaf, dumb, and blind could see how much our parents — especially our mom — prefer Michaela.

"I'm not in the mood today." Michaela cuts the discussion short as we pass by the skater kids and pierced punks loitering around the cube near St. Mark's Place. But then she links her arm through mine, to show that she's not really mad — just worried about being late.

Stink and steam are rising up from the garbage bags heaped on the street corners — a real New York summer smell — and I take a deep breath, gross as it is. I feel like I'm looking at everything harder and closer this morning: the silver skyscrapers glinting in the distance, the yellow taxicab traffic inching toward Broadway, the chattering crowd of girls in black leggings and wedge heels standing outside the Public Theater. They must be lining up for Shakespeare in the Park tickets. I fight down a lump in my throat and remind myself that we're not leaving this minute.

A cloud of heat envelops us as we descend the steps into the subway. On the platform, Michaela and I walk past the newsstand guy, who waves at us. He has no idea what our names are, but he "knows" us, the way that people in the city know each other. I'm sure he thinks of us as the ballet sisters, since we're always walking by him in our tights, with our hair up and our feet turned out (we can't help it — we don't know how to walk any other way). We don't know anything about him, either, other than the fact that he has a bushy mustache and will give us a discount on Dentyne Ice if we ask for it nicely.

"Where's the train?" Michaela asks under her breath, tapping one foot as she gazes down the length of the pitch-black tunnel. "We'll never make it at this rate." It usually takes us about forty minutes to get to dance school, and we have the whole journey down pat — ride the 6 train to Grand Central Station, transfer for the shuttle to Times Square, then catch the 1 train, and get out at West 66th Street. It's a bit of a hike, but I kind of like all the switching of trains, the hurrying through stations, soaking up the mad energy, being part of the crush.

"Don't stand so close to the edge," I warn Michaela, taking her wrist. Our parents enjoy scaring us with stories of lunatics who push people onto the tracks. These are the things, the rules, you learn when you're a city child: Watch your back; keep your bag tucked under your arm; avoid making eye contact.

I wonder what the rules are upstate, in the country. Keep an eye out for rabid foxes? Avoid creepy men in overalls who go by the name "Farmer Joe"? I'm considering these possible terrors when I notice a small shape dart across the tracks.

And I shriek.

The woman standing next to me, who is wearing head-to-toe black, including giant sunglasses, looks up from her BlackBerry and scowls.

"Rat!" I clap a hand to my mouth. "Michaela, there's a rat —"

"It's a mouse," Michaela corrects me, trying to wrestle her wrist out of my death grip. "What's with you? It's not like you haven't seen one before."

I don't answer. The rat — I *know* it's a rat — pauses on the tracks and turns its rodent-y little head in my direction. Its beady red eyes seem to glow at me, and then it turns and sprints away, a second before the train squeals into the station.

"It's an omen," I tell Michaela as the train doors part, blowing freezing air out at us. "Don't you know that? An omen of . . . doom."

"Good God, Katie." Michaela lets out the mother of all big-sister sighs.

I bite my lip as we're pushed onto the train by a swarm of impatient bodies. Everyone has their little New York superstitions, and mine is that rats in the subway equal bad luck. Last night I suspected it, but now I know for sure: The move to Fir Lake is going to be a disaster.

Forty minutes later, Michaela and I have gone from the realm of rats to the hushed, cream-and-rose-colored world of the Anna Pavlova Academy of Ballet. The dressing room is empty as we hurriedly shed our street clothes, and my sister and I wave to each other as we dash into our respective studios.

"Katie Wilder," my teacher, the great Claude Durand, pronounces.

When the great Claude Durand speaks your full name, it can be very good or very bad. Once, *once*, after I performed a decent arabesque, he smiled, patted my arm, and said, "*Oui*, Katie Wilder!" My heart sang that day, even though Claude's smile can be frightening (apparently they don't have proper dental care in Paris).

Today, Claude is standing in the center of the wide,

airy studio, wearing his usual navy-blue leotard and rolled-up gray sweatpants, and glowering as he strokes his neat white goatee. Beams of sunlight fall through the tall windows, lighting up the nine girls standing at the barre: my Lower Intermediate classmates. They are all dressed in black leotards, pink tights, split-sole Sansha slippers, and high, tight buns. Seeing them like this, I can understand why we're called bunheads.

Our eye-patch–wearing pianist, Alfredo, is at the white baby grand, cracking his knuckles. Clearly, they were about to begin before I rudely burst in. And, when I glance into the wall of mirrors, I notice that — as Michaela predicted — my bun is coming undone, rebel curls crowding around my ears in a most attractive way.

Okay. It's bad.

"Pardon me, sir." I smooth my hair and drop in a curtsy, as I have been taught. All I really want to do, though, is blurt out Michaela's bombshell from last night. "I'm kind of spazzing out," I want to say, as I might to a teacher in my junior high, who would want to hear all about my "issues at home." But the great Claude Durand thinks excuses are for the weak and clumsy. Excuses are not for future ballerinas, especially if we expect to grace the stage of Lincoln Center one day, which, truth be told, we all do. We wouldn't be here, at Anna Pavlova, otherwise.

So I simply glide over to the spot behind Trini

and rest my hand on the barre, remembering to keep my neck long and straight. "Like a duck," Claude tells us — meaning a swan, of course. We've learned how to decipher his mangled English over the years.

Trini angles her head toward me as Alfredo starts playing Beethoven. "You okay?" she asks out of the corner of her mouth. Trini and I have perfected the art of talking during class without our lips moving.

I lean forward and whisper, "Later."

Claude lifts his silver-handled walking stick and brings it down hard on the shiny wooden floor. *Thud.* *"Allons-y,"* he commands, still watching me slit-eyed. "Pliés."

Automatically, I shift my feet into first position — heels together, toes pointing outward — and bend slowly, slowly at the knees. Then I rise up, letting my arm follow in a swoop. My stomach is still in knots, but I'm soothed by the thought that, in the studio next door, Michaela is doing the exact same thing as I am. Every dance class, no matter what the level, begins with pliés. Down, up, down, up. I feel a burning in my calves — I didn't have time to stretch earlier — but the motion is so familiar, so built into my body, that it's a little like breathing. Alfredo's fingers fly over the keys, and the music washes over me, along with the sunlight, warm and sweet. I'm already half forgetting about Fir Lake.

This is why I love to dance.

Claude is counting out the beats, banging his walking stick on the floor for emphasis. "*Et* one — *et* two — *et* what is this ugliness?"

I freeze, assuming he means me, but, no, his latest victim is beautiful Hanae Murasaki, who is the best Lower Intermediate dancer — the Michaela of our class. There is a small swell of joy in me, and in all the girls, I'm sure. It's like we're nine movie villains, rubbing our hands together and cackling, "*Bwah-ha-ha!*" Ballet dancers pretend to support each other, but when it comes down to it, we're forever waiting for the star to get sick as a dog so the understudy can take over. I feel a flash of sympathy, though, when Claude taps Hanae's shoulder blades and hisses, "*Alors,* Mademoiselle Murasaki, why do you stand like *une bossue?*"

Only a handful of us girls speak French — I studied it in junior high, and know how to say hello, good-bye, and where are the toilets? — but, thanks to the great Claude Durand, we all understand the word for "hunchback." Because we've all been there. If we dare to let our shoulders droop even the tiniest bit, it's over — we're Quasimodo.

But — *but* — if we stand up straight and carry ourselves with a bit of grace, there is the chance that Claude will call us by our full names, and we will glimpse a slice of heaven.

Which makes all the pain and humiliation worthwhile.

Kind of.

Miraculously, I get through the barre exercises — élevés, piqués, rondes de jambes, attitudes, arabesques — without Claude screaming at me. By the time we all gather in the corner for jetés, I'm pleasantly sweaty and feeling pretty good about myself. We're supposed to cross the floor in jumps, one by one, and I'm last in line. Renée Jackson, the tallest girl in the class, is first, and I watch her take off, the ribbons she always wears in her hair rippling behind her. Alfredo is playing Mozart's Piano Sonata 11 — my favorite.

I lean against the wall and let my eyes drift toward the windows that face the grand plaza of Lincoln Center. It's so fitting; we're close to that dreamworld, but not inside. Sometimes when I study the elegant white buildings, I wonder if the dancers in there ever stare out their windows and wonder about the dancers in here.

And that's when it hits me, with a suddenness that makes me start, that *this is it*.

This is the last time I will stand in this studio and gaze down at Lincoln Center. This is the last time I will watch Hanae and Trini and my other friends leap across the floor. The last time I will hear Alfredo — wonderful, funny Alfredo, who winks at us with his good eye — play this upbeat, sprightly melody. And the last time I will be able to think *I am a student at the Anna Pavlova Academy, the most competitive ballet school in New York City.*

Of course, I know this isn't officially my last class. I still have a few more weeks. But from now on, I'll be split in two — my mind saying good-bye as my body goes through the motions. Something my mom said earlier — about there being a dance school in Fir Lake — creeps into my brain, and I squirm. It's all wrong.

"Katie Wilder!"

It can't be. Not twice in one class.

I lift my head, my cheeks flaming, to see that all the other girls have cleared the floor, and I am lagging behind. Claude, understandably, is frowning at me.

"*Alors,* Mademoiselle Wilder, are you dancing or are you dreaming?" he asks. "Because one cannot do both."

I hear the soft titters of the other girls. In June, when Claude told me that I was a stain upon the face of ballet (it's okay; he said the same thing to Trini once), nobody laughed. My classmates are usually nice to me; being Michaela Wilder's sister commands a certain amount of respect. But today it seems I'm fair game. Even Trini's mouth is twitching; she must be entertained by my spaciness.

Any other day, I would lift my chin and run into the jump, splitting my legs in midair and enjoying the rush of wind across my face. But something about today — the heat and Fir Lake and Lincoln Center and my mother and Claude — is boiling up in me, and I realize that, without a doubt, I am going to cry.

"May I be excused?" I ask, already taking a few steps back. Claude loathes it when anyone leaves during class, but he can't hold us in here against our will. I clutch my belly to indicate a stomach-related problem, and before anyone can say anything, I turn and run.

3

The hallway is empty, with classical music drifting out from behind closed doors. In the dressing room, someone is humming as she changes.

I stand alone with the giant, black-and-white photographs of famous dancers, who appear blurry through my tear-filled eyes: Mikhail Baryshnikov, Suzanne Farrell, Anna Pavlova herself. From another wall, color photos of our teachers in their heyday stare down at me: There's a beardless Claude onstage in Paris, dressed up as the Nutcracker Prince, and Svetlana Vronsky, the headmistress and Michaela's teacher, standing on her toes in a swan costume — the prima ballerina of the Bolshoi Ballet. When I was little, I used to make up stories about those photos; I'd imagine that Svetlana and Claude were secretly in love and hiding it from us. Then Michaela patiently explained to me that Claude was gay. That was so long ago, I almost can't believe the photographs are still here.

Wiping my nose on my arm in a most graceful fashion, I turn toward the bathroom, but then I notice that the door to the Advanced Class studio is ajar. I don't mean to spy, but a half open door is an invitation, isn't it?

I tiptoe over and peer inside. Their pianist is banging out Bach, and Michaela is in the center, performing fouttés. Her back is as straight as if she's swallowed a broomstick — Claude wouldn't *dare* call her *une bossue* — and her arms form a precise circle. I bite my lip. She's risen up entirely on her left toe, the hard box of her pink pointe shoe against the floor. And she's whirling. Once, twice, three times. Her head whips around and her filmy pink skirt twirls. The foot she's turning on moves so quickly, all I can see is a blur.

It's breathtaking. There is no other word for it. My sister's dancing makes your breath catch in your throat.

Michaela's classmates, all in their burgundy leotards with their toe shoes laced up their ankles, stand grouped in one corner, their faces tight with envy and awe. Sofia Pappas looks like a truck is about to hit her. And their teacher, Svetlana, her scarlet-dyed hair loose about her shoulders, is glowing as she observes her star pupil.

My sister is not only a champion sleeper. She is also a champion ballerina.

I'm a fizzing mix of jealousy and pride as I watch Michaela finish the fouttés. *That is my sister!* part of me is shouting. *My best friend.* But another part of me is whispering, *You will never look like that when you are dancing.* No one in this school will. Michaela is far beyond us, in a universe all her own.

The plan — concocted by Svetlana and our mom — has been in place since Michaela was my age: After she graduates high school, she's going to Juilliard, and then straight into a real company, maybe even the American Ballet Theater, to dance with Ethan Stiefel. Or the New York City Ballet, to dance onstage at Lincoln Center. My head spins a little when I think about Michaela's future, because it's all lit up with spotlights.

My future is more like a subway tunnel — dim and unknown.

In the Advanced studio, Michaela is breathing quickly; her collarbone, shiny with sweat, rises and falls as she walks over to the container of toe shoe rosin on the floor. I watch as she grinds the box of her shoe into the white grains — rosin helps you to not slip. The tips of my toes tingle. All I wanted this year was to dance on pointe. But when I tried, when I tremblingly laced up my first pair of toe shoes and performed in them for Claude, he pulled my mom aside afterward and told her I needed to wait another year. I feel a sharp tug in my chest at the memory.

"Everyone, I hope you were watching how wonderfully Michaela performed," Svetlana is saying in her flawless but thickly accented English. Her fingers toy with the ends of the leopard-print scarf around her neck. "That is how each of you should strive to dance."

God. Doesn't she know better? It's that kind of talk that makes girls despise each other.

Then again, Michaela is leaving — which the girls don't even know yet. I can picture the celebrating that will erupt when they find out that Svetlana's pet won't be overshadowing them anymore. Looking at Michaela now, I realize my sister is having the identical thought. She is facing the mirror, her feet in the rosin box, but really she is watching her classmates with a thoughtful, anxious expression on her face. I know Michaela worries what other people think of her; that's why she doesn't bask and preen when Svetlana sings her praises. She's modest — which is another reason to hate her, I suppose.

Michaela's eyes shift, and I see her see me standing in the doorway. Her lips part, and she gives the tiniest shake of her head. I know I'd be in serious trouble if Svetlana caught me, so I slink away from the door and start back to my studio. I dab at my eyes, but my urge to sob has, thankfully, passed. I'm doubly relieved when I reenter my studio and find that class has ended — the girls are sitting on the floor, some cross-legged, some with their legs splayed out on either side to show how flexible they are. Claude is standing before them, saying something in a deep, formal tone. For one crazy second, I wonder if he's telling them about my departure.

"*Entrez*," Claude tells me gruffly, waving me over. "We are speaking of *The Nutcracker* auditions to be held next month."

My heart leaps. *The Nutcracker!* I'd forgotten. Every year, a handful of Anna Pavlova students are handpicked to appear in the New York City Ballet's deluxe, wintertime performance. Michaela has — surprise! — been in *The Nutcracker* many times, as one of Mother Ginger's children, as one of the candy canes, and then as Marie — the star. I was in the show once, when I was five, as a party guest, and all I remember is how scratchy my velvet dress felt, and that the stage lights made my eyes burn.

Now, at fourteen, is the very last time I can squeak through. Almost all the available roles are for young kids, though, on occasion, an older girl will be cast as a snowflake. I know my curves aren't fooling anyone, which is what Claude told me last year when I tried out. "*Chérie*, you do not look like a child," he said in his oh-so-subtle way. But I've been hopeful.

Until now, when I plunk down on the floor and realize I *can't* audition this year. Because I won't be here.

I'm worried I'm going to start crying again, so I purse my lips and put my forehead on my knees. How did this not occur to me last night? How did this not occur to Michaela? It should have been the first thing she said: "Katie, we're moving, and you won't be able to audition for *The Nutcracker.*" She knows — better than anyone — how badly I've wanted this, wanted this one delicious chance to prove to Claude and to our parents that I *could* be onstage with the big girls.

I'd bet good money they don't put on a *Nutcracker* in Fir Lake. And if they do, it's with, like, elderly ladies from the local nursing home.

When Claude finishes going through the list of roles, he tells us we are dismissed, and we all rise and begin to clap. Just like every dance class everywhere begins with pliés, every dance class ends with the students applauding first their teacher, and then their pianist. Claude presses his palms together and bows his head, and Alfredo shoots us a hammy wink. I am about to turn and walk out with Trini — who is shooting me the most impatient, tell-me-what's-going-on glance — when Claude calls out:

"Katie?"

My heart gives a small kick as I face him.

"I would like to speak with you," Claude says, motioning out the door. "*Allons-y.* Into Svetlana's office."

I tense up. Svetlana's office? Is it that I dashed out of class in the middle of floor exercises? Arrived late? Wore a messy bun? I want to start apologizing, but I'm not sure for what. Once again, I consider telling Claude about the move to Fir Lake, but there's no time; he's already leading me to Svetlana's office at the end of the hall. Looking even more intrigued, Trini waves to me and heads toward the changing room. As I watch her go, I see that Michaela's class has let out as well, the burgundy-clad girls streaming out into the hall. But I don't see my sister among them.

My legs are shaking as Claude turns the knob on Svetlana's door and we walk inside. My eyes sweep over the framed images on the pink wall — more photos of legendary dancers, all autographed; the 1980s cover of *Dance Magazine* that featured a close-up shot of a once-beautiful Svetlana; and snapshots of Svetlana's two grown-up daughters, who don't dance ballet.

Svetlana herself is sitting at her desk, smoking a cigarette, with her mile-long legs propped up on stacks of papers. And there's a girl sitting in a chair with her back to the door, her hair in a neat bun that hasn't budged an inch during class.

Michaela.

My sister turns around, and we stare at each other — me in shock, Michaela looking grim. "Um, hi," she finally says.

"What's going on?" I ask, for once not caring if I don't sound respectful in front of my teachers. My legs quake harder now. Did Svetlana see me spying on the class? What? *What?*

"Sit, darling." With her lit cigarette, Svetlana gestures to the empty chair beside Michaela, and numbly, I sit. Claude, clearing his throat, takes the seat next to me.

"Darlings." Svetlana's enormous gray eyes dart from me to Michaela and back again. I notice that she has a few pockets of wrinkles beneath her eyes, kind of like our mom. "Claude and I very much wanted to discuss with the two of you your dance future in this . . . Furry Lake." Her cherry-lined lips twist in disgust at the name.

I feel my mouth flap open, very unballerina-like. *They know?*

"Fir Lake," Michaela quickly corrects Svetlana, and then looks down at her pointe shoes. I can tell she is purposefully avoiding my confused gaze. At a loss, I swivel my head toward Claude, and he is nodding.

"How — when — when did you find out?" I manage to croak, glancing from Claude to Svetlana and back again.

"Your mother called me last week," Svetlana tells me crisply, taking a long drag off her cigarette. "It was crucial that we discuss the consequences of this move on you girls' dancing careers."

I can't even process the fact that Svetlana has said that *I* have a dancing career. No. Instead, my face is hot and I'm clutching the chair's armrests, and my mind is on a steady whirl, like a mouse wheel: *Everyone, everyone knew before me.*

"Of course, I brought up with your mother the interesting possibility . . ." Svetlana pauses and taps her cigarette into the pearl-framed ashtray on her desk. "Of you remaining in the city for the duration of this year. With me, in my apartment. I have the space. My daughters" — she flings a hand toward the snapshots on her wall — "have left long ago." Svetlana is looking at Michaela the whole time she speaks, but then her eyes flick toward me, so I assume when she says *you*, she means both of us.

Live with Svetlana? I try to imagine it — an apartment smelling of Svetlana's rosewater perfume; bird-sized breakfasts each morning ("to keep your figures trim!"); awkward rides to dance school in Svetlana's red I'm-newly-divorced Porsche . . . At least *that* world I can picture, whereas when I think of life in Fir Lake, my mind seems to hit a wall. A wall painted with pine trees and wolves.

Michaela crosses her legs and swings one toe-shoe-clad foot. "Thank you so much, Svetlana," she says with her usual poise and politeness (I kind of want to gag). "But I talked about it with my mother, and I — we —" She coughs into her fist. "We don't think that's the best idea. My parents really want to keep the family together."

I'm surprised by this news. The mom I know, forever serious about Michaela's dancing, would have been all for the move-in-with-Svetlana plan. And the dad I know would have glanced up from his laptop and nodded with a dazed look in his eyes. Then again, what do I know? Zilch, apparently, considering that Michaela and our parents were making life-changing decisions right under my nose.

Svetlana's cheekbones, already rouged, turn even redder. "I understand, darling," she murmurs, even though her tone says she doesn't. "Then it seems I will have to arrange a call with the headmistress of the Fir Lake dance school. A Ms. . . ." Svetlana sifts through the mess of papers on her desk. "Ms. Mabel Thorpe." Again, her lips twist. "To let her know of the training you girls had here, at the Anna Pavlova Academy." Svetlana sniffs and twirls the ends of her leopard-print scarf. "I'd never want that training to go to waste."

Michaela and I exchange a fast glance. We've known Svetlana for many years, so we know that, right now, she's royally ticked off.

"Claude!" Svetlana suddenly booms, and both Michaela and I give a start.

"*Oui*, Svetlana?" Claude asks, sitting up straighter, and I can tell he's been zoning out. I feel a tickle of pleasure; who's been daydreaming *now*?

"Do you have anything *you* would like to say to the Wilder girls?" Svetlana drums her long salmon-pink nails against the top of her desk.

"*Mais . . . euh . . .*" Claude rubs his goatee and blinks at me a few times. "It is *un grand* pity," he finally says, forcing an uncomfortable smile (the teeth, the teeth!), "that you will not be capable to dance this year in *The Nutcracker*, Katie."

I'm sure Claude means well. But all his parting words do is unleash something deep inside me that instantly brings hot tears to my eyes. Stupid, stubborn tears. It's as if, since they didn't get their chance to come out last time, they're *determined* to make an appearance now.

Michaela gets to her feet and takes my hand, pulling me up with her. "We have to be home in time for lunch," she announces, even though our family never eats lunch together.

Svetlana's mouth opens; she's probably about to scold Michaela. Then she seems to remember that she's dealing with her favorite student and catches herself. So she simply waves a hand toward the door, releasing us.

Michaela drops in a quick curtsy and I manage to mimic her, then follow her blindly out into the hallway. "Let's change and get out of here," Michaela whispers, putting an arm around my shoulders as we walk toward the dressing room. "We can talk about everything outside."

The first tears slip out and run down my cheeks. "What's to talk about?" I snap, half angry and half grateful. Without waiting for an answer, I yank open the door to the dressing room. The small, windowless room smells of sweat and rosin, and is teeming with girls all in various states of undress, unknotting their buns and brushing out their hair. The sound of post-class chatter fills the air, but when we walk in, there's a hush. Of course. Michaela has entered. The queen is in our presence.

"Michaela Antoinette," I like to tease Michaela when we're at home, and she's out of Ballet Mode, lounging on the couch in her nightgown and socks, with her hair loose. "That's how they see you, you know." *They* being everyone: from the littlest girls learning their first steps, to the most seasoned teachers, to the moms who sit in the waiting room and whisper to each other when Michaela walks past. *"I heard that one was chosen . . ." "Svetlana says she's never seen anyone as . . ." "She's going to Juilliard . . ."* As the queen's sister, I sometimes get the leftovers of those whispers. The mother hens will glance at me, too. *"Do you think the younger one is as good?"*

"Michaela Antoinette," Michaela will echo thoughtfully when we're at home. "Then let's hope they don't behead me."

Now, Michaela keeps her head down as she walks to her locker, her hands quickly undoing the sash on her pink skirt while two Advanced Beginner girls clear out of her path. Sofia Pappas, whose back was to the door, turns away from her locker and gasps.

"Katie!" she shrieks, flying toward me, yanking her carrot-red waves loose from her bun. "I was wondering where you were — oh, sweetie, what are we going to do without you?"

I sniff hard, letting Sofia crush me into a hug.

"Michaela told me on the phone last night," Sofia says, squeezing me so tight I cough. "I lost it immediately. Just started *wailing*. I can't live without you guys!" Sofia releases me, gripping me by my arms, and gasps again when she sees my tearstained face. "Oh, Katie! You're crying, too! It's so hard, isn't it?"

Sofia beats me in the overdramatic category every time.

I look past Sofia to see that most of the other girls in the room have formed a circle around the two of us. I instantly get that Sofia — whose big mouth is legendary — has filled them in.

"Why didn't you say something?" Trini asks me, her lips turned at the corners. Trini is starting at LaGuardia in September, like I was supposed to, and I'd already agreed not to wear my Steve Madden zebra-print flats on the first day, because she was going to wear hers.

"I just found out," I tell her truthfully, blinking back my tears. "And I couldn't in class . . ."

"I've heard of Fir Lake," Hanae pipes up, undoing her glossy black plait. "My parents went on vacation there once. It's in the Adirondacks — not too far from Canada, I think."

Great. So now it's like I'm leaving the country.

"Ugh, what kind of dance must they have up *there*?" Jennifer Golden groans, tugging on the strap of her tote bag.

Trini perks up at this. "Cow ballet!" she giggles, her eyes dancing, and Hanae and Renée Jackson burst into giggles as well. I feel a blush start around my neck.

"Wait, Katie," Renée cuts in, growing serious. "What about . . ." She drops her voice. "Your *sister*? I bet Svetlana wants her to stay."

In unison, we all glance over toward Michaela, who is sitting alone on a bench in the corner, removing her pointe shoes. The lamb's wool she wrapped around her toes before class is now stained dark red with blood. It's a sight that always makes me wince, but Michaela looks almost bored as she peels off the gory wool and throws it in the wastebasket. Her feet are blistered and bumpy — ideal dancer's feet.

"No, she's coming," I say with a shrug. "I'm not sure why."

I know the girls clustered around me are dying to ambush Michaela, too. But even Sofia and Jennifer, who've grown up with Michaela, who've lent her leotards and braided her hair, even they stand back a little. *I'm* the Wilder sister they can touch and grab and bombard with questions. I'm on their level, or beneath them — beneath the older ones, anyway.

On cue, Jennifer Golden suddenly cries, "My baby!" and pulls me into her skinny chest. Jennifer is all bones and sharp angles, so when *she* walks by the mothers in the waiting room, they put their heads together and whisper, "*Eating disorder . . .*" The twisted thing is, a lot of the Advanced dancers look like Jennifer. There are at least two girls in Michaela's class who I *know* don't eat anything other than Swedish Fish, which I see them devouring in the dressing room on a regular basis.

"No, she's *my* baby!" Sofia snaps at Jennifer, tugging me toward her. Normally, I have fun with this kind of banter between the older girls — I'll even play it up and pretend to choose a favorite (usually it's Sofia), just to watch the others pretend to be hurt. When I was younger, Sofia and Jennifer would come to our apartment and pinch my cheeks and dress me up in feather boas and lipstick while Michaela howled with laughter. I was their living doll, and I ate up every attention-gobbling minute.

Now, I'm finding it hard to breathe, surrounded so tightly by them all. I mumble something about there still being three weeks left. Then I manage to break free and hurry to my locker. There are sighs of disappointment, but eventually everyone scatters.

"I'll call you later?" I say to Trini, whose locker is next to mine, as I pull my T-shirt on over my head and kick off my ballet slippers.

"Mmm." Trini busies herself with something in her quilted tote bag.

My stomach tightens. Trini and I have been attached at the hip since we were tubby little girls in leotards. I can't stand having her, or any friend, mad at me. But then I hear Michaela's voice behind me — "Katie? You ready?" — and I forget about Trini. In the end, my sister is the friend who matters, even when I want to kill her for not telling me things.

"IM me tonight, okay, guys?" Sofia cries as Michaela and I leave the dressing room, and I hear the buzz of gossip start up again as soon as we shut the door.

I exhale. The Inquisition is over.

"I saw you," Michaela says once we've walked past the murmuring mothers in the waiting room, and are out on humid, crowded Broadway. Our bags bump against our hips as we walk, and my T-shirt sticks to my back.

I'm still feeling frosty toward my sister about the issue of Svetlana-Claude-Sofia knowing before I did. "Saw me being eaten alive by our friends?" I ask as we cross the avenue in the direction of Jamba Juice. Crushed strawberry shakes with immunity boosts are our post-class tradition. "Thanks for coming over to save me," I add, shoveling on the sarcasm like sand.

"I meant I saw you peeking in," Michaela replies as we approach Lincoln Center. "On my class. Why were you spying?" I feel her studying me.

She doesn't sound angry or annoyed; just curious. I lift one shoulder. "The door was open," I offer. "And I wasn't spying. Just watching." There's a crucial difference.

The two of us pause in front of the Lincoln Center plaza. Throngs of tourists are posing for pictures on the steps, and girls with their hair in telltale buns and their feet pointed outward — our sisters in dance — scurry by us. The cold spray from the fountain reaches my cheeks. I'm filled with so much missing for this place, even though we haven't left yet, that my gut hurts.

In her silent, semi-psychic way, Michaela puts her arm across my shoulders. "We'll be back," she assures me. "There's Greyhound, you know. And school breaks. This isn't good-bye forever."

I take a deep breath. When *will we be back*? I want to ask. But instead I turn to my sister and ask, "There are buses we can take from this *Furry* Lake?" in my best Svetlana impersonation, with the thickest Russian accent I can muster.

Michaela looks at me, opens and closes her mouth, and then bursts out laughing. I start laughing, too, and I think we're both relieved that it's okay to return to the land of jokes.

"I was going to *die* in there!" Michaela says between gasps. "I was so paranoid she was going to start a fire with her cigarette. I was silently chanting, 'Put it out, put it out."

"And did you see how awkward Claude was?" I giggle, shaking my head. "It was like Svetlana was asking him to do something really abnormal and out-rageous, like, I don't know — take a shower . . ."

This is my talent: making my sister laugh.

"And I didn't expect Sofia to foam at the mouth in the dressing room!" Michaela cries.

"The one-two punch of her and Trini was pretty terrifying."

"They're *insane*," Michaela declares, shaking her head. "Our friends are insane."

"We're insane," I snort, and in that moment, we are — just two crazy sisters, standing in the middle of Broadway, holding our sides and shaking with laugh-ter. The city swirls and jitterbugs around us, and I decide that no way am I going to spend the next three weeks moping. I'm going to lap up Manhattan and relish every moment.

I'll have *plenty* of time to be miserable once we get to the wilderness.

4

This is a historic moment.

The Wilder family is together . . . *in a car.*

Summer vacations to London or Moscow involved airplanes. Weekend trips to Boston or Philadelphia were all about buses. But now, in the last week of August, my parents, Michaela, and I are scaling the Adirondacks in a brand-new, shiny-blue SUV.

A few days ago, when we were still in the sweaty midst of packing, Dad drove the truck (I'm sorry, but it looks like a truck) home from a dealership in Brooklyn, explaining, "We'll be dead in Fir Lake without one." I think we'll be dead without citronella candles. I've been reading up on mosquitoes, and apparently the ones in untamed lands carry fatal diseases.

Michaela and I never even knew our parents had drivers' licenses. Which might explain why they are the world's worst drivers.

"I think I made a wrong turn somewhere," Mom mutters, gripping the steering wheel as we jolt along the highway, passing trees, trees, and more trees (by the way, whoever claims there's a tree shortage in the world needs to visit upstate New York). Mom has said she's made a wrong turn approximately twelve times in the five hours we have been out of New York City. If I weren't so zombie-tired from getting up at dawn to let in the movers, I would laugh. All I can do, though, is roll my eyes at Michaela as I reach for the crumpled sack of Doritos between us. I feel kind of like that bag: stale and wrinkled in my H&M chocolate-brown sundress cinched with a red belt. Michaela, sitting cross-legged in cuffed jean shorts and a striped tank, looks ready to dance *Swan Lake.*

"That last road sign said a hundred miles to Montreal," Dad says distractedly, glancing up from his issue of *The Atlantic Monthly.* The surprisingly cool, crisp wind coming in through his open window ruffles both the magazine's pages and Dad's thinning light-brown hair.

Back around Albany, my usually quiet dad sat up straight and announced that we needed to roll down our windows and breathe in "that fresh mountain air." I don't think there's a more irritating phrase in the history of the world. Air is air. Michaela and I looked at each other, a little alarmed. Up until that moment, Dad had been pretty chill about the whole move, not seeming to care about Fir Lake while Mom drove the crazy train. But he'd clearly joined her on board.

"Are we in Canada?" I ask now around a mouthful of Doritos.

"No, but it could be that we *passed* Fir Lake. . . ." Dad leans forward to turn down the volume on the radio. All that we've been able to pick up for the last hour is crackling static and bad country music. Now some song is on about moons and fences. I miss Z100.

"How should I know if we passed it or not?" Mom snaps, adjusting her tortoiseshell glasses. "Everything on this godforsaken highway looks the *same*."

"No joke," I murmur, pressing my forehead to the cold pane of my window to take in the low white sky and jagged mountains dotted with trees that look like heads of broccoli. As soon as we left the Bronx, that's all the scenery has been — with the occasional dead racoon lying in the middle of the highway.

If this is nature, I am not a fan.

"We haven't passed it," Michaela reports, checking the heavy atlas in her lap. "It's just a couple more exits." How my sister is able to read a road map is beyond me. I suspect she's secretly done more research into Fir Lake. I call Michaela a Googlemaster — she can look online and find answers to the most random stuff. As far as I'm concerned, the Internet was invented for MySpace, IM, and e-mail. The end.

"*Thank* you, Michaela," Mom sniffs, her tone implying that Dad and I are, once again, useless.

My father shoots me a quick smile over his shoulder, and before I can smile back, the car goes over a huge bump and my ears start popping like the time I rode the Cyclone at Coney Island. We're up high now. I swallow hard, and Michaela looks up from her map.

"License plate game?" she offers in her most supportive voice.

I sigh. We've done it all: twenty questions, charades, staring contests, and attempts at three-way calling Sofia (we couldn't get cell reception). I've tried napping with my head in Michaela's lap, and Michaela has tried finger-combing the tangles out of my hair (we were both unsuccessful). We've made four stops to pee, the most recent at a creepy gas station in Lake George, where Michaela and I bought the Doritos and our parents argued over directions with the toothless, bearded guy at the register. There was a deer head mounted on the wall, so I was relieved to get back in the car. Now, though, my butt kind of aches, and I'm ready for a serious leg stretch.

"Are you carsick?" Michaela whispers, inching toward me when most sane people, I think, would move *away*. Michaela has to whisper because our mom would flip out at the notion that someone might throw up in the new SUV.

I've never gotten sick in cars before — not even in

stop-and-start taxicabs — but there *is* a vague, unpleasant feeling in my gut. I'm not carsick. I'm homesick. Already.

The last three weeks slipped by in a stream of funny-smelling cardboard boxes, mountains of clothes, and thick ribbons of packing tape. Michaela did all my packing for me, sitting on my bed and sorting through my shoes and skirts, and I didn't bother to help her. Instead, I snuck out of the apartment every night and walked up and down 1st Avenue, trying to memorize things: the blinking signs of twenty-four-hour diners; the girls in strapless dresses kissing boys in front of the L subway station; the homeless man Michaela and I nicknamed "Cousin Hairy" rattling his change cup on the corner; the smell of refried beans and cilantro coming from the Mexican restaurant across the street.

In between packing, Mom and Dad had their professor and writer friends over for a good-bye dinner, and they all talked loudly about literature and politics over glasses of chilled vodka that Michaela and I weren't allowed to touch. Michaela and I *were* allowed to have our friends over one night, so we invited Trini, Sofia, and Jennifer for Chinese takeout — our favorite cuisine (even if Jennifer only ate the water chestnuts).

After our final class at Anna Pavlova, Michaela packed our slippers and toe shoes and leotards into a suitcase, her face tight. I didn't sleep at all that night, holding my breath and listening for the sound of Michaela's weeping; it was so obvious that leaving

Svetlana was killing her, even if she wasn't saying it aloud. But if Michaela did cry, she must have hidden her sobs in her pillow.

Two mornings later — *this* morning — big-muscled men in jeans and sweat-stained T-shirts came and whisked that suitcase away, along with all our furniture. Then, while our parents watched the movers load up their truck outside, Michaela and I stood in our empty living room and watched the dust bunnies dance across the hardwood floor. On one wall, I noticed a smear of hot-pink paint that used to be hidden by the piano; that was from when I was ten and Michaela was thirteen and we'd decided to redecorate the apartment. "I don't want to go," I burst out, because Michaela was the only person I could say that to who wouldn't tell me I was being childish. My sister took my hand. "Come on" was all she said, and on cue, our mom honked the horn of our SUV. We walked out of our graffiti-decorated building into the August heat, slid into the car, and soon the city skyline was behind us.

And now we're here.

"*Here* we are," Mom murmurs, abruptly swerving the car toward the exit ramp. Someone honks at her, and she honks back. I'm buckled in, but I clutch the seat for good measure. *Family of Four Dies in Car Crash on Way to New Home*, I think. *Fledgling Ballerinas Cut Down in their Prime.* "Right, Michaela?" Mom asks, even though we're barreling off the highway.

"I think so," Michaela answers, checking the map, and it's the weirdest thing — she sounds almost . . . excited.

I study my sister, and it could be my imagination, but her eyes are a little bigger and sparklier than usual. I want to poke her arm and ask her if she's lost her marbles — I like that expression — but then I realize that there's nothing *really* wrong with getting excited about arriving at a new place. I suppose it's pretty normal, in fact. I close my eyes and rummage through my emotions, searching for excitement, but all I can find is dread and terror and a general sense of pissiness.

I hate that our parents have decided our fate, I hate that I'm trapped in a truck the size of our old bathroom and I hate that I won't be able to audition for *The Nutcracker*, or ride the subway uptown to meet Trini for hot dogs at Gray's Papaya. Fuming, I open my eyes to see an endless stretch of green. Horses — or maybe cows — stand in the tall grass, grazing as their tails swish lazily in the damp afternoon air. My heart jumps. *Seriously?* I've been to the Bronx Zoo tons of times, but I've never seen animals roaming around out in the open like that. It's freaky.

But up ahead is something even freakier: a square green sign with white lettering. We've seen so many different signs on this trip: ridiculous town names that cracked me and Michaela up (Poughkeepsie, anyone?); white outlines of leaping deer (I kept imagining one coming out of the woods and diving onto the hood of our car); and a cheery THE LORD LOVES YOU banner when we got lost in a small town in the Catskills. *This* sign, though, sends a wave of nausea rolling over me. It could be that I'm carsick after all.

Or it's just that I now understand that there's no turning back.

YOU ARE NOW ENTERING FIR LAKE, NEW YORK, the sign reads. POPULATION 2,100

And beneath that, in smaller letters:

HAVE A FIR-TASTIC DAY!

Help. Me.

Michaela reaches over to take my hand. I know that she knows what I'm feeling, and I'm glad, but that doesn't stop me from wanting to bust out of the SUV and sprint back to civilization. I squeeze Michaela's hand, hard, and she says, "Ouch."

"Literally two thousand people?" I ask, my voice weak, as we drive into the open arms of Fir Lake. A big gust of wind shoots through the car, blowing my curls up into my face.

"Two thousand, one hundred and four, as of right now," Michaela says, grinning at me, but I can't return her smile. Two thousand people. LaGuardia High School for the Performing Arts, where, in a perfect world, I'd be starting my freshman year in two weeks, has more students than that. My mind hurts trying to imagine a place that small. At the same time, I'm wondering as I stare out my window where those mysterious two thousand people *are*.

Only a smattering of other cars mosey along beside us, and off the road are rolling green pastures that I guess must be farmland. I spot a handful of lonely houses that look saggy and empty, their front porches crumbling. We drive by a tiny bakery called Bread and Roses, and a couple of farmstands with crooked, hand-painted signs reading, FRESHEST CORN THIS SIDE OF LAKE CHAMPLAIN! and MILLIE'S MAPLE SYRUP SHACK.

"Mmm, corn," Dad sighs from the passenger seat. "And look, girls!" he calls as we pass another farmstand with a striped awning. "They make their own cheese! We'll have to buy some for dinner tonight. How awesome is that?"

Dad has, as far as I can remember, never used the word *awesome*. What's happening to him? It's like the fresh mountain air that's seeping in through the window — which, by the way, is now making my arms break out in gooseflesh — has gone to his brain.

Here's the thing about my dad: Before Michaela and I were born, before Mom even met him (they met at a performance of *The Nutcracker*, actually, when Mom sat behind him and kept asking him to move his big head), he was a super-successful writer. His first novel, *Moon Over Manhattan*, came out when he was twenty-five, sold a bazillion copies, and was made into a movie (which Michaela and I aren't allowed to see, because supposedly there are breasts in it).

Sometimes, Michaela and I would go into St. Mark's Books, scan the shelves for Jeffrey Wilder, find *Moon Over Manhattan,* and stare at the black-and-white photograph on the back: our dad, young and thin, with his hair waving back off his forehead and his hands in the pockets of his corduroys. He did publish lots more books after that first one, but none of them were as famous, and in the last few years — ever since I turned eleven, really — he hasn't written anything at all. He's sort of moped around a lot and gotten into arguments with his agent on the phone. Mom says he's "stuck" and tells Michaela and me that we shouldn't ever bring up Dad's stuck-ness to our friends, *or* to him. I guess Mom is now convinced that Fir Lake will magically do wonders for his inspiration.

I'm dubious.

"That *is* awesome," Michaela says, her ponytail bouncing as she nods at Dad. I can't tell if she's just being a good daughter or if she really means it. I let go of her hand, suspicious.

"Jeffrey," Mom snaps at Dad. "We need to be looking out for Honeycomb Drive." She puts one cork-wedge espadrille on the brake, slowing down behind a car with a bumper sticker that reads, MY FAMILY IS 100% ORGANIC. IS YOURS?

Horror hits me. "*Honeycomb Drive?*" I ask Michaela. I remember the rat on the subway, and think: *Bad Omen Number Two.* I can only imagine Trini, Jennifer, and

Sofia's reactions when we tell them our new address. *"What, are you guys living in a beehive?" . . . "Don't get stung!" . . . "Wait, but, what's the cross avenue?"*

"It's better than Bushberry Way," Michaela says, pointing to a street sign. We're out of farm territory now, passing tree-lined sidewalks and snug houses with dogs curled up on front porches. The afternoon is fading and long pink shadows stretch along the ground.

"Or Frog Croak Road," Dad chimes in, gesturing out his open window.

Mom groans, clearly fed up with all of us. A red light — the first we've seen in ages — is swinging up ahead, so Mom comes to a quick stop that makes us lean forward in our seats. We're alongside the car with the organic bumper sticker, so Mom honks her horn — too loudly, it seems, because the driver of the car frowns at her.

When he lowers the passenger side window, I see that a girl about my age is in the seat beside him. She has shiny, stick-straight auburn hair that I'm instantly jealous of, but she can keep the jumble of freckles all over her cheeks and nose. She's wearing a loose-fitting, button-down plaid shirt that looks like it's straight out of Country Miss catalog. And she's gaping at me and Michaela, as if we're a science experiment — lab rats on display. I bristle. My subway-riding instincts kick in, and I want to roll down my window and ask Flannel what she's staring at. Michaela elbows me in the side.

"Excuse me, can you tell us where thirteen Honeycomb Drive is?" Mom shouts to the driver, and I can tell that he's taken aback by her accent and her loudness. I cringe.

Two minutes in Fir Lake, and the Wilders are already doing it all wrong.

"You're new in town, right?" the man asks, showing the slight gap between his teeth when he smiles. His graying hair has red in it, and I understand that the girl must be his daughter. "The new Russian professor?"

My breath stops. *They know who we are.* I feel like we're in a horror movie, and all the townsfolk are crowding around our car like zombies, moaning: *We've been waiting for you. . . .*

"Yes, Irina Wilder," Mom replies crisply. "And this is my husband, Jeffrey." She doesn't seem the least bit disturbed, and even Dad waves at the man in the car.

Flannel continues to stare, unblinking, at me and Michaela, and I wonder if it's just that she's never before seen two girls who *don't* look as if they're on their way to a barn raising.

"Bob Hawthorne." The man gives a salute as the light changes. "Just make a left up there by that weeping willow. Welcome to the neighborhood!" And then he and Flannel are gone.

"So it's true what they say," Dad muses as Mom makes a left at what must be the weeping willow — a tree whose long green leaves sweep the ground. If I was planted in this town, I'd weep, too. "People *are* nicer outside the city." Dad, like me and Michaela, was born and raised in Manhattan.

I open my mouth to say, no, they're just nosier — but then I see it, coming up on the left. 13 Honeycomb Drive. Our new house.

And I'm speechless.

After dinner one night back in the city, Mom and Dad showed Michaela pictures of the house online, but I turned away from the computer, saying that I wanted it to be a surprise. That was a lie; I just couldn't stomach thinking about any home other than our apartment on 5TH Street. Now, I'm kind of wishing I'd had some preparation.

Because this puppy is *scary*.

It's dark gray and spindly, with a black roof that's pointed like a witch's hat and big windows that yawn like mouths. There's a front porch, a red mailbox, and a small patch of grass in front. Ivy creeps up around the windows, like it's eating the house alive. Talk about omens — I knew there was a reason 13 is an unlucky number.

"We paid *money* for this?" I ask, and Mom gives me a look in the rearview mirror.

"We got a good deal," Dad informs me cheerily. "It's a bit of a fixer-upper." I can tell, from the intense, juicy way he bites into that word, that he's been waiting all his life to use it.

"It's not *that* bad," Michaela tells me as Mom brings the car to a jerky stop. But there's a flash of worry in her eyes.

"All I know," I reply. "Is that if *I* were a serial killer, this is where I'd camp out."

Two moving trucks are parked in the driveway, and the muscle-bound guys from that morning are unloading what looks like our couch, all wrapped up and mummified. It's then that I notice that our house (which in my mind, I'm already calling "The Monstrosity") isn't the only one on Honeycomb Drive. It's in between two others, neither of which is as ugly or terrifying. The one to the right of The Monstrosity is actually sort of cute, painted yellow with blue shutters. Why couldn't Mom and Dad have bought that one?

As our parents get out of the car and trot over to the movers, Michaela unbuckles her seat belt and eases herself gracefully outside. I have no choice but to follow. I put one gold platform sandal down on the mushy grass, stick my head out of the car, and am instantly attacked by a swarm of mosquitos.

The tiny demons buzz and dip, forming a cloud around my head. I can't help my scream as I start flapping my hands, trying to get them off me. The more I swat, the more of them seem to materialize, getting in my nose and mouth.

"Katie." Michaela hurries over and tugs me away from the deadly swarm. "They're just in the air because it's evening — ignore them."

"Easy for you to say," I sputter, shaking out my hair and grateful to be alive. "They don't want to consume *your* flesh and blood." Suddenly, The Monstrosity is looking pretty welcoming.

The door to the house is open, with movers coming in and out, and the other movers stand in the driveway, talking to Mom and Dad. As Michaela and I approach the porch, I feel cold, prickly drops of rain on my bare arms. The sky is darker and more ominous than it was before, and I shiver, quickening my steps. Michaela starts to climb the rickety porch steps, stepping hesitantly in her flip-flops. Before I can do the same, I spot a movement outside the house next to ours — the yellow one.

I glance over and see that a young woman, who is maybe in her twenties, has stepped onto the porch and is standing with her palms up, as if to catch the rain. She is so beautiful she almost seems fake, like a creature from a fairy tale; her soft white-blonde hair falls in loose curls down her back and her skin is a rosy pink. She's wearing a green jungle-print sundress, and she's barefoot. I'm so curious about our neighbor that I stop for a minute and stare.

She turns her head, studies the trucks, and then lands her gaze on me. Unlike Flannel, she doesn't go all bug-eyed — she simply smiles in an inviting way.

Are we supposed to be friends with this blonde woman? I don't know. In New York, people live on top of one another, crammed together in cramped buildings. But we barely knew our neighbors, not even the friendly-seeming couple next door who blasted hip-hop until midnight every night (Michaela said at least we didn't hear them having sex, which was something that would have surely scarred me for life).

I decide I need to learn more about our new neighbor before I can return her smile. So I bolt up the creaky porch steps, and run into The Monstrosity. As soon as I'm in the foyer, a solid sheet of rain comes down behind me, making a steady sound like a mother shushing her baby. Michaela, sitting on one of the million boxes heaped in the foyer, grins at me.

"It's kind of crazy, huh?" she asks.

The Monstrosity smells dank and musty — the way I imagine cobwebs would smell. The kitchen — a lone bulb burning in its ceiling — is as huge as the farmlands we saw from the car. In the city, a kitchen large enough to fit a *table* in is an unheard-of luxury. Beyond the kitchen is the living room with an empty fireplace. Our peeling armchairs, comfy and homey back in the city, now seem dwarfed by the vast space.

An oak staircase, with two angel heads as knobs on the banister, spirals up toward the second landing. I hear some movers clomping around upstairs.

"Crazy," I echo.

This is our house.

Mom and Dad burst through the front door, startling me. They're both drenched from the rain, but they're laughing. "That's some storm!" Dad says in the same way he said "fixer-upper."

Mom claps her hands, efficient as always. "The movers are bringing the last of our stuff," she tells me and Michaela. "Don't you girls want to go upstairs and see your bedrooms?"

Bedroom*s*?

Plural?

I glance at Michaela, who is standing up from her box. "Oh, yeah," she says, looking embarrassed. "I forgot to tell you, Katie. We're each getting our own room."

I'm so stunned by this news that I forget to be mad that Michaela forgot. A warmth that feels like delight shoots through me. My own room? It's something I never thought I'd have, so I never imagined it. My own room, where, when I can't sleep, I can switch on all the lights and read until dawn? Where I can practice jetés and pirouettes alone, without Michaela correcting my every step? Where, after a shower, I can take off my towel and see what I look like naked in the mirror — just to see? Where I can lock the door and daydream for hours?

I never considered any of these possibilities.

"Two rooms, Katya," Mom says, and for the very first time that day, I smile. Maybe The Monstrosity won't be so awful after all.

5

Okay, so having your own room?

Sucks.

Especially when it's late at night, there's a thunderstorm rattling the windows of your frightening new house, and your life as you know it feels like it's over.

Just for example.

I bunch into a ball as the thunder crackles outside. I'm in my old bed, on my old sheets, but the blanket over me is too thin for this room, which is freezing. The rain sounds like gunfire, and tree branches knock against the windowpane. From outside my door, there comes a loud groan followed by a creak.

Earlier, after the movers left and Mom and Dad unpacked some lamps and bedding and batteries, we ate dinner sitting on chairs in the living room. Since it was raining, Dad gave up his dream of fresh farmer's cheese, and we had to make do with canned tuna and salted crackers. While we were eating our glamorous meal, Mom told us some facts about houses, since she'd grown up in one in Russia. Apparently, at night, houses "settle," which means they make strange moaning noises. Michaela said she'd read about that somewhere, but *I've* never heard of it and think it makes zero sense.

A pissed-off ghost is much more likely.

There's a violent crack of thunder and I jump, then hug my arms around my middle, feeling like a two-year-old. I miss the lullaby of city traffic. And there, if I was ever antsy or spooked in the middle of the night, all I had to do was lift my head and see Michaela. I feel such a deep ache for our old room that tears spring to my eyes. Out of habit, I squint through the pitch-blackness, expecting to see another bed against the opposite wall. A flash of lightning shows me that I'm surrounded by a closet, my desk, and a few boxes. That's all. The off-white walls are bare and have long, narrow cracks.

Reality check. Michaela is down the hall in a bedroom with a slanted ceiling that overlooks the back garden (my windows face out onto the yellow house with the blue shutters). I fight the urge to race down the hall, and slide into bed with my sister. Michaela was so exhausted after dinner that she could barely keep her eyes open, so she'd be furious if I woke her. She's probably thrilled to have me out of her hair. No one to nag her awake at night, no babyish ballet slippers to take closet space away from her toe shoes. . . .

I sigh and turn over onto my back. Though I was looking forward to flipping on my light and reading in the middle of the night, I can't. My old bedside lamp, when Dad pulled it out of its box, was split clean in two. There's no ceiling fixture in my new room, so I had to use Mom's weak flashlight to climb into bed. And the minute I shut the flashlight off, I learned something important.

There is no light in the country.

None.

Cars don't drive by, and there are no streetlamps or tall buildings with other people awake inside. It's like night falls and electricity ceases to exist.

But what about the moon?

On a mission now, I sit up and wipe my tears with the heels of my hands. I've been such a crying machine lately. Is this what moving does to people? I'm so used to being a tough city girl that this weird, weaker version of myself — the Katie that shrieks and does the crazy dance at the sight of mosquitoes — feels unfamiliar.

I lift Mom's flashlight and flick it on. When my bare feet hit the icy wooden floor, I cringe. Stupidly, I'm wearing my city summer sleep outfit — boxers and my white tank. I have an image of myself in long johns, wearing a stocking cap on my head, and that seems like a really good idea. If this is August in Fir Lake, I don't want to know November.

With the halo of the flashlight guiding me, I make my way toward my window. Pushing aside the makeshift curtain that Mom hung for me — an old flowered bedsheet — I peer outside, trying to see past the driving rain. If there is a moon, I can't make it out amid the heavy clouds and forks of lightning. There is, however, another small spot of light outside, and when I realize it's coming from the blonde woman's yellow house, I feel a shiver of intrigue. There's a light on in her second-story window — her bedroom maybe? — and I can see a shadowy shape inside. A lone figure, sitting very still. What is this woman's *deal*? I'm always suspicious of fellow insomniacs. Maybe she's planning something sinister. Maybe she's waiting for her long-lost love to return home. Maybe —

"Katie?"

I drop the flashlight with a clatter and spin around to see my door half open. I'm certain it's the neighbor lady, somehow transported to our house, but in the next instant, I realize it's my sister.

"What are you doing?" Michaela asks, her voice soft as ever. She's wearing a long-sleeved T-shirt and drawstring pajama bottoms (because she's smart), and carrying a tray that bears two small candles — the flames flickering hopefully — and two white mugs. I'm so relieved to see her that I don't stop to question why she's holding these things. In fact, I'm wondering if I've imagined her, that's how deeply I was craving her presence.

"Me? I was — uh —" *Spying on our neighbor* sounds illegal, so I backtrack to my original goal. "Looking for the moon."

"Let me help," Michaela says, as if I've spoken the most normal phrase in the world. She pushes the door shut with her foot and sets the tray on the floor next to my bed. It's amazing how soothing and warm the candlelight is, as opposed to the wild shapes of the flashlight. I reach down and shut it off as Michaela pads over to me in her gray socks.

"The clouds are too thick," she murmurs as we both crane our necks. "No moon tonight."

I feel a tremor of disappointment. Back home, I'd sometimes catch the moon — bent like a croissant, or round like a bowling ball — traveling between apartment buildings. But usually I didn't think about its presence in the sky. And forget stars — I never saw those, unless you count the scattering of celebrities Michaela and I often spot walking in our neighborhood. Our *old* neighborhood. That's what I need to keep reminding myself. *Former*. Past tense. I glance at the yellow house again and see that the light in the blonde woman's bedroom has gone out.

"So you've been moon-hunting all night?" Michaela asks, letting the flowery bedsheet fall back into place.

My sister has her watch on her wrist and I notice that it's well after midnight.

"Why are *you* awake?" I ask. "I mean, I know it's storming out, but for a pro like you . . ."

Michaela shakes her head. "It wasn't the storm." I can see her sheepish smile. "I guess I kind of . . . missed you."

"Oh, God, I missed you, too!" I immediately fling my arms around Michaela. During and after the long, grueling road trip today, I felt the slightest distance between us. But now, as Michaela and I hug tight, I've never felt closer to my sister.

"It'll be hard, getting used to this separate room thing," Michaela sighs, pulling back and tweaking the end of my nose, like she used to when I was little.

"Is that why you were wandering around the house — making . . ." I gesture to the mugs on her tray.

"Hot chocolate," Michaela fills in. She puts her arm through mine and we start back toward my bed. "The perfect drink for a rainy night."

Leave it to Michaela to practically *cook* on our first night in the new house. As we sink down on my bed and lift the steaming mugs to our lips, I ask, "How did you do it?"

Michaela blows on her drink, then takes a careful sip. "The Swiss Miss mix was in one of the boxes in the kitchen. And . . ." She tosses me a glance that's — naughty? mischevious? I can't quite tell. Michaela's glances are usually neither. "I found a bottle of Maker's Mark in one of the boxes, so I added in a few drops of whiskey."

My lips, on their way to the rim of the mug, freeze. Did my sister — my good-girl straight-laced sister — just speak the word *whiskey*? The two of us have never had alcohol, except for a few sips of bubbly Veuve Clicquot at a fancy New Year's party thrown by Dad's agent. I can't help it — a tiny thrill goes through me at the thought of doing something so forbidden. But the twist of worry in my gut is stronger; what if Mom and Dad found out? I gulp and stare at Michaela, wondering if she's an imposter, a shape-shifter.

"I'm *kidding*," Michaela says after a minute, breaking into giggles. "You should see the look on your face! I was just trying to cheer you up."

"Yeah, I knew that," I say coolly, taking a big sip of my drink to prove my point. I still feel a heartbeat of hesitation — and then a wave of relief — as I swallow and realize it is plain cocoa. Which is thick and sweet as it spreads through my limbs, softer than any blanket. I should have known Michaela would never do something as wild as spiking hot chocolate. "Cheer me up from what?" I ask when I'm feeling more myself.

Michaela gives me a sly, knowing look, and sips from her mug again. "You were kind of losing it in here before, weren't you?" she asks. "I bet you hated how dark it was, and every little noise was making you jump. . . ."

"So maybe I was having a *mild* panic attack," I say, and Michaela laughs again. "I guess it's sort of . . . lonely out here." I didn't think of that word before but it seems to fit exactly what I've been feeling. The knowledge that Michaela and I are in this huge house in separate rooms, surrounded by nothing but farms and mountains and horses — and a few suspect neighbors — makes me dizzy, off balance.

"It's just a matter of adjusting," Michaela says in her practical, patient way. "Besides, think about all the friends you still have back home, Katie." She motions to my tote bag, which is lying in a lump next to my desk. "Did you ever open that envelope Trini and the girls gave you?"

The envelope — of course. After my last class at Anna Pavlova, Trini, Hanae, and Renée sidled up to me in the dressing room and handed me a lilac-colored sealed envelope. "Don't open it until you're out of the city," Trini instructed. On the subway ride home, Michaela convinced me *not* to tear the envelope open, and that evening, I packed it away. Then, in all the mess of the move, the gift completely slipped my mind. I love that Michaela, not me, is the one to remember it.

When I retrieve the envelope and return to the bed, I rub its edges, curious about its contents. I'm hoping for long, handwritten letters from each girl, telling me how much my friendship means to each of them and how they won't be able to live without me. But the inside feels stiff and flat, like a photograph, and soon I find myself staring at a shiny print that Trini must have ordered off Snapfish. It's from about five years ago — I'm *nine*, which is insane to think now — and it's taken on the day of Anna Pavlova Academy's big summer performance. While *The Nutcracker* is the important winter event, everyone in the school gets to dance in our summer show, which takes place in early June, and features a bunch of different dances all choreographed by Svetlana. It's held in the auditorium of LaGuardia High School, and parents take about a million pictures.

This one, taken by Trini's mom, shows me, Trini, Renée, and Hanae posing in slick yellow raincoats and tights — our class's dance that year was set to "Singin' in the Rain." We've all got our hair done up in buns, and our cheeks rubbed red with rouge, and our arms are around one another's waists as we smile, smile, smile. The funny thing about this photo, though, is that Michaela is in it, too — the camera must have caught her by accident in the background. She's only twelve, but looks ethereal and perfect in *her* costume from that year: a pale aquamarine gown, since she was playing a water nymph. My throat swells (again!) as I realize that so many things I love are in this photo: the girls, ballet, Michaela. I flip the photo over and, on the back, Hanae has written, in her precise penmanship, "We'll miss you, Katie — stay strong and keep on dancing!" Beneath that, all three girls have signed their names, with little *x*es and *o*s.

Michaela leans close and traces her long fingers over the photo. "All Sofia and Jennifer gave me was extra lamb's wool, because my toes always bleed so much." She moves her hand away from the photo and smiles at me. "See? Don't you feel better now?"

I nod, gazing down at the message on the back. *Stay strong.* I remember my thoughts from before, about Katie the City Girl losing her toughness here in the country. No more. If I can survive seeing rats on the tracks and getting lost in a sketchy neighborhood in Queens — which happened last summer when I was out there visiting Hanae — what are a few stray cows?

As Michaela and I finish our cocoa and tuck our feet up onto the bed — Michaela covering my bare feet with her socked ones — I want to think that it's my New York City roots that make me strong . . . but really, it's Michaela. Having her in the room now, smelling her familiar powdery scent, I can ignore the thunder and lightning. Only my sister has known me since the day I was born; she says she remembers how hard I kicked my soon-to-be-dancer's legs while lying in the crib, and how she put her hand on my belly to calm me.

Talking in whispers about dance friends and past performances — "Remember when I had to dress up like a doll, and Sofia had to wind up a key in my back?" Michaela giggles — my sister and I stretch across my bed. We manage to fit our heads onto one pillow and pull my blanket over us. Soon my eyelids are getting heavy, the rain sounds like music, and Michaela is breathing in and out beside me. And I pretend that we're back in our room, that we've never left the city, that nothing at all has changed.

6

"*The morning is wiser than the evening*" goes an old Russian saying that Mom taught us ages ago. When I was little, I didn't understand that expression, but this morning — my first in Fir Lake — I get it.

Because, as I pull back my makeshift curtain to see the daylight, I feel, if not smarter, than at least saner than I did last night. The sky is scrubbed clean, a blue so bright it blinds, and I can see mountains in the distance. *They're pretty*, I think. The house next door, home of our mystery neighbor, seems plain and innocent, its shutters open to let in the cool air that hits my face when I open my own window.

I turn around to look at my new room, and again I feel wiser. When I put up decorations and put down a rug, this square little space might be almost . . . pleasant. And the first things I'll hang up, I decide, will be the ballet photograph from Trini, and my subway map from home.

On my bed, I see the crease in the sheet from where Michaela slept. Earlier this morning, I heard her creeping out of the room, carrying the tray with our empty mugs. Knowing my sister, she's been on the floor of her room ever since, stretching in her ballet gear with her hair in a severe bun. If we were still in the city, we would be on our way to Anna Pavlova now, and Michaela believes that it's dangerous to go too long without practice.

As I slip out of my room, even The Monstrosity seems friendlier. The oak walls are colored amber by the sun, and there's no more suspicious groaning. When I pass the spiral staircase that leads up to the attic — a place I plan to explore later with Michaela — I strain my ears for Mom's and Dad's loud voices downstairs. They've got to be brewing coffee or wrestling with furniture. But all I can hear are faint birdcalls from outside. Maybe in a house this size, we don't have to hear one another all the time.

Which is sort of nice.

And is also why I can't tell that Michaela is listening to music at top volume until I open the door to her bedroom.

My sister is not in tights and a leotard. She's wearing her denim shorts from yesterday and a green halter top that I think is new, and her hair is loose and freshly washed. And though she is dancing, it's not the kind of dancing that Svetlana would really approve of. Michaela's iHome, set up on her desk, blasts old Pussycat Dolls — *"Don't cha wish your girlfriend was hot like me?"* — and she is writhing her hips and rocking her head from side to side, her damp hair slapping her back. I stand there openmouthed because I have never seen my sister dance like this before — and she's really, really good at it.

How?

For a second, I wonder if Michaela's been sneaking out to dance clubs at night — there are tons not far from our old apartment, along Delancey and Rivington streets. But I would have heard her leaving our room. And Michaela wouldn't sneak out without telling me.

"Uh, Michaela?" I say when I find my voice, and she spins around.

"Oh, Katie!" she exclaims, her eyes widening. "How long were you — I was just — um — unpacking. . . ." She bites her lower lip, then smiles. "And, you know, getting some exercise." Blushing, she hurries over to her desk to shut off the music, and I watch her, feeling as if I've interrupted a moment I wasn't meant to see. There's something awkward about the silence in the room when the music stops, but that's just stupid. Michaela and I are never embarrassed in front of each other.

I glance around and notice that her room already looks lived in, with a (new) periwinkle rug on the floor and her dresses and jeans hanging neatly in her walk-in closet. I vaguely remember the trips Michaela and Mom took to Crate and Barrel a week before the move. They invited me to join them, but I opted for taking one of my long walks instead, and was only a little envious when they returned laden down with bags and boxes. Now, I see that Michaela even got new bookshelves — beautiful creamy-white ones that run floor to ceiling. She's obviously in the middle of arranging them; a carton of books seems to have exploded on the floor.

Michaela has tons of books. In the city, our bedroom shelves were heavy with mostly *her* novels, though I did fit a few of mine in there as well. When you grow up with a professor mom and a writer dad, it's kind of hard *not* to accumulate a lot of books. But Michaela and I have very different tastes; Michaela likes serious stuff by James Joyce and Joyce Carol Oates and other writers possibly named Joyce. I prefer old-fashioned romances like *Wuthering Heights*, or ghost stories about tragically beautiful women.

I wouldn't mind being tragically beautiful someday. I think that might be fun.

"Hey, I have something for you," Michaela is saying, still looking somewhat pink in the face as she crosses the room toward her window. Her view is striking — our back garden is wild with bushes and flowers and plants I can't identify. Everything looks a little unkempt, and I remember that greenery needs tending to; like the house, the garden is a fixer-upper. I just hope our parents don't expect me and Michaela to take care of it. I'm so bad with plants that I killed a cactus Mom got me for my twelfth birthday. (Though, really, who gets their daughter a *cactus*? All I wanted was a satin envelope clutch, but that never came through.)

While Michaela begins rifling through a stack of rolled-up posters, I wander over to the jumble of books and bend down. Most of the names on the spines I'm glad not to share a room with anymore — Kafka, Camus, Carver. In other words: Yawn, yawn, and yawn. Then I see a book that sticks out from the rest — a picture book. How did *that* get mixed up in there? I take hold of the tattered spine, reading the title on the faded jacket: *City Mouse, Country Mouse: An Aesop Fable.*

Memory rushes at me, smelling of bed linens and Mom's Chanel perfume. Some nights when Michaela and I were growing up, while Dad wrote in the kitchen, we would snuggle into bed with our mom. The three of us would read the story of two mice who switch lives — the city dweller goes to the country, and vice versa. The moral was that, in the end, each mouse was happier with his old life. I remember studying the illustrations in the book and wondering why the city mouse would ever want to leave in the first place.

I get a shiver down my spine.

"I didn't know you had this," I say, turning to face Michaela with the book in hand, just as she's turning to me, saying, "Here you go!"

The poster she's holding out to me is the one of Ethan Stiefel that used to hang over her bed. I get the usual heart-skip from seeing Ethan's gorgeousness, but I'm also confused. "You're giving it to *me*?" I ask. Ethan was always hers — the guy she was going to meet when she was accepted into the American Ballet Theater, marry, and have lots of ballet-dancing babies with. I would live in the apartment next door with my not-quite-as-famous-dancer husband.

"Happy move-in day," Michaela says, handing me the poster as she takes *City Mouse, Country Mouse* from me. "I've been selfish. I think it's time you had Ethan all to yourself."

I roll up the poster and feel a prickle of delight, knowing I'll now get to stare up at His Hotness every night. Then I notice that Michaela is eyeing *City Mouse, Country Mouse* with a frown.

"Oh, I didn't mean to pack *this*," she says, turning the dusty pages. "It was in the throwaway pile back home." She snaps the book shut, then looks up at me with a nostalgic smile. "Remember how much we loved this book? It's so cute. Anyway, I'll donate it the local library."

"Michaela!" It's weird, but there's this part of me that feels like the book in her hands is our entire childhood. Or maybe I'm being overdramatic again.

Michaela reaches out to squeeze my arm, and her face is a mix of sympathy and amusement. "Katie, what's the big deal? Neither of us is going to read this book *now*. This is what people do when they unpack. They figure out what they don't need." She lifts her bare shoulders and raises her brows at me.

I swallow down my hurt, but I'm surprised that my sister doesn't want to keep some reminder of the past. My eyes travel over her shiny new furniture, and I feel relieved that she's left me with our old stuff. I like to hang on to things. The contents of my drawers back home — which are now jammed into some unopened box — were a chaos of movie ticket stubs, bent MetroCards, gum wrappers, Duane Reade receipts. . . . Throwing anything away makes me sad. It's like saying good-bye.

Michaela gives one of her big-sister sighs, and from her expression I know that *my* expression is sour and pouty. "Keep the book, Katie," she says, passing it back to me. "I never knew it meant so much to you."

"It doesn't!" I say quickly, even as I press the book to my chest along with the Ethan Stiefel poster. "Whatever — I should go unpack, too — get my room in order —" Now, it's my turn to blush as I wheel around and start for the door. The absolute last thing I want to do today is open my boxes and organize. I want to do what I'd normally do on a late summer weekend: Pick up iced caramel macchiatos from the corner Starbucks with Michaela, buy *Teen Vogue* from the Universal News across the street, walk to SoHo and window-shop along Spring Street. . . .

Of course I can still do all that stuff today.

In my *head*.

"Wait, Katie," Michaela calls out before I leave her room. "I need extra Scotch tape, so I was hoping you'd come into town with me."

Town?

I pause and feel my ears prick up, like I'm a puppy hearing the word *walk*.

Sure, I knew Fir Lake was a "town," but I figured that town was made up of the farmstands we saw yesterday. Now, it dawns on me that there's an area here that we didn't drive through, an area where one can actually purchase Scotch tape. And Scotch tape could lead to thumbtacks and to chewing gum and to shoe stores and to iced coffee and to movie theaters and streetlights. . . .

My spirits soar. There's hope after all.

Fifteen minutes later, I'm showered, dressed, and hurrying down the staircase, my wooden wedge heels clicking against the oak. I decided to get a little fancy for town; I'm wearing a dark pink tunic over lacy brown leggings, with ropes of pink beads. I'm hoping Michaela and I can do some shopping today, since I need something even more outstanding for the first day of school.

The first day of *high school.*

Which, I realize as my stomach jumps, is only

about a week away. I've been so distracted by The Monstrosity that I haven't given much thought to the *other* beast looming on the horizon. But I forget about school as I weave through the boxes in the living room and hear soft voices snaking out of the kitchen. Mom and Michaela are in there, I realize, and they're whispering. Pausing outside the kitchen door, I can distinctly make out the words "ballet," "barre," "you shouldn't," and "Katya."

More secrets? More surprises? I take a deep breath and sweep into the kitchen, hoping to catch them in the act. They are sitting with mugs of tea at the round wooden table my parents got from Ikea. My mother has papers spread out in front of her — I see the Fenimore Cooper College letterhead on them — and she and Michaela are leaning their heads together, deep in conversation. The second I enter, they jerk away from each other.

"What's up?" I ask, trying to be nonchalant, but I bet I have a semi-crazy glint in my eyes.

"Katya, would you like some tea?" Mom asks casually, gesturing to the pot on the stove. Like Michaela's room, the kitchen is all set up, as perfect as a dollhouse, with checkered curtains on the windows, and cups and bowls stacked on the blue-painted shelves. One more thing my sister and my mother have in common.

"No, I don't want *tea*," I reply meaningfully, hoping my tone will indicate that *I know*. Though what it is I know . . . I don't know yet.

Then I notice that Michaela is watching me with one hand held up to her lips, clearly fighting back giggles.

"Is there a problem?" I ask her, crossing my arms over my chest.

"Aren't you, um, a little overdressed?" Michaela asks, allowing a small laugh to escape before pursing her lips again. "I mean, you look adorable, Katie, but . . ."

I stop bristling. I may be bothered by my sister's chumminess with our mom, but Michaela can critique my outfit all she likes. I know I'm the more fashionable Wilder sister; Sofia guiltily whispered that fact to me at Jennifer's birthday party in December, when I wore a black woolen jumper with big glassy buttons, fishnets, and patent leather flats, and Michaela just had on jeans and a high-necked flowery top. That's why I've never really worn Michaela's hand-me-downs (well, that and the fact that we've never been the same size). Her clothes aren't quite fabulous enough for me.

I guess I take after our mom in that one respect; growing up, I loved going through her closet, letting my fingers slip over her rich fabrics and silks. And I still think half the fun of ballet is the costumes.

As Michaela stands up and pulls on her cotton hoodie, Mom waves us off without asking us when we'll be back. Strange. In the city, whenever Michaela and I went anywhere (except for dance school, which was old hat), we had to leave a detailed list of names, dates, times, subway stops, and, essentially, an oath written in blood that we'd be back. Here, though, Mom simply returns to her paperwork.

And when Michaela and I step outside, I think *both* our parents have gone over the deep end. Because we find our father standing on a ladder, hammering something into the roof. Terror grips me, and Michaela cries, "Dad!" Never in his life — or at least in *our* lives — has our father held a hammer. Or stood on a ladder. Or done both at the same time. I'm prepared to take my cell out of my bag and call 911. I'm thinking an ambulance should be standing by, just in case.

"Making some repairs to the place," Dad says, grinning down at us. His cheeks are red and he continues to hammer away — though *what* he's hammering is unclear. "This is healthy for me, girls. Gets those endorphins going before I sit down to write."

"I'm worried about Dad," I tell Michaela as we walk away, cutting through the back garden. The high grass tickles my calves, and I can feel the mud from last night's rain oozing into my round-toed shoes. I look down and see that Michaela is wearing sneakers.

"He'll be okay," Michaela says, catching my elbow to steady me. "I think —"

Then we both go silent and come to a standstill. My jaw drops and I'm sure Michaela's does, too. Dead ahead of us is a deer. A big light-brown deer, with pointy ears, a long, spotted body, and a tail that sticks straight up into the sun-colored air. She (I think it's a girl) stares at us with her huge dark eyes like we're a pair of headlights. I can't breathe. *There's a wild animal in my backyard.* I try to remind myself of my stay-strong resolution from last night. Would a tough city girl really quake at the sight of Bambi?

Apparently, yes.

I'm trembling like mad, but relieved when Michaela reaches out to take my hand. At least I'm not the only one freaking out. I let out a squeak of fear.

"She's amazing," Michaela murmurs.

"Shhh," comes a female voice to our right. "Keep still. You'll scare her."

We'll scare *her*? I'm about to question this sentiment when I turn my head and see the blonde mystery neighbor in *her* back garden. She's crouched low in a long, patterned skirt with a fringed hem, wearing cloth gardening gloves and yanking up weeds. With one arm, she pushes her light hair off her forehead and nods toward Bambi.

But it's too late. Bambi has already turned and is sprinting down a sloping hill, and then into the distant woods. She runs as gracefully as a dancer and I watch her go with the tiniest swell of sadness, which is weird considering how much she skeeved me.

"See?" Mystery Neighbor says, and I look over to see her standing and removing her gloves. "She's even more skittish than you guys are." Then her face breaks into a grin, and again I think that she should be cast in some fairy tale movie. "You must be Michaela and Katya," she adds.

Oh, my God. My whole body freezes. This town is out of control.

Then Michaela shocks me even more by smiling back at Mystery Neighbor and saying, "You must be Emmaline."

I gape at my sister. The zombies have possessed her!

"Such a pleasure," Emmaline says. She crosses through her back garden into ours and shakes Michaela's hand, then mine. Her grip is warm and dry. "Katya," she repeats, almost thoughtfully, meeting my gaze, and I wonder if she saw me spying on her last night.

"Katie," I correct her automatically, and then feel like a child.

"My mistake," Emmaline says with a quick, light laugh, and I decide that no, she didn't see me. Nor is there anything sinister about her. But who was she pining for in the night?

The minute Michaela and I are a safe distance from Emmaline, heading down a dirt road that Michaela is sure leads into town, I start in on my sister.

"How did you know her name? How did she know ours? Don't you get the feeling she's hiding something?"

"Weren't you listening at dinner last night?" Michaela asks, steering me away from a patch of mud. "Mom and Dad met our neighbors when they came up over the summer. There are the Hemmings, an old couple, on one side of us, and Emmaline on the other. Mom told them all about us, too."

"Which explains why she called me Katya," I murmur, calming a little. I guess I *was* spacing out during dinner. I hate when I miss important information.

"And no, I don't think she's hiding something," Michaela adds with a laugh in her voice. "Why are you always inventing stories about people?"

"I don't *invent*," I protest as the dirt road turns into a hill, and I silently curse my choice in footwear. A breeze whips through the trees that line the dirt road and I rub my bare arms, realizing a hoodie might have been a good idea. "I . . . investigate."

"Okay, Veronica Mars," Michaela chuckles as the wind blows her hair back off her face.

Through the trees up ahead, I see the source of the wind: a sky-blue sheet of lake. It's circled by dark green pine trees — firs, I guess — and its beauty is as undeniable as the fact that Michaela is a great dancer. I still can't comprehend that yesterday, we were driving through city traffic, and today we're smelling fresh mud and wet leaves and sunshine. It feels like we're just on vacation, that in a week, we'll be back at home. Not that we've ever gone to such a rustic, countryish place; Wilder family vacations meant flying to European cities for Mom's research trips. And neither Michaela nor I ever did the camp thing; ballet classes kept us busy enough in the summers.

"Look," Michaela says softly and for one stomach-clenching second I think she's spotted another deer. Instead I see that we've reached the crest of the hill, and there it is, spread out below us: the town of Fir Lake.

Town might be too strong a word for the strip of shops and restaurants that looks as if it's been cut and pasted from a quaint British storybook. As Michaela and I get closer, I see the main road is called, um, Main Street (creative!), and that each store bears a little wooden sign with the shop's name painted in swirly letters. There's a coffee shop called The Friendly Bean, a used-book store called The Last Word, and a scary-looking store with all sorts of ropes and tents in the window called The Climber's Peak.

I pause and take a deep breath. So this is what we've got to work with.

"Come on," Micheala urges, giving my wrist a gentle tug, and we step onto Main Street.

The sun seems warmer here, beating down on our heads, and I almost cry out with joy when I see more signs of civilization: a tiny post office, a library, and *actual human beings*, walking, talking, and carrying shopping bags. Hallelujah! I squeeze Michaela's hand, and she squeezes back, so I know she's relieved, too. There's an old woman tottering along with her walker, rowdy twin boys racing each other to the ice-cream shop (The Simple Scoop), and a man talking on a cell phone. I'm so thrilled by the sight of technology in use that again I want to pull out my cell. But this time it would be to call Trini or Sofia and tell them that guess what? Fir Lake is not as backwater as we were all imagining.

Until I start to notice a few things.

1) Everyone is smiling. At one another, at Michaela and me, at the storekeepers who stand on their thresholds. Isn't anybody stressed, annoyed, or having a bad day? People walking by nod and say, "Morning" to us, even though, for all they know, we could be a pair of serial killers.

2) Everyone is apple-cheeked and glowing, as if they took extra vitamins this morning and, suddenly, I feel like Michaela and I look frail and sickly by comparison. And though the passersby are grinning at us, their eyes are also big with curiosity, just like the Flannel girl yesterday. It's clear that they all know we're newbies. Outsiders.

3) Everyone is wearing T-shirts with cuffed jeans, and *flat sandals over socks*. I'm not kidding. In *August*. It's like there's some official town uniform, and us Wilders haven't gotten the flyer reminding us what today's outfit should be. I glance down at myself, feeling silly in my city-chic ensemble. Michaela, in her hoodie and shorts, looks suddenly fashionable.

4) The streets are so clean they practically shine; I haven't yet seen one food wrapper, newspaper, or crumb on the ground, and even the enormous dogs — many of them St. Bernards — trot along politely, without leashes, acting as if they know how to use toilets.

I glance at Michaela. "Should we run?" I ask in a whisper as we pass by a restaurant called Pammy's Pizza — The Healthiest Slice in the Adirondacks!

"No," Michaela whispers back as we pass the entrance to a blue-and-green shingled motel called The Sleeper Inn. "I need Scotch tape." She scans the colorful awnings. It's really a shame that there's no Staples to be found. "Mom told me about a place that might be helpful," Michaela murmurs. "Right. Hemming's Goods — here we go."

I'm about to ask Michaela what *else* Mom told her this morning, but my sister is leading me into the shop. As we push open the door, the bell above us tinkling, Michaela informs me in a low voice that the store's owners are our other neighbors.

Who are all over us the minute we enter.

"The dancing Wilder sisters!" the twinkly old man behind the counter calls. I picture myself and Michaela posing in sequined dresses on an old-timey circus poster, with that phrase printed above our sepia photograph. From the back of the store, a tiny old woman comes bustling out with her arms open. "They're the spitting image of their mother!" she trills, beaming at us like we're her long-lost grandchildren.

Michaela and I stand motionless, probably looking like the deer in our backyard. Then I get it together and duck out of the way, so poor Michaela gets tackled by Mrs. Hemming. The Hemmings resemble Santa and Mrs. Claus after they've gone on a diet and retired to a small Adirondack town. Mr. Hemming is bald, with a bushy white beard, and he's wearing an apron over a plaid flannel shirt. Mrs. Hemming has short silver hair and wire-rimmed glasses that are bigger than she is, and is also wearing an apron over a checkered housedress. Michaela and I never knew our grandparents, but I've seen photos of them, and they did not look like this.

"So what can I get for you dears?" Mrs. Hemming warbles, releasing Michaela and straightening a nearby rack of disposable cameras. It's then that I notice how insane this store is. It's a wild chaos of *everything*, from trays of gummy bears to goosenecked lamps, from cartons of orange juice to Tom's of Maine toothpaste. There's even a soda dispenser behind the counter, and a handwritten sign above it reads: *We make genuine Lime Rickeys!*, which are these delicious soda-fountain drinks that Dad used to buy me and Michaela at Eisenberg's, a famous deli in the city. There's also a sign above a display of cheeses, which, in the same spidery handwriting, says: WE ARE PROUD TO SELL ORGANIC PRODUCTS!

While Mrs. Hemming is busy unearthing Scotch tape for Michaela, I lean against an ancient-looking gum-ball machine and check out the other customers. A young ponytailed mother is pushing a baby in a stroller and examining the jars of homemade strained pears; a grandpa type in a fisherman cap is picking through a mound of shiny apples, and a blond guy with his back to me, who looks to be about Michaela's age, is studying a rack of Hanes underwear.

I'm a little embarrassed for him.

"Katie, want to pick out some fudge?" Michaela asks, waving me over to the counter. Mr. Hemming is ringing up the Scotch tape and babbling about the weather while Mrs. Hemming is asking Michaela if she's ever hiked up Mount Elephant — whatever *that* is. "We can take it home to surprise Mom and Dad," my sister adds brightly, but the look in her eyes screams: *Please come save me from this crazy old couple.*

I hurriedly join Michaela just as Underwear Boy makes his way toward the register. He has a couple packets of white boxers under his arm, and my face grows hot even before I notice how good-looking he is.

He's tall and well built, with broad shoulders that strain against his orange T-shirt. His hair is a curly, shaggy mop that falls into eyes so pale, pale blue they're almost translucent — but in a good way. He has a high forehead, and a straight nose, and a firm chin with a dimple in it. I don't want to stare, so I glance at my shoes, the heat from my face sliding down into my neck. From the corner of my eye, I see Michaela pay and step aside to make room for Underwear Boy. He doesn't seem the slightest bit flustered about buying boxers out in the open.

"Hello, Anders," Mr. Hemming booms, placing the boxers in a bag. "How are your mother's tomatoes doing?"

Anders? I mouth to Michaela. What kind of a name is that? My sister shrugs back at me.

Anders mutters something about the tomatoes doing fine and then turns around with swift, natural grace that makes me realize he's an athlete. He could also be a dancer, but that's very doubtful.

My heart clutches as Anders stands still for a second and glances from me to Michaela. The corner of his mouth lifts, like he wants to either smile or say something. I'm not sure what to do, so I glance at Michaela for assistance, and to my astonishment, my sister is looking right back at Anders and not even trying to hide it. Her mouth is in a half smile, too. What's *wrong* with her?

Anders lifts his chin at us — possibly his way of saying hello — then saunters out of the store, letting the door bang behind him.

"That Anders Swensen," Mrs. Hemming clucks from behind the counter. "He was such a nice boy when he was younger, always smiling and saying 'please' and 'thank you,' but ever since he was named quarterback — well, Lord help me for saying this, but he's become a bit . . ." Mrs. Hemming pauses like she's about to curse. "Rude," she finally whispers, her brown eyes enormous behind her glasses.

"Too handsome for his own good is what I say," Mr. Hemming speaks up gruffly, counting the change in the register.

"It really is a shame," Mrs. Hemming prattles on, obviously pleased to have an audience. "I hear he's breaking girls' hearts right and left at the high school." At this, Mrs. Hemming pauses and her bow-shaped lips part. "My heavens," she adds, sizing up me and Michaela. "You girls are starting at the high school, aren't you? You know it's right down at the edge of Main Street, don't you now?"

I shake my head, overwhelmed, while Michaela nods.

"Be careful, is all I have to say." Mrs. Hemming drops her voice to a scandalized whisper as the young mother approaches the counter. "Kids today, they can be plenty cruel, especially to newcomers, if you catch my drift."

Oh, *please.* I try not to roll my eyes. You haven't known mean until you've dealt with city kids: uptown trust-fund girls with salon-straightened hair, five-hundred-dollar boots, and tongues like knives and hard-core punk boys wearing studded dog collars who steal your MetroCard out of your back pocket. I've seen it all. And in junior high, though I never rolled with the A-list, I was never shunned, either — and besides, there was always ballet school, where my *real* life happened anyway.

"Thanks for the heads-up," Michaela tells Mrs. Hemming, putting her hand on my shoulder to indicate we should escape while we can. The Hemmings call to us that our family must come over for dinner sometime, and then Michaela and I are safe.

"What were you doing?" I ask my sister, a little breathless.

"I'm sorry!" Michaela says, swinging the bag from Hemming's Goods. "I wanted to get out of there sooner, but those two didn't stop talking —"

"Not the Hemmings." We're nearing the end of Main Street and I see it up ahead, like a hulking brick giant: the high school. "That guy. Anders or whatever. You were *staring* at him! While he was buying boxers." I'm scandalized.

Michaela's face flushes briefly. "What's wrong with looking?" she asks. "Didn't you think he was exceptionally hot?"

"I guess." I watch my feet as they step over the cracks in the sidewalk. I'm not used to debating the hotness of real-live boys with my sister.

By now we've reached the high school, so we come to a stop and gaze up at our future. Carved into the white stone above the entrance are the words FIR LAKE HIGH SCHOOL, ESTABLISHED 1955. The building is sprawling, with a green lawn and flag pole out front, and what look like endless sports fields in the back. Like everything else about Fir Lake so far, it's movie-perfect and picturesque; a world away from the urban plainness of LaGuardia High School. I can practically see the blonde pigtailed girls jumping into convertibles with their pom-poms — until I remember it's *not* 1955. And I know that a pretty building can just be a facade for real ugliness inside. I think of what Mrs. Hemmings said, and for one frightening second, wonder if the country bumpkins at Fir Lake High *might* give city kids a run for their meanness money.

"So how bad do you think it's gonna be?" I ask Michaela, feeling a stab of anxiety.

My sister pauses before answering. "I have a good feeling about this year, Katie. I can't explain it, but I do."

And just like that, I believe her. We *can* handle anything, Michaela and I — even a deer in our backyard and arrogant football players and sandals over socks. I grin at Michaela, and she grins back. Look out Fir Lake High School, here come the dancing Wilder sisters.

7

On the night before the first day of school, I'm up in the attic of The Monstrosity, lying on my stomach with my laptop in front of me. The keys *click-clack* as I IM with Trini. Moonbeams float down from the skylight, and the empty boxes from our move sit silently in their shawls of dust. It's been a week since we landed in Fir Lake, and here are some things that have happened:

I discovered a hornets' nest in the eave above my window (my screaming could probably be heard by the diners at Pammy's Pizzeria — The Healthiest Slice in the Adirondacks!); Dad almost chopped off a finger by trying to trim some bushes (on the car ride to the hospital, Michaela held a piece of cloth over Dad's bleeding finger while I tried not to pass out and Mom yelled at Dad for trying to be "that kind of man"); and a letter arrived in our rusty mailbox welcoming me to

Ms. Mabel Thorpe's School for Dance and Movement, which would commence fall classes in another week.

U must feel so OOS, Trini writes to me now, which is her shorthand for "out of shape." *U been stretching at all?*

Of course, I lie. It's been hard to focus on stretching when I've been busy adjusting to insects I never knew existed.

OK, whatever u say. Hope MT — naturally Trini's already shortened Mabel Thorpe's name, even though I haven't met the woman yet — *goes easy on you.* I narrow my eyes at the screen and, like she can see me, Trini adds a smiley face, her way of apologizing.

I readjust myself on my stomach, flick a curl out of my eye, and change the subject. *Think I've decided on outfit 4 the big day 2 moro*, I type, feeling a pang of nervousness. I should be going to bed soon, since Michaela and I have to get up super-early. According to an e-mail Mom got from the Fir Lake High principal's office, homeroom — I'm in Mr. Rhodes's Room 120, and Michaela's in Ms. Leonard's Room 404 — starts at the ungodly hour of 7:45. Not that I'll be able to sleep anyway.

OMG I need to go 2 SLEEP — *Nutcracker auditions in the AM!* Trini writes back, and my stomach plummets. Right. LaGuardia High School may not start for another week, but Trini, too, has a big day tomorrow. What I wouldn't give to start my morning in the dressing room at Anna Pavlova, putting on my slippers and getting ready to impress Claude and the visiting choreographer. Instead, I'll be getting ready to impress a cluster of kids whose idea of a fun time is milking cows.

R & H & I miss u & M a lot, Trini adds. *Sofia & Jennifer do 2. It's NTSWYG.*

Not The Same Without You Guys. I smile, feeling choked up as I think of Michaela's and my ballet crew back in the city. *Same,* I write. *Good luck.*

Don't fall in the lake, Trini writes back — she's never one to keep things mushy — and then signs off, leaving me alone in the hushed attic.

Creepy as it can be, I've come to sort of appreciate the attic. Ever since Michaela and I scoped it out on our second evening in Fir Lake, I've felt a funny attachment to its low ceiling and musty smell. It's like the attic is the strange, ugly little sister of the house, and its small, confined space reminds me of our old apartment. The Monstrosity is still too big for my taste.

When I hear footsteps on the stairs, I sit up and close my laptop, worried it's Mom. Lately she's been especially short with me; she's stressed about the college's classes starting this week, and is forever driving back and forth to campus. Dad, meanwhile, can't do much because of his injured finger, so he's been grumpy, too, and spends his afternoons wandering through the woods. I'm concerned that he's going to get mauled by something.

My shoulders relax when I see it's Michaela, still dressed in her jeans and hoodie from the day. My sister is not a fan of the attic — she says it makes for good storage space, and doesn't get why I like to chill up here when we have a whole house at our disposal.

"I know, I know, I'm a freak," I tell Michaela, getting to my feet.

"Sure you are, but that's beside the point." Michaela smiles, extending my fuzzy pink cardigan toward me. "Come downstairs and be quiet. Mom and Dad are asleep. I want to show you something."

I don't realize "downstairs" means "outside" until we're tiptoeing through the dark living room, and Michaela is reaching for the knob on the front door. "What's going on?" I whisper as I push my arms through the sleeves of my cardigan.

Michaela holds a finger to her lips. As we're slipping out into the cold night, she whispers, "When I was taking out the garbage after dinner, I noticed this amazing thing."

Garbage is another fascinating new aspect of life in the wild. In the city, we tossed our trash down a chute conveniently located in our building's corridor. Here, we have to brave the outdoors to dump our Hefty bags into — I'm not kidding — a "bear box." A bear box is a gigantic wooden container big enough to hold *two* trash cans, and its lid is weighted down with stones, so, as Mom explained, roaming bears can't get their paws inside. I dare anyone to think the phrase *roaming bears* and not die of terror. Raccoons are, apparently, really into garbage, as well. The whole concept is not only scary, but gross — and grosser still is something called "compost," which involves the recycling of vegetables. Ugh.

Michaela, thankfully, doesn't lead me to the bear box across the street, but around our house to the back garden, which looks eerie bathed in the moonlight. She stands still and tilts her head all the way back. I do the same.

The sky is literally *soaked* in stars. My eyes strain to follow the dizzying stretch of white gems, which seem so close that my fingers itch to touch them. I try to remember what I know about constellations, but come up blank. Michaela and I spent many summer afternoons at the Planetarium in the Museum of Natural History, but that doesn't compare to standing outside, the galaxy within reach. Back in the city, what with all the skyscrapers and artificial light, I figured I'd never see the kind of night sky I read about in romance novels, or saw in movies.

"Thank you, Michaela," I whisper, gazing up in wonder.

"I can't believe I only discovered it this evening," she replies, her voice filled with awe.

I let out a sigh, calmer than I've been in days. "You know what?" I murmur. "No matter what happens at school tomorrow, we can think of this and feel better."

Michaela nods, keeping her eyes on the sky. "And we'll come out here every night, as long as the weather's okay."

"Promise?" I ask, glad to have a Fir Lake tradition, even one that involves the outdoors.

"Promise."

"Maybe that was a bad idea," Michaela moans at 7:40 the next morning as we speed-walk up the dirt road into town. We each have our Capezio totes on our shoulders, only now they're stuffed with sharpened pencils, new notebooks, and the bagged lunches our mom prepared. "Our stargazing." She rubs her eyes and yawns hugely. It did take her a while to get out of bed this morning.

I managed to get an impressive (for me) four hours of sleep, so I'm feeling pretty alert. Or maybe it's just the adrenaline racing through my body. I feel like every nerve ending is awake and on edge in the brisk, clean, September air. The trees around us are still emerald-green, but there are already stray leaves on the ground.

"Don't wuss out, Mickey," I protest, kicking up a leaf with the toe of my zebra-print flat. "You did promise."

"I know, I know." Michaela sticks her tongue out at me, then reaches up and tightens her high ponytail. I notice she's wearing lip gloss, which is not *totally* new for her, but not an everyday occurrence, either.

Michaela and I both spent a little longer than usual getting ready, modeling outfits to each other in the hall between our rooms. "You'd better hurry," Mom snapped, toasting bread for us when we dashed into the kitchen, but Dad only glanced up from his *New Yorker* and murmured, "Don't you girls look nice."

Michaela is wearing dark jeans that make her legs look like they go on forever, flip-flops, a long gray tank under a cropped hoodie, and her gold necklace with the hammered-gold pendant that Mom got her for her sixteenth birthday (no cactuses for Michaela, of course). I'm in a short, black bubble skirt, a black tee with silver sparkles in the shape of the Empire State Building across the front, and a short-sleeved black-and-white blazer. I know I'm not going to fit in at the school, but that's kind of the point — in New York City, there's only one kind of fashion crime you can commit, and that's looking like everyone else.

"Coffee might help," Michaela says in a gentler tone as we reach the top of the hill, and shield our eyes from the glare coming off the lake. "We can stop at The Friendly Bean."

I wrinkle up my nose. I'm still working my way through Starbucks withdrawal.

The baristas at The Bean move as slowly as humanly possible, drawling good mornings to everyone, smiling big, and shuffling along with their containers of farm-fresh milk. So Michaela and I wind up with only one minute to spare as we tear down Main Street, our lattes sloshing. We race by Hemming's Goods, and I swear I can see Mrs. Hemming nosily peeking out onto the street, probably *tsk-tsk-tsk*ing us.

"Being late — on the first day — makes — a terrible — impression," Michaela pants.

"What — do you — care?" I pant back as the high school comes into view. I guess both Michaela and I are a little *OOS*. "You're going to — get into Juilliard — anyway." Michaela doesn't answer, only picks up the pace.

We hear the bell shrill before we reach the lawn. There are a handful of kids by the flagpole, mostly guys with knotty hair playing hackey-sack and smoking. They watch Michaela and me as we tear up the front steps and push through the heavy glass doors. The first thing I notice about the inside of Fir Lake High is how fresh and new it looks, as opposed to my bedraggled public junior high in the city. These empty hallways are lined with windows, and the walls are painted a cheery blue. There's a huge, floor-to-ceiling poster with some sort of orange animal on it, and in gold the words GO TIGERS! are scrawled across the top.

"Go Tigers," I mutter to myself. What are the Tigers? *Are* there tigers in Fir Lake?

From where I stand, I can spot Room 110, so 120 must not be far, and I take a step in that direction.

Michaela, who I'm positive has studied a map of the school online, confidently heads for the marble staircase straight ahead.

Then we both stop, turn, and glance at each other.

"Find me after homeroom!" I cry as she calls, "Text me your schedule!" Then she dashes up the staircase along with a few other stragglers, and disappears.

I throw back my shoulders and walk on until I reach Room 120. There's a cardboard yellow smiley face pasted to the door and red cardboard letters spelling out WE'VE GOT SPIRIT!, both of which I take as bad omens. And the door is closed, which is even worse. I hesitate, then knock.

"Who's late?" a raspy male voice asks, and the door swings open.

Everyone is seated. Fourteen unfamiliar faces point toward me, twenty-eight eyebrows go up, and my stomach tightens as sweat breaks out on my forehead.

"Who is *she*?" I clearly hear a guy in the back of the classroom whisper.

"The new girl — you know, from New York *City*."

"*Oh.*"

"What's on her shirt?"

Last week, I thought: *Here come the Wilder sisters.* Now, I'm thinking: *How fast can I turn and run?*

My city grittiness could never have prepared me for all these peering, wondering eyes. There's a girl in the front row with her golden hair in two braids — I immediately nickname her Heidi — and she looks me up and down in a way that would put the snobbiest city girl to shame. She leans back to whisper to a girl wearing hiking boots, and the two of them break into giggles.

I remind myself that I don't care. I don't need — I don't *want* — to make friends in Fir Lake. I have Trini and Sofia and the girls back home, and most of all I have Michaela, even if she is several stories above me, and not in the studio next door.

So I turn away from the new faces and look at the teacher to my right — Mr. Rhodes, I presume. He is short and pudgy, with a long white mustache that curls up at the ends, and he's wearing suspenders and an American flag clip-on bow tie. He's glaring at me, but I've dealt with Scowling Authority Figures before — namely, the great Claude Durand. I lift my chin, prepared to excuse myself, but then Mr. Rhodes clears his throat and rasps out the longest sentence I have ever heard in my life.

"I wonder who you think you are missy trotting on in here like you're dressed for a funeral long after the bell has rung I'll tell you I've been at Fir Lake High School for going on twenty-seven years today and I have not and will not tolerate tardiness and it's no accident that Benjamin Franklin said, 'Early to bed, early to rise' because he discovered lightning didn't he and missy by the looks of it you have not."

His last word rings out in the deathly silence of the classroom. I try to swallow.

Somehow I've found the one mean adult in all of Fir Lake. And suddenly, I miss Claude so much I want to cry.

"Electricity," someone mumbles from the mass of faces to my left.

"Heh?" Mr. Rhodes spins around and holds his hand up to his ear.

"Electricity," the voice says again, louder, and this time I see it's coming from a girl sitting in the middle of the classroom.

As I take in her shiny auburn hair and freckles, my heart jumps with recognition. It's Flannel, whose father gave Mom directions on our first day in Fir Lake.

Except today she's not wearing a plaid shirt, but a fitted dark purple tee and — I wish I was kidding — denim overalls. And she's not staring at me, but at Mr. Rhodes.

"Benjamin Franklin didn't invent *lightning*, Mr. Rhodes," Flannel continues in a matter-of-fact voice. "The key, the kite, you know . . ." She lifts her shoulders.

To my shock, Mr. Rhodes doesn't have a response right away. He straightens out his bow tie, coughs into his fist, and, checking his clipboard, asks, "Autumn Hawthorne, is it? I had your brother last year."

I resist making a face. Of course her name is *Autumn*. How wilderness-y can you get? She probably has sisters named Summer, Spring, and Winter.

Autumn nods, and Mr. Rhodes starts up again, like an engine revving. "Ms. Hawthorne you are not allowed to speak out of turn in Fir Lake High School but that being said I appreciate your attention as I was clearly testing the students to see how closely you were all listening."

It couldn't be more obvious that Mr. Rhodes is lying through his big, horsey teeth; his wide face even is a little pink. Flannel — Autumn — has clearly knocked him down a few pegs. But I'm both thankful and confused; was she trying to help me? Or was she just showing off? Autumn's eyes meet mine, and she offers me a tentative smile, but I look away.

"Have a seat, missy, so I can finish calling roll," Mr. Rhodes rasps out, pointing me toward the only empty desk in the room — right in the front row, next to Heidi. I collapse into the stiff plastic chair, putting my tote bag between my feet. I've already noticed that everyone else has regular L.L.Bean backpacks.

Sitting on the other side of me is a sort-of-cute boy with short dark hair and sleepy brown eyes. He's wearing a polo shirt with the collar turned up so I nickname him Preppy. I feel like Preppy might be watching me, but I refuse to make eye contact, with him or anyone. If I pretend like I'm riding the subway, that won't be a problem.

As Mr. Rhodes continues with the attendance, I learn that Heidi's real name is Rebecca Lathrop,

Hiking Boots is Meadow McArthur, and Preppy is Sullivan Turner. I want to keep track of the names, but I'm distracted by how quiet the classroom is. Back in my junior high, homeroom was practically a free period — spitballs whizzed across the room as girls swapped iPods, and boys tried to rap like The Game while our frazzled teacher made announcements. Here, everyone is sitting still, and all I can hear — besides Mr. Rhodes's scratchy smoker's voice — are birds twittering outside.

"Katya Wilder?" Mr. Rhodes calls, and I give a start. He pronounces it wrong — "Katie-yah," not "Kaht-ya" — which bothers me even though I don't go by that name. Trying to keep my voice steady, I say I prefer Katie, and a soft murmur goes up behind me, like a puff of smoke. I must be giving these kids a field day: Not only am I new, but I've got a weird, foreign-sounding name that I'm picky about.

"Mm-hmm," Mr. Rhodes says. He studies me for a minute, then bends over and makes a notation on his clipboard. Wonderful. What can he be writing next to my name? *Attempt to Emotionally and/or Physically Destroy Before School Year Is Over?*

I'm last on the list — fitting — so Mr. Rhodes puts the clipboard on his desk and rubs his hands together. "Okeydoke, kids," he says, plastering a wide smile on his face, and I realize that he's whipping out a Jekyll that's even scarier than his Hyde. "First off, welcome to your freshman year at Fir Lake High School, which might I remind you has been standing on this ground since before you were even a glass of beer between your parents."

A few nervous coughs fill the air. I wonder if dying would feel pleasant right now.

"*Most* of you" — Mr. Rhodes lets his little piggy eyes stray to me — "have been together since you were picking your noses in a nursery so we don't need to bother with any of those getting-to-know-you games that some of the lighter-in-their-loafers teachers like to play."

I feel a laugh building in my throat, but I hold it in. Again, I can tell that Preppy Sullivan is looking at me — probably because my lips are twitching — but I wish he would stop.

"So, turning to serious business," Mr. Rhodes goes on, lifting a bright orange sheet of paper from his desk. "The important events of this semester." He skims the sheet and mutters, "Yearbook and the Garden Club are holding their first meetings this afternoon, yes, yes, yes, no loitering in the hallways, yes, yes, we've heard it all before. And then there's . . ." He glances up, and pauses dramatically, and says, "The matter of Homecoming."

The classroom erupts.

It's insane. A second ago, a blanket of peace hung over the room. Now, kids are standing and cheering, Preppy Sullivan is pumping his fist, Heidi Rebecca is clapping and bouncing up and down in her chair, and from the back of the room a loud, long choreographed whoop rises up: "Go-o-o Tigers!"

My blood is roaring in my ears. I'm considering crawling under my desk and staying there, like it's a bomb shelter. What is *Homecoming*? It sounds like some bizarre Martian ritual ("When our spaceship returns, we will have a homecoming."). Or does it have something to do with home*room*? Everything feels like a scattered puzzle in my head, and there's no fitting the pieces together. There's also a part of me that hears the word *home* and thinks immediately of Manhattan — the stoop of our building, the crowds on Broadway, Lincoln Center. . . .

Before I can burst into tears at my desk, Mr. Rhodes speaks again. "Yes, yes, we're all wishing our team lots of luck this year. Homecoming will be held on October sixteenth, so mark your calendars."

Next to me, Preppy Sullivan reaches for his book bag, and I catch a whiff of something cool and sweet-smelling that makes me wonder if he's wearing cologne. As I watch in disbelief, he whips out a spiral-bound datebook and scribbles something inside. He's literally writing down the date?

Thankfully, homeroom only lasts for fifteen minutes, so at eight o'clock sharp the bell rings, and Mr. Rhodes hurriedly passes out our locker assignments and schedules. Preppy Sullivan doesn't even ask — he just leans over my shoulder to look at the white card in my hand and says, "Cool, I've got first-period Social

Studies in Room 306, too." I don't reply, but Heidi Rebecca leans toward *him*, and says, "Bio for me. Hey, Sullivan — your arms got so big from working at The Scoop this summer! You still there through the fall?" She flutters her lashes at him so hard I'm surprised they don't fall out.

"Nah," Sullivan replies, glancing down at his right arm with a smile. "I've got tennis."

As Sullivan and Rebecca flirt, I jump out of my seat, racing past Mr. Rhodes. Before I'm even out the door, I begin texting Michaela my schedule — Social Studies, English, Gym, lunch, Horticulture (*what?*), Biology, and French. I add, *Meet me by the stairs in 5 seconds*, and then step out into the suddenly packed hallway.

"How psyched are you for Homecoming?" someone shrieks in my ear, and I watch as two blonde girls — both in long prairie skirts and Birkenstocks — run toward each other, arms out-stretched. All around me kids are embracing and slapping one another on the back. Mr. Rhodes was right; everyone here *did* grow up together. They've probably all been best friends since birth. As I plow ahead, making my way toward the staircase, a line of girls standing at their lockers watch me, whispering to each other. It's a little like walking through the waiting room at Anna Pavlova, only I know nobody is discussing my dancing.

Michaela, I think, like a prayer.

But when I reach the staircase, my sister is nowhere to be found. I wait and wait, my palms growing clammy, even as the hallways start to clear, because I know Michaela will show. She has to. I asked her to.

"Katie, right?"

The voice is bold, just like it was a few minutes ago, in homeroom. My guts in knots, I turn around to see Autumn Hawthorne.

"Oh, hello," I say, backing up a few paces. She's a *big* girl — not fat, but broad and tall, with high cheekbones. I bet she could snap me over her knee.

"Hey," Autumn replies, smiling again. She's almost pretty when she smiles. "I heard Sullivan saying you were in first-period Social Studies. Me too. Want to head over together?"

Before I can stop it, Trini's voice — or what Trini would say if she were here — pops into my head as I give Autumn a quick up-and-down. *Cute overalls. Do you think she was bailing hay this morning?* I can't for the life of me imagine why someone like Autumn — a country girl if there ever was one — would want to be nice to *me,* the new girl dressed in black. Doesn't she already have a million built-in friends here?

Unless she's trying to lure me into some sort of a trap. I know how girls can work. I've read *The Clique.*

"Thanks, but I'm waiting for my *sister,*" I tell Autumn pointedly. *And I don't need you.*

Autumn shrugs, then tucks her unfairly beautiful hair behind one ear, and starts up the staircase. I'm relieved to see her go, but I'm worried that, with each second that passes, I'm going to be later and later to my first class. I try to peer all the way up to the fourth floor. Why isn't Michaela *coming?*

Finally, when the hallway is totally emptied out, I realize I have to give up on my sister for now. As I'm taking the stairs up two at a time, my cell phone buzzes. I glance down, and see a text from Michaela:

So sorry! Didn't have time. I'll see u @ lunch tho!

I'm so elated that my sister and I have our lunch period together that I forget I'm on a staircase, miss a step, and pitch forward, dropping my bag and banging my knee.

Such a ballerina!

"Are you okay?"

I look up to see Sullivan standing at the top of the stairs, holding his hand out toward me. I turn my head and look down at the staircase, as if I can somehow tumble backward, out the door, and back into yesterday.

"Come on, we gotta go to class," Sullivan says, and then he takes my hand and pulls me up, surprisingly strong. I feel like my heart is beating in my throat as we face each other.

"Are you okay?" he asks again.

No, I'm not. I can't find my sister (not until lunch!),

everybody hates me (homeroom teacher included), and I just made a legendary fool out of myself (who falls *up* the stairs?). And, by the way? I don't know how to speak to boys. I never had a single friend who was a guy, and I'm not sure I can start now. So I don't answer, but instead step around Sullivan and head toward Room 306. I can only hope that the social studies teacher will be a little more understanding about lateness than Mr. Rhodes was.

If not, I may as well file this whole experience under *Worst Day Ever.*

8

"Today hasn't been too bad, right?" Michaela asks as we put our bag lunches down. We're sitting at a two-person table in the orange-and-blue cafeteria, which is decorated with Go Tigers! pennants, and swarming with students.

I can't help it. I start laughing. Beats crying, I suppose.

My knee hurts from where I banged it on the stairs in front of Sullivan. I have a headache from English class, where snooty, bespectacled Ms. Delacorte recited poetry for forty-five minutes. And I'm still sweaty from gym, where the young, handsome, and sadistic Coach Shreve made each of us hold onto a metal rod and do fifteen chin-ups.

Here's a secret: When someone is a good dancer, it does *not* also mean she will be good at gym class.

"What's so funny?" Michaela asks as she unwraps the chicken-and-avocado sandwich Mom made. My sister looks disturbed, and I realize my laugh sounds slightly hysterical.

"Nothing. Everything." I get myself under control, and take a big bite of my own sandwich. While I'm chewing, I see Michaela still watching me with worry in her eyes. I want to reach across the table and hug her. She doesn't even know how glad I am to see her now.

Michaela and I have never attended the same school at the same time (except for dance school, of course). Michaela went to our local public elementary school, but our parents thought I was too "daydream-y" and needed "special attention" so they sent me to a stuffy private school uptown. When I turned twelve, I managed to convince them to send me to Michaela's public junior high. But by that time my sister was already in high school, and I had to deal with all the junior high teachers beaming at me and saying, "Oh, you're Michaela Wilder's sister? Well, we have high hopes for you, then!"

At least that was one annoying thing that *didn't* happen today.

"Tell me about your morning," I instruct my sister, reaching into my brown bag for the miniature bottle of Pom that Mom packed. If I talk about my day, I might start laughing again.

While I'm drinking, I see Autumn Hawthorne walk by our table with her lunch tray. Like all the other kids, she stood in line for the cafeteria cuisine; nobody besides me and Michaela seems to have brown-bagged lunch from home. As Autumn passes a group of guys, one of them — who has messy reddish hair and glasses — punches Autumn in the arm and she socks him back. I watch in wonder as Autumn takes a seat at a table with a handful of other girls. Who was that guy? Does Flannel have a boyfriend?

"Well, homeroom was pretty great," Michaela says, and I can hear what sounds like genuine happiness in her voice. I stop mid-drink and look over at her; I notice that she's reapplied her lip gloss. "Ms. Leonard is so cool," Michaela goes on enthusiastically, taking a sip of her own Pom. "She's really young and smart and she wears these funky glasses and just graduated from Fenimore Cooper College with her masters in —"

"She didn't rail you out for being late?" I ask, marveling at my sister's luck.

"Amazingly, no!" Michaela raises her voice over the din of kids around us. Though I'm caught off guard by her jubilant mood, I'm loving how it's just the two of us in our little capsule, free to catch up. "She said she understood, since it was the first day and all, and she said she liked my necklace. . . ." Michaela grins, fingering her hammered-gold pendant. "So then she told us all about Homecoming, which I have to say

I always thought was a kind of dumb ritual, but when Ms. Leonard explained it, she made it sound pretty fun. And then she handed out sheets about different after-school activities like yearbook and —"

"You know what Homecoming is?" My voice comes out in a stunned whisper. "I mean — you've heard of it before?"

Michaela raises one brow at me, then pats at the corner of her mouth with her napkin. "Katie, what's the matter with you? Haven't you seen any movies? Or TV shows? Come on. You have the same pop culture education as I do!"

I'm not sure what "pop culture education" means but Michaela's I'm-so-much-smarter-than-you-are tone makes me grit my teeth. "Michaela, hello — we're from the *city*. Whatever Homecoming is, we don't have it there."

Michaela puts down her sandwich and shakes her head.

"What?" I challenge her, leaning across the table. At the table behind us, a boy snorts loudly, and says "Of course I can climb Mount Elephant. Haven't you tried?"

"Sometimes I wonder . . ." Michaela bites her lip, meeting my gaze. "How it's possible for you to be this spacey. I mean, on the one hand, you see everything. On the other hand, you — don't. You see what you want to see."

I feel my mouth fall open and an angry heat creeps across my face. I can't remember the last time Michaela spoke to me this way. Maybe because she never has. And I have no idea how to respond. All I know is that these are supposed to be our crucial forty-five minutes of togetherness, and Michaela is choosing to spend them yelling at me . . . for absolutely nothing.

I'm about to tell my sister just that when three tall, very pretty girls crop up behind Michaela, giggling as they balance their lunch trays. One of them has flaxen hair that comes to her chin and shows off both her big hoop earrings and heavily lined gray eyes. She's wearing a green halter dress that comes to her ankles — surprisingly trendy for Fir Lake. The other two girls are identical twins; they both have long, wavy dark hair and full lips, and they're both wearing tight T-shirts (one pink, one yellow), and short tennis skirts with sneakers. The three girls give off an air of breezy confidence; if they were in a comic strip, they'd all be sharing a thought bubble that reads: "Yeah, we *know* we're hot."

They're terrifying.

The blonde one sets her tray down on the floor and motions to the twins to keep quiet. Then she slowly advances toward the back of Michaela's head. My sister, still staring me down, is oblivious to the fact that something horrendous is about to happen to her. My heart clutches, and my hands fly to my mouth. "Michaela — look out —" I cry but I'm too late. The blonde girl is already putting her hands over Michaela's eyes.

"What the —" Michaela gasps, then peels off the blonde girl's hands and spins around.

I hold my breath and almost cover my own eyes, not wanting to witness the humiliation my sister is about to be put under.

Instead, Michaela shrieks with joy, and says, "You guys!" and the three girls start laughing. But not in a mocking way at all.

I don't understand.

"The fabulous Michaela W!" the blonde girl cries as if she's known my sister all her life. Except for the fact that she pronounces her name "Mikayla" — nails on the chalkboard to my ears.

"We were looking for you!" the twin in pink exclaims. "Where'd you run off to?"

"I had to meet my sister," Michaela replies, and maybe it's my imagination, but I think I hear a note of impatience on the word *sister*. Then again, I could be paranoid, because Michaela gestures toward me with a smile, giving no sign that we were just in a semi-argument. "Everyone, this is Katie. She's a freshman. Katie, these are Heather, Lucy, and Faith," Michaela says, motioning to the blonde, the pink twin, and the yellow twin. "They're in my homeroom."

"Hey-ey, Katie," Faith singsongs, giving me a small wave. "That's a . . . neat top." Her lip curls slightly. I wonder if she knows what the Empire State Building is.

"You two look *exactly* alike!" Lucy says, then Faith pokes her in the side and the two of them start cracking up. Wow. Twin jokes. Har har.

It's Heather, the blonde girl, who's obviously the ringleader, because she regards me seriously and says, "You know you have an amazing sister, right, Katie?"

"You mean the Michaela you only met today?" I reply, pronouncing my sister's name correctly and hearing the iciness in my voice. I know I'm being rude, but Good *God*. Why are they already drooling all over Michaela? Did she dance for them or something?

Heather blinks, clearly startled by my out-of-nowhere snarkiness. She might be Alpha Girl in Fir Lake, but I'd love to see Ms. Thing try to survive a day in New York City.

"Katie!" Michaela scolds me. "Sorry," she laughs, turning back to Heather and the others. "She's having a rough first day," she explains in a low voice as if I'm not present.

"Hang in there, Katie!" Lucy chirps, and just like that I *know* she's a cheerleader.

"You girls should come sit with us," Faith adds, pointing toward a table that's positioned right by the wall of windows. Two other girls — both equally pretty, and both admiring their reflections in their pink compacts — are sitting there, so right away I can tell it's the Popular Table. In the city, the social lines and circles weren't as plain and obvious. There was more crossover, more blurriness. In my private elementary school, if you were supersmart or talented or had famous parents, you could rise above dorkiness sometimes. I liked it that way.

Here, I bet nobody would care that our dad is a writer.

Michaela twists around to face me, and for a second I think she *does* want us to join them. I try to tell her with my eyes that this is a bad idea. I don't want to make fake-cheerful conversation with twin cheerleaders and bitchy Heather. I want to keep talking to my sister. Is that too much to ask?

Fortunately, Michaela has always been good at reading my eyes. Turning back to the girls, she shakes her head and says, "Definitely another time."

Uh, yeah. When pigs flap their wings.

"So we'll see you at the yearbook meeting later?" Heather asks Michaela.

"Sure," Michaela says, swinging one flip-flopped foot casually. "Three o'clock in front of Room 201?"

Three o'clock? School ends at 2:45. Michaela and I are supposed to walk home together . . . right? Before I can speak up *or* before Heather can respond, Lucy lets out a gasp and grips Faith's arm. "There he is," Lucy hisses, and I see that she's trembling. "In line. Look." She pauses, then squeals, "Wait, don't look *now!*"

But we're all already looking. And when I see

who Lucy is talking about, a flush comes over me. Standing in line to get his macaroni and cheese is a tall, trim boy with curly golden hair and an easy grin. It's Underwear Boy. I'd forgotten that I might see him in school.

"Oh, come on, Lucy, don't tell me you *still* have a crush on Anders Swensen," Heather murmurs. The five of us all try our best not to watch as Anders swaggers past us and over to a table full of tall, broad-shouldered boys who cheer when he approaches.

"Of course I do," Lucy replies, rolling her eyes, and Faith adds, "But we're not stupid enough to actually want to date him."

"Why not?" Michaela asks, laughing softly and looking away from Anders.

"Because everybody knows that Anders Swensen is yet to be tamed by a girl," Heather answers immediately. "He'll cheat on anyone he hooks up with. It's, like, a rule."

"Sounds like a nice guy," Michaela responds wryly, drinking from her Pom, and the three girls explode into appreciative giggles, as if Michaela has uttered the funniest phrase ever.

No wonder Michaela said she was having a good day. She has new friends.

After Heather, Lucy, and Faith have floated off to the Popular Table, I suddenly find I'm not hungry anymore. I rewrap my sandwich in tinfoil. "So . . . a three o'clock meeting?" I ask Michaela.

"I was trying to tell you before," Michaela responds, not quite meeting my eyes. "I heard about yearbook in homeroom, and it sounded promising. Heather's editor in chief, so —"

"What about dance?" I burst out. Since when has Michaela cared about things like *yearbooks*? "How are you going to have time for after-school stuff once we start classes with Mabel Thorpe next week?"

Michaela picks at the edges of her bread. "Katie, I'm sorry I can't walk home with you today," she says softly, getting — as always — to the heart of what's bugging me.

"It's fine," I say, waving my hand — and promptly knock over my bottle of Pom. Crimson juice runs down the table and drips off the edge, landing on my black skirt.

"Oh, *Katie*," Michaela big-sister-sighs, grabbing her napkins and blotting at the spill. I start laughing again — because I guess that's what I do now when I want to cry. And Michaela looks up from the spill and starts laughing, too, and, we sit there with the bloodred napkins between us and let our shoulders shake. And I forget all about the three girls who stopped by our table, and everything between me and my sister feels absolutely back to normal.

Still, I'm in a gloomy mood as I walk back to The Monstrosity alone.

My feet scatter leaves as my mind turns over my afternoon. Biology and French were neither hellish nor fun. But in Horticulture, a class held in the greenhouse on the roof of the school, the teacher put us into pairs so we could tend to our assigned plants. I was partnered up with Heidi Rebecca. "I'm running for president of the Garden Club," she informed me as we prodded pots of soil, like she'd been picked to perform in *The Nutcracker.*

Halfway up the dirt road, I pull my cell out of my tote and check for new texts. Nothing.

As soon as I pushed out the glass doors of Fir Lake High, I texted Trini to ask her about *The Nutcracker* auditions. Then, for good measure, I texted Hanae, Renée, and Sofia (who isn't even auditioning, but she always gets the gossip first). But no one's responded.

My sister, my friends — everyone's abandoned me.

I'm practically picking out the balloons for my pity party when I reach Honeycomb Drive. The Monstrosity looks dark and empty, and I realize Mom must have gone to her office on campus, and Dad is probably off tramping through the woods. Whatever. I'll let myself in, go up to the attic, and lie there alone. That'll be uplifting.

I'm rooting around in my bag for my set of keys when I see a little red car turn into Emmaline's driveway. The engine shuts off, and Emmaline herself climbs out. It's the first time I've seen her since that day with the deer. She is wearing flowy pants, beaded sandals, and a tank top, and under her arm is a rolled-up green mat. I stand still for a second, knowing she can't see me as she locks her car and starts for her porch. Watching her feels a little bit like watching Michaela's class — I'm hidden, but I see all. I'm safe. Then, Emmaline scares the daylights out of me when she whirls around, smiles, and says, "Would you like to come in, Katie?"

"I —"

I weigh my options. Going home — not home, but The Monstrosity — seems about as appealing as a foot amputation. It's too chilly and mosquito-y outside to try hunting for my dad. *I* don't have Heather and Lucy and Faith knocking down my door asking me to hang out, so . . .

"Okay," I answer, my voice tentative.

"Okay," Emmaline replies, and opens her door.

I tell myself that the chances of Emmaline inviting me in so she can feed me to her dog are slim to none. Still, the drummed-into-my-brain *don't-go-with-strangers* lesson of my childhood is ringing in my ears. My heart is beating faster than it should be as I cross Emmaline's threshold.

"What's your poison?" Emmaline asks, putting down her rolled-up mat.

I stiffen. "Poison?" I echo.

I hear Emmaline's warm laugh. "I mean what do you like to drink? Does tea sound good?"

"Sure," I reply uncertainly. Emmaline's house is smaller than The Monstrosity, but it's stuffed full of beautiful, strange things. Like, for instance, the — no joke — giant gold *Buddha* in the living room. Multicolored, beaded drapes hang over the windows, and ornate vases overflowing with fresh flowers sit on the tables. The air smells sweet and strong, like incense, and there's a rock fountain burbling in the entrance hall. I'm in a daze. For one thing, I'm *in Emmaline's house* — the source of all the mystery. But I can't even focus on investigating, because there's so much to take in.

"You can rub his belly," Emmaline calls from the open kitchen, and I realize I've been standing mesmerized in front of the Buddha statue. "For luck," she adds.

Lord — or Buddha, or whoever — knows I can use a dose of luck today, so I extend my hand and rub the cool belly. A tingle shoots up my arm. I feel like I'm in another time, on another continent. Fir Lake couldn't be farther away.

"I travel a lot," Emmaline explains, coming into the living room. She is holding two pale blue mugs that have no handles, and the scent of jasmine tea floats out toward me. My stomach rumbles; I never did finish my lunch earlier today. "Mostly through Asia," she adds, putting the cups on a small glass table that is painted with flowers. "And I like to pick up little treasures, so that whenever I'm at home, I feel like the whole world is still with me." She motions for me to sit in one of the chairs at the table, then hurries back into the kitchen.

I sit, but keep looking around. The house is quiet, so I gather that Emmaline does live alone. But there's nothing lonely about her home, especially when she turns on the fringed lamps at the entrance to the living room. The light is rosy and soothing. Emmaline sets a plate of cookies down on the table and slides into the seat across from me, her big blue-gray eyes watching me carefully. "Eat, drink, while it's warm," she urges.

My throat is so full of questions — *Why do you travel to Asia? What do you do every day?* — that I'm afraid I won't be able to swallow anything. But soon I'm sipping the hot, fragrant tea with surprising ease and scarfing down the soft chocolate cookies.

"You're a dancer, right? You and your sister both?" Emmaline speaks up after I've eaten for a few minutes, and I choke a little bit on my tea. I wish she would *stop* trying to freak me out. "It's the way you hold yourselves and walk," Emmaline explains after I've managed to nod and stop coughing. To demonstrate, she stretches out her neck, but I doubt I look that graceful. "Also, when I first met your mom over the summer, she told me that her daughters dance ballet." Emmaline grins. "I'm a yoga instructor," she adds, picking up her tea. "I teach classes in the attic of the town library. Yoga's a form of dance, don't you think?"

Oh. Yoga is super-popular back in the city; Sofia's mom does it religiously, and there are studios on every corner in the East Village, but I don't know much about it. Though Emmaline's teaching yoga explains her green mat, and all the Buddha stuff. "Um, maybe," I murmur, looking into my tea cup. "You can take yoga classes in Fir Lake?"

Emmaline nods proudly. "That's why I moved here — to start my own studio. I was living in Japan for a while, and then Thailand, and then San Francisco." I try to grasp the idea of having so many homes, and my head spins. "Then I just needed some *peace* and some nature, so I read an article about Fir Lake — and up and moved here."

"Why would anyone *want* to move here?" I ask Emmaline truthfully, thinking of how painful it was to tear away from the city. "There's nothing to do!"

"There's yoga," Emmaline points out, a smile playing on her lips.

"I should tell my sister about that," I say. "She'd be good at yoga, I bet. She's good at *everything.*" Is it my voice that's bitter, or the tea, now that I'm down to the dregs? I can't tell.

Emmaline tilts her head to one side. "You know, Katie, I'm an only child. Well, not a child — I'm twenty-six. But I've always wondered what it would be like to have a sibling — especially a sister. Someone to tell my secrets to."

Thinking of Michaela and the three girls at lunch today, I reply carefully. "My sister and I are best friends. Sometimes."

"Sometimes?" Emmaline echoes, and laughs fully this time. "Well, that still sounds pretty good to me." It's when she says this and her eyes darken, that I think the word *lonely,* like I did my first night in Fir Lake. Again, I get the sense that Emmaline is one of those tragically beautifully heroines I like to read about, and I wonder about her love life.

Suddenly, I remember Sullivan helping me to my feet, and Anders in the cafeteria, and I blush. I want to ask Emmaline questions about boys, about love — for some reason, I sense she'd *know* about that stuff — but that seems more like something you'd ask a friend. So, after thanking Emmaline for the tea and cookies, I pick up my tote bag and walk to the front door. Emmaline waves to me from her porch as I cross over to The Monstrosity.

"Don't worry, Katie," she calls through the coming twilight. "Your luck will change."

When I get inside The Monstrosity, though, I see Emmaline is wrong, because a message from Trini is waiting on my cell phone:

I'm in! I'm a snowflake! TEFW!

Too Excited For Words.

Woo-freaking-hoo.

I want to be happy for my friend. I do. But at the same time I want to kick something.

Much later that night, when Michaela comes to get me from the attic so we can stargaze, she doesn't say anything about the yearbook meeting or the fact that she stayed in town afterward to have pizza with Heather and Lucy. (When Michaela called to say she wouldn't be home for dinner, Mom said, "No problem!" into the phone; if I tried the same thing, Mom would lock me in a dungeon). And I don't ask my sister any questions.

When we're outside and sitting on a blanket and looking at the sky, I do tell Michaela about *The Nutcracker* text, and how mad and sad and pleased for Trini it made me. And Michaela, her eyes following the stars, tells me it was normal for me to feel that way, and now we'll have a real reason to go into the city to see *The Nutcracker* in December. Which is the perfect thing to say.

Finally, wrapping my sweater tight around myself, I ask Michaela about her evening — it's still nuts to me that she didn't spend it at home.

"Did you go cow-tipping?" I ask, only half teasing. I've read about cow-tipping; bored-out-of-their-minds country kids literally push over sleeping cows late at night.

"*No!*" Michaela laughs. "The yearbook meeting was cool, and then we went to Pammy's. There were a lot of other kids from school there."

"Cool," I say, using her word. I have the feeling that my sister and I are performing a dance, but I'm a few important steps behind. It's like I'm missing my cue to twirl onto the stage, or stumbling into a fall. My knee hurts at the thought.

"How about you?" Michaela asks, leaning back on her elbows and sucking in a deep breath of air. "Did you do anything after school?"

I think of my surreal afternoon tea with Emmaline, and I don't *mean* to keep it secret from Michaela, but I decide not to mention it just now. So I shrug and say, "Homework," which is the first time I've ever really lied to my sister. Immediately, guilt washes over me, and it feels as powerful and immense as all those stars.

9

Here's something I've learned during my eleven years as a student: You can taste Fridays. They taste like recklessness and freedom and the coming weekend. There's relief in the air, but also a tingle of who-knows-what's-to-come. Back in the city, Fridays tasted like smoky hot dogs slathered with mustard from Sunday street fairs, and fresh Jamba Juices after extended Saturday ballet classes, and stale sticks of chewing gum on long subway rides, when the train was running on its slower weekend schedule.

In Fir Lake, my first Friday as a freshman tastes like the buttered popcorn Heather, Lucy, and Faith bring over to Michaela and me at lunchtime, with Heather asking, "Do you guys want to come to the movies with us later?" (Michaela politely declines, probably because I kick her shin beneath the table), like the cloying cotton-candy perfume Heidi Rebecca sprays on her wrists during Horticulture, telling me she has a date with a "cutie from the tennis team" tonight, and like the mint chocolate chip ice-cream cones Michaela and I treat ourselves to on our walk home from school (Michaela's idea even though we both know ice cream isn't the best snack for dancers).

"We made it," I sigh, my mouth full, as Michaela and I pass by Hemming's Goods. Mrs. Hemming spots us through the window and waves enthusiastically. The store is filled to bursting with people stocking up on beer and paper plates and sunscreen. "Saturday's gonna be a real September scorcher so spend it outside!" Mr. Rhodes told us in homeroom. I thought of the deer in our garden and the hornet's nest outside my window. I'm not too fond of *outside*.

"You seriously thought we might not survive our first week?" Michaela asks with a smile in her voice, adjusting the straps on her new blue bookbag. She purchased it yesterday at The Climber's Peak, on an after-school saunter through town with Heather. Michaela invited me along — "They have some adorable parkas there, Katie!" she insisted — but I went home and did French homework instead. As a result, I'm now officially the only girl at Fir Lake High School who carries a Capezio tote bag.

"After that horrible Monday, I did wonder," I tell my sister as we head up the starting-to-be-familiar dirt road.

Truth be told, it was after Monday that the week

picked up a little. Michaela and I walked home together every afternoon except for yesterday, and our small, two-person table was still our lunchtime refuge (even if Heather and the twins did swing by every so often). We ate dinner with our parents and did our homework in our bedrooms like good girls until Mom and Dad went to bed. Then we snuck downstairs and outside, huddling in our sweaters and counting the stars.

Thanks to Michaela, I also stopped being late to homeroom, because she suggested that we lay out our clothes the night before. With Mr. Rhodes off my case, I'd sit at my desk, wishing I'd gotten more sleep, while Sullivan and Rebecca talked over my head. Mr. Rhodes made announcements about after-school activities, like student government, the Camping Club (yikes), and cheerleading, and kids signed up for stuff like crazy — Heidi Rebecca went in for cheerleading, and Flannel Autumn dove straight for the Camping Club sheet — but I held off. I know that once I start ballet classes again, I'll be swamped after school.

Actually, Mabel Thorpe's classes commence this coming Monday and, at the thought, I feel a flutter of excitement in my belly.

"You and your overdramatics," Michaela teases me, patiently licking at her cone. I'm jealous of how carefully and neatly my sister eats ice cream, as carefully as she dances, forming a little whorl that lasts for as long as she likes. By comparison, I'm a mess; my scoop is melting down the sides of the cone, my fingers are sticky with chocolate chips, and I've already swallowed half of it.

"I'm just psyched it's the weekend," I say, crunching on my cone as we near Emmaline's house. I'm about to tell Michaela that I'm hoping the two of us can catch up on our stretching when I notice that Emmaline's red car is in her driveway. I haven't chatted with our neighbor since our strange afternoon tea, though most nights, when I'm up at insane hours, I see that her bedroom light is on, and sometimes I'll catch her pacing. But now, Emmaline is sitting on the steps of her porch, with her forehead in one hand.

And I think she's crying.

I grab hold of Michaela's arm, just as my sister reaches for me. We glance at each other, alarmed, and then I look back at Emmaline. It's unmistakable; her slender shoulders shudder and she lets out small sniffling sounds. She's wearing her yoga clothes, and her skin is all splotchy. My mind reels with the possibilities. Did something bad happen in yoga class? Did her Buddha tip over and break? Or is it something worse — is she longing for, say, her perished love?

"Maybe we should ask her what's wrong," Michaela whispers, lowering her cone as we continue to stare at Emmaline from a distance.

I shake my head. "I'm sure she wants her privacy," I whisper back. In our apartment building in the city,

Michaela and I once ran into our upstairs neighbor — whose name we never knew — sobbing in the elevator. She didn't say anything to us, and we didn't say anything to her, and we rode down to the lobby with her sobbing all the way. "It's only polite," I add as we walk into The Monstrosity.

I'm surprised to see Mom in the kitchen, talking on the phone. She's been home late the past couple of nights, since it's a bit of a drive from the campus. "And you can install it in one day?" Mom is asking, twirling the phone cord around one finger while, with the other hand, she scribbles something down on a notepad. "Tomorrow sounds perfect," she adds as Michaela and I dump our bags on the floor. When Mom hangs up, I start to ask her who she was talking to but I'm interrupted by two things: Dad yelling, "Irina! I need your help!" from his study, and a loud, tinny version of Justin Timberlake's "SexyBack" coming from Michaela's bookbag.

"I told him not to write with that injured hand," Mom mutters, charging out of the kitchen as Michaela kneels down and unzips her bag.

"Sorry about the song!" my sister tells me, laughing, as she retrieves her cell. "Heather downloaded it for me in homeroom today." I make a face.

"Heather!" Michaela exclaims, pressing her cell to her ear as she stands up. "I can barely hear you. Are you guys at the movie theater?" I wonder if there's a spoonful of envy in Michaela's tone. I can hear Heather's voice on the other end, even though I can't make out her words.

I bite my bottom lip. I didn't even know Michaela and Heather had each other's numbers. I certainly don't have the number, or e-mail, of anyone in school.

"Uh-huh, I remember," Michaela is saying into the phone while I shift from one foot to the other in my satin ankle boots. In social studies today, Autumn Hawthorne stared at them as if they were made of moon rock. "Yeah, that would be terrific," Michaela adds. "Let me just ask Katie. Hold on, babe?"

Babe?

Michaela covers the mouthpiece of her cell. "Heather's inviting us to the docks of Fir Lake tomorrow afternoon," my sister gushes, her eyes bright. She's like a social firefly, lighting up at the mere thought of weekend activities. "A bunch of kids from school go there to dive and picnic and take boats out. It's a tradition for the last warm weekend of the year."

"Is it as super-important as Homecoming?" I mutter. Water sports don't exactly equal fun for me. Especially since neither Michaela nor I can swim.

"Katie, don't be a party pooper," Michaela chides me as if she is actually a person who uses the phrase *party pooper.*

"Okay, I'll go," I whisper. Michaela flashes me the thumbs-up sign and returns to Heather.

"We're all set," Michaela reports cheerfully as I wander out into the living room. I'm hoping to head up to the attic and IM with Trini, but something my sister says in the kitchen makes me pause.

"Stop it, Heather!" my sister squeals in a most un-Michaela-like manner. "He does *not* like me!"

My cheeks grow warm. He *who*? Michaela hasn't mentioned one single boy to me this week, other than Cecil Billings, her socially inept lab partner in Physics who kept sneezing on her notebook. And I doubt she's talking about him.

I had to have misheard my sister just now, because if she thought someone in Fir Lake had a crush on her, she'd definitely tell me.

"I'm glad we painted our nails last night," Michaela announces as we bump along the road toward the lake, sunshine and the scent of pine trees spilling into the car. Mom is at the wheel, and she's humming along to the Russian CD that's playing.

I look down at my flip-flops; my nails are a dark scarlet, and Michaela has painted hers in a vivid pink. Michaela and I are experts at do-it-yourself mani-pedis; back in the city, in between dance classes, we spent our weekends sprawled across our bedroom floor with bottles of polish remover and cotton balls. But we've never done our nails in preparation for a lakeside jaunt.

"They complement what we're wearing, right?"

Michaela adds, pulling down the strap of her blue Tigers tank top. Beneath it she has on a fuchsia bikini. I realize that my sister seems almost nervous. Since when she has cared so much about outfits?

"I guess," I say. I'm wearing my navy-blue boy-short tankini under a black cotton dress, but I'm planning to keep the dress on. It's definitely hot enough out for swimwear; the air feels as if it's been toasted. Still, I'm in no mood for Heather and the other girls to see me in something so revealing. My boobs feel unwieldy even in regular clothes, forget a tankini.

To take my mind off my body, I glance out the window. We're driving through an entirely new part of Fir Lake, one that exists on the opposite end of town. Here, there are no sidewalks and no street names, and the houses — huge, mansion-like, pearly white — hide in the hills. Groves of trees cast dappled shadows on the quiet road, and over the music, I can hear the gentle *lap-lap* sound of the lake nearby. Straight ahead of us rises a frighteningly craggy mountain, and Michaela nudges me and murmurs that it's the famous Mount Elephant.

"It does look like a beast," I say, eyeing it cautiously.

"Wouldn't it be cool to try and climb it?" Michaela asks breathlessly. "Imagine getting to the very top, and seeing all of Fir Lake spread out beneath you. . . ."

"That does sound cool," Mom chimes in, grinning at Michaela in the rearview mirror.

"Yeah, when you have a death wish," I add under my breath.

"Make a left up here, Mom," Michaela instructs, slipping on her sunglasses. Once again, I'm impressed by at my sister's uncanny sense of direction. She's probably one of those people you could plop down in the middle of the woods and she'd find her way home.

As quickly as Mount Elephant vanishes, a gleaming sapphire slice of Fir Lake comes into view. On its shore is a makeshift beach, with grass instead of sand, where girls in sun hats are spreading towels and opening coolers. Naked babies toddle into the water on their chubby legs, and kids cannonball off the splintering wooden docks, sending up great splashes. Farther out on the water, where the lake meets the forest, a group of laughing boys are bobbing, and there are small white dots that must be boats. It's all incredibly inviting, like an ad for the perfect vacation spot — until I remember that we *live* here. This realization would probably make another person happy. But I feel sort of deflated.

Before Mom can pull into the parking lot that runs parallel to the beach, Michaela leans forward and kisses her on the cheek. "Right here's great," my sister says in a rush, snatching up her bookbag from the floor of the SUV. "And don't worry about picking us up — Katie and I will get a ride back with Heather."

I wonder where the fire is as Michaela hustles me out of the car, and Mom drives off.

"I need to get my license," Michaela sighs. "No more of this Mom-dropping-us-off stuff, you know?"

A-*ha*. From this safe distance, none of the kids lolling on the beach could spot us getting out of Mom's car. I don't see what the big deal is, though. In the city, none of our friends had licenses, and everyone envied those lucky few whose parents had cars. Plus, I'm surprised that Michaela would care about parental embarrassment, considering she and Mom are BFF.

"Michaela! Over here!"

Heather, Lucy, and Faith are waving to us from their spot by the lake. The three girls are stretched out on a plaid picnic blanket, and lit by the sun, they look like angels. Especially Heather, whose slim figure is clad in an ivory-white bikini. Lucy's dark waves are hidden beneath a straw sun hat, and she and Faith are wearing identical yellow polka-dot bikinis, just like in that old song. Frisbees and footballs sail over their heads, and kids I recognize from Fir Lake High run circles around them. But the girls seem to be untouchable, protected by an invisible shield.

When we reach the three of them, Heather jumps up to hug Michaela tight. "You look beautiful!" Heather exclaims. The girls' blanket is littered with bottles of sunscreen, dog-eared *Cosmopolitan*s, and packs of cigarettes, leaving very little space for two additional bodies. And Faith and Lucy, who blow kisses up to me and Michaela, aren't doing anything to clean up. But Michaela simply sheds her tank and shorts, and eases down onto the blanket beside Heather. I'm a little shocked to realize, as I observe my graceful sister, that in her bandeau bikini, with her hair rippling down her back, she looks as pretty and carefree and nature-loving as the girls who surround her.

She fits in.

"Katie — undress, sit down, relax!" Michaela says, shooting me a big smile, and the three other girls turn to me. It's this sudden attention that makes me feel even more awkward in my black dress and sunglasses — as if I'm a big dark splotch in the middle of this gloriously sunny day. I don't disrobe, but I do wriggle into a spot at the very edge of the blanket, the grass prickling the backs of my knees. Heather begins passing around a white paper bag bursting with fresh strawberries, Lucy puts in her iPod earbuds, and Faith lights a cigarette (I wonder how Mom would react if she knew Michaela's new friends smoke).

It seems as if all of Fir Lake High is here today — or at least the Popular Kids, a sprinkling from each grade. Sitting on the edge of the dock, dipping their toes into the water, are Heidi Rebecca and Meadow McArthur. They are sipping iced teas and shrieking every time they get splashed by the diving boys. One of those boys, I see, is none other than Sullivan, who, I have to say, looks pretty scrawny — but still undeniably cute — without his shirt on. He shouts something up to Rebecca, then holds his nose and disappears under the water, only to pop up again, his dark hair plastered to his head. I feel my cheeks get hot, so I look away.

Heather and Michaela are laughing uncontrollably about an article in *Cosmo*, when an enormous dragonfly, with iridescent wings and a long red body, lands on my knee. I let out a small yelp, but by now, I've had enough run-ins with insects to be prepared. Reaching into my tote bag, I pull out the supersize can of Off! I stole from our bathroom, take aim at the little sucker, and —

"Don't do that!" Heather shrieks, and I drop the can. The dragonfly takes off, zigzagging its way back to the lake while I recover from my mini heart attack. "We're eating," Heather tells me crisply, her heavily lined eyes narrowing at me as she holds up the strawberries — none of which, by the way, have been offered to me yet. "Besides, dragonflies are harmless."

"Bug spray is really, really bad for the environment, Katie," Faith informs me, waving a cloud of cigarette smoke out of her face, and Lucy nods emphatically.

I look at my sister, patiently waiting for her to leap to my defense.

Michaela shakes her head back and forth as a grin spreads across her face. "Katie, my dear, try not to be such a city girl," she says, winking at me to show she's kidding. Heather and the twins burst into gales of laughter, but I can only force a smile. *Thanks a lot, Sis.*

And seriously? What does my sister have in common with these girls, who are not dancers, who are not from the city, who couldn't be more different from her and me? She and I are *both* city girls, will always be city girls, no matter how well Michaela can blend in on a lakeside beach.

I stuff the offending Off! into my bag, get to my feet, and announce that I'm going to wade into the water. I'm supremely grateful that I've kept my sunglasses on this whole time, because I can feel something close to tears welling in my eyes. As I trudge away from the blanket, I glance over my shoulder and see that Michaela is watching me with concern, but then Heather whispers into her ear and my sister turns to her friend.

The water is surprisingly cold for such a hot day, and I'm only brave enough to let it lick my ankles. I take off my sunglasses, letting the wind whip my curls across my eyes, and I have to admit that it feels sort of nice. I notice Sullivan — who is now getting into a paddleboat with another boy — watching me from down the shore, and when I look over, he smiles and waves.

I pretend not to see.

The bottom of the lake feels cool and slimy, and as I study the forest in the distance, I wonder about snakes. Then, without warning, I notice a long shape moving beneath the water, drawing closer and closer to the shore until —

I gasp as a tall boy shoots up out of the water, like some sea god from Greek mythology. It takes me a second to realize it's Anders Swensen.

I've seen Anders twice in the cafeteria this week, and he never looks at me and Michaela as he saunters over to his football buddies. I also saw him outside the gym once, when Coach Shreve gave him a high five and said, "We're rooting for you to score big at Homecoming, Swensen!" Besides that, Anders never seems to walk the Fir Lake High hallways. It's as if he's so cherished and special that he flies to class by private jet.

Now, his hair — made darker blond by its wetness — is slicked back off his face and water runs down his bare, muscular chest and arms. I feel a flush start around my collarbone and slither its way up toward my face. For no reason at all, my eyes stray to a thin line of golden hair that runs down his flat stomach to the waistband of his blue swim trunks and —

Suddenly, two other boys — one with curling black hair, the other with a shaved head — pop out of the water just like Anders did, whooping and hollering. I realize they were all racing each other to the shore. And Anders won. Of course. The three boys make their way around me as if I'm invisible and, shaking out their damp bodies like puppies, lope up the grassy beach. I watch them go, and so does everybody else — it's like a hush falls over the busy lakeside as Anders and his two handsome friends walk.

And walk, and walk . . . and come to a slow stop at Heather, Lucy, Faith's — and Michaela's — blanket.

I stand up on my tiptoes to get a better look. I guess it makes sense that Anders would know Heather and her crew, since they're all seniors, and there are only about fifty kids in each grade at Fir Lake High School. But there seems to be more going on at the blanket than a pleasant did-you-finish-your-home-work? chat. From the way Heather laughs and the way the guy with the shaved head nudges Anders in the ribs, I get the sense that the air by the blanket is charged with electricity — and not the kind Benjamin Franklin dealt with.

Then, to my growing disbelief, Michaela, who'd been reclining on her elbows, sits up and says something to the three boys as well. Calm as you please, she smiles as she stretches her long legs out in front of her. My *sister*! Talking to gorgeous guys! As if she's been doing it all her life! I don't know whether to feel proud or troubled or both.

The three boys linger by the blanket for another minute, and then they turn and head toward the soda machine near the parking lot, still nudging one another and cracking up.

My skin feels even warmer than it did a second ago. I don't know if it's from overexposure to the sun — I *really* am not used to spending this much time out-side — or from what I've just seen. But the next thing I know, I am taking off my sunglasses, and pulling my black dress over my head, and putting them in a messy pile on the shoreline. Then, deciding not to care how I look in my tankini, I close my eyes and surge into the freezing lake water. Goose pimples pebble on my arms, but the water also feels clean and refreshing, like a wake-up call.

"Katie! What are you doing?"

Keeping my feet on the bottom of the lake, I shake my wet hair out of my face and turn around to see Michaela standing up on the blanket, waving her arms at me.

"You can't swim!" my sister adds at a high volume, introducing this fact to the entire lakeside community.

I bend my knees and sink lower until I'm chin deep. I feel suddenly reckless, like a Friday afternoon.

"Neither can you!" I shout back.

Michaela crosses her arms over her chest as Heather and the twins giggle, and I feel a small swell of victory.

But in the end, I'm a good sister. I don't want to upset Michaela. Nor do I want her telling Mom that I acted irresponsibly at the lake. So I stand up, water sluicing down my body, and trudge back to the shore, picking up my dress and shades. As I walk toward Michaela, I offer her a smile, and she smiles back, and the charged moment between us passes.

*   *   *

"Thanks, babe," Michaela says as Heather pulls her silver Prius up to Honeycomb Drive. My sister, who's in the passenger seat, leans over and gives Heather a kiss on the cheek. "You're the best."

She drove us home, she didn't invent the cure for cancer, I think from the backseat as I unbuckle myself. True, Heather went out of her way to drop us off; both she and the twins live right by the lake beach, probably in one of those mansions in the hills. But I still haven't forgiven her for the Off! incident. And she hogged Michaela for the rest of the afternoon, the two of them flip-flopping off to get fresh corn on the cob and whispering together on the blanket. (The twins only smiled at me, then went back to their iPod-listening and chain-smoking).

"No prob, sweetie," Heather tells Michaela, exhaling a stream of smoke. "Maybe I'll see you at Pammy's for slices later tonight?"

"Maybe," Michaela says, climbing out of the car. I'd rather cut off my own thumbs than chill with Heather and the twins over pizza. Then again, it's not like anyone has invited me along.

Heather taps her cigarette out the open window as I slide out of the car. "Bye, Katie!" she adds, raising her voice to a higher pitch, the way one does when addressing small children.

"Later." It's a pleasure to step outside and look up at The Monstrosity. I'm sun-sleepy and still

• 157 •

damp from my swim, so I'm eager to get inside and change. I'm also hoping to get Michaela alone and ask her what Anders Swensen and his friends were saying.

But, I'm distracted by the strange white van parked in our driveway. "Don't tell me Mom and Dad got another car," I moan to Michaela, who doesn't respond. As soon as we step into the entrance hall, kicking off our wet flip-flops, I hear a loud banging coming from upstairs. Occasionally, there's a short drilling sound as well.

"Oh, hi, girls!" Dad says, emerging from the kitchen with his laptop, his glasses askew. "I'm gonna work in the garden, because I can't stand this racket!"

"What's going on?" I ask, raising my voice over the banging, which has gotten more fervent in the last couple of seconds.

"Oh, you know," Dad replies vaguely, straightening his glasses. I realize that in fact, he *doesn't* know what's going on. "I think your mom wanted that — thing — installed. . . ." Dad squeezes my shoulder, smiles at Michaela, and floats out the door.

What thing? As I head through the living room and up the stairs with a silent Michaela, I realize the banging is coming from the attic. We come upon Mom walking down the attic steps, the sleeves of her white blouse rolled up and a checkbook in her hands.

She stops, looks from me to Michaela, and asks my sister, "Did you tell her?"

Oh, God. Here we go again.

"Tell me *what?*" I demand. My heart starts to bang hard against my ribs as if in competition with the noise upstairs.

"Mom is installing a barre and a mirror in the attic," Michaela says. Her face looks pale again, even though she got a nice tan from being in the sun all day. "Like a small studio."

I feel a quick stab of disappointment. The attic has become *my* hideaway and now it's going to be a practice space? Then again, it's pretty nice of Mom to do this for us.

But then my mother elaborates.

"We're creating this studio," Mom says. "because Michaela won't be joining you at Mabel Thorpe's School, Katya."

"She . . ." I wonder if the drilling has affected my hearing. Of course Michaela and I are starting at Mabel Thorpe's together. We'd discussed it with Svetlana. We'd gotten that letter in our mailbox. . . .

Or, rather, *I* got the letter. Not Michaela. A hollowness seeps through me.

"Michaela convinced me — and rightfully so — that Mabel Thorpe's School would not be quite at her level," Mom goes on, her tone still cool and practical. "She might feel held back. If she has her own barre, though, she'll be able to practice whenever and however she likes."

Naturally. Heaven forbid the queen of Anna Pavlova join a small-town dance school! That wouldn't *ever*

• 159 •

be good enough for Michaela Antoinette. Let her peasant-y little sister bother with that foolishness.

"It's not fair," I whisper, anger ripping through me. I can't even look at Michaela.

"Who ever said life was fair?" Mom responds, and I know I walked right into that one. I'm not sure what my expression is, but it must not be too pleased, because Mom takes a step forward and adds, "You can use the barre, too, Katya. But we felt that continuing at a traditional school would be better for you . . . give you a sense of discipline and . . ."

I've heard enough. More than enough. "I have to go shower," I say through clenched teeth.

"I wanted to tell you, Katie —" Michaela reaches for my arm, but I pull away and stalk toward the bathroom. As I close the bathroom door and sit on the edge of our claw-footed tub, I'm shaken by the fact that my sister kept something hidden from me again.

And I can't believe I have to face a brand-new dance school all on my own.

10

Ms. Mabel Thorpe's School for Dance and Movement meets once a week on Monday evenings in the Fir Lake Community Center, which is about a mile outside of town. Mom drives me there after school, gripping the wheel as I sit beside her in stony silence.

I spent all of Sunday avoiding Mom, and feeling so-so about Michaela, who snuck me guilt-ridden glances as she crept up to the attic in her tights and leotard. Eventually, I joined her there, and watched as she stretched her leg out along the barre. The daylight falling into the attic, resting on Michaela's smooth shoulders, made her look like a Degas dancer. I hadn't seen my sister dance in a while and it felt comforting. Michaela told me to change into my ballet gear and come stretch alongside her, and I know she meant it, too, but I refused.

Mom comes to a jerky stop in front of the Community Center and turns toward me. "Your curls," she says, leaning forward and fussing with my bun, which isn't holding together too well. Michaela wasn't home to help me; Mondays are her yearbook, stay-late-at-school days. Automatically, I lean away from my mother, even though I know I can use the assistance. I do want to look impeccable for my first class.

"Katya, I know you're being your usual temperamental self," Mom says as she drops her hands. "But remember that you're here to dance and to be a professional. You wouldn't ever go in to perform for Claude with that face you're wearing now."

I feel how tight my mouth is and I try to relax my features. Once I'm in the studio, breathing in the familiar smells of toe rosin and sweat and Murphy Oil Soap used to scrub the barres, *then* I'll be calm again. Happy. Home.

"See you in an hour," Mom tells me, and I'm relieved that she won't be walking me inside, doing her patented kiss-up-to-the-dance-instructor routine. Then again, she and Svetlana have already had their phone conference with Mabel Thorpe, so that work is probably taken care of. Still, a piece of me is wistful as Mom drives away; it would have been nice to walk into a new dance school with *someone*.

Trying not to think about Michaela, I hurry toward the Community Center, a low, ugly brick building with a lit-up sign outside advertising upcoming events: GOSPEL SING-ALONG EVERY SUNDAY! APPLE PIE-TASTING CONTEST ON OCTOBER 13! WOMEN'S OFFICIAL KNITTING CIRCLE OF FIR LAKE — MEETS TWICE A WEEK!

Clearly, this is the place to *be*.

In the lobby, there's a wipe-off board bearing the words *Ms. Mabel Thorpe's School for Dance and Movement Meets on the Second Floor.* For the first time, I pause to wonder just how many classes Mabel Thorpe has in this "school." Is she the only teacher? How many levels *are* there? I guess I assumed there was an advanced level for Michaela, but maybe . . . there isn't.

I'm not wearing street clothes under my denim jacket, so I don't need to bother with a dressing room — which is lucky, since when I get upstairs, I don't see one. There's a coatrack, a shoe rack, a tiny bathroom, and a door that opens on to the studio. I can make out the familiar wooden barre and a long mirror. I remove my zebra-striped flats, reach into my bag for my ballet slippers, and tug them on, praying that this will finally be the year I'll switch them for toe shoes. I hang my jacket and bag on the coatrack, and hurry into the studio, suddenly filled with nerves.

There are only four other people present, and no sign of a teacher, except for a black boom box (people still use those?) on the floor in front of the mirror. In the center of the room, talking in giggles, are three girls who look to be eleven. One has mouse-brown hair that is held back on either side by two glittery barrettes, another has dirty-blonde bangs that hang into her eyes, and the third has frizzy dark hair and glasses. All three are wearing green Fir Lake Junior High T-shirts over blue sweatpants — and white socks.

Socks. Not ballet slippers. I stare at the offending items in disbelief. If someone dared enter Claude Durand's studio in socks . . . I shudder at the thought.

And aren't these girls a little young *to be in my class?* I wonder as I brush past them. But then I get a closer look at the fifth member of the class, who is standing in the opposite corner, studying herself in the mirror.

She is older than me.

Much older.

Like, my *mom's* age.

She has gray-flecked curly brown hair that comes to her chin and wide brown eyes in a heart-shaped face. She's on the chubby side, and in her pastel green sweatsuit (and socks), she looks as if she should be rolling pie dough in the kitchen, or bundling up her kids for leaf raking. She *could* be the mother of one of the girls, but since she's not interacting with them at all, I have the sneaking suspicion that she really is a student.

It's too bizarre, but I ease myself down onto the floor. I'm certain that when I start stretching, this studio will feel more normal to me. Even if there *are* framed posters of kittens hanging above the mirror.

I close my eyes, trying to conjure up Claude's exacting voice, and the soft, light melodies of Alfredo's piano playing. But it's hard to do so with the constant buzzing sound of crickets outside and the occasional *croh-croh* of a frog just beneath the window. I stretch my legs out and point my toes as hard as I can, wishing for the hundredth time that my arch was as sharp and lovely as Michaela's. Then again, *I* don't have my own special *barre* in the attic.

My legs protest — *OOS!* — as I lower my head to my knees. I hear a few murmurs chase each other across the room like fish in a pond, and when I lift my head, the three girls and the pie-dough lady are all watching me, openmouthed.

"Why is she doing that?" I hear the girl with the barrettes whisper to the dirty-blonde, and the frizzy-haired girl shrugs, gawking at me like I'm a sideshow.

"I'm stretching," I reply flatly. More confused murmurs answer me, so I lower myself onto my back and lift my legs straight into the air.

"Be careful, dear!" The pie-dough lady takes an anxious step forward, ringing her hands. "You could hurt yourself that way! Maybe you should wait until Mabel —"

"Did I hear my name?"

I sit up to see another middle-aged woman sweeping into the studio. She has shoulder-length hair that is dyed platinum blonde and held off her face with a bright pink terry cloth headband. She's wearing a full-body pink leotard (really not a good look for *anyone*, regardless of their age) with hot-pink leg warmers. Her lashes are jet-black and heavy with mascara, and they curl upward, as if she is permanently surprised.

"Mabel!" the pie-dough lady exclaims. "Aren't you a sight for sore eyes?" Meanwhile, the three girls in the center let out appreciative hoots, and the frizzy-haired one cries, "Did you see me on Main Street yesterday, Mabel? My dad and I waved at your car!"

I try to imagine greeting Claude or Svetlana in this manner, and I get a headache.

Mabel lifts one hand and waves, slowly and carefully, as if she's a beauty pageant contestant. It hits me that she very well may have *been* a beauty pageant contestant. "Hello, blossoming dancers," she says with a grin. "Welcome to another year of shape and movement."

I have no idea what that means, but I nod along with everyone else.

"Some of our flowers from last year have left us," Mabel goes on, still flashing her bright white smile. "But we do have a new little green bud with us this year."

I don't realize she means me until everyone turns and stares in my direction again. I also realize I'm still on the floor.

"Hi," I say, getting to my feet. "I'm Katie."

"Molly, Dee, Hayley," the girl with the sparkly barrettes replies in a bossy tone, pointing first to herself, then the dirty-blonde, and then the frizzy-haired girl. I can tell that in Fir Lake Junior High, Molly is the Heidi Rebecca who makes new girls feel awkward on their first days.

"And I'm Pearl," the pie-dough lady says, coming forward to take her place in the center of the floor. "We're so glad to have you, Katie."

My heart sinks as I force a smile at Pearl. *This* is the class? This odd, ragtag bunch? I have the same feeling in my gut that the heroine gets at the beginning of a horror movie: that something is very, very off.

"Katie comes to us *all* the way from the big city!" Mabel announces. Her eyes are the neon-blue of colored contact lenses.

Dee brushes her long bangs out of her face to gape at me. "Whoa — you're from *Albany?*"

I'm at a loss.

"New York City, sweetheart," Mabel tells Dee, and then shoots me a quick, I-feel-your-pain wink. "Katie was a student at the famous Annie Pavlovsky School —"

"Anna Pavlova," I correct Mabel automatically. *Who was, you know, only one of the greatest ballerinas of all time.* Part of me wants to file this exchange away as a funny story to tell Michaela later — until I remember that I'm annoyed at my sister.

"Right, darling," Mabel tells me breezily. "I chatted with your mom and the school's instructor — they both had the most *darling*, funniest little accents — so I know we've got a real ballerina on our hands."

In spite of my mixed emotions about Mabel and this class, I can't help but feel a small flush of pride. I'm more than ready to start dancing, to show Mabel and Pearl and the girls what all my years of training have taught me. There's no Hanae — *or* Michaela — around to steal my thunder, and suddenly I'm the tiniest bit pleased that my sister decided to opt out of this school.

Then, as if reading my mind, Mabel adds, "They mentioned your sister as well. Apparently, she'll be at Juilliard next year?" Mabel looks around to see if anyone else is impressed, but of course no one in the room knows what Juilliard is. And now I feel like second-best once again.

"Yeah," I mumble.

"Well," Mabel says, checking her pink plastic wristwatch. "We're still missing someone, but why don't we go ahead and get started anyway?" Then she bends down, plugs in the boom box, and presses PLAY. An old Kelly Clarkson song — "Since U Been Gone" — fills the studio. I glance at my four classmates to see if anyone else finds this strange, but they are all totally focused on Mabel.

"Let's start with some gentle running," Mabel says, clapping her hands together as she begins to jog in place. "Just go at your own pace. This isn't a competition."

I freeze as everyone around me starts to run in place. Pearl is an emphatic jogger, bouncing on her toes, while the three amigos are lazier, poking one another and laughing as Dee slips in her socks. The sinking, horror-movie feeling returns. How can I show off my ballet skills if we're not going to do, well, *ballet*?

"Mabel, aren't we going to begin with pliés?" I blurt, gesturing to the barre behind me. I know I'm being disrespectful, but I'm getting kind of worried.

Mabel is mid-jog but manages to give me another winning smile. "All in good time, Katie. Now why don't you get into the jogging spirit?"

Translation: Shut. The Hell. Up. I brace myself, take a deep breath, and start jogging. I glance into the mirror and see how ridiculous I look: pumping my fists up and down in my pink tights, black dance shorts, and a black leotard and a high bun. It's like a twisted joke, only I don't want to laugh.

We're halfway through our next exercise — swinging one leg back and forth in time to a Clay Aiken song — when I realize we're probably never going to get to pliés. Or arabesques. Or anything resembling the kind of dance that I'm familiar with. What am I *doing* here? Did Mom and Svetlana know what this school was going to be like? Did Michaela?

I'm starting to plan out a possible escape route when the door to the studio bangs open. It must be that one missing student Mabel mentioned. And when I turn around, I see that the student is none other than —

"Autumn Hawthorne!" Mabel chirps over Clay's voice. "Welcome back! Please come and join us as we blossom together."

Autumn remains in the doorway for a second. It's extremely strange to see her outside of homeroom or social studies or the cafeteria. Especially since she's not wearing her usual plaid button-down or denim overalls. Instead, she has on a stretchy white T-shirt over black leggings, and, lo and behold . . . *pink ballet slippers.* Joy floods through me at the sight. True, they look a little ill-fitting on Autumn's wide, sturdy feet, but who cares? I'm no longer the only freak in the class! Or the only teenager.

Autumn scans the classroom, and when her gaze lands on me, she doesn't look remotely as surprised as I'm feeling. She shoots me a small, tentative smile, and even though we haven't said a word to each other since the first day of school, I smile back.

It's the craziest thing, but I'm almost . . . *happy* to see her.

Looping her hair into a ponytail, Autumn takes her place behind me, and we return to our all-important leg-swinging. I keep a curious watch on Autumn in the mirror as Mabel leads us through a series of floofy knee-bends she calls "pliés" (I imagine Svetlana suffering a heart attack at the sight). Autumn isn't exactly graceful or talented, but she's a hard worker — she watches Mabel with the utmost concentration as our fearless leader instructs us all to "just keep blossoming!" (Pearl, for her part, is surprisingly good at the knee-bends, as are Molly and Dee, but Hayley keeps losing her balance along with her glasses). I'm so busy observing Autumn that when Mabel sends us to the barre, my new teacher channels Claude and asks me to please pay attention and stop daydreaming. I guess I can't win anywhere.

Class ends with a "freestyle" center routine that involves my holding hands with Pearl and Dee and moving in a circle (I survive that by imagining how I'll describe the dance to Trini in my next e-mail). Finally, Mabel releases us, saying that she can't wait to see us again next week.

Yeah, right. When my mom picks me up, I'm going to ask her to get me out of Ms. Mabel Thorpe's School for Dance and Movement as fast as humanly possible. And when I get home, I'm going straight to Michaela's room and demanding that she create a schedule so we can start sharing the barre.

Patting her forehead with a tissue, Pearl waddles up to Mabel, who is unplugging the boom box, and the two of them begin to chat about how challenging our class was, and how expensive the syrup has gotten at Millie's Shack. Meanwhile, Molly, Dee, and Hayley saunter out of the studio with their arms around each other's waists, and Autumn crouches in a corner and removes her ballet slippers. Part of me wants to say hello to her, but I'm not sure yet if she likes me or if I like her. So I turn and head out the door. I'm putting my ballet slippers in my tote bag when I hear Autumn say, "You're really good, you know."

I spin around to see her coming out of the studio, barefoot and holding her slippers.

"You mean, in *there*?" I'm not used to getting too many compliments on my dancing.

Autumn nods, bending down to retrieve a pair of white Nikes from the shoe rack. "It's pretty obvious you studied ballet at a fancy school in Manhattan."

"Oh . . . thanks, I guess," I manage as Autumn sits on the carpet and laces up her sneakers.

And then I realize, with a skip of my heart, that Autumn *wasn't* in the studio when Mabel made my grand introduction.

"Wait, how did you know that?" I ask, as suspicion stirs in me. I grab my jacket off the coatrack and put my bag on my shoulder.

Autumn looks up with a half smile. "The Hemmings," she says simply. "In case you haven't noticed," she adds, standing up, "they're kind of like our town newspaper. During the summer, all they could talk about were the two New York City ballerinas moving to Fir Lake." This is the most I've ever heard Autumn say, and I realize that once she's actually talking, nothing about her seems small-town-country-girl at all.

"I can picture them doing that," I mutter, rolling my eyes, and Autumn laughs, which for no real reason, makes me feel good. She plucks a puffy dark blue vest off the coatrack, and together we start down the stairs. Behind us, I can hear Pearl and Mabel talking as they walk out of the studio. I wonder if they see me and Autumn, and think she and I are . . . friends.

It's a strange thought, but one that makes my spirits feel lighter than they have all evening.

"So I'm sorry if I came off as rude the first time I saw you and your sister," Autumn says as she and I walk into the brisk night. It's crazy that two days ago it was warm enough to go swimming; now the air is as cold as the flat of a knife. "This is going to sound dumb," Autumn goes on. "But it's just that I'd never seen real-life ballet dancers before." She's full-on blushing now — I can see it in the moonlight. "From New York City, at that!" Autumn laughs quickly, a nervous laugh, and I feel my chest grow warm with sudden understanding.

"I get it," I tell Autumn honestly, turning up the collar of my denim jacket as we walk to the edge of the road. I smell wood smoke and burning leaves, and I realize that this is what fall smells like. "I can be pretty curious about people, too," I add.

"Well, yeah, and I'm also sort of obsessed with dance," Autumn says. "Always have been, probably ever since I read *Ballet Shoes* when I was younger."

"I thought . . ." I glance at her. "I thought you belonged to the Camping Club."

"I love camping," Autumn says, glancing up at the sky. "My whole family, we like to go hiking or apple-picking as much as we can before the weather turns. And the Club seems fun so far, though if I had it my way, I'd take dance classes every day after school. But this" — she jerks her thumb back toward the Community Center — "is the best the Fir Lake dance world has to offer."

A bubble of relief floats up in me. "I *knew* you weren't happy in there!" I exclaim. "Are we the only ones who see the truth about Mabel?"

Autumn holds a finger to her lips, and I see Mabel and Pearl emerging from the Community Center, wearing down jackets. We wait until they've walked around the Center to the parking lot behind it. "It's not *that* awful," Autumn finally whispers. "Mabel means well, and it's better than nothing. . . ." She pauses, and her lips part as she studies my face. "Oh, no, Katie! Don't tell me you're planning to drop the class!"

I start laughing. I thought that Michaela was the only person in the world who could read my expression that accurately.

"Katie, are you really — with good conscience — going to leave me to deal with Pearl and company on my own?" Autumn demands, but she's grinning as she says this.

I hear an engine coming up the dark road, and turn to see my family's lumbering SUV. Mom flashes her headlights at me. "I should go," I tell Autumn as Mom brings the car to a stop, but then I see Autumn waving at the car behind Mom.

"That's my ride," Autumn explains. I shield my eyes with one hand to get a better look, and see Autumn's red-haired father behind the wheel. In the passenger seat, there's a tall boy with glasses, and I recognize him as the guy who punched Autumn's arm in the cafeteria. "They probably stopped at my father's office on the way here," Autumn adds, checking her watch. "Jasper — my brother — likes pretending he's already a college student so he's always making up excuses to go to campus with my dad."

Oh. He's not her boyfriend — he's her *brother.* I want to smack my forehead.

"Your dad works at Fenimore Cooper?" I ask Autumn as Mom honks the horn.

Autumn nods, taking a few steps backward. "He's a biology professor — that's how he knew who your mom was. I bet you thought we were stalkers." Again she smiles, and again I think that Autumn is a lot prettier than she seems at a first glance.

"Just amateur stalkers," I reply, waving as I hurry toward the SUV.

"See you tomorrow!" Autumn calls, opening the backdoor of her dad's car.

I can't explain why but I'm beaming as I duck into the car.

"Don't tell me," Mom says as we zoom away from the Community Center. "You hate the class and you want out, even though I've already paid your tuition for the year."

"Oh — well —" I glance over my shoulder to see Autumn's car behind us. "Actually, it was . . . okay."

Mom raises her eyebrows as she navigates the pitch-black road. "When Svetlana and I spoke to Mabel Thorpe, we both got the sense that the school was a little . . . well, not Anna Pavlova."

I open mouth to tell my mom everything: the Clay Aiken, the fake stretches at the barre, Mabel's flower talk, Pearl . . . but then I pause. Come to think of it, I *would* feel guilty leaving Autumn in the class by herself, now that she's asked me to stay. And whining to my mom will only reinforce my status as the family baby. She'd just throw her "Who ever said life was fair?" line back at me.

"It's a change," is all I say, and my voice sounds very mature to my ears.

It *is* nice to be getting exercise again, and I know myself — I'd never really use the barre in the attic if left to my own devices. Maybe Autumn and I can start a ballet slipper revolution. Maybe, after a few more classes, I can even convince Mabel to throw some pirouettes into the routines. As Mom turns the car onto Honeycomb Drive, I realize that if either Wilder sister is going to attend Mabel Thorpe's school, it *should* be me. Michaela in that class would be a crime.

When Mom and I are back at The Monstrosity, I hurry up the stairs, dying to give my sister a recap of the evening. I figure she's doing her term paper for English. The door to Michaela's room is shut, and I'm startled to see a white sheet of paper tacked to it. In Michaela's neat, bubbly handwriting are the words: *Do NOT Disturb!!*

The sign can't possibly be meant for me, since Michaela and I have been disturbing each other our whole lives. Plus, I have an entire dance class — and interaction with Autumn — to describe. Her term paper can wait. This is urgent.

I raise my fist to knock when I hear my sister's laugh, tinkly as a bell. She must be on the phone, but I've never heard my sister laugh quite like that. Intrigued, I press in closer to the door, so close that I can see the grain of the wood.

"That sounds nice," I hear Michaela say in a low voice, and I wonder if Heather is inviting her somewhere again. I decide Heather can wait, too. I go ahead and knock — once, twice —

Michaela opens the door a crack. Her cheeks are flushed bright pink as she balances her cell phone against her shoulder. "What is it, Katie?" she asks, and there's a big-sister sigh lurking behind her words. "Didn't you see the sign on —"

"Are you talking to Heather?" I whisper.

Michaela blinks and fights back a smile. "Um, yeah," she finally answers. "How was dance class?"

"Oh, my God, Mickey, it was crazy — there was like a forty-five-year-old woman in it, and Autumn Hawthorne, the girl who —"

Michaela widens her eyes apologetically. "Katie, can we catch up tomorrow morning on the way to school?" she whispers, cutting me off.

"Aren't we gonna stargaze?" I ask. Michaela's mouth droops, which does not bode well.

"I'm really tired . . ." My sister opens the door an inch more and I see that she's already in her pajamas with the covers on her bed turned down. "Maybe not tonight . . ." She glances meaningfully at the phone in her hand.

"I understand," I say with a shrug. It's the first time Michaela has bailed on stargazing.

Michaela smiles at me, then gently shuts the door. *Click.*

I'm left staring at her *Do NOT Disturb!!* sign, my mind swirling with Mabel Thorpe and Autumn and Michaela's tinkling laugh.

Why did I tell my sister I understood? The truth is, I'm more confused than ever.

11

"Do you confused little whippersnappers have any clue what's happening approximately two weeks from now?"

Mr. Rhodes poses this question to us in homeroom on Thursday, three days after my first dance class with Mabel Thorpe. I'm sitting at my desk with my chin in one hand, fighting back a gargantuan yawn. Sullivan glances at me worriedly, but I'm too exhausted to explain. Three nights in a row without sleep is nothing too new for me, but trying to piece together a mystery involving your sister is particularly draining.

Every night this week has taken the same strange shape: After dinner, Michaela will go to her room, and I'll go to the attic — my sister hasn't been using the barre much. There, I'll IM with Trini, who informed me that Claude said she'll be ready for toe shoes "very soon." When I've had my fill of Trini, I'll go down to Michaela's room, and inevitably her door will be closed, her little obnoxious sign will be in place, and her whispers and giggles will be echoing through the hall. I'll knock and ask Michaela if she wants to stargaze, and she's always holding the phone to her shoulder, wearing her pajamas and an apologetic frown.

On the walk to school this morning, as Michaela and I crunched crimson and rust leaves beneath our heels, I flat out asked my sister what was going on.

"Nothing, Ms. Paranoid," she said, bumping me with her hip. "In case you haven't noticed, it's getting too cold out to stargaze every night."

I couldn't argue with that. In fact, I was shivering in my fashionable-but-not-warm-enough cream-colored peacoat tighter as my breath came out in puffs. Autumn — the season, not the girl — seems to arrive with a vengeance here in the wild.

And the thing is, I can't exactly force my sister to tell me anything. I can only hope that she trusts me enough to open up to me on her own.

If there *is* something going on.

"Well?" Mr. Rhodes prompts, raising his eyebrows and jostling me out of my thoughts.

Heidi Rebecca sits up straight and calls out, "Homecoming!"

When Michaela and I were younger, Mom told us about the Russian scientist named Pavlov who taught his dogs to drool every time he rang a bell. Rebecca's saying "Homecoming!" is like Pavlov ringing his bell, because immediately every kid in the room begins to cheer and stamp his or her feet and possibly even drool.

Slowly, I turn my head to look at Autumn, and she rolls her eyes at me. I smile.

Since Tuesday, Autumn and I have been doing a careful dance around each other. We'll walk to Social Studies together after homeroom, discussing Mabel Thorpe's eyelashes or trying to guess what color sweat-suit Pearl will be wearing next week. Yesterday I tried impersonating Mabel ("Blossom, girls!") and Autumn laughed, which reminded me of making Michaela laugh. But our conversation never strays to anything personal.

Still, I've gotten the sense that Autumn, like me and Michaela, isn't the biggest fan of school spirit. It's subtle things, like her loud sigh in the cafeteria yesterday when one of Anders's football friends stood up to announce a Celebrate The Lake event at the church. I'm pleasantly surprised that Autumn, a Fir Lake native with, as Anders's buddy put it, "the lake water running through our veins, and scaling Mount Elephant on our brains!" can be at all snarky.

But I guess Autumn *is* kind of surprising.

Once the madness in the classroom dies down, Mr. Rhodes begins to read from the orange flyer in his hand, rote as a robot: "Candidates for Homecoming

Queen will be selected by the Student Government this week and announced first thing Monday morning. Voting will take place in homeroom next week, and the winner will be crowned at the Homecoming Gala, to be held following the football game on October 16, in Fir Lake's very own gymnasium."

I groan inwardly. I can only imagine what this "Gala" will look like — orange and blue streamers, a boom box (à la Mabel Thorpe) blasting country music, Heather wearing a paper crown, everyone shimmying in awkward circles. I want no part of it. Back home, school dances and parties were no less painful, but at least there was something to be said for style. Last summer, I went to a friend's Bat Mitzvah that was held on the roof of the Metropolitan Museum of Art: twinkling fairy lights, views of Central Park by night, The Neptunes playing, and mugs of frozen hot chocolate delivered from Serendipity. Even my junior high rented out a grand ballroom in the midtown Hilton for our year-end dance. It's hard to compete with New York City.

Yet based on the rapt expressions of my fellow students, a dance in Fir Lake's gymnasium must be high glamour. Girls titter behind me, and Rebecca pouts prettily at Sullivan. I wonder if it is the kind of dance where dates are involved — a frightening thought.

In the city, dates — at least according to Sofia and a handful of other friends who'd gone on them —

usually involved getting Sicilian slices from Ray's Pizza and eating them on a brownstone stoop, or walking across the Brooklyn Bridge on a sunny day. I get the feeling that dates in Fir Lake might be a tad more formal.

"Hey," Sullivan says softly when the bell rings. I assume he's speaking to Rebecca, so I sling my tote bag on my shoulder and get ready to stand.

"Katie," Sullivan adds, his sleepy brown eyes waking up when he smiles at me. I think of him, bare-chested, at the lake and I feel my heart jolt. "Are you going to the Homecoming Gala?" he inquires.

Wait. Hold on. My pulse is ticking like a speeded-up clock. Is Sullivan *asking* me to the Homecoming Gala? Or is he just asking if I'm going?

"I — probably not —" I stutter. Which is the truth; I can't fathom the idea of attending the dance. I'm sure Michaela and I will come up with some alternate adventure of our own that night, like maybe getting Mom to drive us to Montreal.

Sullivan nods, and then looks past me and starts talking to Rebecca about how tennis practice is getting intense. I feel the smallest pang of regret, but then I stand up and hurry over to Autumn, who is waiting for me by the door. Together, we walk out into the teeming hallway. I'm hoping Autumn won't ask me what Sullivan said and at the same time I'm hoping she will. Maybe she would be able to make sense of the exchange. I want to text Michaela and ask for her advice, but I doubt my sister would even be able to respond before lunchtime. She always seems super-occupied when I catch her between classes, flitting down the hall and saying she has to meet Heather. I let out a sigh I didn't even know was building in me.

"My brother told me all about Homecoming," Autumn speaks up as we pass the trophy case in the lobby. "He went to the dance last year, and he says it's over-the-top cheesiness and the usual Go-Tigers! brainwashing." She pauses, then looks at me. "What? Why are you smiling?"

"Because I figured we were on the same wave-length." I realize that this is the first time Autumn and I are talking about something other than Mabel Thorpe, and it feels totally natural.

"You don't even know," Autumn says darkly as we climb the staircase.

"Tell me."

Autumn shakes her head, the ends of her shiny hair brushing the tops of her overalls. "Football's like a religion around here." She lowers her voice as we near our Social Studies classroom. "If you don't *believe*, people think you're . . . I don't know, the devil or something."

I can't help but laugh, even though I know Autumn's serious. Fir Lake High School *is* like a temple to sports: Behind the school there's a gigantic football field, lined on either side with bleachers, and beyond it, the tennis courts, the running track, and the baseball diamond. All of it bigger and more beautiful than the school itself.

"We can *both* be devils," I tell Autumn as we walk into our classroom. I see that Sullivan beat us there, and he's sitting with his desk pushed close to Meadow McArthur. Is he asking *her* to Homecoming?

Autumn and I settle into our seats — we're diagonal from each other — as our teacher begins drawing a map of Europe on the board. I see Autumn hunch over her notebook for a minute, scribbling something, and then she discreetly passes me a folded-up note. When I open it, I see she's drawn a funny little cartoon image of a devil. And I think, *This girl could be my friend.* Which, like everything else about Autumn so far, surprises me.

Our family doesn't practice any particular religion. Our dad's Jewish and our mom was raised in the Russian Orthodox church, but she says she's an atheist. So every year Michaela and I get a mix-and-match combination of Christmas and Hanukkah, and neither of us is sure if we believe in heaven or hell. Michaela always says, "I can't imagine either."

But I think I have a clear picture of what hell might be:

Freshman-year gym class.

About two hours after the Social Studies, I'm lying with my cheek and my belly against the cold gymnasium floor. All around me, kids in ugly polyester blue shorts and orange T-shirts are doing push-ups, pumping up and down like soldiers in training, while Coach Shreve paces in front of us, barking out commands. His voice bounces off the tiled walls and his sneakers squeak.

I'm doing pretty well in school so far. My homework is always complete, I answered an important question in English yesterday about a William Butler Yeats poem, and last week my French teacher told me I had an impressive working knowledge of the language. (I wanted to tell her that I had a working knowledge of French *curses*, thanks to the great Claude Durand). Gym has been my one stumbling block.

I wonder why it is that when I'm dancing, my body does what I tell it to, but here, in gym class, I become ungainly and unruly. It's like my boobs, which strain against the too-tight T-shirt they issued me on my first day, are in the way, and my limbs get stiff and stubborn. Over lunch yesterday, I asked Michaela if she ever felt the same, and she said, "I *wish* my boobs got in the way." Michaela's completely flat, but on her, it looks good — model-y. And then she said that since she was a senior, nobody took gym seriously; the girls stood around chewing gum and comparing their weekends while the boys shot hoops, and their teacher — not Coach Shreve — pretended not to care.

The squeaking of Coach Shreve's sneakers gets

louder so I know he's getting closer. In the next instant, he's standing right over me.

"Katie, Katie, Katie," he says.

I lift my head from the floor. "I can't do push-ups," I explain unnecessarily.

Coach Shreve's dark eyes look concerned. Last week, in the locker room, Susanna Baker, who eats at the Ninth Grade Popular Table with Rebecca and Sullivan, whispered, "Coach Shreve is so hot he makes me sweat" and then she fanned her underarms, which I thought was kind of gross. All the other girls laughed, though. When I told Michaela the story, she burst out laughing and said, "Oh, Katie, you take things too seriously."

"Let me tell you how I feel about the 'C' word," Coach Shreve tells me now.

I look up at the round clock above the gigantic Tigers mural, and see that it's time for him to send us to the locker rooms. "Everyone, please go shower!" Coach Shreve booms, and then adds, in a lower voice, "Except for you, Katie."

I wonder when my Buddha-rubbing luck is going to start kicking in. Yesterday, when I was closing my window for the night, Emmaline happened to be closing hers at the same time. She smiled at me, and called out, "We need to have tea again sometime!"

I almost asked her, "Why were you crying on Friday?" but that didn't seem like the best thing to yell between our two houses. Instead, I said I'd love to. Then I wondered if Emmaline herself ever rubbed the Buddha's belly, because she didn't seem like the luckiest girl to me.

Everyone thunders past me on their way to the locker rooms, and Coach Shreve sits down beside me, his legs crossed Indian-style. I prepare myself for the worst.

"Katie, do you know what my ex-wife used to say to me?"

Okay, *that* I was not prepared for.

"Um, no . . ." I struggle to sit up.

Coach Shreve stares off into space and rubs his chiseled jawline. "Her favorite word was 'can't.' 'No, Timothy, I can't make this marriage work.' 'Timothy, I can't be happy with you.'"

I look around to see if there are any witnesses. *Can someone call the Too Much Information Police?*

"Do you know where that attitude lands you, Katie?"

"Um, no . . ." *Those* two words seem to be serving me well.

"In divorce court," Coach Shreve replies. "And eating alone in your kitchen for the rest of your life."

"Coach Shreve, I think the bell is about to ring," I say. *And, you know, last time I checked, I'm not a licensed therapist.*

"Sorry." Coach Shreve's head snaps back to me. "I mean to say that thinking 'can't' all the time won't get you very far, Katie. Now why don't you be a sport and try showing me a solid push-up now that your class-mates aren't around?"

Buddha comes through for me then, because the bell shrills. Coach Shreve still makes me show him my halfhearted attempt — I collapse on my belly any-way — and then tells me to practice at home. I nod and scuttle away, trying to pretend like his out-of-the-blue personal-life confession didn't freak the bejeezus out of me.

People are a lot more private in the city.

The locker room is empty when I get there, save for Susanna Baker, who is blow-drying her hair and doesn't need to rush anyway, since there's always a spot for her at the Freshman Popular Table. I speed-shower, dress, and tear toward the cafeteria, knowing Michaela will be irritated if I keep her waiting for too long. Plus, though we've been lucky about snag-ging our two-person table every single day, I'm not sure if it's officially "ours" yet — The Wilder Sisters' Table — the way each class's Popular Table seems to have an invisible RESERVED sign.

I imagine sitting down with Michaela, telling her *You'll never guess what Coach Shreve said to me,* and hearing my sister's shocked laughter. But when I enter the cafeteria, I don't spot Michaela's long neck or flowing light-brown hair. With a flash of relief, I see that our table is available, so I make my way through the thick of students and trays, and sink into a seat.

It's strange that Michaela isn't here by now, but maybe she got held up in Physics lab. Perhaps she's having a moment with her partner, Cecil Billings? I smile at the thought, then pull out my brown bag lunch. As I unwrap my lox-and-cream-cheese bagel (Dad drove all the way to a supermarket in Burlington, Vermont, this week because he had a craving for lox), I feel a spark of worry. Is Michaela purposefully staying out of my way because I pressed her too much this morning?

I check my cell phone, and when I see no missed calls or messages, I stand up and gaze around the cafeteria. I spot Autumn's older brother, sitting with a group of guys, and I glimpse the table where Autumn typically sits with her girlfriends, though Autumn herself is not there. No Michaela. It could be that my sister's getting the hot lunch — she made a point of telling Mom not to prepare a bagel for her this morning. "Everyone knows that bagels outside of New York City suck," Michaela stated plainly.

I'm craning my neck to get a look at the hot lunch line, when someone pulls out the chair across from me.

"Do you mind?" Autumn asks, her voice just shy of hesitant. She gives me a questioning smile as she sets down her tray.

"No, um, I . . ." Between Sullivan and Coach Shreve and now Autumn, I'm *really* eloquent today. "It's just . . . that's my sister's seat," I finally explain.

Then I realize how silly I sound. "But go ahead," I tell Autumn, meaning it. "Michaela can pull up an extra seat when she gets here."

As Autumn and I both sit down, I realize we've completed a new step in our dance; now, it's permissible for us to hang out at lunchtime. I wonder about the group of girls Autumn usually eats with — Camping Club friends, I'd bet — but I'm too distracted by Michaela's absence to ask Autumn any questions.

"Are you looking for your sister?" Autumn asks me as my eyes zigzag across the cafeteria.

"Yeah. She's normally here way before I am."

"Well . . ." Autumn replies, slicing her meatball in half with her fork. "I think I saw her over there. . . ." Autumn waves to a table not too far away, by the wall of windows. A crowd gathered in front of that table splits, and I swallow hard.

It's the Senior Popular Table, and there's Michaela, comfortably sandwiched between Heather and Lucy, as if she's been sitting with these girls every day. She's stabbing at the cafeteria salad with her fork and laughing at something Faith is saying — laughing the way she usually laughs at my impersonations of Svetlana. There are also boys at the table today — Anders, his two friends from that day on the lake, and another guy wearing a football jersey. I'm jealous of the others, that they get to enjoy Michaela's warm presence.

Hurt rises up in me as I stare at my sister. Had she been waiting for an opportunity to ditch me at lunch so she could chill with her new group of friends? I *lived* for our lunches together and I thought Michaela did, too. How could I have read my sister so wrong?

"Oh," I say to Autumn as if the sight of Michaela at the Popular Table isn't making my body quiver with sadness. "Thanks." Then I look down and take a huge bite of my bagel.

Ouch. My jaw aches. The bread is stiff and tasteless, somewhere between cardboard and rubber. Michaela was right. As always. Which makes me even more pissed at her.

"What is that *pink* stuff?" Autumn asks as she leans forward to study my food.

"It's lox," I reply, thinking, *Should I walk up to Michaela now and confront her? Wait until we're home?*

"Like . . . keys and locks?" Autumn asks, and I reluctantly focus on her again.

"No, no, it's fish — smoked salmon," I answer impatiently.

And then I realize, looking across the table at my new maybe-friend, that Autumn truly doesn't *know.* She doesn't know what lox is! This idea is so strange and funny that I can't help but giggle, my mind off Michaela for a moment.

"*Smoked* salmon?" Autumn's eyes widen, and she shudders. "Ew, Katie, that's disgusting!"

"It's not, it's delicious," I laugh, putting down my bagel. "What's disgusting is this bagel. Is there any place to get decent bagels around here?"

"I'm sure there is," Autumn replies, reaching across the table and lifting up the bagel slice to better inspect the lox. "Actually, there's this bakery not too far from my house called Bread and Roses, and I think . . ."

"Oh, my God, Katie!" Michaela appears at my side like a whirlwind. "I'm so sorry, babe, I didn't know if you were coming to lunch at all today —"

I hate that she called me *babe*.

"You could have texted me!" I snap, not wanting to get too riled up in front of Autumn, who has suddenly busied herself with her meatballs.

"I had to stay after class and" —Michaela glances back at her new table — "the girls invited me to sit with them, and you weren't around — so —"

"I got here as soon as I could!" I protest.

I can tell Michaela is struggling to hold back a big-sister sigh as she glances at Autumn. "Hi," she says, smiling her genuine Michaela smile. "You must be Autumn. Katie's mentioned you. I'm Michaela, her sister."

"I know who you are," Autumn says, and I wonder if she means those words to sound as loaded as they do.

It's when Autumn and Michaela are greeting each other that it hits me: I, too, was eating with a friend today. And when I wasn't fuming over Michaela, I was actually having fun. I guess there's no written rule that says that my sister and I must spend every single waking minute of every single lunchtime together. Not that Michaela and I ever get bored with each other, but maybe it's good for us to mix now and then. "Healthy," as Mom would say in her practical voice. "Absence makes the heart grow fonder."

Our mom is fond of sayings.

Looking up at Michaela now as she makes small talk with Autumn, I experience the weirdest sensation. It's as if my sister is drawing away from me, shrinking and shrinking like the city skyline when we drove away from home, until she is out of sight.

"What's wrong?" Michaela asks, putting her hand on my shoulder.

I touch her hand with mine. "I'm fine," I say. "Are we walking home together today?"

"Of course!" Michaela says, looking almost offended — as if any other possibility would be outrageous.

As Michaela glides back to the Popular Table, I watch her for a moment, then turn back to Autumn. "So, the bakery near your house . . ." I say.

Autumn studies me in her quiet, thoughtful way. I can tell that she wants to address the Michaela situation, but she also knows this might not be the best time. So instead she smiles and says, "It smells like heaven. They might have good bagels there."

"I should check it out sometime," I say, giving up on my own bagel and putting it back in the bag. "Where do you live?"

"Not too far from you, actually — right off Frog Croak Road," Autumn glances at her food. "Maybe . . . since it's close by . . . would you want to come over to my house this weekend? The Camping Club is camping out on Mount Elephant from Saturday night into Sunday, but I'm free on Saturday during the day. . . ."

I feel my heart swell. I'm invited to Autumn's house! If that's not a friend move, I don't know *what* is. And despite the overalls Autumn is wearing, and despite her belonging to the Camping Club, knowing that she's probably my first friend in Fir Lake makes me grin.

I can't wait to tell Michaela.

12

"Welcome to Casa Hawthorne," Autumn says when I arrive on her doorstep Saturday afternoon. She gestures with a flourish as I step inside the warm entrance hall. "I know it's not a penthouse on Park Avenue, but . . ."

"Eeeek!" is my response. A large, furry creature is panting in my face, its jagged nails digging into my chest, and its enormous tongue attempting to slobber —

"Ralph Waldo, Ralph Waldo, down boy!" Autumn yells, pointing to the floor as if this might help. Magically, it does, because the creature — a gargantuan St. Bernard — gets down on all fours and stares up at me, his tail wagging so hard it bangs into Autumn's legs.

"He likes you!" Autumn exclaims as I struggle for air.

The only one of my friends who's ever had a dog was Sofia Pappas, and hers was a nervous, yappy little dachshund who zipped from one end of her apartment to the other (her parents eventually took the dog to a pet therapist, which is actually quite common in the city). Trini has a fat cat that naps all the time, and a few goldfish have floated in and out of my childhood. But an in-your-face, wild-and-free mountain dog like Ralph Waldo seems specific to Fir Lake.

"Go on, Ralph Waldo, go play out back," Autumn says, patting Ralph Waldo on his rump, and the dog obeys, galloping through the house and presumably out the backdoor to the yard, where I pray he'll stay. Forever.

"You're not a dog person, huh?" Autumn asks me with a grin as I unbutton my peacoat with stiff fingers. My cheeks are frozen from the short walk, and I can barely feel my feet in my cute gold-buckled flats.

"Let's just say I haven't spent a lot of time around animals," I respond, hoping to sound diplomatic even though I'm considering calling a doctor to make sure I didn't catch rabies.

"Ralph Waldo means no harm, I promise," Autumn assures me as she takes my coat.

"Uh-huh," I say, studying the framed portrait of the dog that hangs in the entrance hall, alongside an embroidered square with the words *Nature always wears the colors of the spirit — Ralph Waldo Emerson* stitched into it. At least now I know where the dog got his weird name.

"So describe your old apartment for me," Autumn instructs as she hangs up my coat in the hall closet. "You know, I've never been to New York City. . . ."

"*Really?* I'm shocked," I tease. When Autumn doesn't answer right away, I worry that my comment offended her. But then she whirls around, laughing appreciatively.

"I know, I'm such the wide-eyed ingenue," Autumn says as we walk through her living room. I wonder what *ingenue* means, but I don't want to seem stupid by asking. Autumn's living room is decorated in shades of forest green and nut brown, so it still feels like you're outdoors even when you're inside. There are tons of science books bursting out of the plastic shelves, and paintings of woodland creatures on the walls. It's kind of ugly, but welcoming at the same time.

"Well, our apartment wasn't a penthouse, and it wasn't anywhere near Park Avenue," I say, sitting gingerly on the arm of Autumn's couch. I'm still expecting Ralph Waldo to fly out at me at a moment's notice. Autumn flops onto a green La-Z-Boy, and listens intently. "We lived in the East Village. Our kitchen fit two people at most, and there was only one bathroom. My sister and I shared a bedroom, too."

"Wow, I would go crazy if I had to share a room

with someone," Autumn says. "I need lots and lots of space. Or maybe that's just what I'm used to."

"Is anyone else home now?" I ask, tipping my head back to see the second landing.

"My dad's on campus — he has office hours on Saturdays," Autumn replies. "And Jasper is probably holed up in his room, reading. As always. Hey," Autumn adds, getting to her feet. "Let's go to the kitchen." I notice that there's no mention of a mom. In my house, my mother's presence is like a storm — loud and strong and impossible to ignore. "I have a surprise for you," Autumn adds. "Are you hungry?"

"Starving." Whenever I spent the day at Trini's apartment, we rarely ate together. I guess that's not what ballerinas do.

"Good," Autumn says as we step inside the kitchen. "Because guess what I picked up at the Bread and Roses bakery this morning?"

"Autumn . . . did you get bagels?" I cry, impressed. The kitchen, like the living room, is green and brown, and there are so many plants along the windowsills that it looks like a small jungle. Plus, there's a white cat snoozing on the counter. How many creatures live in this zoo?

"Oh, my God!" Autumn gasps, and I pause, looking around for the problem. The stove isn't on, the refrigerator purrs peacefully, everything seems in order.

Autumn gestures to a yellow plate on the counter, which is empty save for a few crumbs.

"That greedy little pig ate the bagels!"

"Who? The cat?"

"No! My brother!"Autumn grabs my hand and pulls me out of the kitchen. "This is war. Come on, Katie. I'll need an ally."

I have no choice but to rush up the staircase after Autumn. When we get to the second landing, the door at the end of the hall is wide open, and a Shins song drifts out. "He wasn't even scared enough to close his door!" Autumn mutters, storming over to the room. "Jasper Benjamin Hawthorne, you are *so* busted!"

"I am?" Jasper asks, his mouth full of bagel as he looks up from his book. He is lounging on his dark blue bed, wearing a rumpled black T-shirt, ripped jeans, and black and red armbands on his wrist. His glasses perch on the bridge of his nose and his hair is sticking up in the back, like it usually is when I see him in the cafeteria at school.

I've never been in a boy's bedroom before, so while Autumn glowers at her brother, I scope out the joint. On Jasper's black-painted walls hang framed poems — black type on a white background, with the poet's names on the bottom: Pablo Neruda, William Blake, Percy Shelly. There's also a framed photograph of Mount Elephant in all its snow-capped glory hanging over his cluttered desk. He has no shelves, only crooked, towering stacks of books and CDs. The book he's holding in his lap is a tattered copy of Ernest Hemingway's *The Sun Also Rises*.

I get the feeling that this isn't a typical Fir Lake boy's bedroom. Certainly not the kind of room someone like Sullivan, for instance, would have. There, I imagine, it's all sports posters and tennis rackets and DVDs like *Old School*.

"Those bagels were for me and Katie!" Autumn is saying, pouncing on her brother and trying to wrest the last stub of a bagel from his grip. "I paid for them with *my* hard-earned cow-milking money, and wait until I tell Dad!"

Autumn milks cows? I think, stunned anew by my friend.

Jasper looks lazily up at Autumn, chews, and swallows. "You snooze, you lose," he finally says, speaking in a laid-back, steady tone that I'm sure is making Autumn even crazier. "They were just *sitting* there, and you weren't around, so . . ."

"So you put your grubby paws all over them," Autumn snaps, then starts pummeling Jasper's arm with her fists. Jasper inches farther down the bed, holding the last bagel piece over his head, clearly enjoying himself.

I watch them openmouthed. When Michaela and I are cruel to each other, there's never physical violence involved.

"Autumn — Jasper — stop — I don't care about the bagels!" I cut in.

Autumn and Jasper give me looks that say, *What? We do this all the time.*

"Hey, aren't you from New York City?" Jasper asks me once Autumn releases him, her face red and her hand triumphantly waving the bagel stub.

"Last time I checked," I shoot back, lifting my chin.

"Then you should be tough enough to handle a fight," Jasper points out, his green eyes bright with mischief.

I clench my teeth. "And you should be tough enough to apologize to your sister!" I retort. I don't know if it's my pent-up frustration at Michaela, but suddenly I'm all about ending the Tyranny of the Older Sibling.

"Thanks, Katie," Autumn says, rejoining me in the doorway.

"Okay, okay." Jasper makes a great show out of getting off his bed, standing, and then dropping in a mock bow. "My sincerest apologies, Lady Autumn, Lady Katherine."

Autumn and I look at each other and roll our eyes.

"Actually, it's Katya," I inform Jasper, and for some reason, I don't feel the flush of embarrassment I usually get when I speak my full name.

Jasper nods, holding my gaze for a minute. "Cool name. Russian, right?"

I'm taken aback by his knowing this. "Um, yeah."

"Show-off," Autumn grumbles. She offers me the mangled piece of bagel, and I refuse, so she takes a bite of it.

"So, Katie," Jasper says, crossing his arms over his chest, his mouth curling up in a smirk. "Seems you're adjusting to Fir Lake *really* well."

It's impossible to not hear the sarcasm in his voice. I glance down at my short black velvet skirt, patterned tights, and fuzzy white sweater with red ribbons up the sleeves. So maybe I'm not exactly dressed for a fall Saturday in the country, but who is this boy to tell me so?

"In fact, I am," I reply, putting my hands on my hips. "The problem is, Fir Lake hasn't adjusted to *me* yet." I'm not sure I believe my own words, but in that instant, they feel good on my tongue.

"Well, as a proud citizen of this fine town," Jasper says with a grin. "I look forward to the challenge."

"I hope you're up to it," I volley back, feeling a smile start on my lips. It's weird, but I'm kind of . . . having a good time.

"Okay, you guys, enough sniping," Autumn interrupts, taking my arm, and it's almost like I'd forgotten she was there. "Jasper, can't you at least pretend to act human when I have friends over?"

"What is this 'human' you speak of?" Jasper asks. Then he crashes back onto his bed, flashes me and Autumn a wicked smile, and returns to *The Sun Also Rises*.

"Have fun with Ernest," Autumn replies, and shepherds me back into the hall. "You're so lucky you have a sister," she tells me in a low voice. "Jasper thinks he *is* Hemingway. You know — sensitive writer guy who is all into nature and stuff."

"Speaking of nature, do you really milk cows?" I ask, trying to sound nonchalant.

"Yup, Jasper and I both do," Autumn replies without a trace of shame. "At Mountain Creek Farm, right up the road. We've been doing it forever, on random weekend mornings. It pays well, and it's pretty easy to learn."

"I can't . . . wow." I'm speechless. Then I surprise myself by asking, "Can I come watch you sometime?"

"Sure, but not in that outfit," Autumn replies. She turns the knob on the door at the end of the hall, and we enter her room.

Which is a shrine to ballet.

The walls are papered with clippings from dance magazines, newspaper ads about ballet performances in Montreal, close-up photographs of toe shoes and tutus, and shots of famous dancers. On Autumn's neat wooden bookshelves are the colorful spines of countless DVDs: *Center Stage, Save the Last Dance, Step Up, The Turning Point, Dirty Dancing* (the original *and* the cheesy *Havana Nights* one). . . . I try to take it all in.

"I warned you," Autumn says, shutting her door. "I'm obsessed."

"Oh, only a little," I say, as I brush my fingers over the antique pair of toe shoes that hangs from a nail above Autumn's desk. "All that's missing is, like, the embalmed body of a ballerina hidden in your closet."

"Funny you should mention it . . ." Autumn flings open her closet door to reveal her jeans and flannel collection.

The two of us burst into fresh laughter and collapse onto Autumn's quilt-covered bed. I can't remember the last time I laughed this much with someone other than Michaela. I feel a light prickle of remorse, as if I'm somehow being unfaithful to my sister. But I remind myself that when I told Michaela I was going to Autumn's house, on our walk home from school on Thursday, Michaela's eyes lit up and she said, "That's great, Katie!" I guess she's been worried, since I haven't quite hit the friend jackpot in Fir Lake.

Autumn is still chuckling as I sit up and look at the rest of her room. You can always recognize the desk of a Smart Kid by how crowded it is with school stuff, and Autumn's is practically buried under piles of index cards, yellow highlighters, and shiny textbooks. Autumn doesn't say much in Social Studies, but when we got our pop quizzes back on Friday, there was a big fat 100 scrawled across the top of hers. (I got an 85.)

Among Autumn's study supplies, there's also a photograph in a heart-shaped frame. The photo is of a striking woman with big green eyes and luxurious auburn hair. She's sitting on the green couch that I just saw downstairs in the living room, but something about the picture looks older, faded.

"That's my mom," Autumn says when she catches me staring, and right away I know Autumn's mother isn't alive. My stomach tightens, scared that Autumn is going to tell me her mom was eaten by bears, and, hey, did I want to go for a walk in the woods later?

"She died giving birth to me," Autumn adds.

Oh. Autumn's words wallop me in the gut. That seems a lot worse than death by bears. I try to imagine growing up under that veil of guilt, knowing that you're the reason your mom's not around. Talk about having a tragic past.

I feel too embarrassed to look at Autumn, but out of the corner of my eye, I see that she's watching me. "I'm sorry," I murmur.

"Don't be," Autumn replies with a small shrug. "I mean, it's sad, sure, but it's not like I knew her."

"I'm glad you told me," I say, turning and meeting her gaze.

"Why wouldn't I? It's no secret. Anyway, I guess it explains why I'm not the girliest girl — I mean, except for the ballet thing." Autumn gestures to herself; she's wearing a green long-sleeved Henley and cuffed jeans.

"Growing up with my dad and my brother, there wasn't too much help with things like lip gloss and heels, you know?"

Now I feel terrible for scoffing at Autumn's overalls and flannel shirts.

"Do you think I'm too girly?" I ask, running my thumb over my glossy bottom lip.

Autumn makes a so-so motion with her hands. "For Fir Lake, you sure are. But it's part of your charm," she adds with a smile. "And you always wear the best clothes." Her voice is matter-of-fact, not colored by jealousy or cattiness.

"*You* think so?" I ask, unable to mask my surprise.

"I know how you see me, Katie," Autumn says. "Hick from the sticks, no fashion sense, wouldn't know a trendy outfit if her scarecrow wore one . . ."

Autumn, by the way, really *does* have a scarecrow outside her house.

"Autumn, that's not . . ." I start to protest but her knowing smile is so contagious so that I start to laugh. "Okay, maybe I thought that before I knew you. . . ." It feels weird to be admitting these truths and secrets, letting them all spill out.

"And I thought you were a city snob," Autumn says in the same cheerful, plain manner. "Wearing all-black on the first day of school . . . acting like you were too good to walk to Social Studies with me . . ."

I digest this. "Then why were you nice to me?" I ask.

"You seemed interesting," Autumn replies instantly. "Different from everyone else. I like my friends at school fine, but we all come from the same place, know the same people. . . ." She reaches over and tugs one on of my curls, then grins when it springs back into place. "But even your hair is different."

"*You* have the most amazing hair," I reply. "I'm serious. I bet it blows boys away."

Autumn's face colors and she shakes her head, the hair in question catching the sunlight coming through her window. "Ha. Boys don't even see me."

"No, they don't see *me*," I counter.

"You're joking, right?" Autumn rolls her eyes. "I mean, it couldn't be more obvious that Sullivan Turner has the world's biggest crush on you."

A blush hops onto my face, so sudden and hot that I put my hands to my cheeks. "No."

"Katie, he's always staring at you."

I press my clammy palms together. "But isn't he dating Hei — Rebecca Lathrop?"

"Oh, please!" Autumn. "They went on *one* date this year, but it's not as if he's her boyfriend or anything. Except, like, in her dreams."

"How do you *know* all this?" I ask, bewildered.

Autumn lifts one shoulder, looking world-weary. "Everyone knows everything in this town. There are hardly any secrets in Fir Lake."

"*I* have a secret," I say, tucking my legs up onto the bed. There's something delicious about finally being the one with secrets. "I think Sullivan might have wanted to ask me to Homecoming!" I recount what he'd said to me in homeroom.

"*Katie*, that's awesome!" Autumn cries, squeezing my arm. This is by far the girliest I've ever seen her behave, and I like it.

"Do you think he's cute?" I ask. Our back-and-forth feels new and fresh to me. My ballet friends and I rarely gossiped about boys back home, except for Jason Rosenthal.

"*Yes*," Autumn says, giving me a *hel–lo*! look. "I mean, in that preppy, typical Fir Lake boy way. But still. I like his brown eyes."

"Me too," I say, blushing. Do I have a crush on Sullivan? I'm not sure, but it feels pretty close to one.

"You know what you should do?" Autumn says, her grin widening. "Ask him out!"

"Are you insane?"

"Why not?" Autumn leans back against her wall. "Ask *him* to Homecoming! Turn the guy-girl tables a little."

"No *way*." I unfold my legs and put my feet on the floor. "Forget it. I'd never have the guts." I regard Autumn for a moment. "Come on, seriously. Would *you* ever ask a guy out?"

"Maybe." But she looks hesitant, and I realize that Autumn, like me, has probably never had a boyfriend — which makes me like her even more. "I might. They're just *boys*," she says after a moment, tossing her hair.

This is news to me. "Boys are confusing," I say. "Well, you do have a brother. Maybe boys don't seem as foreign to you. I mean, Michaela and I don't even have any male *cousins*."

"Jasper doesn't count!" Autumn cries. "I can't take *him* to Homecoming. . . ."

"I know, but I guess brothers can be . . ." I pause, trying to conjure up an image of a Wilder brother — curly brown hair, stick-out ears, lanky body. Someone I could watch shaving and ask about sports. I'd always been so content with Michaela that I'd never stopped to wonder about another possible sibling. "Useful," I say. "Like, you can ask them questions about boy behavior."

"You can't go to your *sister* for advice on guys?" Autumn asks me, looking bewildered. "I thought that was the main purpose of older sisters!"

I shrug. "My sister and I don't talk about boys that much. Neither of us has a lot of experience." I hope revealing this fact about my sister doesn't constitute betrayal.

Autumn raises her eyebrows. "But doesn't Michaela have some experience now?"

I feel my forehead wrinkle in confusion. "What?"

"Anders," Autumn says calmly as if she's giving me the weather report. "You know — the gorgeous senior QB?"

"QB?" I ask numbly. My mouth feels clumsy.

"Sorry — quarterback," Autumn explains patiently.

My brain is like a broken calculator. The information does not compute. "Michaela . . . and Anders?"

Autumn nods happily, not yet noticing my distress. "Word is he's been into her since the first day of school. Has Michaela been flipping out about their date tonight?"

I can't move.

"Anders Swensen . . . asked my sister out?" I ask.

In that moment, it clearly registers with Autumn that not everything is peachy keen. I'm figuring it must be the look of utter shock on my face. Autumn's own face falls.

"Wait, Katie. Did you not know?" Her voice is quiet.

I manage to shake my head.

"Michaela didn't tell you?"

Shaking my head seems to be the one motion I'm capable of.

Immediately, Autumn begins to backpedal. "Well . . . it could be I misunderstood. . . . I mean, stupid rumors are flying around all the time, and maybe it's another girl. . . ."

"Right. Another girl named Michaela," I say.

Beautiful, beautiful Anders Swensen. With *my* Michaela? I feel a small burst of pride, followed by disbelief. Could it be? Could it be that he was liking her and she was liking him back, right out in the open, and I was the *only one* who had no clue?

And why does this all feel so familiar?

"You never know," Autumn offers, watching me in the same cautious way I was watching Ralph Waldo earlier.

"I need to ask my sister," I declare, getting to my feet. "It's not like her. This is *huge*! If it were true, she would've told me, right?" My stomach is a ball of nervous tension.

"Definitely," Autumn says, though her eyes only say *I hope so*. She gives me a fast hug. "Let me know what you find out" are her parting words as I hurry out of her room.

I dash past Jasper's room — he waves to me from his bed — and down the stairs, narrowly avoiding a collision with Ralph Waldo, who's returned from outside, panting and wagging.

"Don't bite me don't bite me don't bite me . . ." I mutter as I back up toward the hall closet. Still eyeing Ralph Waldo, I pull out my coat, yank it on, and back out the front door — straight into Mr. Hawthorne, who's just returned from campus.

"Send my best regards to your parents!" he calls after I've apologized ten times.

"I will!" I cry, cutting across their front lawn and accidentally bumping into their scarecrow.

I tell myself that Autumn could be wrong. For all I know, I'll come home to find Michaela in her ballet clothes, stretching on the barre in the attic, and when she sees me, she'll say, "Want to rent a movie tonight?"

Afternoon is bleeding into twilight, the sky a melancholy purple. The air is so cold that it hurts to breathe it in. Piles of leaves are everywhere, like miniature Mount Elephants, and I have to leap over a few, ballet-style, to get to Honeycomb Drive.

"Katie! Is everything all right?" Emmaline, who's getting out of her car, calls to me as I tear past her, my jaw clenched tight.

"Yeah, no, I don't know!" I call back, running up our porch steps. Inside, I rest against the front door to catch my breath.

"Don't spill the mulled apple cider," I hear Mom saying in the kitchen. "Careful now."

"I still think we should be bringing wine," Dad replies.

"This isn't the city," Mom says, and steps into the front hall. She's wearing her black cashmere poncho and her big pearl earrings. A second later, Dad emerges behind her in his long charcoal coat, carrying a silver pot.

"Where are you *going*?" I ask them.

In the city, dressed as they are, they would have said "the opera" or "the ballet." Here, in Fir Lake, Dad says: "The Hemmings."

"They're having us over for an autumn feast!" Mom says, heading for the door. "Isn't that polite of them?"

I want to tell my parents that they're a tad overdressed, but I'm not really one to talk. Besides, I have bigger things on my mind. "Is Michaela home?" I ask. I think I hear someone puttering around upstairs.

Dad nods absently. "She's about to go out with some friends, though. I'm sure she'll want you to join her."

I'm sure she will.

As soon as Mom and Dad are gone, I sprint up the stairs to my sister's room, to find out the truth once and for all.

13

Michaela's door is ajar for a change, and she is standing by her dresser with her back to me, humming. She must have just showered; her robe is lying across her bed, along with a heap of discarded clothes, and the whole room smells powdery and clean. Her hair is wet and hangs down between her shoulder blades. She's wearing a white halter top, jeans, and black, flat-heeled boots that come to her knees.

Anders Swensen is tall, but in heels, I bet Michaela would tower over him.

Still humming, Michaela wiggles her hips a little and slips on a pair of dangly gold earrings. Then she holds up her gold-pendant necklace, surveying it. She doesn't look like she's getting dressed for a night out with friends.

"Do you have a date with Anders Swensen?" I ask, my voice low and even.

"Katie, you scared me!" Michaela spins around, dropping the necklace. Her face is flawless; her eyebrows, naturally arched, are outlined neatly, her cheekbones are brushed with something shimmery, and her lips look as if they've been kissed by a berry.

"Well, do you?" I ask, crossing my arms over my chest.

Michaela lets out a big-sister sigh, and puts a hand to her forehead. "Yes. Who told you?"

Yes. She said *yes*.

I think of all the times Michaela could have told me that the hottest boy in school asked her out. Our walks to and from school. Our lunches together, if she whispered.

I'm so upset that I'm shaking.

"Autumn told me," I say. "She made it seem like it's common knowledge."

Michaela frowns. "That can't be. Only Heather, Lucy, and Faith know. . . ."

"And Anders and his friends," I point out coldly. "News travels fast in a small town."

"Katie, why are you looking at me like you want to *murder* me?" Michaela cries, throwing up her hands. "Look, I was going to tell you, but —"

"You didn't. You told your *other* friends, though." Tears blur my vision, and Michaela appears squiggly and small.

Michaela bows her head for a moment. Then she draws in a deep breath and looks up.

"Katie," she says. "You're my other half. My sister. The closest person in the world to me."

"Same here," I say, softening as I smile through my tears. Maybe this is Michaela's apology, which I'll graciously accept, since I'm the more noble one.

"And you'll *always* be my sister," Michaela goes on. "But . . . you're not my friend."

I've never been stabbed, but I'm guessing this is how it feels.

"That's insane — we're best friends!" I exclaim, swiping at my eyes with the back of my hand. My woolen sleeve brushes my cheek, and I realize I didn't take my coat off.

"We are in a way, but —" Michaela lets out another big breath. "It's complicated. You're *not* my friend in the way that Heather is. I've never had friends like her, or Faith and Lucy —"

"What's so great about *them*? What about our friends back home?" I interrupt, seething. In our last IM session, Trini told me that Sofia had complained to her that Michaela wasn't good about e-mailing regularly. "Don't they count?"

"Of course they do, but, God, Katie!" Michaela tugs on one of her earrings and lets out a frustrated sound. "I wanted to make new friends *here*. To start a new life. It's important. That's why I'm so glad you've made with friends with Autumn! *She's* someone you can confide in!"

"I don't need Autumn! I have you!"

Michaela stares at me, hard. "Katie, there are some things you tell your friends that you *don't* tell your family. That's how life works."

Oh, life. Unfair life. My sister reminds me of our mother.

"So you haven't told Mom and Dad?" I snap, my outrage blooming by the second. I almost want to chase after our parents and reveal to them Michaela's *real* plans for the night.

"See, *that's* why I didn't want to tell you right away, Katie," Michaela hisses. "You'd blab it to them! You know how strict Mom is!"

"Mom wouldn't care," I spit. "She adores you."

"Only when I'm dancing ballet," Michaela fires back. "I can't —" Then she stops herself and looks down at her necklace on the floor.

"What?" I demand, taking a step closer to my sister.

Michaela steps away from me. "Nothing. Leave me alone." She whips back around to her dresser and begins sorting through piles of bracelets.

"We're not done yet!" I shout, storming around Michaela so that I'm facing her profile. "You didn't tell me about Anders because you thought I'd tell Mom and Dad? That's ridiculous! I can keep a secret!"

Michaela doesn't answer. She only purses her lips and paws through her bracelets with greater urgency.

"You know I can!" I insist, pulling on Michaela's

arm. What *I* know is that I'm acting incredibly immature. I try to calm myself.

"Katie, did you ever think that maybe I didn't tell you because you behave in this ludicrous manner?" Michaela bursts out, finally looking up at me. "Maybe the fact is, you're not ready to know that I —"

"Have a boyfriend?" I cut in, feeling my face flame. "You'd really keep that from me?"

"He's not my *boyfriend*, Katie," Michaela says in a quieter tone, slipping on a few gold bangles. "We're just going on one date. That's all." She picks up her compact from her dresser and glances at her reflection. I can see by the glint in her eyes how excited she is.

I lean one elbow on Michaela's dresser, feeling some of my fury drain away as well. "Where are you going anyway?" I ask, my voice steadier now.

"Dinner and a movie in town, I think," Michaela says, a smile breaking out on her face. "How basic can you get, right?"

I can tell Michaela is enchanted by something so basic. "Autumn says he's liked you since the first day of school," I blurt.

Michaela's cheeks turn pink as she walks over to her bed, picking up her gray cotton cardigan from the heap. "I don't know if *that's* true," she says. "We hung out that first night, you know, when I went with Heather to Pammy's Pizza after yearbook?" I nod, and Michaela goes on, holding the cardigan up to her chest and looking at herself in the mirror. "Well, he and I talked a little that night, and apparently he told his friend Todd who then told Heather that he thought I was pretty." Michaela shrugs at this. "And then we kept seeing each other in the hallways at school, and then at the lake that time, and then he asked for my number. . . ."

I'm riveted by Michaela's story, picturing every moment, every encounter. My sister has been leading a whole other life that's been unfolding alongside mine. It's insane.

"What do you think, the yellow or the gray?" Michaela asks, holding up another cardigan for me to review. The air feels quiet between us again, settled. It never ceases to amaze me how fluidly Michaela and I can move from anger to peace.

Well, semi-peace.

"The yellow," I say. "Brighter."

"Yeah, boys like bright colors," Michaela says as she puts on the yellow cardigan and does a spin in front of the mirror.

"They do?" I glance down at my black-and-white ensemble. For some reason, I think of Jasper.

"I don't know, I made that up." Michaela laughs — a short, high laugh. She's nervous.

Suddenly, Michaela's cell phone begins to shimmy on her desk as Justin Timberlake serenades us.

"Oh my God oh my God he's here!" Michaela makes a lunge for her phone. If I weren't still upset,

I'd want to giggle. With her makeup and her bracelets and her Saturday-night date, my sister's like a character from the '80s movies we loved to Netflix back in the city when we were feeling silly — *Sixteen Candles, Some Kind of Wonderful, Pretty in Pink.* . . .

"Hello?" Michaela says into the phone, suddenly calm and composed.

Like she has no idea who's on the other end.

"You're outside?" Michaela's voice is downright breezy, even though her eyes are getting bigger by the second. She licks her bottom lip, and smooths her hair with one hand. "I'll be right down."

From my perch on the bed, I watch as Michaela tornadoes through her room, pulling on her red hooded anorak (another recent purchase from The Climber's Peak), grabbing her black clutch, checking her reflection once more, and then starting for the door. Then she pauses, turns, and runs over to me with her arms outstretched.

I hesitate, but then return her embrace.

"Good luck tonight," I say. Despite everything that's happened, I feel a blip of excitement for my sister. She's going on her very first date! With Anders Swensen!

"Truce?" Michaela asks. "We'll talk more later. I promise."

I want to tell her that promises are as dangerous as secrets, but by then she's floating out the door. I hear her light footsteps on the stairs, and then the front door slams.

It's a Saturday night, and I'm home alone.

I'm *so* cool.

Sitting on Michaela's bed with my hands in my lap, I consider doing my homework — then realize that I have to draw the lameness line *somewhere*. I can't call Autumn, because she's on her awful camping expedition. And if I e-mail Trini, do I *really* want to hear back about her toe shoe–fitting sessions with Claude? Besides, Saturday nights apparently equal *Nutcracker* rehearsals now, as the performance gets closer.

So I stand and begin wandering across Michaela's room, absentmindedly picking up a book here, an earring there. The once pin-neat Michaela has gotten messy; her socks and shoes and leggings lie in a heap on the floor. I guess cleaning takes a backseat to Anders, Heather, and the twins. I stop in the middle of the room to study Michaela's biggest poster. It's swoony and romantic: a black-and-white photograph of a couple kissing on a Paris street.

After Autumn's dance-dance-dance room, it's funny to see my sister's, where there's hardly any evidence of the fact that she's a dancer. Only her burgundy leotard, draped over her desk chair, gives her away. On her desk, there is a scattering of pennies and nickels and wrinkled receipts from Pammy's Pizzeria and The Climber's Peak. All evidence of her new life. When my eyes land on Michaela's laptop, my fingers tingle with the desire to open it. Michaela and I know each other's Gmail and MySpace passwords. I could just take a quick peek at her messages, to see what juicy secrets might have passed between her and Heather, or her and Anders, online.

But I can't bring myself to do it. After all, I have morals. Boundaries. Principles. No matter how much my sister upset me earlier, I can't break her trust.

Plus, if Michaela ever found out I that snooped through her computer, she'd hang me.

So, deciding to put temptation behind me, I grab my coat off Michaela's bed, shut off the light, and leave my sister's room. Maybe tonight I'll treat myself — take a bath, watch TV, and go to bed early. If I can't find out all my sister's secrets, at least I can catch up on sleep.

Ha.

At 11:30 — long after my bath and my TV marathon, and after Mom and Dad have returned from the Hemmings and gone to bed, secure in the knowledge that Michaela would be back by her midnight curfew — I'm still wide awake. I toss and turn, replaying what Michaela said to me in her room. *You're not my friend. I wanted to start a new life.*

Staring up at Ethan Stiefel, I try to calculate how long dinner and a movie might take. Michaela and Anders could have gone to one of those three-hour movies, which I hate, because I inevitably have to pee midway through. And maybe their dinner took forever, since the wait-staff in Fir Lake restaurants hardly move at a snappy pace. Or maybe the date was a disaster and Michaela flew off in a huff and decided to spend the night at Heather's house.

The sound of an engine outside The Monstrosity startles me, and I sit up.

Through my curtains, I see the light in Emmaline's bedroom is on — as usual — so it can't be her car I hear. The Hemmings have probably been dead asleep since nine.

Which leaves one possibility.

My heart hammering, I slip out of bed and creep over to my window. I have to angle my neck, but I can make out a blue car parked in our driveway. The driver's side door opens and out steps gorgeous QB Anders Swensen. His trim figure is clad in an orange-and-blue Tigers jacket, a black turtleneck sweater, jeans, and white sneakers. It's a kind of a dorky outfit, but Anders still looks perfect. The guy would probably be hot in waist-high pants and a pocket protector.

What was it Mr. and Mrs. Hemmings said? *That Anders Swensen . . . Too handsome for his own good . . . I hear he's breaking girls' hearts right and left.*

And for the first time that night, I wonder if Michaela might be just one of Anders Swensen's many victims. Does my sister know what she's doing, dallying with a boy like him? Isn't she in way over her head?

Anders walks around the car with his easy athlete's grace, opens the passenger side door, and takes my sister's outstretched hand. The word *gentleman* comes to mind as he draws Michaela up and out of the car. Michaela's hair streams down her back, glowing in the moonlight, and her legs look as long as a fawn's. Anders says something to her and they laugh.

I guess the date went well.

I'm barely believing what I see as my sister — my sister who used to stretch across my bed in her night-gown and socks, laughing so hard she snorted — puts her arms around Anders Swensen's neck. Anders slides his arms around Michaela's waist and pulls her closer to him. And they kiss.

It's a real kiss, a serious kiss, one that involves their mouths opening and their heads tilting, and their bodies pressing together.

"Did Jason Rosenthal stick his tongue in your mouth?" I remember asking Michaela when she returned home that day and recounted the subway kiss.

"Yeah." My sister hugged a pillow from her bed, a smile tugging at her lips.

"Ew!" I cried, putting my hands over my face, and Michaela big-sister-sighed and said, "*Katie*, that's what happens when you kiss!"

Apparently so.

I feel a strange sort of tingle pass through me at the sight, and my face grows hot. I rest my forehead against the frosted windowpane and watch, my pulse racing, as Michaela ends the kiss. She is smiling — a slow and dreamy smile that I don't recognize as hers. She rests *her* forehead against Anders's, and he gazes into her eyes like he's searching for something in them.

For a moment I forget myself, and it's like I'm watching an impossibly romantic movie that I want to go on and on. Then I remember I'm watching innocent, good-natured Michaela and smooth, suave Anders. The guy in the movie who's too good to be true.

Don't do it! I want to shout out the window. *Don't fall for a boy who's going to break your heart!*

If Michaela hears my thoughts, she pays them no mind. Instead, she laughs softly as Anders kisses her neck, and she rubs her hands up and down his arms. Is she crazy? What if Mom and Dad wake up and see them? Doesn't she know people might be watching from their windows?

Or maybe it's just me who is.

Michaela whispers something into Anders's ear, and I see him nod and smile. I assume they're saying their good-byes, but no — Anders takes Michaela's hand and together they stroll around The Monstrosity, disappearing behind it. Are they heading to our garden?

There's only one way to find out.

It's for Michaela's own good, I tell myself as I duck out of my room. I have to see if this Anders person can be trusted.

And, okay, maybe I want to see what happens when a guy and girl are alone together.

Treading softly in my socks, I hurry down the hall into Michaela's dark bedroom, creep over to my sister's window, and peer outside. Michaela and Anders are sitting on a blanket of leaves, in the very spot she and I used to sit in every night. They're cuddled together, with Anders's arm wrapped around Michaela's shoulder, and their breath trailing up into the air like smoke. The nearly full moon hangs over them, beaming down is approval, as they tilt their faces skyward.

They're stargazing.

Our Fir Lake tradition. The one Michaela said it was too cold for.

I can't watch, but at the same time I can't stop watching. Anders points up to the sky and says something to Michaela, who listens raptly. Is he showing her the Big Dipper? Orion? I bet he knows every single constellation. I bet he can find the North Star. I bet he can teach Michaela all sorts of things.

Frustration and envy bubble up in me, a potent brew. Why does Michaela always have to be the one to learn everything first, to move ahead while I remain stuck? Why couldn't *she* be the Wilder sister trapped behind a window, watching as I kissed a boy beneath the stars?

Then I remind myself that I wouldn't ever shut Michaela out of my life the way she's shut me out of hers.

I back away from the window and break into a run. Safe in my room, I flip on the light and study myself in the mirror — my flattened curls, my thick eyebrows, my crooked nose. No guy will ever want to cuddle with me. I'll be stargazing by myself for the rest of my days.

I turn off the light and crawl into bed, but my Ethan Stiefel poster seems to mock me so I pull the covers over my head. I lie still until I hear a car door slam outside, and Anders's engine start up. Our front door opens, followed by Michaela's gentle footfall on the stairs, and her light humming. I stiffen when I hear her come to a stop in front of my door and slowly turn my knob.

"Katie?" Michaela whispers, and the light from the hallway pierces through the blanket. "You're awake, right?"

"Mmm," I mumble against the material, terrified she's going to yell at me for spying.

"It's okay, don't get up. But guess what? Anders just asked me to Homecoming!" Happiness oozes through her words like honey.

"That's great," I manage to grunt. I roll over onto my stomach and press my face into the pillow. I know Michaela is expecting me to leap up and down and celebrate with her, but I can't. Not after what I've seen.

Finally, Michaela whispers good night and retreats. And somehow I drift off, dreaming uneasily about constellations and kisses.

"Is this a bad time?" I ask Emmaline on Sunday morning.

Emmaline peeks out her door, her hair a riot of curls. She's holding one of her light blue mugs, and wearing a silk kimono decorated with pink and black flowers. "Not at all, Katie," she says after a minute, opening the door all the way. "Shall I put on some more tea?"

"No, thanks." I glance at her painted glass table and see that she was in the middle of break-fast — a bowl of pears sits beside an open *Fir Lake Gazette*. I feel a surge of guilt. "Listen, I can come back if —"

"Don't be silly." Emmaline ushers me inside. "You know, I was hoping you'd come by. I'm just surprised to see you *now*, is all. Aren't Sundays for sleeping in until noon?"

"I'm not a big sleeper," I reply. Understatement of the century.

Her bell sleeves fluttering, Emmaline leads me into her living room. The burbling sound of the rock fountain is soothing, and Buddha smiles serenely. The drapes that half cover the windows make it seem as if we're in a dim tent, as if secrets will be safe here.

"Neither am I," Emmaline says, sitting down at her glass table and gesturing for me to take the chair across from her. "I keep strange hours. Don't tell anyone, but . . ."

She leans across the table toward me. I lean toward her, my breath catching.

"I think those of us who can't sleep dream better than anyone else," Emmaline whispers with a smile. "After all, we get to own the night."

A shiver tiptoes down my spine. "Owning the night" sounds even more magical than sharing a blanket of leaves with some boy. Or at least it does when Emmaline says it. I knew coming here this morning was a good idea.

"Sometimes I see your bedroom light on," I dare to admit, my cheeks flushing.

"Oh, no — *I'm* not keeping you awake, am I?" Emmaline asks. She pushes the bowl of pears toward me, along with a fork.

Only because I'm curious about you, I think, but I shake my head no. I spear a pear slice and pop into it my mouth. The pear melts, butter-like, on my tongue, and tastes of fresh fall mornings. "It's my thoughts that keep me up," I say truthfully. "They're always spinning." I laugh at how foolish this sounds.

"I'm the same way," Emmaline says immediately, setting down her teacup. "So, tell me. What are some things you think about when you can't sleep?" Then she puts a hand to her lips, and her eyes go wide. "I apologize, Katie," she adds. "I'm prying, right? A lot of people in this town have no boundaries, and I'm afraid it's rubbing off on me."

I think about boundaries, about Michaela closing her bedroom door in my face, and Autumn opening up to me in her bedroom. I think about the way Michaela leaned into Anders's kiss and the way I ran from Sullivan. Everything, in some ways, is about boundaries — who you let in and what you leave out.

I decide to let Emmaline in a little.

"All kinds of stuff," I begin, reaching for another pear slice. "Dance and Fir Lake and my friends back home and how I wish my boobs were smaller. . . ." I blush at this but Emmaline is listening seriously, so I go on. "And my sister and school and then last night . . . um, boys."

My embarrassing monologue complete, I look down at my hands and wonder if I should have kept my mouth shut.

Emmaline is silent for a moment, and then she lets out an understanding laugh. "Ah, boys," she says knowingly. "Always the culprits."

I glance up at her, glad that she's latched on to that topic. "They make everything so complicated," I sigh. I can't believe how much my simpler life was before Anders swaggered into it with his broad shoulders, and Sullivan dropped by with his sleepy brown eyes.

"You're telling me," Emmaline says, propping her chin up in her hands. That sadness I've seen in her expression before appears again, but then flits away, like a pigeon. I open my mouth to ask her if something is wrong — at last, a piece of the Emmaline mystery revealed! — but then she asks, "What's your issue with these bizarre creatures we call 'boys'?"

I lift my shoulders, overwhelmed. "Where do I start?"

Emmaline tilts her head to one side. "Well, I always tell my yoga students to take things one pose at a time. So . . ."

I smile, realizing that Emmaline must be a good teacher. Probably far better than Mabel Thorpe. And definitely more encouraging than Claude Durand.

"Well, Michaela has a boyfriend," I begin haltingly, my skin flushing again. "*Kind* of a boyfriend. In any case, there's a boy she kisses who asked her to the Homecoming dance. But I don't know if he's to be trusted."

Emmaline nods, sipping her tea. "That might be something Michaela needs to find out for herself. Now, do *you* have a boyfriend?"

I burst out laughing. "Me?"

Emmaline starts to laugh, too. "It's not *such* a crazy notion, you know. You're quite beautiful, Katie. Trust me on this."

No one's ever called me beautiful before — with the exception of Michaela, but she has to, she's my sister — and it makes my heart kick. Still, it's not like I believe Emmaline. I reach up and pat my springy curls. "I don't have a boyfriend," I say, poking holes in a pear slice with my fork. The fruit seems to be working a strange magic, loosening my tongue. "And the thing is, I never gave much thought to boys before Fir Lake. Now, there's this guy in my grade, and my friend is convinced he likes me, but how can I know for sure? It's all such a jumble. . . ."

"Can I let you in on a secret?" Emmaline says. "As confusing as we think boys are, they find *us* a hundred times more baffling."

"No way." How could someone find me baffling? I'm like the opposite of mysterious.

Emmaline gives me a just-you-wait-and-learn look. "I know they don't *seem* insecure, Katie, but guys — especially guys your age — often are. A guy friend of mine once told me that he used to *pray* that girls would ask him out, because he was too scared to make the first move!"

"Really?" I'm stunned.

"Really." Emmaline sips her tea. "So, as a girl, it pays to be brave sometimes."

It pays to be brave. Suddenly, I feel myself filling with resolve. Last night, seeing Anders and Michaela together made me want to hide under my covers and disappear. But on this wiser morning, sitting across from Emmaline, the thought of my sister and her boyfriend lights a fire under me. Maybe I don't want to be the girl who watches life go by outside her window.

Maybe I don't have to be. If Michaela is blazing her own path here in Fir Lake, I don't see why I can't as well.

As long as the path is paved and not covered in mud and grass.

"I know what I need to do tomorrow," I murmur, more to myself than to Emmaline, but she smiles at me across the table and says, "That's good."

"It's all you, Emmaline!" I exclaim, sitting up straighter. "You . . . inspired me." I gaze at my neighbor in awe while she chuckles modestly. "How do you know so much?" I add.

"Oh, experience is a harsh teacher," Emmaline says vaguely, tracing a circle along the rim of her teacup. "But, Katie, you might not want to take love advice from me."

"Why not?" I ask, my interest newly piqued. I remember how Emmaline cried on her porch.

"Well, I suppose because I'm just a girl eating alone in her kitchen every night, " Emmaline replies, her eyes distant.

I'm not sure how to respond to this, Emmaline's sudden opening up to me. I want to know her secrets, and yet I don't. I shift in my seat, and am about to ask Emmaline if she lost her truest love in the war (it doesn't matter which war — I've just always wanted to use that expression) when Emmaline clears her throat. "Blah blah blah," she says with a wry smile. "That's more than enough about me."

No it isn't! I want to cry, but Emmaline is already rising to her feet, the silk of her kimono shimmering in the weak sunlight. I don't want to leave yet — Emmaline has such a light, easy presence that it's difficult not to feel better around her.

"Emmaline?" I blurt as I stand up. "Would it be okay if . . . I mean, would you mind . . . if I came to one of your yoga classes someday?" There's something scary in asking this — in choosing to try something new, something that in no way involves Michaela.

Emmaline's grin lights up her face. "I'd love that, Katie. Anytime. Here, let me run upstairs and get you a flyer with the schedule on it."

I watch as Emmaline ascends the staircase. The living room is quiet and I glance over at Buddha, who watches me knowingly.

Once more can't hurt.

I stride across the rug, look Buddha in the eye, and rub his belly. If I'm going to ask Sullivan Turner to Homecoming tomorrow, I'll need all the luck I can get.

14

Monday morning. 7:15. Prey not yet in sight.

I am lurking in the shadow of my high school, wearing my cream-colored peacoat and matching hat, clutching a hot latte, and stomping my feet to keep them warm. Thanks to some research I did on my school's Web site yesterday — it seems I, too, can be a Googlemaster — I learned that boys' tennis practice lets out at 7:20 sharp on Mondays, since the girls' team uses the courts in the afternoon.

Getting up before daybreak was dreadful, but hopefully worth it. Because there is no way I'm sort-of-maybe-kind-of asking out Sullivan in front of Heidi Rebecca and Mr. Rhodes.

Yesterday, I'd considered telling Michaela about my Sullivan plan, but whenever I looked for her, she was either (for once) stretching on the barre, or (stunner!) on the phone with her door closed. Then I realized that if I really wanted to be brave, I'd have to tackle this task on my own. So when Michaela came to my door at night, looking sheepish and asking me if I wanted to stargaze, it was I who faked a yawn and told her that I was beat. I knew that if the two of us sat on a blanket and looked at the sky, I'd burst into tears and confess that I'd seen her and Anders.

No. It'll be much simpler to just never stargaze with my sister again.

I squint out toward the tennis courts, where I can make out a gaggle of boys trouping toward the school, swinging their rackets. The rest of the sports fields are empty, a vivid green-brown color beneath the sun.

It's funny how I'm already used to seeing rolling fields and open space everywhere. A few weeks ago, I was still on the lookout for errant skyscrapers. Now, if I saw a building that was taller than four stories, I'd probably faint from the shock.

As the pack of boys gets nearer, I pick out faces: short, well-built Elvin Harrington who sits at the head of the Freshman Popular Table at lunch; sandy-haired, serious Byron George III, who was just elected freshman class president, and . . . a pair of familiar brown eyes. Instantly, my stomach does a jeté that would make Michaela jealous.

I shut my eyes and try to remember what it was Emmaline told me about bravery and guys being insecure. When that doesn't work, I think of Michaela kissing Anders, and then sticking her face into my room to say she had a date to Homecoming.

There. That worked. Now I'm ready to take action. All I have to do is open my eyes and —

"Katie?"

My eyes fly open and Sullivan is standing before me, grinning. His cheeks are pink from his workout, and he looks like an advertisement for All American Cuteness. I lift my neck as tall as it will go — "like a duck," as Claude Durand would say. I hope my curls spilling out from under my hat look luscious and romantic, not wild and frizzy.

"I'll catch up with you guys later, 'kay?" Sullivan calls to his teammates, waving his racket as they pass by us. I can hear cars pulling up to the front of school and the laughter of kids as they congregate on the front lawn before the bell.

"What are you doing out here?" Sullivan asks me, shielding his eyes from the sun's glare.

I freeze. I didn't count on him asking me that.

"Oh . . . I . . . I was thinking of joining the girls' tennis team," I lie like I've never lied before. "I thought I'd watch the guys practice to get a feel for the sport."

"From over *here*?" Sullivan asks dubiously, glancing from where I stand at the backdoors of the school to the far-off tennis courts.

"I have really good eyesight." I gulp down the rest of my latte, burning my tongue. "And speaking of which . . ." I ransack my brain for a segue.

Here it comes: disaster. It's barreling toward me like a subway train.

"Yeah?" Sullivan raises one eyebrow.

"I'm really *looking* forward to Homecoming," I spit out, my heart thumping. "Get it?"

Oh, my God. I did not just say that. What's *wrong* with me?

To his credit, Sullivan does not double over and howl. In fact, his grin widens. "Man, so am *I*," he enthuses. "It's going to be ah-mazing — the parade, the pep rally, the game, the dance."

The *wha*? I didn't know Homecoming involved so many activities. I keep a smile glued to my face, though. Each time I start to second-guess what I'm about to do, I remember Michaela and am newly resolved.

Sullivan is still talking, and I hear him finish with, "I've been waiting for Homecoming since I was, like, five years old!"

I'm not sure that's something to be proud of, but I don't say so. I have to keep my focus. So I take a step closer to Sullivan — that's what Michaela did with Anders on Saturday night — and lower my lashes in what I hope is an alluring way. What I also hope is that Sullivan won't notice I have no idea what I'm doing.

"You're going to the dance then?" I purr — or at least, I think I purr. Sullivan nods and I add, "See, I'm not too familiar with Fir Lake customs," which is one of the few non-lies I've uttered this morning.

"Yeah?" Sullivan seems fond of that word.

"Well . . . I'm wondering if . . ." I dig my fingers into the sides of the environment-friendly Friendly Bean cup. "If people have to show up with, like, dates."

I want to throw up. I can't believe I, Katie Wilder, am asking out a boy. "Are you wild, Katie Wilder?" Darryl Williams, who sat next to me in my junior high math class, used to ask me with a sneer. The joke being that I was anything but wild. Michaela told me that the kids in her high school made the same cracks about her. Our parents should have changed their last name to Safe. Or Well-Behaved. Anything but Wilder.

I meet Sullivan's gaze as he smiles at me and slowly nods his head. "Dates are pretty important, yeah."

I swallow hard, waiting for him to tell me that he's psyched to be going with Rebecca and that they'll see me there. Instead Sullivan adds, "So maybe, you know, you and I could . . ." He points to himself, and then to me, and he shrugs.

I breathe slowly and steadily, the way I imagine one might breathe in a yoga class.

"Sure." I shrug back.

"All right," Sullivan says with a grin, and then lopes off toward the building.

And that is how I, a suddenly wilder Katie Wilder, wind up with a date to Homecoming.

In homeroom, I feel like a new woman. I lean back in my seat, beaming, with my legs crossed and my pen tapping the desk. Rebecca, as if sensing the reason behind my burst of confidence, scowls at me and tugs on the end of one of her braids. I wish Autumn would get here already. Sullivan has not arrived yet, but even the sight of his desk makes my skin tingle with satisfaction.

I have a date!

I can't believe how easy it all was. Aside from my stomach acrobatics, crushed coffee cup, and mind-blowing anxiety.

I'm not even bothered by what I saw a few minutes ago, as I was walking to the school's front lawn: Anders's blue car pulling into the parking lot, and Michaela stepping out of it. She closed the passenger side door as if she'd been getting into and out of cars all her seventeen years, as if she'd never heard of a subway. When Anders got out, he gave Michaela a long hug, and then the two of them touched lips ever so softly. Everyone hovering around the front entrance gawked at them, but I looked away. Earlier that morning, I'd felt bad leaving the house before my sister. But apparently, Michaela no longer needs a walk-to-school companion.

Thankfully, in homeroom I'm far removed from

Michaela and her transformation into Miss Fir Lake. Nothing can bring me down. When Autumn enters the classroom, I wave to her excitedly, and my new friend mouths, "What?"

"You were right," I mouth back. I'll fill her in on the walk to first period.

Mr. Rhodes is about to call roll when Sullivan himself bursts into the classroom, out of breath and racketless. As Mr. Rhodes scolds him for his tardiness, Sullivan heads over to his desk and shoots me a fast wink. Rebecca gapes at us and I grin.

When Mr. Rhodes is through with attendance, he picks up an orange flyer from his desk and says, "I will now announce the candidates for this year's Homecoming Queen. I'm sure most of you know how this important tradition works, but for those of you who live with your heads in the sand: The student body elects a queen, who chooses her king the night of the dance. And as those amoral people in Hollywood say, the nominees are: Lucy Benedict . . ."

Sullivan's elbow is only a few inches from mine. What would happen if I touched it? Am I *supposed* to touch it? My thoughts are racing.

"Heather Jennings . . ."

I have to tell Trini; she'll be shocked that I'm dating a non-dancer. Or dating at all. I have to tell *Michaela*, although I'm still miffed at her.

But I can feel my anger toward my sister waning. We'll have so much more in common now that I have a guy in my life, too. Maybe we can even go on double dates to Pammy's Pizzeria. It's as if, for the first time ever, my sister and I are on an even playing field.

"Michaela Wilder," Mr. Rhodes calls.

I snap to attention and look around, half expecting to see my sister in the room. Then I wonder if Mr. Rhodes mistakenly meant *me*, the way my teachers in junior high would sometimes flub and call me "Mi — Katie."

But it's when Mr. Rhodes sets his orange flyer back on his desk that hits me.

Hard.

He said Michaela's name because she is one of the chosen, one of the candidates. How can it be? Do people even *know* her? How did she catapult to these heights? I turn in my seat and see Autumn watching me sympathetically. At least *someone* understands.

"Whoa, that's your sister, right?" Sullivan asks, and I can tell by the sparkle in his eyes that he's now especially pleased I'll be his homecoming date. After all, I have good pedigree. Kind of like a purebred dog.

"I guess so," I reply because the thing is, I'm not even sure anymore.

At lunchtime, the Senior Popular Table is so swarmed by drooling fans that I have trouble spotting Michaela. But I know she's sitting there today — she sent me a text telling me so during second period. I texted her back, *Congratulations, Homecoming Princess,* and she responded, *Oh, it's a crazy fluke! Don't tell Mom, OK?*

I'm not sure why Michaela would avoid a golden opportunity for Mom to worship her even more, but I text back a simple *OK*.

Now I can see my sister's light-brown head, close to Anders's flaxen one, and — are they *sharing* a lunch tray? Oh, gag. I watch as Heather, sitting on Michaela's other side, playfully slaps my sister's arm, and the whole table bursts into laughter.

Autumn, who is seated across from me, confirms that every girl sitting at that table has been nominated for Homecoming Queen. I wonder out loud when the backbiting and competitive bitchery will begin.

"My guess is right about now," Jasper says, sitting on the edge of our table and scaring both of us to death. "I'm with you, Katya," he adds, half smiling at me. "Those girls are vicious."

"Katie," I tell him, rolling my eyes.

"Ew, Jasper — go away!" Autumn groans, trying to push him off the table. "Remember the rule? We're supposed to pretend not to know each other at school."

I imagine inventing this rule with Michaela and am not sure if I should giggle or bawl.

"I can't tear myself away," Jasper says, batting his lashes at us. They're dark and long — wasted on a boy. "Your conversation is too, too fascinating."

"Are your friends discussing something more important?" I ask, wracking my brain for what the boys in my junior high used to talk about when I eavesdropped on them during lunch. "Like . . . the latest technological upgrades to the original *Star Wars* trilogy?" I wish I could be this articulate around Sullivan.

"Katie, have I told you lately that I love you?" Autumn asks, and even though I know she's being silly, it's nice to hear someone speak those words.

"You wound me, Katya," Jasper says, clutching the front of his shirt. Then he adds, "Actually, that's not a bad idea. How about a *Star Wars* marathon at Casa Hawthorne on the night of Homecoming? I'll supply the popcorn."

For a split second, I think Jasper's suggestion sounds worlds better than a high school dance. Then I remember Sullivan.

"Katie has a *date*!" Autumn crows, grinning at me. "A good one, I might add."

"Which means you *have* to come, too," I tell Autumn, giving her a meaningful look. The idea of being alone with Sullivan all night while Michaela slow-dances with Anders across the gym is freaky. I'll need someone to escape to the snack table with, someone who'll laugh when I impersonate Heather accepting her tiara.

"Maybe I'll go after all," Autumn replies with a shrug. "What do you say, J?"

"I'm too horrified to even dignify that with a response," Jasper answers coolly, then hops off our table and ambles over to where his friends are sitting.

"He's right," Autumn says, picking up my Pom bottle and sneaking a sip. "Homecoming's so not my thing. You've brainwashed me, Katie."

"Please don't let Jasper sway you," I beg Autumn. "Maybe you can still find a date." It's weird that *I'm* the one now dispensing boy advice.

I continue to plead with Autumn during that evening's dance class. In between the leg swings and Mabel Thorpe urging us to "blossom, lovelies, blossom!" I whisper things like, "We can go dress shopping together!" and "You know you want to!" Autumn shakes her head and fights back a laugh. Mabel doesn't appear to notice our chatting; it could be that her mascara is so weighing down her lashes that she can't even see us.

As Clay Aiken warbles his final note and Mabel announces that she'll see us next week, I put my hand to my forehead and realize I'm not sweaty at all. At the end of a Claude Durand class, I'd feel like I'd just emerged from a sauna. But I'm not getting much of a workout from Mabel and her touchy-feely "movements." However, the other students — even Autumn — are staggering to the water fountain outside the studio, and Dee cries, "You kicked our behinds today, Mabel!" It's one of those moments when I wish for Michaela's presence, just so I could roll my eyes at my sister, and she'd roll hers back.

"Would you ever take a yoga class?" I ask Autumn

as we wave good-bye to our ragtag bunch of classmates and start downstairs.

"You mean with Emmaline Miller in the library?" Autumn asks, buttoning up her quilted knee-length jacket. It shouldn't surprise me that Autumn knows who Emmaline is, but I'm still not used to the web of small-town connections. "I heard she's weird," Autumn adds.

"She lost her boyfriend in the war," I inform my friend dramatically as we exit the lobby. Mr. Hawthorne's car is idling outside; he's going to give me a lift home, which is a relief to my mom, who still isn't wild about driving down country roads after dark.

"Wow," Autumn replies, but she looks dubious. "Well . . ." she adds, her breath coming out in cotton-puff clouds. "I guess I'd rather brave a yoga class than go to Homecoming, if I had to choose between the two."

It's not what I want to hear, but it's probably the best I can get.

That night, over dinner, I consider floating the yoga option by Michaela as well. But as soon as I broach the topic — "What are you doing after school this Thursday?" — my sister tosses her hair over one shoulder and exclaims how *busy* she is this whole week. Of course, Michaela doesn't specify what — and who — she's so busy with. Mom and Dad probably assume it's schoolwork, which Michaela has still been acing. I'm not sure who she's trying to impress with her good grades, since her acceptance to Juilliard hinges on a ballet audition.

As soon as Michaela's plate is clear, she's up out of her seat, pulling on her red windbreaker, and telling us that Heather's driving her to the docks with the other girls to see if the lake has frozen over yet. I frown at Michaela. If she's lying, that's an excuse that would set off *my* parental alarm, and I'm not even a parent. If she's telling the truth, that sounds like a horrific way to spend a Monday night — a second runner-up to cow-tipping. But Mom just tells Michaela to be home by midnight.

Naturally, I'm still awake when I hear the familiar engine outside The Monstrosity at five to the witching hour. Again, I watch from my window as Michaela and Anders get out of the car and kiss deeply. I wonder if Sullivan expects *us* to kiss at Homecoming.

I'll cross that narrow, rickety bridge when I come to it.

Michaela and Anders don't stargaze, but Michaela is obviously starry-eyed from her date; in the morning, I find her windbreaker thrown haphazardly across the living room sofa. When I pick it up, I smell the distinctive reek of cigarette smoke. The same scent lingered in Svetlana's office and in the bathrooms of my junior high school. So Michaela really did meet up with the girls, then; I have an image of all the seniors chilling on the docks at night, wearing their hats and scarves. Maybe somebody started a small campfire while Heather chain-smoked and Faith tapped ash into the lake. Maybe Michaela took a couple drags off the cigarette, too.

I guess my sister *is* busy. Having fun.

I get busy in my own way. After homeroom that day, gathering every shred of courage, I give my cell phone number to Sullivan, and he gives me his. That evening, when my cell vibrates and Sullivan's name appears on the caller ID, I drop the phone as if I've seen a bug on the screen. I almost want to run to Michaela's room and ask my sister for guidance. But the conversation lasts exactly five minutes and four seconds; Sullivan and I quickly run out of things to say once we establish that I don't know how to swim or play tennis, and that he's never heard of Lincoln Center.

I also throw myself into homework, which is more pleasant than it sounds because Autumn makes for a great study partner. One Wednesday evening in my bedroom, Autumn and I read the cheesiest lines from *Romeo and Juliet* out loud, cracking each other up. I know Michaela, who is down the hall doing her own homework, can't hear us, but I wish she could.

When we vote for Homecoming Queen in home-room, circling our choices on anonymous ballots, I spend forever hovering over the form. I stare at my sister's name and chew a hole in my pencil, and before Mr. Rhodes can tear the ballot from my hands, I circle

Heather's name, and feel like a monster. I don't tell Autumn who I voted for, and she doesn't ask.

Thursday, after school, Autumn accompanies me to the town library for Emmaline's yoga class. That morning, I told my mom I'd be trying yoga, and she looked up from her copy of *The Idiot* and said, "Well, that should be interesting." It's obvious she doesn't like the idea, but as long as I keep up my dance classes, I know Mom won't protest.

"It's got to be better than Mabel Thorpe," I murmur to Autumn now as we walk past the circulation desk. I'm not sure what one wears to a yoga class, so I'm in my black leotard and loose cotton pants from American Apparel, and I've left my hair down. Autumn is wearing a T-shirt and leggings. It's surprisingly comfortable to not be in the full ballet getup.

In the upstairs studio, the lights are dim, the walls are brick, and mellow music made up of lutes and harps flows softly from an iPod hooked up to speakers. There is no mirror and no barre, and everyone is barefoot. Emmaline, her fairy tale hair tumbling down her back, is unrolling a green mat onto the floor. Before her, students of all ages sit cross-legged, each on their own individual mat: two sophomore girls I recognize from school, three middle-aged women who look as if they might belong to Pearl's knitting circle, the young mom I saw shopping that first day in Hemming's Goods, and . . .

I hear myself gasp.

Coach *Shreve?*

I do a double, then a triple take, but yes, it's really him. The same dark-eyed, strong-jawed Coach Shreve who, that very morning in gym class, told me I needed to "be more aggressive" when playing basketball.

Right now, he's not looking too aggressive as he sits on a navy blue mat in a T-shirt and sweatpants, his expression serious. He's the only guy in the room.

Autumn and I turn toward each other, scandalized. "Why is he here?" Autumn whispers.

"Following us?" I whisper back as Emmaline appears at my side. She gives me a kiss on the cheek, which makes me feel special in front of all the other students, then hands bright blue yoga mats to me and Autumn, and points us to the two remaining empty spots on the floor, which are, mercifully, far away from Coach Shreve. As Autumn and I are spreading out our mats, however, I see the coach glance our way. Eek.

It could be worse. Sullivan could be here.

Emmaline sits cross-legged on her mat, resting her palms against her knees. Everyone follows her lead, including Autumn and Coach Shreve, so I scramble to do the same. Emmaline flashes me a small smile, then faces the class. I'm a little nervous, wondering if I'll be able to grasp yoga at all.

"Let's sit still and close our eyes," Emmaline instructs. "Draw your back up as straight as possible, as if your head is a balloon drifting toward the ceiling."

Okay. Doable. I almost feel as if I'm in Anna Pavlova, trying my best not to be called a hunchback. I open one eye, ready to check myself out in the mirror, when I remember that there is no mirror. Which is pretty cool, if unfamiliar.

"Now breathe in, and think about your day, the different things you went through." Emmaline pauses, and adds, "Then when you exhale, let go of it all."

I take a breath and find myself thinking about how my windowpane was coated in a layer of frost this morning, and how I smelled snow when I leaned outside. I think about how Michaela offered me a ride to school in Anders's car, and how I icily declined. I think about how Sullivan winked at me in homeroom and how my stomach somersaulted.

There's something kind of great about being in a studio and following instructions, yet still being allowed — no, asked — to daydream. And when I push the breath out, letting it whoosh from my lungs, I *do* feel myself relax. For the first time in a long time, my thoughts are at rest.

Emmaline's slow, steady voice guides us as we get to our feet and lift our arms, and as we bend forward until our hands touch the floor. Everything we do seems to flow together in a dance and, at the same time, this is nothing like the dance I've always known. "We call this pose Downward-facing Dog," Emmaline explains, and normally that phrase would make me want to giggle, but somehow I'm taking things seriously. Emmaline asks us to flatten our backs and hang our heads down. All the blood rushes to my face, but I press my palms into the floor and rise up on my toes. My body surprisingly obeys.

Emmaline starts moving between the rows of students, throwing out a critique or praise here and there. "You must be new. I didn't get your name," I hear her say to someone.

There's a brief pause, a deep voice replies, "Timothy. Tim."

I know that voice. It's Coach Shreve.

"Tim, if you could try raising your backside a little more," Emmaline says sweetly.

Still hanging upside down, I smile at the idea of someone else telling Coach Shreve what to do. And I feel even more empowered a few seconds later when Emmaline stops in front of me and exclaims, "Excellent, Katie! Really excellent for a first-timer. Everyone, watch how Katie holds this pose."

In all my years as a ballet student, no one has ever asked me to demonstrate. True, Emmaline could just be favoring me because we've bonded over pears and tea. But my legs feel strong and the position of my body feels natural. As Emmaline leads us through different poses with intriguing names like "The Warrior" (lunging forward with your arms up) and "Happy Baby" (lying on your back, bending your knees and holding your feet), the sweat of hard work trickles down my neck. Each movement is a challenge, so that when I get something right, I glow. And here, it doesn't matter how sharply you can point your toes. There are steps to follow, but there's also room to invent.

At the end of class, Emmaline has us bow to each other, which feels much more fair than humble curtsying and applauding. I feel achy but also refreshed as I roll up my mat.

"That was *hard*," Autumn tells me, wiping sweat off her brow. "Mabel's class is a breeze compared to this." The two of us are padding over to Emmaline to return our mats when a male voice behind us speaks our names. We both turn.

"Coach Shreve!" I exclaim, feigning shock. "We didn't see you!"

"We didn't know you took yoga," Autumn adds, not even bothering to hide her curiosity.

Coach Shreve shrugs, looking a little embarrassed. "I don't," he says, awkwardly holding his rolled-up mat under one arm. "An old football injury of mine was acting up, so my chiropractor recommended I try it."

I hope Anders won't show up at yoga class with his own football injury. This town is *way* too small.

"So all my newbies know each other?" Emmaline laughs, coming up beside me. "Welcome, you guys. You all did great today."

Coach Shreve's eyes bug out of his head. "Katie, this was your first ever yoga class?"

"She's something else, isn't she?" Emmaline says while I blush and Autumn grins at me. My heart soars at Emmaline's compliment. For the first time, well, ever, I think I know what it feels like to be talented. At four years old, Michaela planted her feet just so in her first pair of ballet slippers. It's taken me countless hours of practice and training to get good at ballet. But it's taken me one breath to feel comfortable in my skin doing yoga. Maybe yoga is what I should have been doing all along.

I'm afraid Coach Shreve is going to reveal that Emmaline that I can't perform a push-up to save my life, but instead he smiles at her and says, "Well, she has a good teacher."

Hold up. Is Coach Shreve *flirting* with Emmaline?

Emmaline ducks her head, her face rosier than usual, and mutters a quick "thanks." She doesn't seem particularly flirtatious in return.

Still, as I glance between my neighbor and my gym teacher, I feel a flash of inspiration. There's definitely *something* — a spark of possibility — there. I know Michaela would scoff that it's my overactive imagination at work. But my sister isn't here today. This studio is in no way marked by her presence. Besides, my idea isn't entirely crazy. Yes, Emmaline is delicate and thoughtful, and Coach Shreve seems boorish and rock-dense . . . but then again, here he is, in her yoga class. They're around the same age (I guess — I've never been very good at figuring out how old people are when they're not teenagers). They're both single. . . .

As Coach Shreve leaves the studio, I remember what he said that traumatizing time in gym class, something about "eating alone in a kitchen for the rest of your life." And what was it Emmaline said to me the day before I asked out Sullivan? *I'm just a girl eating alone in her kitchen.*

Could it be any more obvious that the two of them are soul mates?

I'm itching to tell Emmaline that I can try to get Coach Shreve's number for her, but my neighbor/teacher has already been swallowed up by her other adoring students. So as Autumn and I slip out of the studio, I tell my friend about my matchmaking plan.

"I'd wait and see," Autumn recommends. "You don't exactly know each of their stories."

Autumn has a point. There's no need to rush. And with Homecoming a heartbeat away, I have my own romantic fate to worry about.

15

The sixteenth of October, a brisk and drizzly Friday that we get off from school, finds me squished between Sullivan and Meadow on bleachers full of screaming kids. I'm wearing my coat, hat, and scarf, balancing a Super Big Gulp Vanilla Coke — someone at the concession stand stuck a Go Tigers! sticker on it — between my denim-clad knees and, against all odds, watching a football game.

"Watching" is probably a loose term for it. The shining white numbers on the scoreboard mean zilch to me, but judging by the shrieks of my classmates, I guess the Fir Lake Tigers are doing well. So well, in fact, that the cheerleaders — Lucy and Faith among them — are spontaneously leaping into the air, their microscopic orange skirts flaring. They are shaking their pom-poms and singing a song that has weaseled its way into my brain:

Go Tigers, show your spirit!
Growl and roar and go-go get it!
Go-o-o Tigers!

I don't even know who our team is playing against, which would probably be sacrilege to admit.

"Look at Anders Swensen!" Sullivan shouts as he points to the small helmeted figures sprinting across the field in their funny tight pants. "Man that guy is on *fire*." Sullivan cups his hands around his mouth and bellows, "Kick their butts, Tigers!"

"Anders is the best!" Rebecca, who is seated on Sullivan's other side, chimes in. "Katie, your sister is so-o lucky!"

By now, everyone knows that Michaela Wilder is the girl Anders Swensen has chosen to kiss . . . for this month, at least. Since Michaela and I hardly have alone time anymore — she rides to school with Anders every morning, sits at the Popular Table at lunch, and stays after school for yearbook every afternoon — I get the scoop on her and Anders the same way everyone else does. I see them in the hallways, tucked into each other — Michaela's hand inside Anders's back pocket, Anders's arm across Michaela's shoulder. I see her sitting on his lap at lunch, and I see her peck him on the lips after they get out of his car each morning. When we're at home, though, Anders is not up for discussion. Mom and Dad still know nothing about Michaela's other life.

"Lucky," I echo, forcing a smile at Rebecca. She is holding mittened hands with Byron George III, and they're passing a thermos full of hot cocoa back and forth. On my left side, Meadow and Elvin Harrington are making out, oblivious to the game. Sullivan's knee is resting ever so slightly against mine, which is making my stomach twist into complicated yoga poses.

I know *I* should be feeling lucky, suddenly sitting in the company of the Popular Freshmen. It does seem as if a warm spotlight is focused on me, as if the arms of acceptance have tightened around my waist. It's all thanks to Sullivan, who called me last night to suggest we attend every Homecoming activity together. After we got off the phone, I raced to Michaela's room and began to hyperventilate. "Would you *chill*?" Michaela said, rolling her eyes. "So you'll spend the day together. Big deal. You were going to the dance with him anyway." In front of the old Michaela, I would have given in to my meltdown, but for this new sister, I faked nonchalance. "You're right," I said. "Whatever."

But today I'm full of nervousness as I sip my too-sweet Coke and try not to move my knee any closer to Sullivan's. To add to the pressure of the moment, it's not just the Popular Freshmen who surround us; we are ensconced in the center bleachers, with the Popular Sophomores behind us, the Popular Juniors in front of us, and in front of *them* — the Popular Seniors.

Michaela is there, of course, wearing a leather-sleeved, orange-and-blue football jacket with SWENSEN 3 emblazoned on the back, jeans, and her knee-high black boots. She, Heather, and the girls around them all have blue and orange stripes painted beneath their eyes, making them look like wild women. Michaela and Heather are linking arms and singing along with the cheerleaders, and there's a lit cigarette resting between Michaela's fingers. I've suspected that my sister started smoking, but it's startling to see her actually do it. I remember her walking out of Anna Pavlova, muttering, "I love Svetlana, but I can't believe she smokes. It's so unhealthy for a dancer." Now, I watch as my sister takes a long drag off her cigarette, exhales, and then purses her lips at Heather, who runs her wand of gloss over Michaela's mouth.

"Are you having a good time?"

Sullivan's voice pulls me back to myself, and I turn my head to see his brown eyes studying me through the drizzle. He's wearing a polo shirt and a denim jacket. I'm the only person in the vicinity who is wrapped up head to toe. Thank God I drew the line at bringing an umbrella.

"Sure," I tell him weakly. I'm exhausted. The morning kicked off with a parade along Main Street that swarmed with students, teachers, and parents (except for my own, of course — Mom was on campus and Dad was writing). All the shopkeepers came out of their stores, and I saw the Hemmings clapping for the furry-hatted Fir Lake marching band. Sullivan watched, openmouthed, as a huge flatbed float decorated with stuffed orange tigers, bearing the entire Fir Lake football team, slid by. Anders Swensen had orange confetti in his hair and was waving his arms in victory, even though the game hadn't been played yet. That float was followed by the one Michaela had mentioned to me — the convertible car holding the candidates for Homecoming Queen. The preening girls flung their hair and threw hard candies to the crowd.

I couldn't take my eyes off Michaela, who was perched beside Heather, doing a fake royal wave, her mouth open in a laugh. I saw my sister scan the crowd, and then she threw a small handful of candy in my direction. I suppose her gesture was sweet, but I ducked, and a Jolly Rancher smacked Sullivan right in the forehead.

Next, there was a pep rally in the high school auditorium, where the cheerleaders did flips and twirls, and the pep squad — a bunch of dorky sophomore guys in orange vests — stood on one another's shoulders. Autumn wasn't at the pep rally or the parade, and neither she nor Jasper came to the football game. Autumn had warned me that they'd be no-shows and would spend the day hiking on the paths around Mount Elephant. I'm not sure tramping over mud-damp ground and getting whacked in the face by bare branches would beat watching a football game, but at least I'd have Autumn for company.

Though being at Sullivan's side all day makes me feel adult and dizzy and excited, even if we haven't been talking very much.

"We won!" Sullivan shouts, grabbing my arm as he leaps to his feet. "Woot, Tigers!"

Everyone around me is waving pennants, hollering, and jumping up and down. I glance toward the front row bleachers and see Michaela blowing exaggerated kisses to Anders, who has been lifted onto his teammates' shoulders. As I stand up to join Sullivan, my Vanilla Coke slips from my hand and spills all over my pink Ugg boots. Sullivan doesn't notice, and just keeps cheering.

Am I really here? The Katie of a few months ago, City Katie, would never deign to attend a football game. That girl, Katie of the subway, Katie of wedge heels and black clothes in the summer, would mock the girl I am at this moment. "Vict-or-y! Victor-y!" the cheerleaders chant, but I feel like a loser.

"Man, tonight's going to *rage*," Sullivan says and, without warning, leans over and kisses me on the cheek.

My pulse spikes. No boy has ever done that to me before. City Katie wouldn't be caught dead at a football game, but she probably wouldn't have gotten her first kind-of-kiss, either. Maybe I need to be more open-minded about this Homecoming business. That attitude has done wonders for Michaela. Why not me?

So I flash a smile at Sullivan and, startling myself, clap my hands and shout, "Go Tigers!" as loud as I can.

I am Country Katie, hear me roar.

Back at The Monstrosity, I put on the black spaghetti-strap dress I got over the summer at a SoHo boutique. I'd forgotten how deep the V-neck is; if I lean forward, you can see my cleavage. But I have to admit the dress looks kind of . . . nice. For once, I'm not minding my boobs. I do a pirouette in front of the mirror, smiling. Sometimes, curves can be a good thing.

I pull my hair into a ballerina bun, checking to make sure my lip gloss is on okay. It feels strange to be getting ready in an empty room, with no Michaela down the hall to offer me fashion advice or paint my nails. After the Tigers game, Michaela went straight to Heather's house with the rest of the girls, where they're no doubt squealing over eyeliner colors and boys. I have no idea what Michaela is wearing to the dance because she and Heather went shopping in Montreal over the weekend, where — according to a rumor Autumn heard from a Camping Club friend — they also got fake IDs.

I wonder if Michaela is planning on using hers tonight.

I'm sliding my feet into my black pencil heels when Mom calls from downstairs that it's time to go. I wish I was old enough to have Sullivan pick me up. When I clatter downstairs with my coat, Mom is waiting by the door, talking to Dad, but when she sees me, her face softens. Dad takes off his glasses and squints.

"Stop it," I groan, putting on my coat. "Please don't do the whole our-baby-girl-is-growing-up shtick, okay?"

"But you look lovely, Katya!" Mom exclaims, and there's definitely surprise in her voice.

"Gulliver will be happy to see you," Dad says earnestly, patting my shoulder.

"Sullivan, Dad, " I correct automatically. I guess I should be relieved my dad manages to remember my and Michaela's names. His new book is almost finished, so he's been even more out of it than ever.

"Yes, Sullivan Turner," speaks up Mom, who I bet has Googled my date.

"You're crazy to tell them," Michaela declared after I revealed, over dinner last week, who I was going to the dance with. But I hate keeping things from my parents.

In the car ride to the high school, Mom lectures me on the importance of being "safe" and "keeping your wits about you." I want to tell her that I'm not the daughter to worry about — that Michaela is the one who's getting fake IDs in foreign countries and dabbling in various Parents' Worst Fears. Yet I feel loyal enough to my sister to keep her secrets safe. When Mom pulls up to the brightly lit school and makes some remark about "weird American traditions," I have to bite my lip to keep from saying that Michaela is a candidate for queen of this tradition.

I'm dropped off with the instruction to be waiting outside the school at eleven P.M. Then I join the legions of jabbering students crossing the front lawn. It's stopped raining and the night air is thin and cold. Mr. Rhodes and Coach Shreve, both in suits, are taking tickets at the entrance to the school. I'm wondering if I should ask Coach Shreve what he thinks of Emmaline — he wasn't at the second yoga class — when I feel one of my spiky heels sink into the mud.

I take another step forward, but all that accomplishes is getting my other heel stuck. I let out a faint cry of distress, but nobody pays attention as they hurry by. I flail out my arms to keep my balance, the opposite of graceful.

So far, Country Katie isn't doing too well.

"Katie, what are you doing?" Sullivan sweeps up beside me, his hair freshly gelled.

I'm too relieved to even be embarrassed. "Thanks," I say as Sullivan takes my hands and yanks me free of my muddy trap. My shoes are pretty much ruined — clumps of dirt and grass cling to the heels — but I'm not going to stress about that now. When Sullivan and I walk into the school, I see that other girls are taking off their muddy sneakers and putting on their dressy shoes inside. I shake my head. So simple, yet so brilliant.

"They don't have mud in the city?" Sullivan asks teasingly as we walk into the gym.

"In Central Park they do," I reply defensively, as if that helps my case at all.

"Oh," Sullivan says.

I hope our conversation picks up a little during the dance.

I'm surprised by how completely the gym has been transformed. Yes, there are the orange and blue streamers I had envisioned, but glittery drapes hide the basketball hoops, and long tables boast bowls of punch and platters of orange cupcakes. A platform is set up in front of the locker rooms, complete with microphone stands and a drum kit. The gym's usual scent of sweat and basketball rubber has been replaced by competing colognes and perfumes, and the floor is packed with guys in brown suits and girls in shimmery peach and green dresses. I'm the only person wearing black.

That is, until I spot a boy in a black button-down and black slacks standing across the gym, by one of the snack tables. Beside the boy is a girl with familiar, long auburn hair. I perk up immediately, and turn to Sullivan, all grins.

"Byron's over there with Rebecca," Sullivan is saying, pointing to a group of freshmen gathered near the stage. He reaches for my hand. "Come on."

"Uh, I have to find my sister. I'll meet you there in a minute," I fudge.

As I push through the colorful hordes, I do keep an eye out for Michaela, but I can't spot her or any of her cohorts. Apparently, they'll be arriving fashionably late.

"What happened to *Star Wars?*" I ask, popping up between Autumn and Jasper, who are bickering over a cupcake. The siblings give a start when they see me.

"We wanted to surprise you!" Autumn says, wrapping me in a hug. It's the first time I've seen her in a dress, and it's a ridiculous plaid number with puffed sleeves — so hideous it's almost cool. But I don't care what Autumn is wearing; I'm so glad to see *her*. "I couldn't stand the thought of *not* witnessing you dancing with Sullivan Turner," Autumn adds, dropping her voice.

"Autumn bribed me," Jasper says flatly, inspecting his cupcake. "Laundry for a week, or something. I can't turn down that kind of offer."

"Gee, that's flattering, Jasper," I laugh, rolling my eyes.

"It was *your* idea to come, liar," Autumn tells her brother, poking him in the chest.

Was it? I wonder why learning this makes my heart flutter the slightest bit.

"Check out the hard-core band," Jasper says, and I turn toward the stage.

The lead singer, a rail-thin man with a silver ponytail, is stepping up to the microphone. Behind him is the rest of the band — a collection of aging guys with beards, bellies, and thinning hair. My stomach drops in surprise when I see that the drummer is none other than Mr. Hemming and the saxophonist is the man who owns The Simple Scoop. At any minute I'm expecting Mabel Thorpe to sail out, shaking a tambourine.

"It's a fine evening to be playing for you, Fir Lake High," the lead singer says in a deep baritone. "Hearty kudos to the Tigers on whupping the Pine Crest Elephants!"

As everyone screams and stomps on the floor, I turn to Autumn and Jasper and ask, "Why are our teams named after animals that don't exist here?"

Jasper shoots back, "It's questions like those that keep me up at night."

The lead singer waits for the cheers to taper off, and adds, "We're The Fir Lake Geezers and we're honored to be playing for you. Now . . . get your groove on!"

"Oh, Lord, " Jasper mutters.

"I think they're sweet," I protest.

"Maybe you should ask Mr. Hemming to dance," Jasper offers, giving me a sly smile.

"She has someone to dance with," Autumn reminds her brother. "Wait," she adds, scanning the gym. "Where *is* Sullivan?"

Oh, yeah. Sullivan. I turn and begin searching the gym as well. People are crowding onto the dance floor;

the band has started playing an upbeat, catchy song that sounds old-timey and vaguely familiar.

"Give me land lots of land under starry skies above . . . don't fence me in."

I think of the slick hip-hop the DJ blasted at our junior high dance. My legs tingle at the thought of dancing — *really* dancing. Mabel Thorpe's class has only gotten more boring lately. I've never let loose on a dance floor, but, maybe tonight is the time to try. I sway my hips, and am about to tell Autumn and Jasper to follow my lead when Autumn takes my elbow.

"Hey, there's Michaela," she says. "Wow, she looks . . . wow."

My sister is drifting through the gym doors with her entourage of Heather, the twins, the girls' three handsome dates, and Anders. Michaela has clearly washed off her war-paint from the game. Her hair, newly highlighted (when did she do *that*?) frames her face in lush waves, and her pale blue satin sheath falls straight to the floor, hiding her famously long legs. Gold shoulder-dusters dangle from her ears and a white orchid corsage encircles her slim wrist. No wonder Autumn is at a loss for words.

Michaela finds me in the crowd as easily as she did at the parade this morning and gives me a quick smile. Before I can smile back, my sister turns to Anders and the two of them start dancing, Michaela moving her body in a way that reminds me of her Pussycat Dolls tribute.

"Yeah, she's stunning," I say, feeling as if someone's punctured a hole in my side.

"Well . . . that's good, because you guys look exactly alike!" Autumn says brightly, clearly trying to cheer me up.

"No, they don't." Jasper glances from Michaela back to me.

"Shut up, Jasper," Autumn says through gritted teeth.

"What? It's true," Jasper replies. His light green eyes travel across my face, and I feel the heat in my cheeks. "Anyone can see that you two are related, but you both have totally different features. I mean, for instance, your eyes are bigger, and your hair . . ." Jasper reaches out, as if he's going to touch my hair, but then he lets his hand fall. "Anyway. Totally different," he finishes, looking down.

My heart is thudding so hard I wonder if Jasper and Autumn can hear it over the music. I feel free and loose, like I'm a ship that's been unhooked from its dock. I'm not my sister. And she's not me.

I gaze at Jasper, who's avoiding looking at me. I want to tell him that his eyes are very nice and I wish he wouldn't hide them behind his glasses. I want to say that he and his sister are lucky to share the same gorgeous auburn hair. And mostly I want to thank him for saying what he said, but I can't speak.

The next thing I know, Sullivan is back at my side, asking if I want to dance. Flustered, I manage to accept, and wave to Autumn and Jasper, who have gone back to arguing over cupcakes. I follow Sullivan out onto the dance floor to a spot right near Rebecca and Byron. Sullivan puts one hand on my waist, takes hold of my other hand and starts to move in a back and forth, swaying motion.

"Ouch," he says.

"Sorry," I say, stumbling off his left foot. Heels were obviously a bad idea tonight. "I swear I'm usually a good dancer," I tell Sullivan. I laugh, but he doesn't look amused.

The band shifts to a new song, one that seems perfect for dreamy slow dancing.

"It's a marvelous night for a moondance, with the stars up above in your eyes . . ."

Funny how all these songs are about nature in some way. About falling in love with nature. I think about saying this to Sullivan, but I'm not sure he'd understand.

"A fantabulous night to make romance, 'neath the cover of October skies . . ."

The song is achingly beautiful, and for some strange reason I find myself looking past Sullivan, over his shoulder at Jasper, who's now joke-dancing with Autumn. He's spinning his sister around, cracking up, and I can't help but think what a pleasant, open smile he has. My heart squeezes and I unconsciously squeeze Sullivan's hand.

Sullivan squeezes back and starts looking at me in

an intense, serious way. Only he's not really looking at my face. His eyes are sort of focused on my chest area. *Oh, no.* I fight the urge to fling my arms around myself, to duck and hide. I *shouldn't* have worn this stupid, revealing dress tonight. I feel like my body has betrayed me once again. How mortifying.

"You look pretty tonight, Katie," Sullivan tells my chest. Then he tilts his head to one side and draws me in closer to him. I feel a huge jolt of nerves. My ankles wobble. Is this *it?* Is Sullivan Turner going to give me my first real kiss, right here in the Fir Lake High gymnasium, in front of a trillion people, including my own sister?

I really, really want to know what it's like to kiss a boy. To know what Michaela feels when she's alone with Anders. Sullivan's lips are inches away. It would be so easy to tilt my head, too, and make it happen.

The problem is, I don't want to kiss Sullivan Turner.

I don't want to kiss a boy who I can't talk and laugh and banter with. I don't want to kiss a boy who only cares about tennis, football, and possibly my breasts, and doesn't see the humor and horror in my getting stuck in the mud. Most of all, I don't want to waste this romantic song about dancing under the moon with a boy I feel nothing for.

Sullivan must sense my change in heart — maybe it's the fact that I'm pulling away from him — because he wrinkles his forehead and asks, "What?"

I swallow hard. "I can't —"

"Ladies and gents, can we request your attention, please?" the lead singer of the band asks. I didn't even notice the music had stopped. Sullivan and I unclasp hands and everyone turns to face the stage.

Ms. Leonard, Michaela's pretty, dark-haired homeroom teacher who is also chair of the Homecoming Committee, walks across the stage in her pale pink dress and matching heels. She hands the lead singer a white envelope, and then stands off to the side, holding a faux diamond tiara in her hands.

"I'm told that what I have here is the name of this year's Homecoming Queen," the lead singer says, holding the envelope up to the crowd, and raucous cheers shake the gym. I look around for Michaela, with no success.

The lead singer opens the envelope, pulls out a piece of paper, unfolds it, and clears his throat. Then he leans into the microphone, grins at the crowd, and says, "And the Fir Lake Tigers's Homecoming Queen is none other than . . ." Mr. Hemming starts a drumroll. "Miranda Warner!"

Thud.

Silence.

"Who's that?" Sullivan whispers to me, but my throat feels stuck.

"Golly, excuse me, folks," the lead singer says, patting his pants pockets. The guitar player steps forward and hands the singer a pair of wire-rimmed glasses. There are low chuckles as the singer slips on the glasses, squints at the paper, and says, "Sorry about that. Is there a Michaela Wilder in the house?"

The whoop that goes up in the back of the gym sounds fuzzy to my ears. I seem to observe through a veil of cotton as my sister gracefully dodges through the crowd, and ascends the stage. If she suddenly burst into pirouettes, *that* might make things more normal. But seeing Ms. Leonard lower the tiara onto Michaela's head, and watching as a student council member hands my sister a bouquet of roses, I feel completely out-of-my-body surreal. I don't think I've ever seen Michaela's face so full of pride, even when she danced in *The Nutcracker*. And for the first time, Michaela doesn't look modest. She is lapping up the crowd's adoration.

I'm ashamed and proud and top-full of tears. I'm so, so happy for my sister but part of me understands that the tiara on Michaela's head is just another sparkling wedge between us.

"I have to go to the bathroom," I whisper to Sullivan. "And — uh —"

"Yeah?" Sullivan looks distracted, snapping his head between me and the stage. Ms. Leonard is asking Michaela who she'd like to choose as her Homecoming King.

"This was really fun and all, but I should probably head home soon," I babble, taking a few steps back in my muddy heels. "I mean, I like you, Sullivan, but I don't think —" God. How does one go about breaking up with someone they're not even dating?

"Huh?" Sullivan is still focused on the stage, on Michaela, who is saying, "Anders Swensen!" into the microphone her clear, sure voice. Sullivan glances back at me, and says, "Um, okay, Katie . . . whatever . . ."

Fortunately, Anders is now getting up onstage, so nobody is looking at me as I fight through the crowd, practically bawling. I tear out of the gym and click-clack loudly down the deserted hallways until I get to the girls' bathroom. *Your sister is Homecoming Queen,* I tell myself as I stare at my pale reflection in the mirror.

Why can't Michaela and I return to the way things were?

I feel like I might be sick. I lean over the sink, splash water on my face, and take the deep, steadying breaths I learned in yoga. Thank goodness for yoga.

It's only ten, but I know Mom will be all too happy to pick me up if I call her now. Still, I owe Autumn and Jasper a good-bye — they were kind enough to come to the dance for me. And I should probably collect myself and congratulate Michaela so I don't look *completely* psycho.

When I reenter the gym, Michaela and Anders are no longer on the stage, and the band is playing a fast-tempo song that everyone is whirling around to. Autumn and Jasper are dancing, and I'm about to go join them when I feel a hand on my bare back.

"Katie!" Michaela gasps. She is holding her tiara on her head with one hand and her black-lined eyes are huge. "I'm so glad I found you! Can you do me a favor?"

"I can't believe you won," I tell her. I reach out and touch her arm. It's been so long since my sister and I had any contact.

Michaela grabs me in a fast hug, catching me off guard. "Oh, isn't it stupid and fantastic?" she cries. "Katie, we have so much to talk about!" Her energy seems over the top, and I wonder for a split second if she's had a beer or something.

"We never talk anymore," I say into Michaela's hair, but I'm not sure she hears.

"Listen," Michaela says as she releases me. "You're getting a ride home with Mom and Dad, right?" I nod, and she breathlessly adds, "Can you tell them I'm spending the night at Heather's house? I'll be home first thing in the morning."

Without waiting for me to respond, my sister kisses my forehead and then flits back into the pulsing crowd. I see her run into Anders's open arms, and he lifts her off the ground.

"I'm going home now," I tell Autumn when I reach her and Jasper, and she nods understandingly. Jasper watches me with his hands in his pockets, frowning a little. I feel bad for ruining their fun. "I'll text you before I go to bed," I promise Autumn, and then turn away.

I call Mom from the bathroom, and wait for her outside the school, shivering in my coat. Thankfully, it's Dad, not Mom who's in the SUV, so the ride home is blissfully free of questions. I tell him about Michaela staying at Heather's, and that I had an okay time at the dance, and then Dad says that he's glad we moved to Fir Lake, and I try not to sob.

Locked in my room, I take out my bun and turn off all the lights, but I don't bother getting into bed yet. I walk, fully clothed, over to my spot by the window. The lights in Emmaline's house are off for once, and a sliver of a crescent moon shows through the clouds.

I wonder if Michaela really is sleeping at Heather's house tonight. I wonder why I thought of Jasper when I was dancing with Sullivan. And I wonder if I'm ready to face any of these truths.

16

"Guess who called last night?" Mom asks over breakfast on Saturday. It's been two weeks since Homecoming. The trees are bare, Michaela's tiara sits on top of her dresser, and Sullivan and I are very maturely avoiding each other.

Last night was Halloween. In the city, Michaela and I used to trick-or-treat inside our apartment building, going from floor to floor in our masks and itchy costumes. Here, I went to a pumpkin-carving party at Casa Hawthorne (my jack-o'-lantern fell apart and Jasper cackled), and Michaela attended a lavish bash at Heather's house (she went as a ballerina). Mr. Hawthorne dropped me off at The Monstrosity around eleven P.M., but Michaela didn't come home until four in the morning (I was awake, of course).

"Hmm . . ." Michaela says, pouring milk onto her cereal. "The Dean of Fenimore Cooper College, to give you a raise!" she offers, and if I squint across the kitchen table, I swear I can see brown on her nose.

"No, though that would be nice," Mom says with a smile, passing Dad the orange juice.

"Um . . . Dad's agent, to say she sold his book?" I pipe up, just to give Michaela a run for her money.

Dad sighs and puts down his toast. "That's kind of you, love. Alas, that would be difficult considering I haven't finished my manuscript yet."

Michaela snickers into her coffee. "Leave it to Katie to not pick up on that," she murmurs.

I feel a rush of anger. *What a bitch*, I think, before I can stop myself. I have never once cursed at Michaela — not even in my head — but now the sentiment seems appropriate.

For the past two weeks, there's been an icy distance between my sister and me. When Michaela isn't sleeping over at Heather's house, she's locked in her bedroom. After school, I'll go to Autumn's to study or up to the attic to practice yoga poses. I can't look at my sister and not see her accepting that tiara, and Michaela seems all too fine with letting me slip away.

"Well?" Mom prods, glancing from me to Michaela with an excited grin.

I'm still seething at my sister, so I put down my butter knife and say, "Anders Swensen?"

There's a sharp intake of breath from Michaela's side of the table.

"*Who?*" Mom and Dad ask at the same time, glancing at me in confusion.

My sister's eyes are shooting fiery arrows at me. As much as I want to bring her down right now, I can't bring myself to utter the words "Michaela's boyfriend."

"Nobody," I grunt.

"Katya, don't be fresh," Mom says, blowing on her tea. She's clearly abandoned her patience. "It was Svetlana who called," she announces.

Michaela knocks over her coffee cup. Autumn thinks it's crazy — in a "city folks" way — that our parents let me and Michaela drink coffee. This is what I'm thinking as I watch the dark brown liquid run down the tablecloth in rivets. I'm usually the big spiller in the family, so I also feel a small burst of enjoyment at the sight.

"Michaela, what's gotten into you?" Mom asks as my sister hurriedly sops it up with her napkin.

Michaela's cheeks look a little pale, and I wonder if she caught a cold from staying out so late. "It's nothing . . . I'm just surprised. What did Svetlana want?"

"What do you think?" Mom says as Dad carries the wet napkins to the trash can. "To personally invite you girls to opening night of *The Nutcracker* over Thanksgiving weekend!"

"Really?" I exclaim, sitting up straighter. Svetlana. I haven't given a thought to my old headmistress in forever. I think of her now, with her dyed-red hair and dramatic flair, putting on her diamond-tipped eyeglasses to punch in the unfamiliar Fir Lake phone number. I imagine her speaking to my mom in Russian, her voice shaking with glee at the thought of seeing her star pupil again. (Oh, yeah, and the runty little sis.)

"Really," Mom affirms. "She has two extra orchestra seats reserved for the Friday night show. And she'd like you both to stay at her apartment from Thursday through Saturday." Mom pauses, glancing from me to Michaela with a big smile. "Pretty amazing, no?"

Pure happiness blooms in me. *Beyond amazing.* I'd been figuring, and had even told Trini, that my family would drive down to the city in December to see a performance. Never in any of my most fervent daydreams had I imagined that Michaela and I would go on our own and so soon.

Oh, the city — solid concrete beneath my heels and the blasting horns of yellow cabs, all the museums and boutiques and street vendors, and apartments that don't creak or settle. Ordering greasy Chinese takeout — which I haven't had since August — with Trini and Sofia and Jennifer, and catching up on the Anna Pavlova gossip. Better still, Michaela and I will be seeing Manhattan at its prettiest, right at the start of the holiday season: white lights laced around lampposts, sidewalk Santas clanging their bells, the scent of sugared chestnuts. The wave of homesickness that washes over me is so strong, I'm surprised it doesn't knock me out of my seat.

I glance across the table at my sister. I know, I just *know* that as soon as Michaela and I are sitting side by side in Lincoln Center, watching glorious, real ballet onstage, things will be peaceful between us again. They have to be.

But Michaela isn't beaming like I am. She looks . . . hesitant.

"You and Dad won't mind if Katie and I aren't here for Thanksgiving?" she asks after a moment, twirling her spoon through her bowl of cereal.

Mom chuckles and Dad shakes his head as he sits back down. "Now, you know that's silly" is all Mom says.

Our family has never really *done* Thanksgiving. Mom, coming from Russia, feels no real connection to the tradition, and Dad decided ages ago that he didn't want the rest of the country to dictate when to have family time. Sometimes Mom would pick up a turkey from Zabar's on the Upper West Side. But mostly Michaela and I would go to our bedroom, put on our ballet clothes, and perform made-up routines for each other. Not really a sacred day in the Wilder home.

"I guess." Michaela plunks her spoon up and down in the milk. "But people make a bigger deal out of it here, you know. Like Heather's family? They decorate the house with strung-up leaves and dried corn on the cob, and they invite at least twenty people. . . ."

What is my sister *doing*? Is she trying to get out of going to the city?

For once, Mom has the same reaction as me. "Michaela!" she snaps, and I realize how incredibly rare it is to hear Mom scold my sister. "You should be honored! Do you know how thrilled Svetlana is to be seeing you? She even said she'd have a private lesson with you, to prepare you for your Juilliard audition in January."

"I'm sorry," Michaela says after a minute, letting out a short laugh. "I'm just zonked. Of course I can't wait to see the performance and Svetlana. It's going to be incredible."

Mom leans back, looking enormously pleased.

"It really will," I sigh, relieved that Michaela has come to her senses. Our gazes meet across the table. "Maybe we could look for bus tickets online after breakfast," I add hopefully. I don't want to push my luck.

I'm expecting Michaela to roll her eyes and say that she has plans with the girls, but my heart leaps when she smiles. "Let's do it," my sister says, getting to her feet, and there's a flash of her old warmth in her eyes. It's as if the mere mention of Manhattan and ballet and Svetlana are bringing the two of us back together. "Last one to my room has to take the garbage to the bear box tonight!" Michaela adds, and then sprints away from the table.

I'm instantly up out of my seat and racing out of the kitchen in hot pursuit. I hear Dad calling after us to slow down, but Mom — usually the parent who's all about discipline — laughs and says, "Oh, they're just excited, Jeffrey. Let them play."

Michaela and I do sound like children as we thunder up the stairs, squealing and shouting "I don't think so!" and "Eat my dust!" My face feels flush with joy. Michaela is in the lead, her agile dancer's feet skimming over the wooden floors, but as we approach her room, I overtake her. I wonder if she's letting me win, then decide I don't care.

I burst into Michaela's bedroom. It's even messier than the last time I was in here; her bed is a tangle of sheets and pillows, and clothes carpet the floor. Her tiara glimmers on her dresser top. And I notice one new detail: a corkboard above her desk that bears a Post-it note on which Michaela has written *Application deadline: 12/20*, and a snapshot of Michaela, Heather, the twins, and Anders posing on the shores of Fir Lake, all of them fresh-faced and wearing puffy vests and duck boots. In a far corner of the board is a photo of me and Michaela from back in the city —we're sitting on our front stoop in sundresses, squinting up at the camera. I remember Dad taking that photo, and I'm surprised Michaela has kept it.

"Garbage duty for me, " Michaela groans, collapsing against her shut door. "I can't *bear* the indignity. Get it?"

We look at each other, then break into giggles. It's like we've gone back in time — like Anders doesn't exist and Homecoming never happened. I'm not about to question this change. I'm loving it too much.

Michaela pulls her laptop off her desk, sinks down onto her bed, and pats the space beside her. Déjà vu dizzies me for a second, and then I join her, tucking a pillow beneath my head. It feels cozy and warm, loafing together as the pale November sunlight pools on the blankets.

"Okay, Greyhound from Fir Lake to Port Authority in New York City," Michaela says, her fingers moving over the keys. "So we'll get there Thursday night, and come back Saturday?"

"Thursday?" I have yoga then, and would hate to skip it. "Maybe instead we could —" I pause, distracted by the small Gmail Chat box that has popped up in the corner of the screen.

Anders: Morning my beauty. U busy?

I glance at my sister. Wow. *My beauty?* I can't tell if that's romantic or gross, I'm leaning toward gross. Then again, after my smooth moves with Sullivan, I can't call myself an expert on love.

Michaela's face colors, quickly, she types back, A little. Call u later? In another second, Anders replies: Looking forward 2 it already. ;)

Oh, please. Could he lay it on any thicker?

"Do you guys talk every day?" I ask as Michaela closes the IM box.

Michaela blinks at me. The two of us haven't discussed Anders since the night of their first date.

"Yes," she replies, smiling softly. "Of course. He's my boyfriend."

I know this, obviously, but it's like when I saw Michaela smoking at the football game — getting confirmation makes the back of my neck prickle.

"Are you guys serious?" I ask, although I'm not even sure what *serious* is supposed to mean. The first time I heard that term used, I pictured a guy and a girl sitting side by side, their mouths set in straight lines.

Michaela props herself up on one elbow, wriggling closer to me. "I think so," she whispers. Is my sister about to *confide* in me? "I mean . . ." Michaela gazes at the space above my head. "What I feel for him is so much more intense than anything I've ever experienced. And Anders feels the same way." It's unsettling to hear Michaela — practical, focused, feet-on-the-ground Michaela — talk this way, her eyes all moony.

"How do you know?" I burst out. "How can you be *sure* he feels the same?" The dam has been broken, and my thoughts pour out. "He's so popular and handsome and a big-time quarterback, so what if . . ."

"What if I'm not good enough for him?" Michaela demands, bolting upright. "Because I'm not a cheerleader or something? Is that what you're implying, Katie?"

Good God. Why can't the two of us get along for more than two minutes? "No . . ." I fumble for the right words. "What if he's a *player*?"

"Katie." Michaela's face grows tight, and she lets

out a sigh that's less big-sister and more rampaging dragon. "You. Don't. Understand." She pauses, then adds in a low, meaningful tone, "Do you see why I can't tell you anything?"

Her words sting — my sister's becoming a pro at that — but I reach for her laptop and grumble, "Fine. Forget it. I'll figure out the tickets."

"Good." Michaela stands up and reaches for the burgundy leotard on her chair. "I was going to go use the barre anyway."

That's a first, I think, but I focus on the Greyhound website, furiously clicking on different dates. Michaela pulls her nightgown off over her head. I haven't seen my sister without clothes on in a long time. She doesn't remotely have my curves, but the shape of her body is softer than it was back in the city. All that day-after-day dancing kept Michaela stick-thin and hard-edged. It's undeniable that she looks better this way. Even her feet seem smoother, less bruised.

My sister finishes putting on her tights, leotard, and toe shoes. Then she fixes her hair into a bun, and stalks out of the room.

"Don't rush on my account," I say coolly, and flinch when she slams the door.

Fuming, I purchase our tickets — departing on Thursday, as Michaela suggested — and am about to close the laptop when curiosity overtakes me. Maybe it's because I felt so close to Michaela before she rudely shut me out again. Maybe it was the sight of that little

IM exchange. But suddenly *I need to know.* I need to know about Anders. I need to know about the things my sister claims I don't understand. The things she won't tell me.

I minimize the Greyhound screen, and Michaela's Gmail page stares at me. I'm a criminal. I know I am. Or maybe I'm just a detective. I guess the line can be thin.

She's right upstairs. She could be back at any second.

I tell myself that I'm not actually sneaking. Her Gmail account is already up there, for all the world to see. My heart racing, I let my eyes travel down the page. There are a bunch of e-mails from Heather, with subject headings like "got so wasted on saturday!" and "congrats!" These messages are definitely worth investigating, but it's Anders's communication with my sister that's on my mind. However, Anders's e-mails have benign subject headings such as "see you tomorrow, my beauty" and "pammy's pizzeria at 6?"

I spot several e-mails between Michaela and a Ms. Tennyson, who is Fir Lake High's college counselor. She's probably helping Michaela plot her glorious entrance into Juilliard. Then I click on the Chats link. Almost all of Michaela's most recent IMs are with Anders, though there are a few with Heather, Lucy, and Faith, and one or two with Sofia, back in the beginning of September. It's like reviewing a journal of Michaela's time in Fir Lake.

The doorknob rattles. I look up in a panic, then realize that it's The Monstrosity doing its settling/groaning thing. Michaela is probably beginning her pliés now. My palms are so damp I can hardly feel them. Acting on instinct, I click on the Chat that took place between Michaela and Anders the day after Homecoming.

> **Anders:** miss u already.
> **me:** miss u 2, silly boy.

This is nauseating. I have to remind myself that the "me" refers to Michaela — not me, Katie. I always seem to develop a minor identity crisis when dealing with my sister.

> **Anders:** am so tired. ☺
> **me:** u don't even kno. cant survive on no sleep, unlike my little sis.

I raise my eyebrows. Michaela mentions *me* when she's talking to Anders? I'm not sure if I should feel flattered or suspicious. After checking the door to make sure Michaela isn't about to barge in, I go back to reading.

> **Anders:** r u really ok w/ what happened last nite?
> **me:** yes. freaked out by how I'm not freaking out.

Anders: LOL. kno what u mean.

My stomach tightens. *What* happened?

me: we were ready. we knew the time was right.
me: and im glad we were safe & everything.

I bite my bottom lip. Am I reading what I think I'm reading?

Anders: same here. ur very smart, miss.
Anders: 1 of the many things i luv about u.
me: *blushing*
Anders: and i promise it'll b better next time.
me: *blushing even more*
me: shut up it was perfect
Anders: ok now I'M blushing.
me: ☺
Anders: i love you
me: i love you too.

I click out of the Chat, trying to breathe. Can it be? Maybe I'm misunderstanding. Maybe it's my over-active imagination at work.

Trembling slightly, I start opening other e-mails, the ones from Heather, looking for more answers: *babe, i think u left ur copy of Sense and Sensibility @ my house*, one reads. *Should i bring to school tomorrow XOXO, Heather.* Nothing too outrageous there. Then

I click on the e-mail dated the day after Homecoming, the one with the subject line "congratulations!"

And the e-mail simply reads: . . . *on no longer being a virgin! XOXO, Heather*

I slap the laptop shut. The room tilts around me.

Okay. So now I know.

But I wish I didn't.

"Yoga breaths, yoga breaths," I say out loud. Michaela could easily be walking down the hall right now. I have the presence of mind to reopen her laptop and minimize her e-mail screen, covering my tracks like any decent criminal. Then I spring off the bed and start pacing back and forth, my mind reeling.

Michaela had sex. Michaela had SEX!

So Anders has seen my sister naked. I look back at her bed. Did it happen in *here*? No. Probably not. It must have been at Anders's house. Does he have a big bed? Were his parents home? Does one *need* to do it in bed, or can it happen anywhere?

Was she scared? Does she really love him?

How could she keep this from me?

I'm furious at my sister and, at the same time, I regret that I dug so deep. Sometimes one can be too good of a detective. Because there are some things you're better off not discovering.

I stop in front of Michaela's desk and look at the picture of us on her corkboard. It was taken in June. We didn't know anything then. We didn't know we were moving. There'd been no talk of dating or sex or Homecoming Queens. No wonder our smiles were so easy and natural. No wonder my arm rested trustingly in Michaela's lap, and our cheeks pressed close together.

That was before my sister betrayed me.

Which is how I feel now, standing alone in her room. Betrayed — like my fellow soldier has run off and left me in the trenches. Like my partner in a pas de deux has decided to bow off the stage. Like my best friend in the world has escaped to a universe that is hidden from me.

I reach out to take the photograph off the cork-board — I'm not sure what I'm going to do with it — when the bedroom door opens.

"You're still here?"

I drop my hand and turn to regard my sister. She's all glowy with perspiration, and she's wearing her familiar ballet gear. This is how I often picture Michaela in my mind's eye — the constant dancer. This is my sister in her truest form.

Yet I feel as if I'm looking at a stranger.

"I bought the tickets," I say, my jaw stiff. I'm sure my face is ghost-pale. I'm worried that Michaela's penetrating gaze is going to pierce through my shuddering heart. That, in her half magical Michaela way, she's going to figure out what I did.

Michaela nods. "Thanks." There's a pause. "I need to change out of my toe shoes. They're killing my feet," she adds, bending down to unlace the thick pink ribbons around her ankles. I watch as she carefully slides one foot out. Her toes are bloodied, as always. But this time, the blood seems more significant — symbolic, somehow. *My sister had sex.*

"I need to be alone," I say. I've never spoken those words to my sister, so it makes sense that she looks up at me with concern.

"Is it — what I said before?" she asks, her voice tremulous. So *now* she feels bad.

I don't answer, only back out of the room. I can't be near her — this stranger — right now. I can't even be in the same house as her.

In my room, I pull my coat on over my pajamas, cram my feet into my Uggs, and hurry downstairs. I slip past my parents, who are still in the kitchen, and walk outside into the cool, windy morning. It's flurrying — the first snowfall of the season. Light, white, butterfly flakes land on my nose. Some winters in the city, it didn't snow until the middle of January.

I guess here, everything happens sooner than you expect it to.

I hold out my hands, catching the snow, and I remember when I first saw Emmaline, standing on her porch touching the rain. Maybe she, too, was trying to forget something that had hurt her. I glance toward Emmaline's house now; her lights are on and her car is in the driveway. We haven't talked since I started taking yoga, but today I have no desire to go next door and pour my heart out. Nor can I stand the thought of calling Autumn to fill her in on Fir Lake High's hottest couple. No. Michaela's secret — my secret now — feels too unwieldy to be let out. I will try my best to keep it safe.

As long as it doesn't eat me up first.

17

"*You* have a secret," Autumn announces as we're leaving the yoga studio on Thursday. My lime-green mat that I bought last week at The Climber's Peak is tucked under my arm, and my hair is down.

"Why do you say that?" I ask, my smile fading. For one blissful hour and a half, yoga took my mind off my troubles, as it always does. I can feel myself improving every week, getting more comfortable with the poses *and* the notion that I'm loving something other than dance. My mom knows I'm taking yoga, but she has no idea how much I enjoy it. I've been paying for classes with saved-up birthday money (Emmaline gives me a discount anyway), and even though I still go to Mabel Thorpe every week, my heart isn't in those classes at all. In a way, it feels like a mini-betrayal of my own.

Though nothing as serious as Michaela's.

"It's scribbled all over your face," Autumn replies as we pass through the ground floor of the library, nodding to the librarians behind the circulation desk. "All week, you've looked like you're holding something back," she adds, glancing at me.

Having an observant friend is both a blessing and a curse.

Autumn doesn't realize how close I've come to spilling everything to her. At lunch today, my friend looked at the Senior Popular Table and whispered, "Did Michaela and Anders have an operation that got them to be attached at the mouth?" I opened my own mouth, so ready to release my secret, but I stopped myself in time.

"It's just family stuff," I say, not wanting to lie but not wanting to get into the gruesome details, either. And though Autumn possesses a streak of small-town nosiness, she's polite enough not to press me.

"Speaking of family secrets . . ." Autumn begins, and I perk up, wondering if she's going to reveal something about Jasper. Not that I should care about Jasper.

Unfortunately, Coach Shreve chooses that moment to pop up behind us.

"Tough class, huh, girls?" he asks, looking as if he's having trouble walking.

I have to say that it's delightful vengeance to be *better* at a physical activity than Coach Shreve is. Today, he had trouble mastering the Happy Baby pose, which is one of my favorites, and Emmaline asked me to demonstrate for him. I have a feeling that he's going to start being kinder to me in gym class from now on.

As we walk through the library doors into the blustery evening — somehow, without warning, it's really become winter — I turn to Coach Shreve and ask, as casually as I can, "So . . . what do you think of Emmaline?"

Coach Shreve looks startled. "Well . . . ah . . ." He tugs his wool hat onto his head. "She's a very capable teacher."

Capable teacher doesn't really translate to *I love her madly and want to have lots of Happy Babies with her*, so I don't push the topic. Coach Shreve tells me and Autumn he needs to stop by The Climber's Peak, and quickly limps off.

"It's a lost cause," I sigh, resting my head on Autumn's shoulder. "Someone who's never had a boyfriend should probably never be a matchmaker."

"I'm sorry things didn't work out with Sullivan," Autumn says, leaning her head against mine.

"It's weird . . . but I'm not," I say, surprised at how well I've been handling the post-Homecoming awkwardness with Sullivan. At the thought of boyfriends, however, I remember Michaela and Anders, and my stomach tightens. *Don't go there.* So I ask Autumn, "What's up with your family secret?" We're walking past Hemming's Goods, and we wave to Mrs. Hemming, who blows us a kiss.

Autumn grins. "The first weekend in November, my dad, Jasper, and I hike up Mount Elephant."

What kind of secret is that? By now, I'm more than used to Jasper's and Autumn's outdoorsy, cow-milking ways. I shrug at my friend. "Sounds . . ." *Torturous*, I think. "Fun," I fib.

Autumn draws a breath and says, "It is. And I want you to come with us."

Me? Hiking up the biggest mountain in Fir Lake? Did Autumn's brains rattle during yoga?

"Um, isn't it a little cold for hiking?" I ask, pulling my scarf up to my nose as we walk past the half frozen lake. "I mean, yeah, global warming and whatever, but, come on. . . ."

"Once you live through a December here, November is warm by comparison," Autumn tells me patiently. "All you need to wear is like, some thermals, maybe a quilted vest, and gloves. As long as it doesn't snow . . ."

I flash to a terrifying image of Autumn, Jasper, Mr. Hawthorne, and myself buried under snowdrifts, crying out for help. I don't even know what "thermal" is.

"We don't have to sleep in a tent, do we?" I ask warily. "I have enough trouble sleeping in my bed."

"I realize, then, that now two more people know I'm an insomniac: Emmaline and Autumn. Maybe it's not such a secret anymore.

Autumn assures me that the hike is just a day trip.

"Katie, it would be really great to have you there," she adds in a quieter tone, and I realize that this hike might mean a lot to her. Maybe she's been waiting for a friend to share it with. In that moment, as I meet her eyes, I understand that Autumn thinks of me as her best friend. But is Autumn *my* best friend? I'm conflicted. In spite of everything, I still feel loyal to Michaela, to Trini and Sofia and all my ballet girls. Having a best friend in Fir Lake would be like closing the door on the city forever.

At the same time, ever since Michaela and I started drifting apart, Autumn has been my lifesaver. I owe her a friendly gesture in return. And now that I'm thinking about it, a jaunt with the Hawthornes *would* provide the perfect excuse for me to escape my crazy family for one day.

And maybe there's a tiny, heart-pounding part of me that likes the idea of spending time with Jasper.

When I tell Autumn to sign me up, her freckled face brightens, and she begins listing instructions: "Wear your sturdiest shoes. Buy hiking boots, if possible, or sneakers will do. Pack lots of bottled water in your backpack, though we always have extra. Don't forget to put sunscreen on your nose and ChapStick on your lips, because the wind can be intense up there. . . ."

What have I gotten myself into?

*   *   *

I'm wondering the same thing on Saturday, as I trudge up a treacherous, sloping trail behind Jasper, Autumn, and Mr. Hawthorne, who are all wearing anoraks, fingerless gloves, and backpacks. The three of them are singing at the top of their lungs, even though we've been walking uphill for hours. It's some song about hiking, though I'm much more focused on *not* tumbling off the side of the mountain than I am on listening to the lyrics. Every once in a while, Mr. Hawthorne will stop to point out the tracks of striped skunks, patches of poison ivy, and owl pellets, which only serves to strike more fear into my heart.

The wind slices through the fir trees, and I clutch at my white earmuffs, wishing I'd worn a hat (the earmuffs looked cuter). Following Autumn's instructions, I'm wearing sneakers, but they're thin-soled baby-blue Pumas, and I can feel every rock, stick, and leaf through them (the Hawthornes are all in lace-up hiking boots). My Capezio tote hangs from my shoulder, cumbersome and heavy (I packed three bottles of water, ginger Altoids, my cell phone, a tin of smoked almonds in case we get stranded, my compact mirror, and lip gloss — which I figured could double as ChapStick).

Obviously, I've made several mistakes.

"I'm so jealous!" Michaela cried this morning when she ran into me in the hallway and I had to explain why I was wearing sneakers. "I've been wanting to climb

Mount Elephant forever. Heather and I went for a hike on a trail near there last week, but it got too cold to go climbing."

She was in her short robe, heading for the shower and, looking at her, all I could think about was Anders and the IMs. "I guess you can't get everything you want," I told her cryptically, and then drifted off to my room, feeling her gaze on the back of my head.

Why my sister would want to scale this crazy mountain is beyond me.

Up ahead, Jasper stops singing, pauses in his tracks, and glances back at me with an amused smile. "Ready to throw in the towel?" he calls.

"No!" I snap between pants. But the truth is, I kind of am. Nobody warned me that the trail was going to become as steep as a wall. A while ago, I decided not to bother keeping up with the corn-fed Hawthornes, and simply struggled along at my own pace, which is basically that of a snail on sleeping pills.

Autumn, too, stops singing and comes to stand beside her brother. "Katie, come *on!*" she hollers, and her tone isn't teasing like Jasper's was. In fact, it's borderline annoyed. "You don't have to be so scared. Just take bigger steps!"

"Easy for you to say!" I shout back. "You could do this blindfolded!"

I actually think I'm doing well — for me. Back in September, when I thought of Autumn as Flannel, and she thought of me as a city snob, I wouldn't have even made it past the trail sign.

"She has a point," Jasper says, elbowing Autumn. She glares first at him, and then at me, and stomps up the incline to catch up with her father. But Jasper reaches out his gloved hand to help draw me up. "It's just another hour or so to the top," he promises. "And the way down is always easier than the way up."

Usually, I get a kick out of me and Jasper volleying insults back and forth, but today it's kind of nice to have him be, well, nice to me. As my hand touches his, I hate how there seems to be a direct line between the nerves in my fingers and the blood in my cheeks.

I'm surprised when Jasper doesn't let go right away. He keeps a tight grip on me as we navigate the rough terrain. He's obviously just being polite — Autumn's dad is big on his kids having manners — but being this near to him is doing strange things to my heart. I study his profile — his auburn hair curling out from under his woolen hat, his glasses, fogged up from the cold, his short nose and smooth, thin lips.

What is going *on* with me?

"Thanks for taking my side back there," I tell Jasper lightly, trying to pretend I'm speaking to someone utterly ordinary — like, say, Autumn's older brother.

"Yeah, Autumn's just cranky 'cause she's hungry," Jasper replies, adjusting one of the straps on his bookbag with his free hand. "Usually she thinks you're adorable, like some terrified domestic cat that's been let loose in the wild."

Do you *think I'm adorable?* I want to ask, but that question feels even scarier than the ravine below us. "I'm glad I provide endless entertainment," I grumble instead.

"But you know," Jasper says, and I feel him looking at the side of my face. "Your princess act does get a little old after a while."

Princess act? I come to an abrupt stop and turn to glare at Jasper. Suddenly, I'm hyperaware of my fluffy white earmuffs, Pumas, peacoat, and tote bag. "It's not an act!" I spit, jerking my hand out of Jasper's. "This is how I *am*. I'm not a Fir Lake native. I don't milk cows." Now the heat in my cheeks is from anger. "I don't go on hikes. I don't wear flannel. I'm a city girl. Deal with it, Jasper."

And with that, I flounce away from him — or I flounce as best I can, what with all the rocks in my way, before I find myself on a quiet plateau with Autumn and her father. Open sky and rugged mountaintops surround us. We haven't reached the top yet, but the view still makes my head whirl. Fir Lake itself looks like nothing more than a puddle of bright blue water. The town — the roads I walk every day, stressing over school and boys and Michaela — is miniature, cardboard.

"Wow," I whisper, forgetting Jasper's princess jibe.

"No kidding," Autumn says, sidling up to me.

"Doesn't everything seem less important up here?" I sense that she feels bad about snapping at me before. And suddenly, I'm filled with the urge to tell Autumn about Michaela. Maybe it's that my confrontation with Jasper has left me feeling restless and jumpy. Or maybe it's that I finally see how well Autumn understands me. Either way, my secret is ready to come out.

"Who's ready for lunch?" Mr. Hawthorne asks, unzipping his bookbag and taking out a thermos, baggies filled with sandwiches, and a folded-up blanket. I'm ravenous — an hour ago, the bark on the trees had started to look like milk chocolate to my eyes — but I can't believe we're about to picnic in the dead of November.

Jasper appears on the plateau, red-cheeked and wind-tousled, and he crosses his eyes at me. I ignore him.

"I have to pee," Autumn announces and, unfortunately, I realize that I do, too.

"There's got to be a Porta Potti around here somewhere, right?" I ask, glancing around.

Jasper bursts into uncontrollable laughter while Mr. Hawthorne says, "Now, Jasper Benjamin. Behave yourself."

"What?" I ask Jasper, my face hot with indignation.

Autumn takes my arm. "Katie, there are no toilets on the mountain," she tells me softly.

"So, you mean . . ." My stomach sinks.

Autumn nods grimly, even though I can tell she sort of wants to laugh, too. "The woods, Katie. Nature's bathroom."

Within seconds, I am reluctantly following Autumn down a narrow path that leads off the plateau and into a thicket of trees. "I can totally hold it," I say, even though my bladder is telling me something very different. Also, the goal is to hike up to the top of the mountain after lunch, so who knows when I'll even see a real bathroom again?

"You go first," Autumn tells me, motioning me toward a shaded spot behind the trees. "I'll stand guard."

Jasper's *princess* taunt is echoing in my head, so I try not to cringe too much as I unzip my jeans and crouch down. I also try my best not to think about what kind of strange plants and grasses — and bugs — might be on the earth below me. I finish as quickly as I can, then hurry over to Autumn, who — ever-prepared — passes me a bottle of hand sanitizer. Then I wait for my friend to take care of business and she strolls back to me casually, accepting the Purell.

"That was a Fir Lake rite of passage," Autumn tells me with a smile, but I'm too traumatized to smile back. "Okay, let's return to our men," Autumn adds, but then I stop her.

This is it. The two of us have this one moment alone, deep in the woods. This is my chance to divulge the truth about Michaela, to unburden myself of this heavy secret.

"Autumn, remember how you thought I was hiding something?" The words rush out before I have a chance to think them through. "Well, you're right. I am. And it's about Michaela."

"Oh, my God. Is it bad?" Autumn whispers, studying my face.

"Pretty bad." And just like that, standing in the shadow of the bare-branched trees, I let out everything, from Michaela's mysterious sleepovers at "Heather's" to the IM Chat with Anders to the huge e-mail revelation. When I'm finished, I let out a long sigh. It's as if someone has removed a bookbag of rocks from my back. I look at Autumn, expecting her to huff over Michaela's lies, or to curse out Anders (although Autumn never curses), or to smile and whisper to me whatever she might know about sex.

Instead, Autumn is silent and hard-faced.

"Are you okay?" I ask, worried that she's caught poison oak or something.

"Katie, how could you do that?" Autumn replies in a low, controlled voice. "How could you disrespect Michaela's privacy, go through her personal things?"

She is staring at me as if I've just told her I kick cats for fun.

"That's not the *point*, Autumn!" I cry. "Michaela has been totally dishonest with me, *and* with our parents, and —"

"But you're no better!" Autumn replies immediately, her eyes burning. "You snooping through her e-mails is *just* as dishonest as Michaela lying about where she's sleeping over."

Autumn's logic does not sit well with me. "So you don't even care that my sister is having sex?" I demand, lifting my chin.

"It's none of my business," Autumn replies coldly, throwing back her shoulders. She towers over me, but I refuse to let her intimidate me.

"If you were really my friend, you wouldn't feel that way," I lash out, and then wish I'd kept silent.

Autumn's expression turns from outraged to thoughtful. "I don't understand you, Katie. You're a dancer, you're amazing at yoga, and then you can be so clumsy in real life. Sometimes you notice the tiniest details, and then you'll miss the big picture. And for the city girl you claim to be, you're as small-town-nosy as they come."

Did Autumn and Jasper band forces this morning and decide to say The Most Insulting Things to Katie? "What do *you* know, Flannel?" I snap, too angry to cry. "You've spent your whole life in Fir Lake." I look Autumn in the eye. "You don't know *anything*."

I turn on my heel and storm back up to the plateau, where Mr. Hawthorne and Jasper are seated on the blanket, eating their tofu dogs. Autumn is right behind me, but I refuse to look at her, and I mutter something to Mr. Hawthorne about not feeling well and needing to get off the mountain.

Mr. Hawthorne jumps up and tells me to wait, he'll walk down with me and drive me home. Autumn and Jasper — my new enemies — look on silently. I know I'll never make it down Mount Elephant by myself — with my luck, a bear would choose today to cross my path — so I stand off to the side, swallowing my tears as the family packs up their picnic. I've definitely messed up their hiking trip, which only makes me feel worse.

While we make our descent, I'm relieved to lag behind, and nobody stops to check on me this time. What was it Jasper said? *The way down is always easier than the way up.* And it's true that this time my shins aren't burning as much. But on the way up, my heart wasn't breaking. I've lost my one friend in Fir Lake, as well as the boy who — okay, now I can admit it — I may have had my first real crush on. I've betrayed Michaela's secret. And I was forced to pee in the woods.

Thanksgiving weekend can't come soon enough.

18

Hemming's Goods is having a sale on candied yams, and the farmstands are hawking jelly jars of cranberry sauce. Paper turkeys dangle from the school ceilings, and Mr. Rhodes pasted a rust-colored sign that says GOBBLE GOBBLE on our homeroom door. Normally, Autumn and I would have a field day with that one, but it's kind of difficult to laugh with somebody when they're not speaking to you.

The first few days after the hiking disaster, I waited graciously for Autumn's apology, but when she remained silent, I realized there would be none. Now, she's stopped coming to yoga class, and I've started skipping out on Mabel Thorpe (I told my mother that the class was put on hold for Mabel's audition trip to Las Vegas, which seems like a realistic excuse). At lunch, Autumn sits with her Camping Club friends again, and rather than admit to Michaela that I'm friendless and ask to sit at *her* table, I've taken to eating in the school library. I hide behind a romance novel as I scarf down my sandwich. The few times I've spotted Jasper in school, I glance away, my stomach jumping.

All I'm living for now is the trip to the city — *The Nutcracker*, Svetlana, my ballet girls. I've literally started *X*ing off the days on my Degas calendar, the one that hangs next to the photograph Trini and my friends gave me. My parents don't know it, but I'm entertaining a fantasy that involves my moving in with Svetlana . . . permanently.

The only other person as psyched for the trip as I am is my mother — and she's not even coming. She's been a whirlwind of activity lately, driving to Montreal to buy a new pair of white toe shoes for Michaela, and skipping office hours to scrub the attic barre with Murphy Oil Soap, just so — as she put it — Michaela's extra practice time will take place in a clean environment. I wonder if Mom knows and/or cares that Mabel Thorpe's studio has dust bunnies the size of Mount Elephant.

One week before the trip, I'm slouched at my desk, highlighting pages in my social studies textbook as snow pours down outside my window. I'm wishing I could call Autumn to ask her a question about the rice crops in Southeast Asia when I hear Mom outside my room, swearing loudly in Russian. There are a couple of crashing noises followed by a *bang*. Dad, who just finished his manuscript, is downstairs, shoveling the front walk (he was thrilled to have to buy a shovel), but I can't imagine what Mom is up to.

I find her in the hallway, my and Michaela's suitcases at her feet as she tries to cram the vacuum cleaner and countless boxes back into the giant hall closet. "Mom, you know we're not leaving for another week," I say, feeling a pang of impatience at these words. If Mom asked, I could tell her how much time was left down to the hour.

"Of course I know," Mom says as she unbuckles Michaela's dark pink suitcase. "I thought we could get a jump start on seeing how much you had to pack." My mother is possibly the world's most organized human being — I have no idea where she got me. "We should sort out the outfits you and your sister would like to take along," she continues. "You'll probably want to get your lavender silk dress dry-cleaned, and Michaela needs —"

"I need to go, because I'm late!" Michaela exclaims, emerging from her room. "Oh, hey, Katie," she adds, smiling at me.

As the trip back home looms closer, my sister has been reaching out to me in small ways, like insisting I ride to school with her and Anders whenever it snows (I sit buckled in the backseat like an infant while she and Anders blast Rooney and giggle over private jokes). She doesn't bring up stargazing anymore, but last night, after dinner, she asked if I wanted to have a mani-pedi meeting in her room . . . and I declined. It's the old Michaela I long for, anyway, the Michaela I used to share everything with. The new Michaela may as well be a moon-dweller.

Tonight, the new Michaela is wearing an oversize sky-blue sweater (I suspect it might be one of Anders's), and an itty-bitty denim skirt over tights and these hideous maroon duck boots she bought at The Climber's Peak. The bookbag slung over her shoulder looks stuffed to the brim, as if she's planning on spending the night elsewhere.

"Michaela!" Mom puts her hands on her hips. "Where are you rushing off to?"

I know very well where Michaela is rushing off to. I can tell by the shimmer in her eyes and the high color in her cheeks.

"Heather's house, for an emergency yearbook meeting," Michaela replies, and I'm shocked by how swiftly and easily she can now lie. She's probably still sleeping like a baby every night. "She's waiting for me outside."

Mom sighs. "Darling, we need to figure out which dress you'll be wearing to the performance, and then which leotard you'll take along for your private lesson with Svetlana —"

"Ugh, *Mom*." Michaela rolls her eyes. I can't recall if I've ever before heard my sister talk back to our mother. "Do we have to do that *now*?" She pushes up the loose sleeve of her sweater and checks her watch.

Mom clucks her tongue. Is she *disappointed* in her Michaela? Hope soars in me. "What could be more important than this trip?" Mom asks my sister.

"Nothing," I speak up, coming to stand beside my mother. I mean it, too. "*I'll* go through my clothes with you, Mom," I add. Maybe the two of us can huddle in my room, bonding and laughing, while Michaela is off hooking up with her boyfriend. Maybe Mom will finally see that while I'm not the most talented, I'm the daughter who's more deserving of her affections.

"Well, to be honest, it's Michaela I'm concerned with," Mom tells me with a dismissive shake of her head. "*You* won't be dancing for Svetlana, Katie, so all you really need to do is pick out your evening dress. And the lavender silk still fits, right?"

No, it doesn't fit. I wore that dress to *The Nutcracker* last year, and since then my boobs have grown an entire cup size.

Standing with my mother and my sister among the chaos of suitcases, I feel like my head is going to explode. *She'll always prefer Michaela, won't she? No matter what.*

"I'll wear my burgundy leotard," Michaela groans, stepping around a surprised-looking Mom to get to the stairs. I'm blocking her path so she attempts to maneuver past me. "Katie, move it," she says teasingly, and lightly hip-checks me. Then she waves her hand in front of my face. "Earth to Katie," she singsongs. "Stop spacing out again."

Something in me snaps. Where the *hell* does my sister get off thinking she can act like things are the same between the two of us?

"Why don't you tell us where you're really going?" My voice comes out strangled, almost not my own.

Michaela's eyes go round. "What are you talking about?" she asks. She clears her throat.

I look past her at our mother, whose brow is furrowed. This is it. No going back now.

"Why don't you admit that you're going to sleep at Anders Swensen's house?" I ask Michaela, all the while watching Mom.

"Who is this Anders Swensen?" Mom demands, glancing from me to my sister.

I take a deep breath.

"He's Michaela's boyfriend," I reply.

I dare a peek at my sister. Her skin is chalk-white, her mouth is turned down at the corners, and she stares at me in disbelief.

It's all over.

But I can't stop. I'm reckless with power. Words begin pouring out of me in a torrent. "He's the QB at high school — that's quarterback — and *super*-handsome. He's the one who comes to pick Michaela up in his car every morning, not Heather. He's the one Michaela's on the phone with every night. On weekends, when you think she's out with her girl-friends? Yeah. She's with Anders."

Michaela is frozen, silent. And my mother is listening to me, her mouth a small circle of surprise. It's immensely satisfying to get this kind of a reaction. But at the same time I feel cruel and small and ugly, revealing everything my sister doesn't want me to.

Still, I keep going. "She went to Homecoming with Anders," I add, my arms quivering now. "See, Michaela's too busy having a boyfriend to even think about ballet anymore —"

"Shut *up*, Katie!" Michaela cries, and lunges for me, grabbing my arm. She's suddenly ugly herself, her delicate face twisted with rage and her teeth bared. "Just shut up! You have no right — where do you get off —" She's shaking.

It's terrifying to see Michaela this upset, and for a second, I back up a few paces. Never in all my fourteen years of knowing her has my sister lost her cool. It's as if I'm seeing Michaela as human for the first time.

Which makes it all the easier for me to regain my courage.

"You can't tell me what to do!" I shout, coming forward so that Michaela and I are face-to-face. Our mom watches us, her jaw dropping farther by the second. All the stored-away hurt of the past three months is rising to the surface, scalding my skin and flowing out of me like lava. "I'm not as blind as you seem to think I am," I say through gritted teeth. "And I'm *not* being overdramatic," I add. "You feel like it's cool to shove me aside for all your new friends, to stuff me in the backseat, but guess what, Michaela? It's *not* cool! It makes you look like a really big bitch!"

"Katya!" Mom cries.

Michaela's eyes, much to my horror, well up with tears. "It's not *my* fault that you've refused to adjust to Fir Lake," she hisses at me. "I tried to include you —"

"That's bullshit and you know it!" I cut her off.

"Katya, we do *not* use that kind of language in this house," Mom snaps, coming over to me.

I turn on her, my face burning. "My name is Katie," I say, squaring my shoulders and lengthening my neck. Like a duck.

My mother's eyes widen, and it's as if she's seeing me for the first time.

Then she looks at Michaela and swallows. "Is this true?" Mom asks Michaela quietly.

I glare at my sister, my arms crossed over my chest, silently daring her to try and weasel out of this situation.

"It's true," Michaela speaks up and now tears are streaming down her cheeks. I feel an overwhelming rush of sadness at the sight, and my first instinct is to reach for her — but I resist.

Mom's hand goes to her throat. "Michaela . . ."

"Michaela, there's someone here to see you!" Dad calls cheerily. "What's going on up here?" he adds, tromping up the stairs with the huge shovel in his hand, and his jeans caked in snow up to the knees. His glasses are off, his cheeks are ruddy, and he's smiling; it seems as if he's finally gotten the hang of doing country-type chores. Then he sees us and his face falls.

"Well, the latest news is, our eldest daughter has gotten herself a boyfriend," Mom says crisply, looking at Michaela.

My stomach aches. I don't know if I wanted it to come to this.

"What — I —" Dad sputters, and then glances behind him at Heather, who is slowly advancing up the stairs.

It's strange to see Heather in our house, especially since she's not looking like her usual put-together self. She has on wire-rimmed glasses and no makeup, her hair hangs limp, and she's wearing a ratty hoodie over denim overalls. Yes, overalls. The kind Autumn would wear.

"Michaela! I've been waiting downstairs forever!" Heather says, her voice tight with stress. "We have to get back to my house before the copy editor arrives, because senior ads are due out first thing in the morning —"

Heather comes to a standstill when she sees the whole Wilder family looking stricken.

"Oh," she says, and glances at Michaela, who's sniffling and wiping her nose with one hand. "My God, Michaela, are you *okay*?" Heather asks in a hushed, frightened tone.

Realization forms in the pit of my stomach. Heather isn't part of some elaborate act. Michaela really *did* have to go to a yearbook meeting at her house.

Great.

"Can I go to Heather's house, please?" Michaela asks our parents, her voice cracking. There's a note of pissiness in her tone — understandably, I guess.

"Will there be *boys* there?" Mom asks Heather pointedly, and I want to bury my face in my hands out of embarrassment for Michaela.

Heather looks completely blindsided. "Um, boys?" She shakes her head, then nods. "Well, uh, there's Lance, the Photography Editor, but he doesn't really like girls. . . ."

"Yes, go ahead, Michaela," Dad says, which surprises me — he rarely speaks up when Mom is ordering us around. Mom gapes at him.

Michaela starts walking toward Heather, wiping her tears with the heel of her hand. As triumphant as I feel in many ways, it physically pains me to see my sister crying. It always has. When I was little, if I lost my favorite stuffed toy, or I didn't get my food in time and started crying, Michaela's own tears would automatically start up and then I'd cry even harder. A cycle of sympathy sobs. Maybe that's what being a sister is about.

I take Michaela by the arm, even though my own arm hurts from where she grabbed it, and say, "Mickey, wait —" My throat is thick with tears, too.

Michaela glances back at me, her eyes cold and hard. "I hate you, Katie," she says, firmly and decisively. "And I am never speaking to you again."

She turns and marches down the stairs, Heather scampering after her.

It was worth it, I tell myself. There are no more secrets now, everything is exposed. Yet I can't stop myself from bursting into tears. Dad steps forward and starts saying something reassuring, but I pull away and run to my bedroom. The one person I want to chase me, to comfort me, to say that she was wrong and that she loves me, is the one I have alienated forever.

A week later, I experience the longest freaking journey of my life.

On a Greyhound bus bound for New York City, Michaela and I sit side by side in absolute silence. Michaela is practically smushed up against the windowpane in order not to look at me. It's growing dark outside, evening descending softly on the bare trees and snowy hills. Michaela's iPod earbuds are crammed into her ears and she's clutching her cell phone in her fist, even though we haven't been able to get service since we left the Fir Lake bus station.

With no iPod of my own to distract me, I only have my thoughts for company as we bump along the highway and the old couple behind me snores in tandem. I gaze through the windshield at the bright taillights of cars glowing in the dark. The more ground the bus covers, the more the snow diminishes, and the lower the mountains dip, until they're all gone.

I think about how different everything felt when we were driving up to Fir Lake at the end of the summer: Michaela and me in the backseat, sharing Doritos and daydreams as we climbed higher and higher into the sunny sky. Now, as we slide down, down, toward the Hudson Valley, I'm not sharing a single word with the girl next to me. *The way down is always easier than the way up*, Jasper said.

Not Quite.

I think about the past week of unspoken war in the Wilder household, a war made all the worse by the pre-Thanksgiving revelry going on outside. While Mrs. Hemming came by to drop off pumpkin pies, Michaela was ignoring our parents, and Mom was ignoring me. Mom had grounded Michaela for a week—an event as rare as a comet, and Dad, who tried to give Michaela a lighter sentence ("no staying out on school nights") got the cold shoulder from Mom. The only people who spoke in The Monstrosity were me and Dad, though neither of us addressed That Night by the Stairs. At school, I remained invisible to everyone — especially Autumn and Jasper. I'd never felt more alone in my life.

As tall, blocky buildings start to crop up between the trees, I remember how relieved I was this morning when I saw Michaela's packed suitcase parked next to the kitchen. I'd been certain that she'd skip out on the trip in anger, but she must have been thrilled to escape the confines of The Monstrosity, even if wasn't to see her precious Anders.

Blech.

I've been sitting with my legs up on the seat, but I put my feet down on the grimy bus floor. The city is coming into view, the long, illuminated spans of bridges and the sharp shapes of the skyscrapers. Happiness rises in my throat. Even Michaela leans all the way to the right so she, too, can watch the city draw nearer. I feel as if the whole bus is holding its breath. Or maybe that's just me.

And just like that, we're in Manhattan, weaving through the traffic-clogged streets of midtown. It's Thanksgiving night, so the sidewalks aren't as full as they'd usually be, but hordes of people still stream across the avenues and crowd into bars and restaurants. I cannot believe that we're turning down brightly lit streets I've known since I was a child and pulling into the bustling Port Authority station. As the bus groans to a stop, Michaela finally turns her head away from the window. She stretches, then glances at me, her expression flat.

"It's good to be home, isn't it?" I ask her, because it feels silly not to acknowledge our arrival in some way.

Michaela's mouth curves up in the smallest of smiles, and she murmurs, "It is."

I'll take that as a positive sign.

As Michaela and I join the crowd of passengers waiting for their luggage outside the bus. It still hasn't sunk in that we're back. Port Authority smells like it always does — overflowing trash bins, cheap coffee, car exhaust. The bus driver is yelling at people to be patient as he passes suitcases along, and a man behind me is squawking into his cell phone. Was the city always this loud?

"Michaela! Katya! My darlings!"

I turn, suitcase in hand, to see Svetlana Vronsky racing toward us. She's wearing black leather pants and high heels, and her scarlet hair and leopard-print scarf trail behind her. It hits me then that Svetlana is the city version of Mabel Thorpe. How had I not made that connection before? Svetlana used to seem so much more elegant to my eyes.

Before I know it, she has me and Michaela wrapped in her arms, squeezing tight and smelling of rose water. Trapped against Svetlana's bony chest, my sister and I exchange looks of mingled horror and amusement. Then Svetlana holds each of us out at arm's length. "Katya, you've become rather pretty," she remarks, not bothering to mask her surprise. "And my prima ballerina?" Svetlana casts her eyes up and down Michaela's figure, and a look of displeasure crosses her face. "Michaela, you naughty girl! You've been indulging in too much farm-fresh cheese up there, no?"

I raise my eyebrows at Svetlana's dig, and Michaela gives her former teacher a tight-lipped smile. "Well, it *is* pretty tasty," she retorts. I do a double take at my sister, hardly recognizing her sarcastic tone. But I'm also a little proud of her.

Svetlana slides her arms around our waists and hurries us out of the bus terminal, clucking about dinner reservations uptown. The night is warm compared to Fir Lake, and I stop to pull off my scarf as Svetlana and Michaela head to the corner to hail a cab. "*Excuse* me!" a woman barks, shoving me out of her way. I knock into my suitcase, and by the time I've turned around to snap at the offender, she's disappeared. I take a deep breath. *Keep up, Katie.* I guess I've fallen a little behind the city's mad-dash pace. Three teenage girls — ropes of dark beads around their throats, trendy leather satchels dangling from their arms — giggle at me as they pass. I know what they're thinking, because I used to be one of those girls.

They think I'm a tourist.

As if to prove them — or myself? — wrong, I hold up my arm and wave toward the oncoming traffic. Like magic, a taxicab slows to a stop in front of me, and I can't help my victorious smile. My city savvy hasn't left me.

Svetlana is all gossip and chatter on the ride uptown, telling us that Claude shaved his goatee, Sofia Pappas "lost a ton, really a ton" of weight, and our *Nutcracker* seats are the "best in the house." Michaela and I can't get a word in edgewise, and I'm sort of glad, because I'm too busy soaking in the city. The flashing lights of all-night diners, even the numbered street signs, make me giddy. The cab dislodges us on Amsterdam and 80TH Street, in front of Svetlana's apartment building. At Svetlana's suggestion, Michaela and I leave our bags with Svetlana's white-gloved doorman so we can head to the restaurant unburdened. As soon as the three of us are back out on the sidewalk, Svetlana lights a cigarette.

"Do you have another one?" Michaela asks in her soft voice. I enjoy watching the stunned expression that slips over Svetlana's face.

"What's this, my Michaela?" she demands as we cross Amsterdam against the light, narrowly missing being hit by a fleet of cabs. Svetlana blows out a circle of smoke for emphasis. "A dancer like you should not be ruining her beautiful lungs with this junk."

I'm walking between the two of them, so I get to see the *oh, please* look Michaela shoots her former teacher. "And you, Svetlana? You're a dancer as well."

This is kind of awesome. I agree with Svetlana, but I also wish Michaela would have talked back to

Svetlana like this when we were students at Anna Pavlova. That might've given ballet school a little extra kick.

"I'm *old*, my darling." Svetlana pauses outside a chic-looking restaurant called Bistro Japonaise and puts out her cigarette on the heel of her shoe. "And I'm not about to audition for Juilliard. Now, come — I have a surprise for you girls." She opens the door to the restaurant.

Bistro Japonaise is so dimly lit I can barely make out the wispy-thin hostess in her black micromini dress and spike-heeled boots. The lanterns hanging from the ceiling provide the only light, and the music blaring over the speakers is obnoxious French techno. As we weave past a table full of skinny women sipping hot-pink drinks from martini glasses, I notice the wall behind them. On it is a floor-to-ceiling, black-and-white photograph of a Buddha. I think of Emmaline's house, and something like longing washes over me.

"Surprise!" Svetlana cries, and I blink when I realize we've arrived at our table.

At which Trini, Sofia, Hanae, Renée, and Jennifer are seated, all of them grinning madly.

"I don't believe it," Michaela says flatly.

"Oh, my God! What are you guys wearing?" Trini manages to shriek and laugh at the same time as she bounds up out of her seat. *She's* wearing a yellow satin skirt, a cropped black sweater layered over a long black tank, and leggings with glittery gold flats. The other girls, who are also jumping up to embrace us, are in a variety of skirts, dresses, and heels. Meanwhile, Michaela and I are dressed for a road trip — jeans, boots, sweaters.

Or maybe we're just dressed for Fir Lake.

I want to ask Svetlana if we can pop into her apartment and change, but Trini is already running toward me with her arms outstretched. I prepare to bear-hug my friend, and then I remember how Trini hugs; she presses her cheek to mine for a millisecond and jerks away. Before I can feel disappointed, I'm being greeted by each girl in turn. Svetlana was right — Sofia *has* lost a lot of weight, so her body feels hard when we hug, just like Jennifer's does. Hanae, prettier than ever, kisses my cheek, and when I tell her how grown-up she looks, she blushes and says, "Well, I'm dancing on pointe now. Claude moved me to the Advanced Class."

"Of course he did," I say, expecting to feel a pang of jealousy, but none comes.

Then Renée whispers, "And Hanae hasn't stopped mentioning it yet."

"The Wilder girls are back in NYC!" Sofia crows once we've all sat down, lifting her glass of water to toast us. "It's been way too long." I see her gaze linger on Michaela, and I remember how their last Gmail Chats were back in September.

"Here, here!" Svetlana chimes in, knocking her knife against her glass. I feel my mouth smiling, but all I want to do right now is curl up under a comforter, not laugh and joke in a noisy restaurant. It must be the long trip. I'm sure I'll regain my energy tomorrow.

Renée scoops out a salted edamame pod from a bowl in the center of the table. "Why do you guys look like two deer in the headlights?" she asks, chuckling.

We do? Michaela and I glance at each other, and I realize I must be wearing the same dazed expression as she is.

"That's what happens when you *live* with deer!" Trini cries, around a mouthful of edamame. I wish I hadn't told her about Bambi in our backyard.

"The bus ride down was rough," Michaela explains, sounding a tad ticked off.

I set my jaw. *Yeah, it was, sis.*

"Appetizers!" the waitress announces, appearing with a tray. As she sets down plates of dragon rolls, I remember what Autumn said when I mentioned liking sushi: "Does everyone in New York City have an obsession with uncooked fish?"

I smile at the memory, then shake my head as I reach for a spicy tuna roll. Why am I thinking about Autumn — who isn't even technically my friend anymore — when I'm here in Manhattan, surrounded by my true friends?

"So, Trini!" I say, attempting to liven myself up. "Are you insanely nervous about tomorrow?"

"Tomorrow?" Trini cocks her head at me, holding up an avocado roll up in her chopsticks. "Oh, *tomorrow*! Right! The *show*!" She laughs heartily, slapping the table. "You know, not really," she says with a wave of one hand. I'm unimpressed by her performance. I know Trini, and I know she's been stressing over the show every second. It's upsetting that she'd try to fake her confidence for *me*.

"Oh, come on, Trini," I snort, rolling my eyes. Hanae and Renée giggle at this, and Sofia says, "Yeah, she's basically been a wreck since September."

"Claude suggested she take Xanax," I hear Svetlana whisper to Michaela.

Trini sets her roll down on her plate. "Why would *I* be nervous?" she asks slowly and pointedly, looking right at me. "*I'm* not studying under some tacky teacher at a hick school."

This comment elicits even bigger laughs from Hanae and Renée, who have their mouths full of sushi. "Now, now, girls," Svetlana chides, pulling a plate of salmon-and-cream-cheese rolls away from them. "Go easy." I'm not certain if she means the eating or the mocking. I swallow down my spicy tuna roll with difficulty.

"Trini told us about your teacher's full-body leotard, Katie!" Jennifer cries, clapping her hands, and her stacked coral bracelets clank together. "We even made up a word for it — *leo-tarded*. Get it?"

Sofia sprays her water from laughing so hard.

I cringe. I wish I hadn't been so descriptive in my

IMs to Trini. I don't know why, but all I want to do now is defend Mabel Thorpe. To defend Fir Lake.

"If you guys did a little research, you'd know Fir Lake is actually not a hick town at all," Michaela speaks up, and a hush settles over the table. The former queen of Anna Pavlova Academy is addressing us. "It's full of professors and interesting people and they have these great indie shops —"

"Micha*ela*!" Sofia brays. "Katie *told* us that people keep scarecrows on their lawns." She joins Svetlana and the other girls in their laughter, effectively shutting Michaela up. I study Sofia — her plum-red lips and her elongated neck — and I think, *Maybe there's a new queen now.*

"You know," I begin, "the dance school in Fir Lake might not be outstanding, but they have an awesome yoga teacher in town." I take a big gulp of water, then announce, "I'm kind of . . . taking yoga now."

Stunned silence.

"You *are*?" Svetlana and Michaela ask at the same time, gawking at me. I realize I hadn't ever told my sister about yoga. Svetlana signals to the waitress and asks for a lychee martini.

"Wow!" Jennifer sighs, cupping her chin in her hands. "Katie doing yoga. What *else* happened in the time you've been gone? Tell us *everything!*"

Everything? I think of Anders, of Homecoming, of all that's passed between me and my sister.

Fortunately, the waitress comes back then to take our orders. Michaela and I both order the salmon teriyaki with sticky rice, and I ask for a large Coke. Everyone else orders miso soups.

Trini waits until the waitress has left and then she says, in a fake Southern accent, "Gee, I guess all that country living really works up an appetite!"

"OMG, I was *just* going to say that!" Sofia shrieks, tossing the wrapper of her chopsticks across the table at Trini.

"Um, we didn't move to Tennessee, Trini," Michaela mutters. Svetlana says nothing, only sips from her martini and shoots Michaela an unabashed *I-told-you-so* look.

My blood is boiling. Were my friends always this judgmental, this competitive?

I turn away from the table, my chest tight, and look at the Buddha photograph again. I may not have many friends in Fir Lake, but I do have Emmaline, who'll always listen and never criticize. And Autumn would never, ever regard me with the scorn Trini has in her eyes now.

Autumn. I feel my throat constrict and realize that I want her to be here. Sure, she'd be wearing her overalls, and gazing around in bewilderment, and mixing up all the names of the foods when she ordered. But I wouldn't care. I would be so, so glad to have her beside me.

As the conversation at the table picks up again — Sofia starts talking about how bloody her toes were that morning, and Svetlana laughs approvingly — I tune out and play with the folds in the tablecloth. Out of the corner of my eye, I see Michaela tracing her finger along her chopsticks. I wonder if she's miles away — thinking about Anders, or Heather, or her room in The Monstrosity. But when my sister glances up and gives me a small, sad smile that's a distant cousin of her smile on the bus, I know we're actually thinking the same thing:

Being home doesn't feel quite so good anymore.

19

Lincoln Center is never so magical as it is on the opening night of *The Nutcracker*. The great fountain is dancing, and the red Chagall mural that peeks through the windows of the Metropolitan Opera House glows. Men in black coats cross the plaza alongside women in cashmere wraps, everyone jabbering in anticipation. And then there are the hordes of hyper little girls, decked out in faux-mink chubbies, dresses with lace collars, and shiny Mary Janes. One or two even have ribbons in their hair, and they all have the most enormous, glowing, hopeful eyes this side of the Hudson. This is *their* night; their night to dream, to fantasize that *they* might one day be up on that stage, pretty as Marie.

As I head toward the New York State Theater, I see a ten-year-old with brown bottle curls performing a clumsy tour jeté for her mother, who applauds.

I glance away, sticking my gloved hands into my coat pockets. I was so that girl once upon a time that I can't even look.

This is the beauty and culture I've been craving — *this is where I belong* — but somehow I can't work up the excitement I know I should be feeling. Maybe it's because I'm arriving at the show alone. Michaela and Svetlana went straight to a one-on-one dinner after Michaela's private lesson, so I spent my afternoon visiting the old neighborhood. I wandered the streets of the East Village, stopping by familiar landmarks, but in the short span of three months, a few of the bars, restaurants, and bodegas had been vacated or replaced with new ones. I couldn't even find Cousin Hairy, our corner homeless man.

As dusk was falling, I bought a slice of pizza on Avenue A, and ate it on our old stoop. Halfway through my dinner, the door to our building opened and out came a trendy-looking young couple pushing a baby in a Bugaboo stroller. I had to stand up to make room for them, and suddenly, I *knew* that the family was living in our old apartment. I could picture the baby crawling across the floor I'd once crawled on, and the wife turning my and Michaela's bedroom into an art studio. I wondered what they had done with the streak of hot-pink paint in the living room. I stopped myself just short of asking, and let them pass into the coming night.

I hand my ticket to the usher, who, in return,

hands me a glossy program. GEORGE BALANCHINE'S THE NUTCRACKER is splashed across its front, but my heart doesn't leap with wonder the way it used to at those words. I try to shake myself out of my funk as I open the program, and I do get a funny jolt when I see Trini's name listed under "Snowflakes." It's odd to think that I could have been listed there, too, had Fir Lake not come calling.

I make my way to the third row from the stage, where I find Michaela and Svetlana. My seat is on the aisle, next to Michaela. The two of us shared Svetlana's guest room last night, our twin beds a few feet apart, like old times. And for one second, as horns honked on Amsterdam fifteen stories below us, I felt as if we were both going to break down and apologize. But then Michaela buried her face in her leopard-print pillow and slept. In the morning we addressed each other in grunts ("Shower first?" "No, you"), which I considered decent progress.

"Hi," I say coolly as I take my seat, and then I notice that Svetlana looks as if she's been crying. Her eyes are watery and her normally fire-engine lips are pale. Meanwhile, Michaela's cheeks are very pink, and she's absorbed in her program. They are obviously ignoring each other.

I'm stumped. This morning, Svetlana and Michaela couldn't have seemed chummier as the three of us sat on Svetlana's wraparound sofa and sipped chai.

Svetlana, her hair in curlers and an anti-aging mask on her cheeks, gushed about how much she loved our mother, and Michaela said that Irina Wilder was a tough woman to please, which made Svetlana laugh. What could have changed in a matter of hours?

I'm on the verge of elbowing Michaela and asking her, when the house lights dim and the masses scurry toward their seats. I take off my coat, and settle back in my seat. Maybe it's a sign that the lights went down when they did, before I could press Michaela for this latest secret. I tell myself that I don't need to know everything. That even if I never find out what transpired between Michaela and Svetlana today, I'll live.

I almost believe it.

And when the orchestra begins playing, and the curtain goes up on that lavish Christmas party scene, I forget about everything. I'm swept up in the sparkle of the costumes and the gilded gift boxes. All the dancers are oozing professionalism, their movements exacting, precise. Marie, sporting a big white bow on her head, is danced by a gorgeous little girl with a cat-like way of moving across the stage. I remember when Michaela danced that role at age ten, and the people sitting behind me and my parents said, "That girl is *something else*," and I turned around and told them, "That's my *sister*."

Now, I glance at my sister beside me, and she's watching the stage with a fond, distant expression on her face. She must feel me studying her, because she turns her head, and parts her lips as if about to say something to me over the soaring music.

"What?" I mouth. But, as she's been known to do lately, my sister lets me down and turns back to the stage. I sigh and follow suit.

By now, I know the story of *The Nutcracker* by heart, but I sink into it anyway — Marie receiving the gift of the nutcracker doll from spooky Herr Drosselmeier, Marie dancing with Drosselmeier's cute nephew, then falling asleep as her dolls come to life around her. When I was younger, I was convinced that everything that happened in the ballet was real, but now I can see so clearly that it's all an elaborate dream. I'm no longer frightened by the grotesque Mouse King with his seven heads. A few years ago, every mouse I saw on the subway tracks was a relative of the king, every doll on my and Michaela's shelves had the ability to become human.

I can't deny that some of the power of the ballet has been drained away. And maybe it's this new clarity that keeps me mellow when Trini makes her appearance on stage. I easily spot her among the white, glittering snowflakes — her spindly arms holding up the fake white branches and her novice feet moving quickly to keep up with the other girls on pointe. She looks pretty, and perfect, and utterly terrified, and I'm wearing a big, stupid grin as I watch her. I can't believe it, but I am truly, completely happy for Trini right now. I search my soul for the smallest hint of jealousy, but I find none. *I don't want to be up there*, I realize. I'm glad to be in my seat, my toes intact, and my nerves calm. And I'm excited to be returning to Emmaline to practice my Scorpion pose. I might be crazy to feel this way, but who cares? I'm not going to fight it.

The dance of the snowflakes closes Act One, and I'm still smiling as the lights go up for intermission. Immediately, Svetlana is grabbing her gold clutch and squeezing past my and Michaela's legs, saying, "Excuse me, girls, but I have to run to the powder room." Only Svetlana would say "powder room." I'm relieved to see she's looking less teary.

Michaela and I remain seated in silence, and I drum my fingers on the seat rest between us. *That was nice, if a little cheesy, right?* I imagine myself saying. Or possibly, *Did you see how well Trini hit her jumps?* I keep drumming, and I hear Michaela take a deep breath. *Do you think the two of us should maybe start talking again?* is another option.

Then I look at my sister, and my stomach collapses. Tears are hovering on her lashes, her lower lip is trembling, and she's gripping the program tight in her fists.

"Michaela!" I reach for her hand. A crying emergency trumps our argument any day. I don't ask any questions, though. I just wait.

And Michaela speaks. She turns her face to mine, and she whispers, "I have to tell you something."

You think?

I nod at her. Michaela dabs at her eyes, her hand shaking. "God, I'm sorry," she murmurs. "Just — watching this — I'm really emotional right now."

My feet are going numb. I'm convinced my sister is about to reveal that she's pregnant. Or dying. Or maybe that I'm adopted, and see, that's why she was acting weird to me this year. Or —

"I don't want to be a dancer," Michaela says.

Or anything but that.

We're both so quiet that I can hear the orchestra moving about in the pit.

"Like —" I gesture to the stage, my tongue failing me. "You mean — not at all —"

"I'm not going to Juilliard next year," Michaela continues, wiping her tears with one finger as they fall. "I'm not even auditioning." Her face is so full of raw emotion that I know she's been bursting to say this all through the first act.

"Why — why not?" I ask. I glance over my shoulder, worried someone is going to overhear Michaela's outrageous confession. I am vaguely aware of the opulent theater around us, of the soft velvet seats we're sitting in. I can't grasp that my sister is telling me these things in Lincoln Center, this land of a ballerina's deepest wishes.

"Because I can't be a doll anymore," Michaela replies. Another person might not understand her, but I do. Ballet dancers *are* like dolls — dress them up, wind them up, watch them go.

"But —" I'm only functioning in one-syllable land. *But if not dance, then what?* I intend to ask. *What about all those years of practice, and your crazy dedication, and Svetlana, and Mom?* This is so different than finding out that Michaela and Anders had sex. Then, my perspective changed. Now, my world has been turned inside out.

"I want to go to college," Michaela tells me, and her voice is firm despite her tears. "Real college. I've been meeting with the college counselor at school, downloading applications. I want to live on a campus. I want to study literature and philosophy and history. I want —" She pauses to sob.

I want.

I realize, as I study my sister's tearstained face, that I've never really heard her speak those words. She's forever been duty-bound Michaela, binding up her hair with her serious face on, and binding her feet into toe shoes. I guess I never knew *what* Michaela wanted.

Other than, maybe, a boyfriend. Friends who aren't dancers. Homecoming. An ordinary seventeen-year-old's life.

Suddenly, I feel my heart expand with understanding.

"How long have you felt this way?" I whisper, and I notice that our hands have locked together. My sister's fingers entwine with mine.

"A long time," she says.

"Before Fir Lake?"

"Before Fir Lake." Michaela nods. "I know I kept it hidden pretty well, but I was kind of losing it. I was dancing in school — at LaGuardia — most of the day, and then it was on to Anna Pavlova in the afternoon, and we didn't even get the summers off."

"I thought you loved it," I say, bewildered. I'm rethinking every moment of our life in the city, of our years at Anna Pavlova. I thought I loved it, too, but maybe that was only because I believed Michaela did. When you're the younger sibling, there are not too many chances for *I want*, either.

"I used to," Michaela replies after a minute, releasing my hand to wipe her tears with the back of her arm. "I used to love it so much. Until high school. Then it became all about pressure, all about how much better I could be. There was no more pleasure, no more beauty." She is speaking quickly now, her words rushing together. "It was all about answering to Mom and Svetlana, and being the girl they wanted me to be."

My throat burns with sudden tears. Of course. How could I have been so blind? All I ever wanted was for Mom to treat me as she did Michaela. Now

I see that maybe my mother was doing me a favor by giving me a break.

"Fir Lake was the first time I could ever feel *normal*," Michaela adds, and then three bells sound, signaling the end of intermission. People begin to drift to their seats. Svetlana will be back soon.

"So you told Svetlana today," I say, imagining what their lesson and their dinner must have been like. Ouch. "And she took it badly."

Michaela lets out a small laugh. "Picture a disaster, okay? Then multiply that by a hundred."

I laugh, too. It feels so good to laugh with my sister again.

"I wish you had told me," I say. Not because I'm hurt this time. But because together, the two of us could have come with a plan, with the best way for Michaela to approach Svetlana.

Suddenly, Michaela squeezes my hand and meets my gaze. "I wanted to tell you first, Katie. Before Mom and Svetlana or anyone. I haven't told Mom yet, obviously. I figured being grounded wasn't the best time to try. I'm going to need your help with that when we get back."

"No kidding," I giggle, sniffling, and Michaela cracks up, too.

"I was going to tell you before we left for the city," Michaela adds, "but then we got into that fight —"

"I feel awful about that," I murmur, tears now trickling out of my eyes. "I should never have invaded your privacy —"

"I know," Michaela whispers, and leans her forehead against mine. "But I should never have kept so much from you. Believe me when I say that nothing feels real until I tell it to you, Katie. Nothing."

Okay, this is bad. The Wilder sisters are now sobbing in the middle of Lincoln Center, and the lights are going down, and Svetlana is appearing at my elbow. At the same time, I can't remember ever feeling so at peace. Michaela and I hug quickly, a silent promise that we'll talk more later, and then we lift up our legs to let Svetlana pass. Svetlana's face is newly made up, and she still looks slightly wounded, but I know she'll get over Michaela's betrayal. She'll have a whole new generation of dancers to shape and torment. No one will ever be another Michaela Wilder, but there are plenty of girls willing to kill their toes to try.

Act Two passes in a haze — the Land of the Sweets is a beautiful blur, the Sugar Plum Fairy's pitch-perfect pas de deux barely registers. It's only at the very end, when Marie and her prince sail off in their flying sled pulled by reindeer, that I feel the tug in my gut that only *The Nutcracker* can give me. I wipe the last of the tears from my cheeks. Maybe the story is not a dream after all. I don't know. I guess I don't have to decide quite yet.

When the snowflakes come onstage to take their bows, I clap so hard for Trini that my palms burn. Michaela puts her fingers in her mouth to whistle, and Svetlana *tsks–tsks* her.

Still, Svetlana's eyes are bright as she stands up, taking several wrapped bouquets from the shopping bag at her feet. "I must find my students backstage," she tells me and Michaela. "I will meet you girls outside, yes? We'll take a cab back to my apartment." She's not really meeting Michaela's gaze as she speaks, and I hope our last night in the city with her won't be too strained.

But I'm glad to have a moment alone with Michaela as we leave the theater, our arms linked. The plaza is quieter now, people casually milling about in the cold, their programs tucked in their coat pockets.

"I'm going to miss this," Michaela sighs, and I know she doesn't just mean Lincoln Center. "Ballet," she explains unnecessarily, motioning to the theater from which we emerged. "This whole . . . *world.* I never stopped loving dance."

"I know." We come to a stop in front of the fountain, and the two of us watch the water jump and tumble. "But you can keep dancing, Michaela. Even in college. For fun."

"Fun," Michaela echoes. "You're right, Katie. I stopped thinking of dance that way. I wanted different kinds of fun."

I'm silent, listening to the gush of the fountain as I think about my sister at the Homecoming Gala, laughing and dancing with her friends.

"When Mom and Dad told me we were moving to Fir Lake," Michaela goes on, looking at me. "I felt like the luckiest person alive. I had this year, this one incredible year, to change everything."

"That was one way of looking at it," I say, amazed once again at the differences between my sister and me. I didn't want a single thing to change. But I suppose stopping change is like trying to stop the leaves from falling every autumn.

"I knew how you felt about the move," Michaela says, giving me a gentle nudge. "I probably should have been more patient with you."

"I was jealous," I blurt, studying my wedge-heeled boots. "Jealous of all your new friends, of you winning Homecoming Queen, of all the good things that kept happening to you. You've always been lucky, Michaela. You *are* the luckiest person alive." But even as I say this, I'm thinking of my sister keeping her desire to break away from ballet locked inside for so long. She couldn't have felt too lucky then.

Michaela starts laughing, softly at first, then harder, until she has to lean against me, and I start to laugh, too. "And *you've* always been superstitious, you dork — believing in omens and all that." Michaela lets out her big-sister sigh, and I'm happy to hear it again. "There's no such thing as luck," Michaela adds practically. "You make your own destiny. I was determined, when I started school in Fir Lake, to find new friends. I wanted to know what it was like to have a boyfriend, I wanted to know what it was like to go to the movies and the pizzeria on a weeknight, not go straight home from dance school."

"You're nothing if not determined," I murmur, remembering the look of concentration Michaela wore when pirouetting across Svetlana's studio. "But it doesn't *work* like that," I add. "Not for most people. All those girls loved you from day one, because you're cute and —"

"Katie, you started Fir Lake High School determined to hate everyone," Michaela says flatly, and I have no defense for that. "You write people off so quickly. The thing is, all the kids in school thought we were *cool* because we were the new girls. Couldn't you tell? They all grew up in each other's backyards. Everybody was set in their roles. But then we came along, and we were different! People actually *wanted* to be our friends."

I swallow hard, thinking of Autumn, and how I'd written her off at first. What if I'd *never* given her a chance? Maybe Michaela's right, and luck has nothing to do with it. Maybe it's all about opening up.

"Let's not argue anymore," Michaela says as we

make our way down the steps of the plaza to the street. "It's our last night in Manhattan, and we should enjoy it."

The tall buildings are lit up, the traffic is roaring, and the city is bopping and booming like jazz. *My home*, I think. I remember how Michaela and I stood in front of Lincoln Center in August, saying our good-byes to the city. Back then, I never considered that there was any other place, any other way, to live. I tilt my head back, looking up at the sky. It's hard *not* to hope for stars, though there are none I can see. But there'll be plenty tomorrow, hanging over our house in Fir Lake.

"We're *both* lucky," I announce, and glance at Michaela. "We have the city, and we have the country. We have it even better than those mice in our book."

Michaela smiles at me, so big that her eyes crinkle up. "Yeah? You're not going to be too city-sick when we pull into the Fir Lake bus station tomorrow?"

I shake my head, feeling a burst of resolve. "No way. I won't have time. There's too much I have to do when we get back home."

20

"I brought you a souvenir," I tell Autumn when I find her milking cows on Sunday. I hover in the door frame of Mountain Creek Farm's small shed, watching as my friend turns around on her stool. She is wearing her tan hat with the long earflaps, a down jacket, and a deeply suspicious expression.

"What is it?" she asks as if the two of us are having a normal conversation — as if we haven't been ignoring each other for the past several weeks. She nods toward the brown paper bag I'm holding in my arms.

"Nothing that should be opened in here," I reply, taking in the alien scene. Autumn is positioned at the flank of a large brown cow, and a pail sits beneath the cow's udders. There are four other cows behind a gate, making loud lowing noises. Sawdust covers the floor, the scents of animal sweat and manure hang thick in the air, and I can hear chickens squawking.

It's the first time I've ever been on a farm, but I refuse to show Autumn that I'm even mildly grossed out.

I'm sure she can tell though, from the way her mouth twists into a smirk. "How did you find me?" she inquires, her tone aloof.

"Well . . . you know me, I'm always sticking my nose into other people's business," I say, taking a gamble and offering Autumn a smile.

As soon as I got up this morning, I headed to Autumn's house. Mr. Hawthorne, who answered the door, told me that Autumn was working at the farm and gave me directions. I wanted to ask him where Jasper was, but I held my tongue. Then I made the short walk to the farm, climbing over giant snowdrifts (I don't care if people say the boots are played-out — I have sworn my eternal fidelity to Uggs).

To my relief, Autumn smiles back — a quick, sheepish smile that softens her face into prettiness. "Hey, I missed you," she says offhandedly.

My heart jumps with hope. "Same here," I say, and we both allow our smiles to widen. Buoyed by this exchange, I take a few steps into the shed. "So who's this?" I ask, pointing to the cow Autumn is milking.

Autumn gives the cow's side a hearty pat. "This is Edith Wharton," she says. "Edith, Katie. Katie, Edith."

Edith moos.

"Wait," I say. "Isn't Edith Wharton someone famous?"

Autumn nods, resuming her work. I watch in mingled awe and disgust as she expertly tugs the cow's udders with her hands. The milk splashes straight into the pail. I'm mesmerized. "She was an author who wrote about New York City in the 1900s," Autumn explains. "I'd think *you'd* know about her, New York City Girl." There's a barb to her voice when she says this, and I know the two of us aren't one hundred percent yet.

I laugh, gingerly moving closer. "I'm not half as well read as you are, Autumn," I say truthfully. Then I pause and study the bell that hangs from Edith's neck. It reads BESSIE. "Edith's not her real name, is it?" I ask.

Autumn shakes her head. "No, that's just my name for her. And those are Virginia Woolf, Jane Austen, Charlotte Brontë, and J. K. Rowling." The four other cows in the shed moo back in return. She flashes a grin up at me. "I have to keep myself entertained *somehow*."

"I'm sorry," I say in response, biting my lip. "I'm sorry I said you didn't know anything, when we were up on Mount Elephant," I go on, looking at the sawdust on the floor. "That was ridiculous because —" I pause and flick my eyes toward Autumn, who's still milking Edith, but obviously listening. "You're basically the smartest person I've ever known."

Autumn pushes a strand of hair off her face with one hand, her cheeks red. "That's not true," she argues. "You're smart in ways I can never be, Katie. Could you imagine me navigating the New York subway system?"

"Why not?" I giggle, and I feel a tickle of excitement at the idea of bringing Autumn back to New York with me sometime.

"Look, I'm sorry, too," Autumn says, jerking her head toward a stool a few feet away to indicate I should drag it over. I do, and sit down beside her, careful not to get too near to Edith. The cow moos and stamps her feet, as if she senses a novice is around. "I probably deserved whatever you said to me," Autumn continues, glancing from Edith to me. "I was totally out of line, yelling at you like that."

"But you weren't," I say quietly, hugging my brown paper bag to my chest. "I needed someone to tell me that what I did was wrong. That's what friends — best friends — do for each other." I know now what Michaela meant when she said friends and sisters were different. Autumn may not be my Michaela, but that's okay. She's not supposed to be.

I hear Autumn swallow. "Are you going to come back to Mabel Thorpe's class?" she asks after a minute.

"I don't know," I reply honestly. "I want to see if I can take more yoga classes instead. I should probably sit down with my mom and tell her so." *That'll* be fun. "Are you going to come back to Emmaline's class?"

Autumn tilts her head to one side. "I don't think so. I want to try and really give this dance thing a shot, you know?"

I smile. "You should. You love it enough." Then, looking down at Edith's hooves, I add, "But we're going to sit together at lunch again, right?"

"God, I hope so!" Autumn exhales. We laugh together, and I feel how okay things are going to be between the two of us.

"I'm not distracting you, am I?" I ask Autumn as she focuses on Edith once more. Yesterday I was hailing cabs. Today, I'm inches away from a cow. Edith sneaks a peek at me out of the corner of one eye, then swishes her tail.

"Well, I'm almost done," Autumn replies, gesturing to the full pail of steaming, foamy milk. "But it's nice having you here. Maybe next weekend I'll even give you a quick lesson."

I imagine the squishy feel of Edith's udders in my hands. "Why don't we start with my just watching?" I ask with a small laugh. "Baby steps."

After Autumn finishes up with the farmer in his office, she and I walk toward Casa Hawthorne. The snow crackles beneath our feet, and I think of the hard pavement of Manhattan, on which I walked twenty-four hours ago. But I don't feel the usual pang of sadness. I know the city is still there, where I left it.

As we pass Millie's Maple Shack, which is surrounded by a tent of plastic to keep out the cold, Autumn asks about Michaela. I say the two of us are doing better and fill her in on the no-more-Juilliard news. Since we're on the subject of siblings, I nonchalantly ask

Autumn if Jasper's at home and she says she thinks he's sledding with some girl. *His girlfriend*, I think, pushing down a seed of jealousy. Whatever. Jasper's just a friend anyway. A buddy. It was foolish of me to ever see him as anything more.

When Autumn and I tumble into her kitchen, we scrub our hands with hot water and sit at the table. I ceremoniously open the brown paper bag. "Prepare yourself for a treat," I announce as I remove toasty-brown H & H bagels, slabs of lox wrapped in white waxed paper, and a tub of cream cheese. "I present to you the perfect New York City brunch," I say, fanning my hands open as Autumn's jaw goes slack. "Courtesy of Zabar's and other fine food shops on the Upper West Side."

"Katie!" Autumn exclaims. She eyes the lox warily. "I don't know. . . ."

"Okay, okay, no pressure," I say, moving the lox away. "But try the bagels —"

"Hold on." Autumn pulls the waxed paper back from me. "You hiked most of Mount Elephant. You watched me milk a cow. I can taste some lox."

Which she does — on a bagel spread with cream cheese — scrunching up her face in fear at first. Then Autumn chews, swallows, and smiles.

"So?" I ask, leaning across the table.

"That was . . ." Autumn wipes a spot of cream cheese off her lips. "Pretty damn good."

I beam.

"You know . . . you're right," I say, slicing a bagel in two.

"Well, yeah," Autumn says, taking a huge bite. "But you always liked this stuff, didn't you?"

"No, not about the lox. I *did* hike Mount Elephant. I even peed in the woods! I'm not . . . such a princess after all, am I?"

I've given a lot of thought to what Jasper said to me on the mountain that day. Maybe I don't need to be one or the other — Country Katie or City Katie. Maybe there's a way to blend my two selves — Katie, who milks cows in the morning, and then has lox and bagels for brunch.

"Who said you were a princess?" Jasper asks then, ambling into the kitchen.

My heart seems to contract, then stop, then start ticking again very rapidly.

Jasper, with his auburn hair and the glint of mischief that is forever in his sea-glass eyes. He's not wearing his glasses, and I think he looks handsomer than I've ever seen him, even though he's in a wrinkled black T-shirt and jeans that are barely staying on his skinny hips. Compared to Anders Swensen or Sullivan Turner, Jasper Hawthorne is downright quirky-looking. But I don't mind.

"Come on, Jasper," I say, having trouble looking directly at him. "You know who said it." *Well put! Excellent work, Katie!* I want to choke on my lox and die.

"Ugh, *Jasper*," Autumn groans, her mouth full. "Can you *always* tell when there's food within a two-mile radius?"

"One of my many talents," Jasper says, coming over the table and reviewing our spread. "Did Katya bring us these goodies from the isle of Manhattan?"

"It's *Katie*, you moron," Autumn snaps, but in that instant I realize I like the way Jasper speaks my real name. I'm not sure why, but something about the syllables in his voice makes me go fluttery inside. I blush deeply at the thought.

"Besides," Autumn adds huffily, walking to the fridge to take out a container of orange juice. "Katie didn't bring them for *us*. They're for me. And her. So scram, Jasper. Didn't Belinda Watts invite you to go sledding with her today?"

I KNEW it! I don't know who Belinda Watts is, but I'll have to promptly begin stalking her on Monday morning.

"Eh, Belinda's boring," Jasper says. "What's the fun of being outdoors with a girl who can identify every animal track and every path? It's much better to have someone, oh, I don't know . . . a little *princess-y* accompany you, don't you think?"

Now my blush is so fierce that I feel like my curls are going to catch fire.

Autumn looks from me to Jasper, and I see something complicated cross her face — understanding mixed with envy mixed with happiness — and then pass. I wonder what she's thinking. I wonder what she knows.

"Jasper, stop torturing Katie," Autumn finally says, slamming the fridge door shut.

"All right, all right." Jasper holds up his hands, and then backs out the kitchen. "But leave some food for me, okay?"

Ralph Waldo bounds into the kitchen then, his tail wagging, and I shrink away until Autumn ushers him out. Cows I can sort of handle, but Ralph Waldo will still take some getting used to. As Autumn and I finish eating, we don't bring up her brother, and I don't address the fact that Jasper has started my heart thrumming beneath my woolen sweater. Afterward, Autumn has to go shower off her farm gook, and we both have a ton of homework to do before tomorrow, so she walks me to the door, and we hug tight.

"Can I ask you something?" Autumn says, as she opens the door for me. "Why did you call me Flannel when we were on Mount Elephant?"

"Oh," I say lightly, waving one hand in the air. "It's silly. I'll tell you another time." No need to rock the boat of our friendship now.

I'm halfway down the Hawthorne's path, passing their weather-beaten scarecrow, when I hear the front door open again. I turn, worried that Autumn's going to demand I tell her all about this Flannel business.

But it's Jasper.

"Wait up," he says, jogging toward me in just his hoodie.

"Aren't you freezing?" I ask, even though my own temperature is rising.

"I didn't mean to hurt your feelings that day," Jasper says, coming to stand right before me. We look at each other, both us hidden momentarily inside a world made of snow-heavy trees.

"You didn't," I lie, but I'm positive that Jasper can see through me.

"I guess I was —" Jasper pauses and looks at his boots. Is he *blushing*? "I guess I was kind of nervous," he finishes in a rush, glancing back up at me.

"Why were you nervous?" I ask, my breath short.

Jasper shrugs, then gives me that half smile. "But we're cool now, Katya?" he asks.

"We're cool." I grin at him.

Jasper nods and sticks his hands into the back pockets of his jeans. "Maybe . . . you know, sometime you, me, and Autumn could go ice-skating. Fir Lake's all frozen over now."

"Maybe," I manage to reply. Skating's the one winter sport I can actually do. Michaela and I used to go to the rink in Rockefeller Center every year.

"Maybe," Jasper repeats. He holds my gaze for a long beat, and the crisp air between us suddenly feels full of electricity. I don't know if Jasper feels it, too, but I'm certainly not going to ask him.

What might it feel like to kiss Jasper? I wonder, all of me buzzing at the thought. *Nice*, I think, answering my own question. *It might feel nice.*

Jasper lifts his hand in a wave, then jogs back into the house. I can feel myself glowing as I turn and start toward home. Possibility flutters in my belly. Will there be that strange crackle between us when Jasper and I see each other again? When we go ice-skating, perhaps? Or maybe we'll go to Hemming's Goods for Lime Rickeys sometime.

My head is in the clouds the whole walk back, and I don't even notice that I'm on Honeycomb Drive until I hear Emmaline shout my name.

"Welcome back to town!" she calls, waving to me from her porch.

I'm overflowing with such goodwill that I run up and throw my arms around her. She chuckles, returning my embrace. She's wearing a long, flowy gray cotton dress under her jacket, and fuzzy slippers on her feet. "I was taking out the trash," she explains, gesturing over to the bear boxes. "But come on inside the house. I have something for you."

A gift? I'm speaking to both Michaela and Autumn again, and I may be going ice-skating with Jasper Hawthorne. What else could I need?

"Did you do any new poses in yoga class on Thursday?" I ask Emmaline as I follow her into the den, which is jam-packed with boxes and bags.

• 357 •

"Actually, I canceled class and flew out to San Francisco to visit old friends," Emmaline says, digging through a plastic bag in the corner. "There was something I needed to do. And look what I picked up there!" When Emmaline turns around, she's holding a miniature gold Buddha in her hand. "An up-and-coming yogi should have one of these."

A yogi, I think, feeling a flush of satisfaction as I thank Emmaline for the Buddha and close my palm over it. *Yogi* sounds much more mature than *ballerina*.

"Plus," Emmaline adds. "This way, you'll have luck with you wherever you go."

Emmaline and I settle in her living room, and I catch her up on our trip to the city, and how beautiful *The Nutcracker* was, though I don't divulge Michaela's secrets — any of them. Emmaline asks me about my Homecoming date, and I say it was a bust, but that there *might* be a new boy on the horizon. "I don't want to jinx it, though," I say, unconsciously rubbing mini-Buddha's belly.

"Well, you don't have to tell me anything until it's more developed," Emmaline says pragmatically, tucking her knees up under her chin.

Then I remember that it's really *Emmaline's* love life we should be discussing. This is my chance. I take a deep breath. "Emmaline?" I say, clutching my Buddha as I face her. "You know Coach Shreve? Who comes to yoga class sometimes?"

Emmaline looks at me blankly.

"I mean Tim!" I correct myself. "Timothy..."

"Oh — oh, yes." Emmaline nods. "What about him? He's your gym teacher, right?" Her face *might* be pinker than usual, but that could just be the rosy light of the living room.

"Well..." I fidget on Emmaline's sofa as she watches me. "I was thinking... I know he's single and he's kind of good-looking, and the two of you are both into exercising and staying healthy... Could it hurt to... maybe slip him your number while you're adjusting his Child's Pose?" I say this breezily, as if I haven't been concocting this plan for weeks now.

"Katie!" Emmaline cries, putting her hands to her cheeks. "Me... and Tim? You've really put some thought into this, haven't you?"

I shake my head, and then nod. "A little. See... I feel like you should be with someone nice... and Coach Shreve is nicer than I thought he was, so..."

Emmaline sighs and wraps a blonde curl around one finger. "Katie, thank you for looking out for me. I appreciate it. I do." She puts her hand on my knee and gives it a shake. "The thing is, you know how I said I went to San Francisco over Thanksgiving? It was... to see a guy."

"Ah." My heart sinks. Autumn was right. I only knew a little piece of Emmaline's story.

"But it's not what you're imagining," Emmaline adds hurriedly. "See, this guy, Mitoki, — we lived in Japan together, and then in San Francisco, and when

I came out here, we tried to make things work, but it was plenty hard."

Oh. The love of her life hadn't died. He was just far away.

"So I finally called Mitoki and said I wanted to end things," Emmaline continues, looking at me steadily, and I can tell that she's relieved to be able to tell this story to someone, even if it's her fourteen-year-old yoga student. "I went to California over Thanksgiving to say good-bye, to wrap everything up, I guess." Emmaline lifts her shoulders. "And being out there with him, I realized I made the right choice. He's changed and I've changed, and I'll always love San Francisco, but Fir Lake is my home now. Until another land calls." She smiles softly.

I'm beyond embarrassed. "God, Emmaline, I'm sorry I invented this whole thing about you and Coach Shreve —"

"It's okay, Katie." Emmaline laughs a little. "I'm just in no real shape to start dating again. But, to be honest . . . I have thought Coach Shreve is cute."

"You have?" I feel my spirits lift. "I think he thinks you're cute, too. I don't know. Sometimes I think I may have a special feeling for these things."

"You might." Emmaline raises one eyebrow at me. "But do me a favor and please don't slip Coach Shreve my number while you're doing layups in gym or something?"

"I won't," I swear, although that's not a half-bad idea.

"Get some sleep, okay?" Emmaline says as I leave, and I wonder if her light won't be on as much now.

My thoughts are dancing around with Emmaline and Coach Shreve and me and Jasper as I walk over to The Monstrosity with my little Buddha. So, of course, the last person I'm expecting to see when I step onto the porch is Anders Swensen. I must have walked right by his car without noticing.

"What are you doing here?" I gasp. Not too polite, I know, but I want to warn Anders to duck and cover — our parents are going to freak when they see a strange boy lurking.

"Oh, hey, Katie," Anders says, flashing me his dimpled smile. The times Anders has given me a ride to school, I always felt like he was ignoring me. But maybe that was because I was so intent on ignoring *him*. Now, his smile actually seems. . . genuine. Maybe Anders has finally figured out that, often, the way to a girl's heart is through her sister.

"I'm here to pick up Michaela," Anders adds, taking off his wool hat as I push open the front door and we walk into the foyer. "We're —"

Both of us stop short at the sight of Mom and Dad in the living room. The fire is crackling in the fireplace, casting soft shadows on the room. Mom is in one chair, reading *Anna Karenina* and drinking chai, and Dad is on the sofa, holding manuscript pages in his lap, an ink stain on his cheek. *They look at home*, I think, and realize that it must have been a hard road for my parents, too, adjusting to rural life. I guess we all needed some time to settle in.

"Well, hello," Mom says in her most imposing college-professor voice, closing her book. She zeroes in on Anders with her own penetrating gaze. "You must be the famous Anders."

Anders comes forward as Mom and Dad rise from their seats to greet him. I can't believe my parents are meeting my sister's boyfriend. Anders jovially shakes Mom's hand, and says to Dad, "Mr. Wilder, it's an honor to meet you."

It is? I doubt Anders has time for reading my dad's novels in between football practices. I'd bet good money Michaela trained him to say that, but in any case, it works; Mom's face lights up as Dad pumps Anders's hand.

"Please, call me Jeffrey," Dad says.

Oh, Lord. What's next? *Call me Dad?*

"Mrs. Wilder will do fine, thanks," Mom adds, giving Anders a scrutinizing look. I know she's not going to let him in that easily. "Where are you and Michaela going this evening?"

"To The Friendly Bean, for s'mores and hot chocolate," Anders says, citing the Most Innocent-Sounding Date in the History of American Romance. The weird thing is, I believe him, too. "I'll drop Michaela back before midnight," he adds, raising his chin.

So no sleepovers tonight, hmm?

"Eleven," Mom says, crossing her arms over her chest. "It's a school night."

"Fine, eleven!" Michaela grunts, galumphing down the stairs in her duck boots, freed from her punishment at last. She's dressed plainly, with her hair in a low ponytail and no makeup. But as Anders gazes up at her, his mouth slightly open and his hooded blue eyes bright, he appears — without a doubt — smitten.

Michaela kisses Mom, Dad, and me good-bye, and Anders leads her out the door, putting an arm across her shoulders.

"Michaela looks happy," Dad says, giving Mom a level look as the three of us stand in the living room together. "And Anders seems very sweet, doesn't he?"

"No seventeen-year-old boys are sweet," Mom says darkly. This sounds like it might be a new favorite expression. Then she glances at me. "Katie, what are you doing hanging around here? If memory serves, you have a good deal of homework to do before tomorrow."

"What did you call me?" I ask, certain I've heard wrong.

Mom pushes her bangs out of her eyes. "Katie. What's the big to-do?"

The blood rushes to my face, and I can feel Dad

watching the two of us. "If you want to keep calling me Katya, that's okay," I say, thinking of Jasper.

"Okay, okay." My mother nods a few times, clearly uncomfortable with this moment of semi-affection. "Now, unless you have anything to add about Michaela and her boyfriend, I suggest you go upstairs."

"Well . . ." I fiddle with the sleeve of my coat. "I think he really cares about her, Mom. I think you can trust him."

Mom makes a *pfft* sound and looks at Dad. "Will you listen to our daughter?"

"She's right, Irina." Dad sits back down with his manuscript. "You should take it easier on people, be a little bit less of a cynic."

I'm not sure I've ever heard my father speak to my mother like that. Is it because Dad finally got unstuck here in Fir Lake, that he's been acting bolder? Last week, The Last Word, our local bookstore, called Dad up to see if he'd like to do a holiday reading of *Moon Over Manhattan*. "It'll be exotic for town folks," the store's owner said. I can tell Dad likes the idea of being a small town semi-celebrity. Suddenly, I'm curious to read his latest book. I wonder if it's about this move, about our strange new life. And how does it end?

As I climb the stairs with the mini-Buddha in my hand, I think about what Dad called Mom: *a cynic*. I've always felt that my father and I were on the same side in our family, and Michaela and Mom on the other. But I, too, have trouble trusting people.

Maybe I'm more similar to my mother than I ever realized — a thought that pleases and disturbs me at the same time.

At a quarter to eleven, I'm finishing up my math homework, when I hear Anders's engine outside. This time, I don't get up to spy on him and Michaela from the window, but continue doing my equations. Still, X seems to equal *Are they kissing?* and Y shouts *YES!*

Antsy, I look up at the ballet photo of Trini, me, and the others that hangs above my desk. It's been reassuring to see it there every night, alongside my New York City subway map. But, maybe because of the recent trip to the city, or even everything that's happened today, I reach up and remove the photo from the wall. I don't tear it up, but simply slip it inside my desk drawer. It could be time for a new decoration, though I'm not sure yet what that will be.

As I close my drawer, I hear the front door open and my sister's footfalls coming up the stairs. "Katie?" She knocks on my door, then sticks her face inside. "I knew you'd be awake."

"When haven't I been?" I put down my pencil. "Was your date fun?"

I know Michaela will understand the weight of this word.

"Lots of fun." My sister gives me an understanding smile. "Listen, if you're done with homework, it's pretty mild outside . . ." She gestures toward my frosted-over window, which is shut tight.

"Is it?" I'm not making the connection between my homework and the great outdoors, but then Michaela big-sister sighs and says, "Stargazing, Katie! Do you want to go stargazing?"

"Stargazing." Our tradition. But the activity has become so fraught. I give Michaela a meaningful look. "You didn't stargaze with Anders tonight?"

"Nah." My sister points and flexes her booted toe, out of habit. "He had to go do homework, and it's been a long time since you and I . . ."

"Fine, but only for a couple minutes," I say, rising from my chair.

"I'll meet you outside," Michaela replies gleefully.

My sister must be nuts to think it's mild; outside, the cold night bites into my skin with fanged teeth. But in the garden, Michaela is sitting on a fleece blanket with another half-wrapped around her shoulders. She holds the other end up for me, and I sit beside her. Not since the bus ride home — and that didn't really count, since there were lots of people around us — have Michaela and I been by ourselves. We lean our heads back. *Ahhh.* The sky is as it should be — dripping with white jewels. I want to pluck down four of them and hang them from my and Michaela's earlobes like souvenirs.

"Hey, Mickey?" I whisper into the silence. I haven't

used my sister's nickname in so long. "You haven't told Mom yet, have you?"

Michaela shakes her head. "I need to proceed carefully. First, let her accept that I have a boyfriend. Then, let her know that when I say I'm going to do 'extra-credit homework,' I'm actually working on my college essays."

"Where are you applying?" I ask, my heart contracting at the thought of Michaela moving away, just when the two of us have become close-ish again.

"A lot of places," Michaela says. "Fenimore Cooper, for one. Vassar, for another. University of Vermont — I hear they have a cool dance program." She pauses and licks her bottom lip. "I just hope Mom doesn't kill me."

"She won't," I assure her. "Things went well with Anders, after all."

Michaela brightens at this and moves in closer to me. "They did, right?"

"Anders isn't like I imagined him to be at first," I say.

"Mmm?" Michaela wraps the fleece blanket tighter around our bodies. "Let me guess. You pegged him for a pompous, redneck QB who eats with his feet."

I laugh. I'd forgotten how wonderful it is to spend time with my sister.

"That was my first impression of him, too," Michaela says, her breath warm on my cheek. "I know

I said I set out to have a boyfriend here, but Anders was not who I had in mind. I thought I wanted someone smarter, more introspective. And Anders can be kind of a jerk when he's doing his macho jock thing." Michaela rolls her eyes. "But you can't help who you fall for, Katie. I fell fast and hard, and Anders fell, too, and soon we were changing each other in small ways." She pauses and brushes some snow off her boots, which peek out of the blanket. "Maybe he's not my destiny, but I guess I'll figure that out when I need to."

It's a lot to take in, all this relationship stuff. "Hey . . . how does sex feel?" I ask. The words jump out of my mouth like naughty schoolchildren rushing out of class.

Michaela blushes, but only slightly, and puts her hand on mine. "Kind of weird and scary at first, but then better," she says. "It can be special, if you make good decisions. Tomorrow, after school, why don't you come to my room and we can really talk about it?" she suggests. "I want you to learn about condoms, Katie. . . ."

"Michaela!" I half shield my ears. "God. What are you? My health teacher?"

Michaela cracks up, then nudges me. "No way in hell, Katie. I'm your sister. If I'm not going to give it to you straight, who will?"

She has a point.

"I can't believe you were walking around with so many secrets this year," I say, but not in an accusatory way. I really am impressed. "I would've buckled."

Michaela raises her eyebrows at me. "You have secrets of your own, Katie. What's this about you taking yoga? And whatever happened with you and Sullivan Turner?"

Right. There's a whole world of information I have yet to share with my sister — from my feelings about Jasper to Emmaline calling me a *yogi* today. But I'll wait. We have time. Not everything has to come out in one breathless moment.

"Oh, you *know* how it is," I say dramatically, flipping my hair. "You're my sister, Michaela, *not* my friend. I can't tell you —"

"You are so bad!" Michaela shoves me, and I tumble back onto the fleece blanket. "I know that sounded awful," Michaela goes on, lying down beside me and leaning her head against mine. The smoke of our breaths winds up into the air. "But don't you realize? Most friends are temporary. Look at how our friendships with the girls in the city have changed."

My throat swells with melancholy.

"But we'll always be each other's sister," Michaela adds. "We'll always love each other, right? Whether we like it or not."

Our quiet laughter rings out into the still night, and an owl hoots at us in return. For the first time in a long time, I feel loose and untethered and pleasantly tired. I feel unstuck.

The full November moon hangs over our heads, ripe and juicy. What would it be like to sail up there for real, on a flying fleece blanket, to explore its ridges and rocks? I'd want my sister with me, of course. She'd remind me to wear the proper boots and bring along food for the voyage. We'd probably bicker the whole way up. And I suppose I could take my first steps on the moon on my own. But without Michaela, I wouldn't be able to dance up there.

I close my eyes and let the fresh mountain air settle on my face.

I think I'm going to sleep well tonight. Better than I have in ages.

Acknowledgements

My most heartfelt thanks to:

Anica Mrose Rissi, the original small-town girl, for her superb editorial guidance and boundless patience.

Abby McAden, for her psychic abilities, and Morgan Matson, for her humor and her calm. Craig Walker, Steve Scott, Bonnie Cutler, Amanda Jacobs, Lisa Ann Sandell, Sheila Marie Everett, Ann Reit, Siobhan McGowan, and all my talented colleagues and friends at Scholastic, for their support.

Jennifer Clark, for lending me both her country expertise and her photography skills, and Robert Flax, Elizabeth Harty, Jon Gemma, Martha Kelehan, Adah Nuchi, Emily Smith, Jaynie Saunders Tiller, and Nicole Weitzner for welcoming me back after my disappearance. Daniel Treiman, for introducing me to Lime Rickeys and being wonderfully distracting. And my parents, my sister, my brother-in-law, and my nephew, for being first readers, constant listeners, sound-advice-givers, and sources of comfort and joy.

Don't miss

Sea Change

The romantic new story from
New York Times bestselling author

AIMEE FRIEDMAN

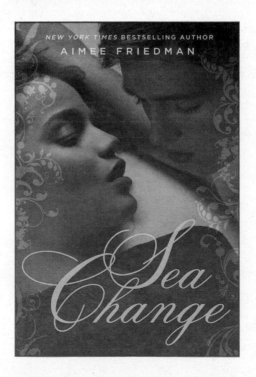

An Excerpt from *Sea Change*

I wasn't expecting to see the boy.

I had been walking along the beach for longer than I'd intended, trying to make sense of my interaction with T.J. and the image of Mom talking to Mr. Illingworth. The kids building sand castles and the couples frolicking in the water barely registered. I only noticed the shards of seashells and the cawing seagulls, and before long, that was all there was to see. As the water grew rougher and slammed into jagged rocks, the beach grew less populated, and I realized that The Crabby Hook and the boardwalk itself were quite a way behind me.

Which was why I was startled by the sight of a tall, tanned guy with dark blond hair striding toward me from the opposite end of the beach. He was carrying a bundle of rope and a fishing rod, the muscles in his arms visible under his faded red T-shirt. He wore ragged carpenter pants that had been hacked off at the knee, and his sun-browned legs were as muscled as his arms. I guessed him to be around my age, but he did not look like someone the kids at the Heirs party would know.

For some reason, I stopped walking, my flats sinking into the sand. Behind the boy, the beach seemed to disappear into a well of fog, and I realized how alone I was. I felt a quick twist of fear and considered turning and racing back to the boardwalk. Then I chided myself; why was I getting so irrationally spooked lately?

"You lost?" the boy called, waving one arm at me.

"Not at all," I replied defensively, squaring my shoulders. "I was just exploring."

The boy came closer. "It's not a great idea to go exploring by yourself on Siren Beach," he said. His voice was deep but a little raspy, and his Southern accent was different from CeeCee's and the others' in a way I couldn't quite define.

"Why?" I demanded, suddenly annoyed that this boy had appeared out of nowhere to break into my thoughts. I could feel my patience running low, like an uncharged battery. "Because of the 'sea serpents'?" I asked, making air quotes.

"You know about the sea serpents?" He was standing before me now, a smile tugging at his full lips. His eyes were a clear, brilliant green, unmuddied by traces of brown or gray.

"I know they're nonsense," I replied, crossing my arms over my chest.

The boy swept his gaze over my face, and my heart flip-flopped. What was he thinking? First T.J., now him. Trying to figure out the inner workings of boy-heads was a daunting task; *two* boys in one hour felt impossible for a novice like me.

But, back on the boardwalk, T.J. hadn't studied me as intently as this boy was studying me now. Almost against my will, I remembered the funny looks Greg — shaggy-haired, bespectacled, chess-team-captain Greg — used to sneak me back in February, when I was no more than his physics tutor. Then, one night, as I'd been explaining the principles of electromagnetism, he'd kissed me, and I'd understood what those glances had meant. And it had seriously freaked me out.

"It's your first time on Selkie, right?" the boy asked, his tone slightly teasing. For some embarrassing reason, the phrase *first time* made my skin catch fire.

"Is it that obvious?" I asked, giving a nervous laugh.

"Well, I would have recognized you," the boy replied, his smile widening.

To Do List:
Read all the Point books!

Airhead
Being Nikki
By **Meg Cabot**

Suite Scarlett
By **Maureen Johnson**

Sea Change
The Year My Sister Got Lucky
South Beach
French Kiss
Hollywood Hills
By **Aimee Friedman**

The Heartbreakers
The Crushes
By **Pamela Wells**

*This Book Isn't Fat,
It's Fabulous*
By **Nina Beck**

Wherever Nina Lies
By **Lynn Weingarten**

*And Then Everything
Unraveled*
By **Jennifer Sturman**

Summer Boys
By Hailey Abbott
Summer Boys
Next Summer
After Summer
Last Summer
Summer Girls

In or Out
By Claudia Gabel
In or Out
Loves Me, Loves Me Not
Sweet and Vicious
*Friends Close,
Enemies Closer*

Point

www.thisispoint.com